I0783903

leaf and let die

KIRBY FALLS

BOOK 3

LANEY HATCHER

content warning

While this is very much a banter-fueled, rivals-to-lovers romcom, there is an on-page panic attack of a secondary character. I wanted to be sensitive to any readers who may find that triggering.

To my hometown,

The people, the backroads, the memories that shaped me. The place that keeps my secrets and welcomes me back no matter how long it's been.

BRADY

Spring 2012

I tossed my gym bag on the metal bleachers and collapsed beside it. A moment later, Floyd and Abby joined me in a similarly exhausted heap.

Soccer practice had been brutal today. It was mostly conditioning since the boys' team wasn't in season. So that meant a lot of running. I didn't mind a hard work-out, but it was finally May, and the first hot temperatures of the year were sneaking through.

I loved living in the mountains of North Carolina, but I wasn't ready for the summer heat—not when I had to run sprints at three in the afternoon with the sun beating down on my shoulders.

I yanked my tee shirt off and brought my water bottle to my lips. I figured I'd just skip the locker room altogether and head straight for the eleventh-grade parking lot and drive home.

"Man, that suuucked," Abby said. Cole Abernathy—Abby to nearly everyone—had been my best friend since kindergarten, but I'd only recently talked him into joining the soccer team. He was probably cursing that decision now. Abby was naturally athletic, though. He'd be fine.

"Yeah, it's hot as hell," I agreed. I took the rest of my water and dumped it over my head.

"Know what else is hot as hell?" Floyd murmured before whacking the side of my leg with the shoe he'd just pulled off.

"What?" I asked, blinking water out of my eyes and digging in my duffel for a clean shirt.

When Floyd didn't answer, I raised my head. But he wasn't looking at me. He was gazing off in the distance. I followed his attention to the opposite side of the field where the girls' soccer team was warming up. They *were* in season and had a game tonight. Sometimes, the boys' team stayed to watch, but I was ready to go home and shower. Plus, it was Friday. That meant there was a bonfire at Abby's.

"What's so hot, Floyd?" Abby repeated my question.

"MacKenzie Clark," Floyd replied with a smug tone in his voice that made me frown on instinct. His eyes were still focused on where Mac was stretching in her maroon uniform. Impulsively, I sought her out, too. Mac's long, dark pony-tail trailed down her back. She straightened and shouted something to one of her teammates before taking off at a jog.

Mac *was* hot. Objectively so. But she was also a gigantic pain in the ass. I'd known her since preschool. Hell, we all had. That was what happened when you lived in a tiny town and everybody was in everybody's business.

The Clarks owned Grandpappy's—the farm across the highway from my own family's orchard. Our two businesses had been in competition for tourist dollars since before Mac and I were born.

While we'd shared classes over the years, we'd never really been friendly. We were . . . something else.

MacKenzie Clark might have been my closest neighbor for miles, but she was no girl next door.

We'd grown up pestering the hell out of each other. I'd teased her, and she'd given it right back, just as good. In first grade, I'd cut the end of her pigtail with safety scissors during nap time. Mac hadn't tattled. Instead, she'd gotten even by holding me down and making me eat dirt at recess. I had dozens of similar stories. Teachers had eventually learned not to pair us up for projects. We argued and bickered like it was our job, but mostly, it was fun. Typically, my behavior was habit and familiarity. I enjoyed getting a rise out of her. I reckoned Mac felt the same.

That was why, for the life of me, I couldn't figure out why one of my best friends would be commenting on how hot she was. Yeah, we were seventeen, and girls had become more of a priority in recent years, but it was strange that Floyd would bring up Mac, of all people. The realization that he could be into her had me shifting uncomfortably on the bleachers and my heart racing. And not from the workout.

Returning my focus to my friend, I tried to make my voice sound casual. "Mac? You think Mac is hot all of a sudden?"

Floyd's expression sobered. Then he glanced between me and Abby. "You can't say anything."

Abby held up a hand in a poor approximation of a Boy Scout salute. "I swear."

I swallowed, feeling even more uneasy. "I won't say anything," I confirmed.

Floyd couldn't seem to resist smiling then.

His smug grin tilted up the corners of his lips, revealing the wide gap in his front teeth, and my chest went tight with a sense of foreboding that I couldn't put a name to.

"Well, my aunt and uncle came to visit this week, so my momma wanted to take them around, show them the sights," Floyd explained. "We ended up at Grandpappy's."

Briefly, I wondered if the disquiet I felt was even warranted. Mac worked on her family's farm. She'd been helping out at Grandpappy's since she was a kid. But what could that possibly have to do with Floyd and his aunt and uncle?

"I got tired of following my family around," Floyd continued, "and went off on my own. I ran into Mac, and we *hung out* for a while in the barn."

Frowning, I asked, "Hung out? What does that mean?"

Floyd bit his lip, gaze straying back across the field. "We made out. She let me feel her up."

My heart—already pounding—went double time. "Wait—what? Why? Do you even *like* her?"

I felt the weight of Abby's gaze on my face from where he sat on Floyd's other side. But I ignored him and focused on the way Floyd shrugged, nonchalant as hell.

"Nah, not really," Floyd replied. "I was just bored. But she seemed easy enough. I bet she'd let me do more."

Disgust had my eyebrows pulling low.

I'd known Floyd Ellerby since preschool, too. We'd been friends and teammates for a long time. I'd heard him talk about hot actresses or models, but this was different.

I dated girls my age. I flirted and fooled around, but I definitely wasn't spending time with anyone out of boredom. I wasn't a saint. I didn't know a teenage guy who was, but I didn't talk about women like that—as if they were a commodity, like they were disposable.

Mac had gone out with a few guys earlier in the year. Granted, Connor Pritchard—her last boyfriend—was a self-absorbed dick bag, and I didn't know why she wanted anything to do with him in the first place. Whatever. Mac was free to be "bored" with whomever she pleased. It wasn't any of my business.

Yet, the thought of my friend hooking up with her made me feel like someone had hollowed out my stomach with a melon baller.

Instead of berating Floyd for being disrespectful—something my daddy would have done—I said something altogether worse. "I don't know why you'd even waste your time with Mac. She's not even pretty. She'd probably give you a disease. And, sure, she seems easy enough, but that's because no one else wants her."

Silence followed in the wake of my statement, as heavy and oppressive as the day's sudden heat. I counted out ten thundering heartbeats before Abby whistled a low note.

"Jesus, Brady," Abby admonished before standing and hoisting his bag.

But, Floyd was nodding. "Yeah, man. You're probably right. She hasn't dated anyone since Pritchard, and he talked all kinds of shit about her. I'm not looking for drama."

I swallowed what felt like a mouthful of glass and looked down at the shirt still in my hands. With jerky movements, I slipped it over my head and zipped up my bag.

"I'm out of here," Abby said. "I'll see y'all later."

Floyd called out a goodbye, saying he'd see Abby tonight at the bonfire.

I couldn't seem to find my voice. With a quick glance, I could see the girls' team had moved on from stretching to some passing drills. I couldn't bring myself to search out Mac after what I'd said.

I didn't let myself think about the relief that flooded my veins when Floyd said he'd back off. Nor did I want to consider the reason behind it. While I was at it, I ignored the guilt and disgust twisting my stomach into knots, too.

With a quiet "See you later" for my friend, I grabbed my stuff and went home.

Mac was at the bonfire that night. The entire girls' soccer team had come straight over after their 4–1 victory over the Cookeville Red Devils.

The temperature had dropped as soon as the sun went down. Mac still wore her uniform but with a Kirby Falls Bobcats hoodie thrown over it to ward off the chill.

Floyd wasn't here yet, and Abby was chatting up Lara Dillion over by the fire.

I watched as the pack of soccer girls finally dispersed, making their way toward the chairs scattered around the glowing flames. Mac hung back, digging through one of the coolers.

Without any common sense or forethought, I started walking in her direction.

"Good game tonight," I said when I reached her side.

Mac glanced up and did a double take as if surprised to find those words coming out of my mouth, which was, okay, fair. We didn't go around complimenting one another.

Her storm-gray eyes narrowed suspiciously.

"I heard you had two of those goals," I tried again. "Nice job. Cookeville is tough."

"Thanks," she said cautiously as she straightened, pulling a blue sports drink out of the ice chest. "Yeah, they're pretty aggressive."

My instinct was to reply, *Good thing you're basically feral*. But I didn't say that. Instead, I offered a smile.

Her frown stayed firmly in place as she watched me edge closer and reach inside the cooler for a drink.

This close, I could see the tiny wisps of dark hair that had escaped her ponytail. Despite her casual appearance, there was nothing about Mac that was relaxed. She was on high alert with me in range. I might as well have been an incoming warship on her radar. She was at battle stations, prepared for attack.

And I couldn't blame her. That was how it had always been between us. We gave each other shit and expected the worst.

But maybe it didn't have to be that way.

Abruptly, Laramie Burke came over and threw an arm around her cousin's shoulders. "Whoa! Any bloodshed over here?"

I grabbed the first drink my hand touched in the icy water and took a step back.

"Not yet," Mac answered, still stone-faced as I cleared my throat awkwardly.

Laramie—everyone called her Larry—slapped me on the back. "Well, then you owe me one for saving you, Brady."

I gave an awkward laugh and popped the top on my can of—I checked the label—Natty Light. *Great.* "No need. Just saying hi. Weapons are set to stun."

Larry's smile wilted in obvious confusion, but Mac's nostrils flared, and she countered, "Speak for yourself."

I took in Mac's unwavering glare and the animosity that radiated from her in waves. Then I gave a slight nod and stepped away. I didn't always know when to back off and retreat, but, right now, it seemed like a good idea.

As I returned to the circle of chairs surrounding the bonfire, I shook my head at what an idiot I'd been. I'd walked over there without a game plan, but I'd known that I didn't want to fight with Mac tonight. Maybe the idea of a truce had been swirling around with all that guilt and confusion from earlier.

I spent the rest of the night avoiding MacKenzie Clark and whatever complicated feelings were preventing me from thinking straight.

A week later, when I ended up at her table during study hall, I once again attempted a civil conversation, but Mac looked at me like I was something she pulled off the bottom of her shoe.

Our encounters for the remainder of junior year were few and far between, but whenever our orbits did collide, Mac seemed extra combative. No matter what I said or how I said it, she took offense and responded in kind. I chalked it up to hormones or just being a terrifying teenage girl. Or maybe our patterns and mannerisms had long been established, and it was too late now to do anything about it.

It was easier to revert to learned behavior anyhow.

Mac loved to hate me.

It didn't seem to matter that I didn't hate her back.

one

MAC

Eleven Years Later

Every single day in Kirby Falls had the potential to be a class reunion, especially when half the people I'd graduated with never bothered to leave.

It was the first Friday in September, so I knew, without a doubt, that the bonfire on Cole Abernathy's property would be full of former classmates. Barring any county or statewide burn bans, the bonfire happened every week, no matter the weather. And, without fail, this particular seasonal shift meant that Kirby Falls High alumni would be out in droves. There was just something about September, when the setting sun meant chilly nights. People were more than ready for the choking humidity of August to give way to crisp, clear skies and cozy flannel.

Obviously, I wasn't immune as I parked my Jeep in the bumpy field beside Abby's barn and grabbed a six-pack and my maroon flannel from the passenger seat. The smell of woodsmoke permeated the air as soon as I opened the door. My boots sank into the dry ankle-high grass, and I heard the sounds of people gathered, laughing and talking—folks I'd known my whole life. The bonfire was a tradition born out of boredom and familiarity, one that was as reliable as death and taxes and Connie Hixson's hummingbird cake taking home the blue ribbon at the county fair.

The faces had changed a bit over the years as former classmates went away to college, paired off and got married, or had kids. But they usually cycled back around as they came home to visit and mingle with us townies who hadn't managed to escape.

The crowd around Christmas was usually the biggest as folks returned to celebrate the holiday but managed to sneak away from their families long enough to get drunk in a field with their friends.

The invitation was always open for Friday night bonfires at Abby's. It had been a tradition since high school, and I didn't see it changing anytime soon. Things rarely did in my hometown.

You could count on familiar faces and the usual suspects. Hell, I wasn't one to talk. I still showed up at least once a month.

After all, I'd never bothered to leave Kirby Falls either.

I slipped through the crowd easily, greeting friends and acquaintances, slapping backs, and giving hugs. I dropped off my six-pack of Firefly cider in one of the coolers beneath the covered patio on the other side of the barn, snagging one of the bottles for myself.

My cousin Laramie was busy hanging out with her best friend elsewhere tonight, so I was on my own until I found someone I wanted to join around the fire. Or there was always the off chance that my sister, Bonnie, would show. She was two years older than me, but everyone knew her and loved her. The bonfires hosted a wide range of Abby's acquaintances. He was a popular guy, so you never knew who was going to show up.

I spied an open camp chair on the opposite side of the massive blaze and changed direction to try to nab it before anyone else.

Most of our graduating class got along pretty well—with a few exceptions. There'd been Lara Dillion, head cheerleader and colossal bitch, but she'd gotten married in college and moved away and never came back. I'd dated Connor Pritchard in eleventh grade and was definitely not a fan. And Floyd Ellerby had turned out to be kind of a dick. Although he still lived in Kirby Falls, he rarely came around. The last time I'd seen Floyd at a bonfire was a few years back, and he and Brady Judd had gotten into it about something. I'd never seen Brady so worked up. The guy was annoyingly friendly and unflappable—unless I was the one doing the flapping.

A devious smile had the corners of my lips twisting upward as I rounded the corner. Yes, irritating Brady was one of my talents. Like Beethoven and his symphonies. Leonardo da Vinci and his masterpieces. Some people played an instrument or could sing real good. There'd been a girl in our graduating class who'd become a famous dancer and performed all over the world. And much like Mandy Jessup, I'd found my calling. Unfortunately, it wasn't anything as lucrative or notable as being a principal ballerina. I was Brady Judd's nemesis, and no one could get his goat like I could.

The vacant camp chair I'd been eyeing came into view, and my boots halted as I pulled up short. A body attached to a pair of long, jean-clad legs slid onto the dark green nylon just ahead of me.

Speak of the devil, and he shall appear.

Unfortunately, the nemesis thing seemed to work both ways. As much as it pained me to admit it, Brady was just as gifted at getting under my skin. He was a tick on my backside and had been for as long as I'd known him. Growing up, we'd practically been neighbors. His family ran the apple orchard across the street. And even now, I had to see his stupid face nearly every day when we closed our respective businesses.

I'd petitioned my family to close the farm thirty minutes earlier or later so I could drag the chain across the driveway without having to interact with Brady, but they hadn't gone for it. As it stood, most evenings, I was forced to walk down the path from Grandpappy's parking lot to the main entrance and watch as Brady did the same from directly across the two-lane highway.

Judd's Family Orchard had a billboard advertising the entrance to their property with a giant photo of eight-year-old Brady holding a basket of apples. The image had faded over the years, but I was still inundated regularly by his gap-toothed grin and the dimple in his right cheek. The cheerful script across the bottom advised motorists to "turn here for wholesome family fun."

Whenever I saw that sign, I was reminded of the boy who'd snipped off the end of my pigtail in the first grade. Or the time he swapped out my banana pudding for mayonnaise at a church picnic.

As classmates since preschool, we'd been gleefully torturing each other for decades at this point. Back in high school, I'd played on the girls' soccer team, and Brady had played on the boys' team. Our paths had crossed a lot as a result. Our weird torture competition probably (definitely) wasn't healthy, but grudges were seldom rational. And while most of our childhood and adolescent battles had been good-natured teasing interspersed with occasional hell-raising, the spring after I'd turned seventeen, I'd sworn I'd never forgive him.

Maybe it was juvenile to keep a promise I'd made to myself eleven years ago, but no one had ever accused me of being the most mature.

Now, from his place in the camp chair, Brady glanced up. A smirk was already formed on his surprisingly full lips. The orange glow from the fire cast his features in harsh relief, making him look demonic, possibly rabid. His smirk widened into a grin as he watched me stand there frozen, two feet away. The asshat had probably stolen the chair on purpose.

"Hi, Mac Attack. I didn't see you there." His voice was delighted, the good-ole-boy Southern accent dialed up to ten.

Sure, I lived in the mountains of Western North Carolina too, but Brady exaggerated his twangy drawl and sounded more like an inbred yokel than anyone else I knew. One time, in second grade, he'd missed *wash* during the spelling bee. He'd spelled out "w-o-r-s-h" because that was literally how he said it. There was country and then there was Brady Judd: shameless flirt, unrepentant annoyance, and backwoods-sounding hillbilly.

"I *bet* you didn't," I challenged.

Brady's grin went full-blown megawatt. His even white teeth appeared to glow in the firelight like some sort of deranged maniac.

I eyed his smooth jaw and styled hair. The brown strands were longer on top and artfully arranged. I imagined if I ran my fingers through them and gave a good yank, my hand would come away sticky with product. Beneath the scent of crackling flames and woodsmoke, I got a good whiff of cologne—probably Axe body spray.

"What?" Brady asked when I'd clearly been staring too long.

I sniffed and crossed my arms. "Nothing. I just don't see why you feel the need to get all gussied up—"

"Thank you," he interrupted like I'd complimented him.

"It's just a bonfire at Abby's. Same one you probably came to last Friday and the Friday before that."

"If this lowly bonfire is so beneath you," he replied, unoffended, "why do you keep showing up? You must not mind hanging out with all us peasants when you have such an engaging social calendar, Your Majesty."

I scowled in response, not bothering to explain myself to him.

I just meant that *I* didn't feel the need to curl my hair and put on a bunch of makeup to impress the same people I saw all the time. Most of them knew me back when I had a mouth full of braces or that obsession with One Direction in the fifth grade.

And now I was just Mac, the smart-mouthed Clark who did the bare minimum to get by. Twenty-eight. No children. No boyfriend. Hell, no prospects. I was basically a Jane Austen heroine in flannel.

My gaze shifted to the chair Brady occupied, and I sighed. No fireside seat was worth this.

"Oh, I'm sorry. Did you want this here chair?" He wiggled his butt a little like I didn't know which folding camp chair he was referring to. Then he spread his thighs wide to get comfortable, and I swallowed and looked away.

My eye roll was instinctual at this point—a conditioned response to this idiot. I might as well have been Pavlov's dog . . . but with better hair.

"There's a seat right here," Brady said, patting his thigh.

I made sure my glare was baleful and unflinching. "Not a chance."

As if I would ever lower myself—literally—to sit on his lap. I couldn't imagine a scenario where that would ever happen. Two broken ankles? Nah, I'll pass. Just finished a marathon? I'd rather stand, thank you very much.

With a huff of annoyance, I tightened my hold on the neck of the bottle in my hand and turned away. I'd find another damn seat. Even the uncomfortable logs positioned around the perimeter would be a better option than spending my evening with Brady Judd. I'd rather have my butt go completely numb than have it contact any part of his anatomy.

However, before I'd made it a single step, I felt a hand close gently around my wrist. I didn't get the chance to threaten violence or demand he unhand me. Brady released his hold immediately and stood in one fluid motion.

I hated how tall he was. I was a respectable five feet, six inches, but Brady towered over me at six three. He was long and lean from years of running and playing soccer. While I wasn't intimidated, per se, I didn't like how small and insignificant I felt standing in his overgrown shadow. I much preferred our interactions nonexistent, but if I had to pick, I'd rather he be sitting down.

"Here you go, Mac Mac," he said, sweeping an arm out to the camp chair. I ignored the nickname. It was one of many he cycled through, and I'd learned a long time ago not to give him the satisfaction of challenging him on it. If you cracked the door even the barest amount on your annoyance, Brady would come strolling through it with a two-hundred-piece marching band.

My eyes narrowed suspiciously. "What are you doing?"

Shrugging, he stuffed his hands in the pockets of his gray puffy vest. "I *can* be a gentleman when I want to be."

My gaze drifted to the chair and then back to Brady, trying to decide if there was a catch. We'd played plenty of pranks on each other over the years. It wouldn't be unheard of for him to yank a chair out from under me or to have sabotaged it in some way that had the nylon collapsing or the whole thing folding up with me in it.

He chuckled at my obvious distrust. "Just take it, Clark. I swear I'm being good."

With that, he shuffled forward to slide around me. I didn't make it easy on him. I stood my ground in the pathway that formed the perimeter of the fire. His tall body curved by, just shy of touching me. As he passed, his head dipped low, and he said quietly in my ear, "But something tells me you prefer it when I'm bad."

His hushed tone and soft exhale against my skin had me fighting a shiver—one of disgust, no doubt.

My eyes snapped to his face just in time to watch him smirk and then turn away. He ambled off toward Jase Wilcox and Cole Abernathy, who were lit beneath the twinkle lights under the awning. Brady clapped both men on the shoulder in greeting before he reached inside a waiting cooler and pulled out one of my five remaining ciders.

I let out an impatient breath when I realized I'd been staring after him like a damn schoolgirl. What had that been about? And why was it so hot out here? Oh, right. The bonfire. What was wrong with me tonight?

Cursing quietly, I slid onto the seat Brady had vacated, noting the warmth left over from his body.

Hazel Bradford was on one side of me, and it didn't take long before we started up a conversation. She'd been a couple grades ahead of me in school and a cheerleader to boot. But we'd been friends a long time.

Hazel asked me how things were at Grandpappy's, and we talked about the upcoming season at my family's farm. Then I asked after the pottery she made and sold at the farmers' market downtown. It wasn't hard to talk to someone you'd known all your life. Like I said, most of us got along with one another. *Most.*

My eyes snagged on Brady as something Abby said made him laugh. He threw his head back, completely unselfconsciously.

I tuned back into the conversation as Hazel asked how my family was doing. I told her my sister, Bonnie, had just started back to school, and that was why she hadn't joined me tonight. She was the art teacher over at Kirby Falls Elementary. While that was all technically true, Bonnie was also pretty busy with her husband, Danny, and his family. Bonfires and going out weren't priorities for my sister anymore, which was fine. We were in different places in our lives. She was older and married. I fully expected her to start popping out kids and living that mom life soon.

"Are Junior and Nola gone for the season yet?" Hazel asked as my thoughts drifted away from my sister.

I nodded. "Yeah, they loaded up the RV this week. They'll be in St. Pete until Christmas."

It was common knowledge that my grandparents were snowbirds. They took their retirement from Grandpappy's seriously, and they deserved it. My grandpa Junior—J.R. or William Jr. to some—and my grandma Nola had worked the land and helped run the farm and orchard until the next generation could take it over.

My parents and aunt and uncle and cousins had all found places within the Grandpappy's legacy. I worked there, too, chipping in and doing what needed to be done on the tourism side of things. I'd helped out in the fields when I was younger but left that part of the family business to my uncle William and his farmhands.

"I saw Larry at the bank this afternoon, so I knew she wasn't coming out tonight," Hazel said. "Why doesn't Will ever come around? I know he's practically famous, but everyone knows him. He'd be welcome."

I got where Hazel was coming from. Will would definitely be welcome. He'd also hate every minute of it. A decade and a lifetime ago, my cousin had been a professional baseball player. An injury had stopped his career in its early stages, and he'd returned home to Kirby Falls to help manage the farm. He hated being recognized by the *leafers*—the tourists who visited our town in search of fall foliage—and he hated reminiscing about his past. Inevitably, some well-meaning local would bring up his baseball career. Some wounds went deeper than we liked to admit. Will was bitter and guarded, and I could understand his tendency to hermit himself away.

On the other hand, I thought his shitty attitude and resentment made life harder for everyone else. Our relationship was complicated, and oftentimes, he was more my boss than my cousin. I knew he thought I coasted through life, content to half-ass my job and everything else I did. Maybe he was right in some regard. But I was never going to live up to his standards. Why bother trying?

"Will keeps busy" was all I eventually managed. But Hazel nodded like she understood.

Our conversation continued as former classmates came and went over the next hour. The temperature dropped even more, and the heat from the flames was welcome as I tugged my flannel tighter around my torso.

A few times that evening, I caught sight of Brady—holding another bottle from *my* six-pack, the ass—with Jase and Abby. They'd found seats at a picnic table away from the fire, beneath the awning near the coolers, and seemed content to hold court there.

Around eleven thirty, I decided it was time to head home. I'd nursed one cider all night, so I was fine to drive.

I said my goodbyes and made my way under the awning to drop my empty in the recycling bin. But just as I released the bottle, I felt a body stumble into mine.

"Damn it, Abby," Brady mumbled roughly as his hands found my waist, steading me and keeping me from tipping into the side of the giant blue trash can.

Just as quickly, Brady pulled away, stepping back and mumbling out an apology.

I frowned, annoyed that I was once again in his proximity and that he'd crashed into me. "Watch it, Judd."

Brady glared at his snickering friends before holding his hands up in surrender. "I'm sorry, Mac. That wasn't intentional." Then, with one last parting scowl for Abby and Jase, Brady turned and headed toward the parking lot.

I stared after him in confusion. He wasn't really going to drive? The drunk ass had *just* staggered into me.

In stunned dismay, I watched as Brady ambled away. He then reached into his vest pocket and produced a set of keys.

Turning to his still-amused friends, I demanded, "You're not just going to let him drive home, are you?"

Abby waved me away. "He's fine."

My eyes bulged. "Clearly, he's not."

"Surely you're not worried Brady might hurt himself?" Abby's dark eyes sparkled.

"No," I protested. "He could kill someone else, though. That idiot would probably walk away without a scratch." I glanced back to see Brady winding his way through the cars parked next to the barn.

Returning my gaze to Abby and Jase, I asked, "You're really not going to stop him?"

Jase shook his head, and Abby grinned, unrepentant.

"Cole Abernathy, you are responsible for whatever happens next." Then I turned and took off toward the sea of vehicles, already regretting my decision and my unfortunate morals.

"Oh, I hope so!" he shouted after me.

I didn't give him the satisfaction of a response.

Brady was just reaching for the door handle of his truck when I jogged up behind him.

"Hey," I called, and he turned automatically. Obvious surprise had his brows going high on his forehead. Yeah, well, I couldn't believe I was chasing him down either.

"You can't just drive in your condition," I said before he had a chance to speak. "I saw you drinking—my ciders, by the way—all night. You should go back to the bonfire. Make Jase or Abby take you home."

Brady ignored all the important parts of my speech and replied with a dopey smile, "Been keeping an eye on me, have you?"

I sighed in aggravation. I hadn't been watching Brady, not really. I'd just . . . noticed him occasionally, over the course of several hours. He was loud and distracting. It wasn't my fault I'd looked in his annoying direction and happened to see a bottle in his hand every time.

"Will you just go give your friends your keys?"

"No, I don't think I will."

We watched each other. Me glaring, and Brady smirking.

I did not want to insert myself into this situation, and I didn't see why I had to be the responsible one here.

"Give me your phone," I said, holding out my hand.

Brady straightened and reached into his front pocket. "Why? Want to give me your number?"

"No, I'm going to call your sister, you idiot."

He released his cell, and I watched it disappear back into his jeans pocket. "Hmm, I don't think so."

"Brady," I groaned, overwhelmed by irritation. I didn't want to spend my valuable free time arguing with him. I wanted to drive home and go to sleep. I had to work in the morning.

His quiet chuckle made me homicidal. It also made me realize he could stand here and give me shit all night long. Or at least until he sobered up.

Apparently, it was up to me to put a stop to this round-and-round and make sure Brady didn't crash into anyone on his way home. I could do this. I could be the bigger person. I would not let my nemesis win this battle.

"Fine," I snapped. Reaching out, I snagged the front of his stupid puffy vest and dragged him in the direction of my car.

"Whoa! Okay, I always knew you'd want to be in charge." He followed along like the dog that he was. "I'm fine with being manhandled. We should probably decide on a safe word, though. I think it should be 'meat loaf.'"

I stopped abruptly and spun to face him. "Why meat loaf?"

Brady replied solemnly, "Because I would do anything for love, but I won't do that."

I blinked, and then I bit my lip hard. "You are such an idiot."

"You're trying so hard not to laugh right now."

I ignored that. "And we do not need a safe word because I am driving you home." He opened his mouth, but I didn't give him a chance to interrupt. "And I'm leaving you there to sleep it off."

He eyed me for a moment. "Okay, you can drive me home."

I eyed him right back. Brady was giving in, but, for some reason, I didn't feel like I was winning. "Get in the Jeep."

His lips curled, and a dimple popped in his right cheek. "Yes, ma'am."

The eight-minute drive to downtown Kirby Falls tested nearly all of my patience, but I tried to remember that I'd brought this upon myself. Everyone knew that drunk people were annoying, but Brady was a pain in the ass even when he was sober. He entertained himself by digging through my glovebox and center console, keeping up a running commentary all the while. He dissected my music choices and criticized everything from my smudged windshield to the air freshener I had dangling from my rearview mirror.

By the time I slowed the Jeep on the empty street in front of his second-story apartment, I was ready to shove him from the moving vehicle.

"Thanks for the lift," he said as I turned on my blinker and pulled to a stop.

"You really shouldn't have even thought about driving drunk."

"I'm not drunk."

I narrowed my eyes at him. "Yes, you are."

"No, I'm not. I drank one cranberry cider all night."

My mind spun as I thought back to Brady laughing and carrying on, drink in hand. Could that really have been the same bottle all night? "But you practically fell over your own feet on your way out. Right into me," I argued.

"Oh," he replied, completely unbothered. "That was because Abby kicked me when I stood up from the picnic table. I'm not drunk, Mac. I'd never drink and drive."

I stared at him while fiery anger—so scalding and familiar—filled my chest. My hands tightened involuntarily around the steering wheel.

"Are you telling me you let me think you were drunk so I'd drive you home?" The words were gritted out, my jaw tense and set.

"You were the one who insisted," he argued. "You practically dragged me into your backseat."

"Front seat," I corrected.

"Semantics."

I took in a slow breath through my nose. "Get. Out."

His quiet laughter made my grip tighten on the steering wheel once more, the leather groaning beneath my palms as I imagined his clean-shaven throat in its place.

Brady opened the door and unfolded his tall frame out onto the empty sidewalk. At least there weren't any witnesses.

With a cheerful wave, Brady called, "See you later, MacBook Pro."

As soon as his door closed, I took off, my headlights illuminating the pavement.

This was exactly what I got for trying to do the right thing: a headache forming in the base of my skull.

An hour later, I'd showered off the smell of woodsmoke and settled into bed with wet hair and my cell phone. My headache had eased, what with Brady Judd being clear across town. I figured a little doomscrolling would help me settle down.

I clicked off the news pretty quickly. Next, I checked a few of the travel blogs I followed but didn't find any new posts.

Then my curiosity got the better of me, and I did this thing I do sometimes. I typed in "flights AVL to Reykjavik" in the search bar. A list of options unfolded, and I smiled softly. "Only two stops," I mumbled to myself in surprise. I'd expected more.

I equated this silly little exercise to people house-hunting on Zillow for homes they'd never be able to afford. It didn't matter. I wasn't going anywhere. What was the harm in checking flights to New Zealand or Greece or Italy?

I released a wistful breath and almost put my phone away.

But then I decided to pull up my favorite social media app, Chatter. Thoughts of lava fields, black sand beaches, and the auroras were suddenly abandoned as my blood pressure started to climb.

Rising onto one elbow, I tapped the mention in my notifications from forty-two minutes ago. With the glow from my screen searing my retinas, I scanned the post from Judd's Orchard, eyes widening.

Brady ran the social media account for Judd's. I handled that side of things for Grandpappy's. At least once a week, I found a teasing snipe on the orchard's account. Luckily, I gave back as good as I got.

Shaking my head, I read . . .

@JuddsFamilyOrchard: Beware, good people of Kirby Falls. There's been a string of incidents where strange women try to force unsuspecting victims into their vehicles. Watch out for a bright yellow Jeep Wrangler. Look alive, @GrandpappysApples.

After years of pranks and premeditated torture, the score between us was too high to count. But if I only took today into consideration, it would more than likely stand at Brady Judd: 1 and MacKenzie Clark: 0.

BRADY

"You don't actually believe that Mac had something to do with the vandalism on your property, do you?"

I stared in bewilderment at my best friend. "Abby, I have literally been explaining exactly why MacKenzie Clark is the culprit. Were you not listening to me?"

Abby sighed. "Yes, I was listening for the first twenty minutes. But honestly, I've been pretty checked out for the last five. You can't *really* believe Mac would sneak over to the orchard in the middle of the night and paintball the side of the Apple House for you to find the following morning."

"Yes!" I practically shouted, and several heads turned in our direction.

I'd texted my friend earlier to see if he wanted to grab a beer after work. With the day I'd had, I needed it. Plus, I'd wanted his advice, even if he was clearly misguided and too trusting.

We were sitting in the brand-new dining room of Abby's latest restaurant while a cleaning crew put the finishing touches on the space. Flyers was a casual wing-and-burger-type place, and the grand opening was tomorrow. Abby had invited me here to have a beer since he was busy prepping for the celebration and finalizing menu items. He was feeding me dinner, so I guessed I couldn't complain too much.

Earlier this morning, my siblings and I had stumbled across the vandalism to Judd's Orchard's main building. The mostly open-air Apple House welcomed tourists and patrons on days the farm was open to the public. It also housed our pre-picked produce, sales counter, apple-washing station, one small administrative office, and the equipment for pressing.

Now, though, the outside of the faded white building was speckled with red, yellow, and blue paint splotches.

"She left a calling card," I reminded him and pulled out my phone to show him the pattern I'd detected.

Abby held up a hand to fend off the device I held up to his face. "I've seen the picture, and I'm sorry, man. I just don't see a letter *M* in all that splattered mess."

"She would definitely do something like this," I argued. "You know she hates me."

Abby narrowed his eyes and reached for his beer. "You know my feelings on this."

I groaned and let my head fall back to stare at the ceiling ductwork. "And your theory has been noted and disregarded."

He laughed—a sound that was part scoff and part audible eye roll. "You're too close to the situation. You always have been."

I returned my head to an upright position and met his amused gaze. "We are not in love with each other. Mac hates me, and I find her incredibly annoying."

"Ah," he countered, "I didn't hear you say you hated her back."

Abby had been harping on this since middle school. Typically, I let it roll off my back because the idea was so ludicrous, but then he did shit like trying to force-proximity us.

My mind drifted to the bonfire the other night when he'd seen Mac approaching and basically shoved me into her like an immature preteen.

Being close to her was like touching a hot stove. The heat, the awareness, the high likelihood of personal injury.

Much to Abby's dismay, his latest attempt had ended with me annoying the hell out of Mac on the drive to my apartment, and not with declarations of love. But I'd had fun torturing her, so I hadn't scolded him about it like I should have.

I examined the three remaining chicken wings on my plate and grabbed the cherry jalapeno one. "I don't hate anyone."

And that was the truth. Neighbors, acquaintances, tourists at the orchard. I could —and did—get along with nearly everyone I met. There were a couple of notable exceptions, but for the most part, I was an affable, lovable goofball.

While I didn't hate Mac, I did love to get a rise out of her. It was part of our game. Hell, it was part of our existence at this point. But where I resorted to friendly teasing and humorous antics, she tended toward outright violence and deliberate attacks.

In middle school, she'd snuck self-tanner into my body lotion in my gym bag. There had been the time she'd let the air out of my tires senior year as well as the Elmer's glue incident—don't ask. Then a few years back, she'd drawn a penis on my face when I passed out at Jolly Adams's divorce party. In permanent marker.

If I thought back to when we were kids, I could—maybe—see Abby's perspective. There had probably been a time when I had a crush on the dark-haired spitfire who lived across the street. But I'd done what any prepubescent boy would have. I'd sought her attention in the most effective way possible. I'd teased and tormented and made myself memorable. Growing up, I didn't know how to manage my complicated feelings any more than I knew how to handle my hyperactivity or focus on classwork.

And then later—when Mac and I had been in high school—I'd had a moment of wishful thinking, a desire to change things between us. Mentally, I waved that thought away. None of it mattered now.

I wasn't going to admit any of that to Abby anyway.

"But to damage your family's property seems a bit extreme, even in this unhinged game of one-upmanship y'all have going on." Abby's words brought my wavering attention back to the conversation and my righteous indignation.

"Well, who else could it be?" I demanded.

He shoved a rosemary French fry in his mouth and shrugged. "I don't know, Brady. Maybe that's why you should let the sheriff's office do their job."

"Pfft. They don't know what the hell they're doing."

Inwardly—and outwardly—I'd vowed to handle this myself. Mac had gone too far this time. I'd had to help my sister Candace paint the Apple House to cover up the damage.

I turned my neck, noting the stiffness there and in my shoulders from working the paint roller all afternoon.

Abby opened his mouth to respond, but I cut him off. "And I expected you to be on my side. Mercer and Joan and Candace aren't taking me seriously," I complained, noting how none of my siblings or co-workers thought Mac was to blame either.

My friend winced. "Just keep an open mind is all I'm saying. You've never been very . . . rational where Mac is concerned." I made a rough sound of indignation, and Abby raised his hands in surrender. "It could very well be a dumb teenager with nothing better to do."

"I'm going to get to the bottom of this, and you're all going to eat your words. Also, why does everyone want to blame hypothetical teenagers when there is a violent offender with motive right across the highway?"

"Well," Abby speculated, "we were teenagers once, and we did stupid shit."

I thought about it for half a second and then nodded. "Alright. Fine. You got me there."

"Just don't go off half-cocked and throw around a bunch of accusations."

I shifted in my seat, thinking about the portrait I'd commissioned just this afternoon.

Abby's gaze narrowed. "What did you do?"

"Nothing!" I said, sounding more defensive than I liked. I lowered my voice. "I didn't do anything." *Yet* went carefully left unsaid.

Because one thing was for sure: I wasn't letting this go. And when I proved Mac was behind this diabolical deed, I was fully prepared to retaliate.

***

Early October at the orchard meant things were hectic. We were busy with tourists Thursday through Sunday, and then busy in the fields the rest of the time trying to get as much ripe fruit off the trees as we could before the first frost hit. I pitched in where I was needed. Sometimes, that meant throwing on a picking bag and joining my elder sister, Joan, and the orchard's only non-relative co-worker, Mark Mercer. Other times, I worked in the Apple House, selling to customers or washing, grading, and pressing apples. Today, I was manning the sales counter with Candace.

She was back in Kirby Falls for the first time in years. Candy said she was just taking some time off before changing jobs and wanted to help Mom and Dad with the orchard, but I could tell something else was going on with her. My little sister was being squirrely, but I'd let her tell me in her own time.

You couldn't force the truth out of someone, especially when they weren't ready to hear it themselves.

"What's happening with your face?" Candy asked.

I finished putting the cash in the register from the last sale and glanced over at her. "What are you talking about, Candy Cane?"

She pointed to her own upper lip. "That thing. Right there."

"Oh, I'm growing a mustache." I popped a handful of orange Tic Tacs from the container I kept beneath the counter.

She blinked hazel eyes that looked just like our mother's. "It's not really coming in even."

I knew that, but I was sticking with it. I'd always been so baby-faced that I hadn't been able to grow a beard when it was the trendy thing. Now, at the ripe old age of twenty-eight, I was going for a mustache. Besides, it looked distinguished. Or it would once it started growing.

"Well," I said, determined to ignore her teasing, "Tom Selleck wasn't built in a day, baby sister. Give it time."

Candy cringed. "Yeah, but I still have to see your face until it looks normal. And who knows how long that'll take."

"Very funny, butthead," I said and pulled her in for a headlock.

Candace was three years younger than me. We'd fought like cats and dogs growing up, but I'd missed her when she'd been living in New York for the better part of the last decade. She was a good sister, and we were close.

Now, she squirmed and shrieked with my elbow gripping her head, and I felt a sense of diabolical sibling satisfaction along with gratitude that Candy had finally come home. I eventually released her when a kid ran up to pay for a turn on the farm's giant bounce pillow.

Once the youngster scurried off with his wristband, Candy punched me in the shoulder.

Then she finished smoothing her hair and said, "You know, I've been meaning to ask you about the prices for the u-pick buckets. Why were the numbers on the signage marked out and replaced?"

I fidgeted with the zipper on my vest before admitting, "I saw Grandpappy's advertising their prices and thought we should stay competitive."

Her gaze narrowed. "So you lowered them by one penny so it would be cheaper than the farm across the street?"

"Yeah, Candy, I did. They're our rivals. Can't win the war if you're not thinking about the next battle."

Candy shook her head. "You and Mac are the only ones who consider us competitors."

While it was true that our farms were very different, you couldn't ignore the fact that most leafers picked only one orchard to visit when they came to town. Sure, some folks wanted the flash and bells and whistles of Grandpappy's, with their giant General Store and their corn maze and their hayrides. You could even pay to target shoot with an apple cannon, for crying out loud.

But some people had discerning taste and preferred a smaller family operation that welcomed and educated. Judd's was just better than Grandpappy's, and that's all there was to it.

"Don't even speak her name," I warned. "That delinquent."

"You're ridiculous. Have you heard anything from the sheriff?"

It had been three weeks since Mac—presumably—vandalized our Apple House, and the sheriff's office hadn't done a damn thing about it.

"No, but I still call them daily for an update on the investigation."

Candy patted me on the shoulder. "Good luck with that, Brady. Hopefully, it was a one-off, and we won't even need all those automatic lights and security cameras you installed."

I nodded, but I was ready. If my calculations were correct, there'd be a development in the investigation shortly. Sometimes, you had to draw out your enemy, and I'd made a pretty big move earlier in the day. I had a feeling something would be happening very soon.

I got my answer a few hours later.

It was closing time and I'd just latched the chain across the gravel entrance to the orchard when I spotted Mac barreling down the path from Grandpappy's, driving a baby-blue side-by-side.

I couldn't resist my smirk as she crossed the highway and pulled to stop three inches from my shins.

Mac climbed out of the vehicle with a furious expression and marched up to me, holding a white paper in her hand. She extended her arm—pretty far because I was so much taller than her—and held up the printout in front of my face.

"What the hell, Brady? Do you know how many people have texted me and, if that wasn't bad enough, called me on the damn phone to ask if I was the one who vandalized the Apple House? I did not paintball your family's property! Did you seriously post this ridiculous mug shot in the Kirby Falls Facebook group accusing me of vandalism?"

Yes. I had done that.

My buddy Jase's little sister was a freshman at Kirby Falls High School and a very talented artist. She'd whipped up this drawing of Mac, and I'd posted it in the town's Facebook group, asking if anyone had seen any suspicious individuals fitting the description purchasing paintball rounds.

I peered around the eight-and-a-half-by-eleven sheet to meet Mac's blazing gray gaze. "I actually think it's a flattering likeness."

"I am going to murder you," she snarled.

I patted my pockets for effect. "Damn. I should have recorded this conversation. That sounded like a threat the sheriff would be interested in."

She rolled her eyes. "I'm sure you already have a letter stashed among your things that says if anything happens to you, MacKenzie Clark is the likely suspect."

I grinned. "That was a good one."

"And really"—she flipped the page around so she could read it—"this description is grossly inaccurate. I do not have a 'prominent forehead,' and I'm five six not four eleven, and you know it."

"Huh," I mused, stroking my chin. "I could have sworn you were shorter than that."

Mac growled, and I tallied another point in my column.

But then her attention dropped to my mouth, and my hand abruptly fell away. She took a step closer, and I straightened to my full height.

"What—what are you doing?" I asked as she leaned closer, a searching look on her face.

She ignored me. "What's on your face?"

Her finger extended out and up like she was going to poke me, and I raised a hand to ward her off.

"Hands to yourself, Big Mac."

"No, seriously." She squinted. "There's something above your lip."

I crossed my arms and gave her my best unaffected stare.

"Oh my God," she wheezed. "Are you trying to grow a mustache?"

"No," I denied automatically. Damn it.

She grinned, her blood-red lips stretching wide to reveal straight white teeth.

I swallowed, momentarily distracted by the bright splash of color she nearly always wore.

"You really are." She was flat-out laughing now, and I'd had enough.

"Well now, why would I try to grow a mustache when it could never hope to compete with yours," I said, deadpan.

She gasped and covered her mouth with the hand not holding the mug shot. "I do not."

It was my turn to grin. "It's even there in your portrait." That had been an extra special request.

Mac's attention snapped to the paper in her grasp. Angry heat flared, and color bloomed in her pale cheeks.

I raised a hand to my ear and cocked my head.

Her brow furrowed. "What are you doing?"

"Just listening for a fire alarm for that wicked burn."

She rolled her eyes.

With a final angry huff, she pushed the paper onto my chest and backed away. I placed a hand over my heart to keep the printout from fluttering to the ground.

Glaring from behind the windshield of the side-by-side, she said, "You're going to regret this, Brady Judd."

It wasn't even an effort to keep the smile on my face while she peeled out and headed back over to Grandpappy's. I assumed she was off to sacrifice puppies or write in her diary about how much she hated me. You know, whatever she did for fun.

The mug shot and the post had done exactly what I'd hoped—drawn Mac's ire. And I'd solidified it with this little encounter—one I'd foreseen from a mile away. God, she was predictable. Now I just needed her to act out in retaliation. Maybe she'd hit the Apple House again. I doubted Mac had the wherewithal to think up a new plan of attack. And if she did decide to bring her paintball gun to the farm, I'd be ready for her. Then my family and everyone would know I wasn't the ridiculous one for thinking Mac was capable of taking things too far.

I looked down at the paper I still held. It really was a nice drawing. Jase's sister was talented as hell. She'd even captured the way Mac's eyes looked like gray storm clouds. And the sort of elegant way her neck curved into her—

A loud blast and an answering explosion had me ducking for cover. There wasn't much cover to be had in the middle of the gravel driveway, and soon enough, I felt a sticky liquid raining down from overhead.

"What the hell?" I murmured. My gaze shot up toward the Judd's Orchard billboard poised above the entrance to the farm just in time to hear another boom and witness the corresponding apple splinter on impact.

"Damn it, Mac!" I hollered, but there was no way she could hear me from this far away, and not over the sound of the apple cannon she was firing.

I awkwardly crab-walked over the chain blocking the entrance and retreated onto our property. While crouching under the trees on the side of the path, I watched as another apple came from the direction of Grandpappy's. This one exploded against the faded billboard right between my eyes—well, the eyes of my younger self advertising wholesome family fun.

Six more propelled attacks struck the image of my youthful face as bits and pieces of obliterated apples fell to the ground and fruit juice burst in time with each impact. Finally, the barrage stopped. I figured she was out of ammo, or one of her saner family members had intervened.

I made my way back to the orchard's parking lot and to my car. Briefly, I wondered if Mac and I had taken things too far. But then I thought, *Nah*, and started the engine of my truck.

Later that night, when my brain was too active for sleep, I made my way into my kitchen and started working on a batch of coffee cake mini loaves. Baking was something I'd done with my momma growing up. It gave me something to do with my hands when I was too busy or agitated. The rote actions of following a recipe helped give me focus and took the pressure off my mind.

I was scrolling through step four of the recipe when a notification popped up at the top of my screen. I placed the spatula on the edge of the mixing bowl and navigated over to the Chatter app. A vineyard near the farm had tagged Grandpappy's in a post, and Mac had mentioned Judd's in her reply.

@TheLonelyMountainWinery: That you taking shots after hours, @Grand-pappysApples?

The reply featured an attached image of a row of four apple cannons with the following text:

@GrandpappysApples: Well, they weren't Jell-O shots, but they were just as satisfying. Right, @JuddsFamilyOrchard?

My snort of laughter rang out in the stillness of my apartment. Instinctively, my gaze sought Mac's mug shot. I'd affixed the printout to the front of my refrigerator with a magnet.

God, she was a menace.

But I was still smiling when I retrieved my spatula and got back to mixing.

three

MAC

I was watering the African violets out in the sunroom when I heard a commotion from the backyard.

After the apple-cannon incident two days ago, I was sort of expecting a retaliatory attack. It wouldn't have been surprising to see Brady standing in my backyard with a twenty-four pack of single-ply, ready to toilet paper the whole house. His only hobbies seemed to be running his big mouth and annoying the hell out of me.

But it wasn't Brady Judd completely dismantling the standing birdfeeder.

"Damn it," I mumbled.

I set down the small watering can on the end table and walked to the other side of the room. The fall breeze ruffled my hair as I slid the door open on its tracks.

I clapped three times and hollered into the yard. "Get on out of here!"

The big black bear didn't even look up from where it stood, pulling the top of the birdfeeder over toward the ground. The metal pole it was attached to groaned and bent under the animal's massive strength. I tried yelling and clapping some more, but the bear spared me a single bored glance before it sat down heavily with its haul of birdseed that I'd just put out this morning.

As the beast shifted to paw at the contents of the feeder, I noticed its left ear. I sighed and shut the door, knowing there was no use bothering to try to scare it off.

When you lived in the mountains of Western North Carolina, a bear sighting was not out of the ordinary. Usually, bears were shy and more interested in the contents of your trash can than in interacting with humans. This particular black bear had been visiting our property for several years. The chunk out of her ear made it easy to keep track of her. Occasionally, in the late winter, she'd appear with a bear cub or two in tow. But since it was early October, she was alone, and from the looks of things, stocking up on reliable food sources.

My grandma Nola loved this pain-in-the-ass bear. Despite the troublemaking, I knew she'd want to hear about our little visitor.

My grandparents were currently in St. Petersburg, Florida, living that retired life. They usually spent the spring months traveling the country in their RV, returning home to Kirby Falls for the summer and holiday celebrations. Since they were away so much of the year, their house needed looking after. I'd been living in the big farmhouse overlooking the pond at Grandpappy's since high school. The arrangement worked for all of us. I had my own space—the whole second floor —for nine months out of the year. And when Grandpa Junior and Grandma Nola were home, we coexisted pretty easily. They were fun grandparents, always had been.

I finished watering the rest of my grandfather's plants and then grabbed my phone and took a seat. The sunroom was large and open. It was glass on three sides but heated and cooled along with the rest of the house. With the afternoon sun streaming in, it was a little warmer than the kitchen it was attached to.

I snapped a picture of the animal still going to town on the birdfeeder and fired it off with a text.

Me: Your friend is back.

My phone vibrated with an incoming call almost immediately, telling me my grandmother wasn't at dinner with my grandfather or visiting friends in the condo community where they lived part of the year.

"Is my sweet bear having a good dinner?" she said in lieu of a greeting, her voice a soft coo for the giant, furry troublemaker.

"Yes, she's happily destroying the birdfeeder I just refilled this morning."

"Speaking of destruction of property . . ."

My groan was loud enough that the damn bear looked over from her place in the grass.

Grandma Nola chuckled. "Word on the street is you shot up Judd's with a paintball gun *and* an apple cannon. You sure do keep busy, MacKenzie Eloise."

"First of all," I replied tartly, "word on the street? Seriously, who says that? And I did not paintball Judd's Orchard."

"I noticed you didn't address the apple-cannon part."

I shifted in my seat a little before replying, "Okay, I did do that. But I went over the night before last and cleaned up all the exploded apple bits."

"That's my girl," my grandmother replied warmly.

"You should really stay out of that nosy Facebook group," I advised.

"I know. I love it."

I fought a smile at that. My grandmother was a wildcard. She was sassy and willful and probably my favorite person in the whole world. She supported and believed in me no matter how much I didn't deserve it. Of course I loved my parents and my sister and my cousins, but Grandma Nola was my ride or die.

Clearing my throat, I changed the subject. "Shouldn't you be off playing shuffleboard or something?"

"Nope. Just lying by the pool with a mojito. Plenty of time to call and give you shit."

I snorted. If I listened closely, I could hear cabana music playing through the pool speakers.

"Braggart," I accused.

"Jealous," she retorted happily.

"Damn straight."

She laughed.

"Have a good evening, Grandma. I love you."

I heard her straw suck up the last of her mojito and smiled.

"Love you too, sugar. Replace the birdfeeder for my bear."

My eyes drifted to the beast and I rolled my eyes. "I will."

"And stay out of trouble, young lady."

Grinning, I replied, "I make no promises."

We said our goodbyes and hung up. My amusement lingered until I heard the unmistakable crunch of plastic outside. RIP birdfeeder.

Apparently, I'd have to make a trip to the hardware store this weekend. Clearly, that bear wasn't going to feed itself.

The following day, I strolled up to the little trailer we used as a ticket booth at the main entrance. It had a long counter across the front and two windows for Grandpappy's visitors to purchase entry to a variety of entertainment. We had the corn maze, hayrides, apple-cannon shooting, the pumpkin patch, the sunflower maze, and, finally, the pick-your-own-apple side of the operation—the reason why I'd dropped by. I knew Larry was on the schedule to work the ticket booth this morning. She'd be on her own until lunchtime when business would pick up and Lori, one of the part-timers, would be in to help out.

"Hey, Larry, do me a favor," I said by way of greeting.

My cousin glanced up from inside the trailer where she was counting out cash from the till. Her winged liner was spot-on, as always, and if I was a betting woman, I'd say she was wearing her beloved black combat boots. Larry's dark hair was in a little topknot, and she eyed me as I propped my arms on the counter and stared up at her.

"What do you need?"

I laid my chin atop my forearms and made my eyes real big. "Lower the u-pick bucket cost by a penny."

Larry sighed. "A penny? Again, Mac? Come on."

"It's important. I'm thinking of the farm."

"This is a waste of time."

"Competition is healthy," I argued. "Capitalism, baby."

She rolled her dark eyes heavenward.

"Just do it, Larry." I pulled out the big-cousin scowl. We were the same age, but that was beside the point. "And don't tell Will."

Larry shook her head but reached for the chalkboard sign propped up in her ticket booth window. "You and that Brady Judd have a problem. It isn't natural or healthy to be so obsessed—"

"Don't start," I interrupted and began backing away. "I'll see you for lunch. Pizza with Becca. I'm buying."

"Fine," she called, visibly buoyed at the thought of Apollo's delivery with our new friend. "And I want pineapple on my half!"

I kept walking and lifted my arm, giving her a thumbs-up.

Becca Kernsy had shown up back in August as a tourist on an extended work-from-home vacation, but I had a feeling that girl was here to stay. My family was half in love with her. Except for my cousin Will. That man was gone—head over heels and never coming back. I couldn't wait for the day he realized it. Will needed something to shake him up, and Becca might just be up for the task.

Work stayed steadily busy throughout the day and into the evening. Leafers were in town in droves. They spent their tourist dollars in our small town while they took in the sights, snapped Instagram-worthy photos of fall leaves, and visited Grandpappy's for apple picking. Since it was October, the pumpkin patch and corn maze were especially busy, too.

My regular duties as a full-time employee included rotating in and out of different positions. One day, I might work in the General Store alongside my parents, Robert and Patty, or the next, I could be scheduled to man the corn maze entrance or the apple cannon. I usually filled in where I was needed. I didn't have a specific role on the farm like most of my family members.

My aunt Maggie wielded her spatula over at the Orchard Bake Shop, making pastries for the morning rush and cakes for special occasions. Maggie's husband

—my uncle William—was the head farmer and stuck to tending the fields. My cousin Will was sort of the overall manager at Grandpappy's. He handled the accounting and ordering and just generally had to put out fires all over the place. I did not envy him that position. Sure, it would be nice to know what my schedule looked like from week to week. And maybe having some authority on the farm was something to aspire to, but with all of that came responsibility. Duty and obligation and accountability made things messy.

I just showed up when I was supposed to and did what I was told. There was freedom in that. I didn't *love* working with the tourists, but who really enjoyed their day job? It wasn't like I'd gone to college and studied business like Will. I didn't have a specialty or specific skill to offer. I was just another cog in the machine that kept Grandpappy's moving, and that was good enough for me.

One of my regular tasks was working the seasonal farmers' market in downtown Kirby Falls. Grandpappy's had a booth there, and we set up weekly, selling homegrown produce and goods from the bakery, like jams and jellies and scone and muffin mixes. I usually had to take a farmers' market shift every few weeks.

And, lucky me, tomorrow was Saturday. I was expected bright and early.

I arrived on Main Street the following morning with two travel mugs of coffee and very little patience. I didn't know why my weekends downtown constantly lined up with Brady's or why our tents were always next to one another, but that seemed to be the way of things. He was working the Judd's Orchard booth with his sister Joan. I could hear his big mouth before I even got halfway down the block.

Maybe if I ignored him, we could get through the next five hours without bloodshed or a black eye.

"Will came early and set everything up," Larry said when I joined her.

I rolled my eyes. This wasn't new, but it sure as hell was getting old.

Will, former professional athlete and overachiever extraordinaire, thought he was the only one capable of doing anything. He acted like Laramie and I were just dumb teenagers who couldn't be trusted to drive the farm truck, much less set up the market booth. I knew he meant well, but sometimes I didn't need to be reminded that I was a directionless twenty-eight-year-old who still lived with her grandparents. The very same grandparents I shared with Will. He treated me more like a wayward employee than a cousin. But Larry and I were used to it at this point. We loved the guy, but he drove us fucking crazy.

"Of course he did," I groused, passing her the thermos with dark roast and hazelnut creamer.

"Thank you," she moaned appreciatively, popping the lid and taking a deep inhale.

Despite having three more minutes on the clock, early birds were already wandering down Main Street and approaching booths. The road was closed to traffic so that pedestrians could mosey.

We sold to tourists and chatted with locals easily enough for the first hour or so. Eventually, Sheila Jessup—retired schoolteacher and active busybody—approached Judd's tent next door. She was loud enough that I could hear her asking about the vandalism, undoubtedly eager for gossip for the town's Facebook group that she ran, as well as the local podcast she recorded weekly. I noticed she sure wasn't buying any apples.

I rolled my eyes as Brady's equally loud voice indulged her in all the gossip she'd been seeking.

"Just let it go," Larry murmured from my side.

"I didn't say anything," I grumbled.

"Yeah, but I can hear you grinding your molars. For the sake of my sanity and your tooth enamel, just ignore him."

Honestly, I hadn't planned on inserting myself one bit. I *did* have self-control, despite what my family thought. But Brady just would *not* shut up.

"Yes, ma'am," he exclaimed at full volume, drawl as thick as molasses. "It's just such a betrayal to be so blatantly attacked by someone in the community."

"Oh, I do agree," Sheila cooed sympathetically. "Our neighbors should be sources of friendship and comfort."

My gaze drifted to the side against my will, and I caught Brady leaning back casually in his chair, a solemn nod aimed back at Mrs. Jessup.

As if sensing my attention, he glanced my way and smirked.

I could probably trace back a number of my angry outbursts over the years to the way Brady's lips tilted up arrogantly at the corners. Like cause and effect. Pavlov's slobbery dog and that damn bell all over again. And today was, regrettably, no different.

Heat gathered behind my sternum in a furious swarm, like hundreds of restless hornets ready to direct their wrath onto a specified target. I'd always hated that Brady could get such a reaction out of me, but I wasn't going to sit here listening to him talk around me, insinuating crimes, placing blame, and spreading rumors, all without defending myself.

An instant later, I stood and faced the Judd's booth, arms crossed and ready for a fight. "Maybe you just like the attention, Brady Judd. Did you ever think of that?" I heard Larry groan dramatically behind me. "Maybe you paintballed your own Apple House to get sympathy, media attention, and sales. That's the theory I'm leaning toward."

The front two legs of Brady's chair hit the ground, and he turned to face me, bright blue eyes sparkling. "Now, why in the world would I ever do a thing like that?"

I tapped my chin like I was thinking hard. "You have always been jealous of Grandpappy's. I have no doubt you'd cheat in an effort to outperform your rivals."

He grinned, delighted. "So you think I'm outperforming you?"

I smiled too, all teeth. "Not a chance, Axe Body Spray."

Brady frowned and ducked his head toward his armpit as if to sniff and then caught himself, replying haughtily, "Well, luckily, the sheriff's office isn't interested in your opinion."

"And from what I've heard, they aren't interested in yours either."

My friend Mary Beth worked down at the sheriff's office answering phones, and she'd told me that Brady called every day to check on the case. The deputy assigned to it tried to avoid Brady at all costs and had even given Mary Beth a standing order to tell him that the deputy was out of the office on important police work.

Brady gasped like I'd wounded him, clutching figurative pearls like a giant man-baby.

"She's got you there," Brady's sister Joan stated diplomatically from his side. "Now, if you two are done scaring off all the customers, I'd really like to get back to work. I have no interest in hauling all these apples back to the farm this afternoon."

I blinked and then looked around. Sheila Jessup was long gone, her retreating form already mostly down the block.

Brady scowled at me as if *I* was the one who'd gotten him in trouble with his no-nonsense big sister.

I scowled back just as hard.

"Obsessed," Larry singsonged when I finally regained my seat.

"Not. A. Word," I said pointedly, the angry hornet's nest now a dull buzz in my veins.

My smartass cousin mimed zipping her smiling pink lips and tossing a key over her shoulder.

The tension broke when a customer approached. A leafer, judging by the tall boots and the bright white sweater tied artfully around their shoulders. Larry and I—and Brady and Joan, for that matter—got back to work, and I managed to ignore the neighboring tent and its occupants for the rest of the day.

At one point just before closing up shop, Larry's best friend, Kayla, wandered over from the direction of the parking garage. Kayla had been a classmate of ours, and we'd known her since Sunday school before that. She and my cousin had always been close. They were even neighbors, living side by side in a duplex over on Elliott Street.

Kayla was tall and gorgeous, with long blond hair and big blue eyes. She resembled the stereotypical surfer girl with sun-kissed skin and a laid-back attitude. Back in school, she'd played volleyball and been a lifeguard in the summers. She was well-liked and popular, and we'd always gotten along.

"What's up, y'all?" Kayla said casually as she approached.

Larry made a surprised little squeak that had me glancing her way as I greeted Kayla.

Eventually, Larry formulated a passable "hello," and I wondered vaguely what was up. Maybe they were in a fight or something.

"Did you make it home okay the other night?" Kayla asked, directing the question to my cousin. "Sasha said you were trashed."

"Yeah, of course." Then Larry laughed brightly, and it was so fake that I wondered if Kayla would call her on it. She knew Larry just as well as I did, after all.

There was definitely something going on.

Kayla and Sasha worked over at Magnolia, a bar on the end of Main Street that catered to tourists. Respectable locals didn't go there, but Larry did visit occasionally when Kayla was on shift. The bar was polished to within an inch of its life, and they only served wine, craft beers, and fancy cocktails. It was the local establishment version of someone who'd gotten too big for their britches. But they made a killing during tourist season, which was growing longer and busier every year.

Hell, Grandpappy's did the same thing. We wouldn't survive without tourist dollars, so who was I to judge uppity Magnolia Bar?

"Did you have fun with Sebastian?" Larry asked suddenly.

Kayla laughed. "Was that his name?"

I detected an audible swallow from my side. "Uh, yeah," Larry confirmed.

"Anyway," Kayla said after a moment of awkward silence, "you want to grab lunch after the farmers' market? I feel like I haven't seen you in forever."

Larry was tense, but she nodded. "Yeah, that sounds good. Unless you need some help loading up, Mac?"

I looked at the very few items we had left on the table. "No, I can manage. Y'all have fun."

Kayla told Larry to meet her at Montell's Sandwich Shop down the street when she was finished and then strolled off, phone already in her hand as she focused on the screen.

Larry and I sat quietly until I all but blurted, "Want to tell me what that was all about?"

She shifted in her seat. "Not really."

"Laramie Annabeth," I scolded.

"Jesus, fine." She sighed. "Last week, I was hanging out with Kayla while she was bartending. She met some guy and went home with him. I decided to stay at the bar and enjoy myself, but I may have possibly overindulged."

Surprise lit my features. Larry was fun-loving and extroverted and exuberant, but she was not one for public intoxication. "Were you dancing on their fancy table-tops or something?"

She winced. "More like puking and passed out in their fancy powder room."

My shock turned to concern. "What the hell, Larry? Why didn't you call me to come get you? How did you get home?"

"I got a hold of Becca, and she took care of me."

My cousin looked sheepish and a little ashamed. I liked Becca a lot, but I couldn't figure out why Larry would have called her instead of me.

"Oh."

"I knew you were at the bonfire," she rushed to explain. "And, honestly, I don't know what I was thinking. I was so far gone."

"Any particular reason you felt the need to get shit-faced?" I asked, proud of the gentleness in my tone when my instinct was to be accusatory.

Larry just shook her head.

I watched my cousin for a moment, the expertly applied makeup that gave her confidence and the vulnerable hunch of her shoulders suddenly at odds. I felt an ache in my chest at her obvious hurt and discomfort. "You know you can talk to me, right? About anything. I know we give each other a hard time and joke around a lot. But you're my family and my best friend. I love you."

She didn't look at me as she replied, just kept staring at the ground as she picked at the decorative rip in her black jeans. "I know that."

Larry was often so carefree and joyful that I rarely saw this side of her. It was stark and unsettling, and I didn't like feeling powerless in the face of it. How did you help someone who was reluctant for it? Could you wrap them up in your love and protect them from the world if you didn't know what you were protecting them from?

Finally, her head rose, and she gave me a smile—a fraction of the one I was used to seeing from her, but a smile nonetheless. "I love you too, you maniac. And you better check your phone. I saw a notification pop up a minute ago."

I took the distraction for what it was and didn't call her on it.

Reaching for my phone on the tabletop, I scrolled through and swiped away various notifications. There were a few emails. A new article had been posted for this travel e-magazine I liked. Finally, my eyes caught on a particular social media notification, and I felt that hornet's nest buzz to life. I'd changed my alerts the other day to let me know anytime Judd's Orchard posted on Chatter. For . . . reconnaissance purposes. And it was a good thing I had.

@JuddsFamilyOrchard: With all due respect, imagine going to work every day and polishing your apple cannon.

Larry leaned into me to look at the screen. "Yikes. Shots fired."

I glared at her for the pun and then started typing.

"Maybe you should take five before you reply. Just, like, a brief cooldown period. For safety," she advised.

"Whose safety?" I asked. "His or mine?"

"Why not both?" she answered with a cheesy grin.

"Yeah, I'm not going to do that."

I reread my reply before hitting post. Didn't want any typos for Brady to draw attention to. Lesson learned. That had been a bleak day a few months back.

But, nope. This looked all good. I grinned wickedly.

@GrandpappysApples: @JuddsFamilyOrchard, With all due respect, aka none . . . that's it. That's the post.

BRADY

I was running late.

I *hated* running late.

Sticking to a schedule helped me focus. It kept me on track and prevented distractions. I knew that Abby—or anyone else, for that matter—wouldn't notice or care that I was late for a Friday night bonfire. It had always been a casual event. But I could feel the shift and upset to my own inner timetable.

Candace had recently started adding local bands and food truck events to the calendar at Judd's Orchard. They'd been popular so far, and tonight especially. She'd asked me to stay a little late to help wrangle the crowds. Since I was an accommodating and benevolent brother/co-worker, I'd said yes. Plus, I didn't want her closing up alone.

But staying over at the orchard meant I was getting to Abby's property at nearly ten o'clock. There were only a handful of vehicles left in the field beside the barn. I figured the early-October weather was scaring people off. This was the first really cold night we'd had this fall. But it was clear and beautiful. I spied an ocean of tiny stars scattered across the sky when I hopped out of my truck.

I breathed in the familiar scent of woodsmoke and made my way toward the bonfire to warm up, but before I turned the corner of the barn, I spotted MacKenzie Clark leaning against the side of the building. Her head was tipped back, resting on the rough wooden planks, and she was breathing deliberately—in through her nose and out through her mouth. Her breath created a plume of white with every exaggerated exhale. This looked very much like the exercise of a person trying very hard not to puke. I recognized it well from my years in undergrad.

"You okay over there, Macaroni Salad?" I asked as I slowly approached her.

Her eyes shot open, but she didn't move away from the wall. "Please don't talk about macaroni salad," she slurred.

I grinned. "Did you overindulge? Are you regretting your life choices?"

"I'm regretting your life choice," she grumbled and closed her eyes once more.

I chuckled. "Do you want me to go get someone for you so they can take you home? Is Larry here? Or Bonnie?"

Mac started to shake her head and then immediately halted. "No, don't. I won rock, paper, scissors with Larry, so I got to drink, and she has to drive."

I peeked around the edge of the old barn and saw Mac's cousin in among the half dozen or so people who were still gathered around the fire.

"Well," I said when I faced Mac again, "I think you nailed the drinking portion of the evening."

"Don't start." But there was no heat behind her words, and those typically fiery gray eyes stayed firmly shut. "You know what it's like."

I frowned. "I know what what's like?"

Mac took a steady inhale through her nose before releasing another cloud of warmth into the air around her. I noticed her eye makeup was a little smudged, and her patented red lipstick had worn off.

"Dealing with the leafers," she finally replied. "I just needed a break."

Grandpappy's was open to the public seven days a week during apple season. Mac undoubtedly saw her fair share of tourists. I could understand where she was coming from. The leafers could definitely try your patience. There were always feral children running wild while parents didn't pay them a bit of atten-tion. We had folks wandering the fields well beyond the rows labeled ripe for picking. And at least once or twice a year, I caught someone back by the pressing equipment "just trying to get a closer look."

So, if Mac wanted to blow off a little steam on a Friday night, I couldn't fault her for it. Especially when, in all likelihood, she'd be right back at it tomorrow, selling apples, answering questions, and wrangling chaos.

"Yeah," I agreed. "I get it."

Mac nodded, and the movement had her suddenly unsteady. She wobbled like a foal on the deck of a pirate ship, and I darted forward to catch her before she listed perilously to one side and her face met the ground.

"Whoa, there."

"I'm not a horse," she groused as she attempted to right herself and get away from me all at the same time.

I rolled my eyes but was inwardly amused that she'd read my mind. "Why don't you sit? Here. Let me—" With a hand around her upper arm, I guided her down toward the dead grass beneath our feet. She was so squirmy and unstable that I ended up going down with her and landing hard on my ass.

We were side by side, and she was breathing purposefully again. I wondered if I was about to get puked on.

Mac closed her eyes and pulled her long, dark hair out of the collar of her puffy jacket and swept it off to one side. Her skin was pale—paler than normal. I stayed quiet while she attempted to get her nausea under control.

I could have hopped up and wished her good luck with the vomiting. I could have joined my friends around the bonfire and told her cousin where to find her drunk ass. But this was maybe the longest, most civil conversation we'd had in recent memory. I still thought she was a delinquent vandal who needed anger management classes. But I also liked the idea that she'd needed my help—just a little bit—a moment ago. I could probably hold it over her head at a later date. Oh, I could even blackmail her with video footage of her getting sloppy drunk on a random Friday. I'd still hold her hair back if she did get sick. I was a gentleman, after all. I had two hands. I could use one to hold her hair and the other to steady my phone and film the destruction.

Maybe in her present state, she'd admit to paintballing the Apple House.

There were lots of diabolical reasons for me to stay right here with her warm thigh pressed against mine and her bony elbow poking into my side. At least, that's what I told myself.

My gaze drifted over her face—watching for signs of impending upchuck. Her plump lips parted with every exhale, and her face was relaxed, dark brows neutral when they were typically drawn together in irritation or lowered in scrutiny.

Mac looked so different than normal. Ninety-eight percent of the time, she was firmly in charge of her faculties. She was quick on the uptake and always ready with a comeback—usually an impressively wicked zinger. Defensive was her default with me. Always had been.

Mac was a wrecking ball and a ballbuster. Basically, she would wreck your balls.

But right now, she looked softer and, despite the threat of vomit, approachable in a way I rarely ever witnessed.

She had this divot in her chin—just a slight dip, really. I was pretty sure I'd started the nickname "butt chin" that had clung to her during grades two through six.

Anyway, when we argued, sometimes I daydreamed about shocking the daylights out of her and grabbing her chin. I'd always thought that little divot would be the perfect spot to rest my thumb. But I'd never actually done it. See the aforementioned ball-busting.

"You don't have to stay," Mac slurred suddenly.

I jumped in surprise, jerking my eyes away from her profile.

"I know," I said, waiting for my heart rate to slow from being startled. But it didn't. For some reason, the muscle in my chest kept pounding out a frantic rhythm. Maybe it was used to all the battles with Mac over the years, and fight or flight seemed safest where she was concerned.

"Why don't you want me to go get Larry?" I wondered aloud.

Mac groaned, and my muscles tensed, preparing to dive out of the splash zone should the need arise. But she only admitted, "Because she watched every time I grabbed a new bottle and told me to slow down at least three times with a handful of knowing looks and one very telling eye roll thrown in for good measure."

I nodded even though Mac couldn't see it. "Gotcha. Trying to avoid the familial 'I told you so.'"

"Exactly," she agreed and then forced another slow breath through faded red lips. "I don't want her to know I fucked up and she was right about it. That's probably why I drank so damn much in the first place."

"To prove her wrong?"

Mac swallowed with a concerted effort. "Yeah."

Quiet settled around us, and I was surprised at how comfortable it was. Mac was warm against my side. I hardly noticed the cold anymore. There was only the scent of woodsmoke and about a million stars overhead. No witnesses to whatever unexpected peace was happening between us.

"I'm tired of making decisions—the wrong fucking decisions—because I'm always overreacting or overcorrecting based on someone else." Mac's voice didn't disrupt the night so much as part it neatly around us, creating a bubble of honesty—an alternate dimension where we shared truths with one another instead of spite. "But at least then I can blame things on them and not myself."

For once in my loudmouthed existence, I had no idea what to say. Part of me worried that if I spoke or even breathed too loudly, she'd remember I was here and stop talking altogether. I'd never heard Mac sound so open or vulnerable. I didn't know she was capable of it.

Mac continued unprompted, "Drinking too much because Larry warned me off. Half-assing everything at the farm because Will doesn't expect any better from me. Living with my grandparents because that's what's easy."

My heart had picked up again with each confession. I knew it was the alcohol talking. She was so far gone that she likely wouldn't remember this conversation tomorrow. I should make myself get up and leave. Give her privacy for whatever she was going through.

But then Mac said, "Dating all these guys because Brady Judd gives me shit over them," and I knew I wasn't going anywhere.

Truthfully, I didn't think I could move. I felt rooted to the ground, a painful spike of realization holding my limbs hostage. "What?" I choked out. In contrast, my own voice sounded rough and unpracticed. It destroyed the illusion of peace and cut through the quiet night like a rusty blade.

Head tipped back and eyes still closed, Mac snorted, and a twisted sort of amusement lit her features. "Remember last month at the farmers' market? David came to pick me up."

I rifled through my memories of working the Judd's booth on Main Street back in September and came up with the image of a generic man in his early thirties with brown hair, khaki pants, and zero personality. The guy—David, apparently —had been meeting Mac to take her on a daytime date, of all things. I'd been nosy and taken the opportunity to rile Mac up over this guy who'd been so obviously wrong for her. I'd introduced myself and made some crack about him being her new boyfriend and how he shouldn't feed her after midnight. Mac had gotten steamed, and we'd traded insults before she'd stormed off with a very dazed-looking David in tow.

Confused, I asked, "The dentist?"

"Yeah," she confirmed. "The dentist. That was our first and only date, did you know that?"

I couldn't remember seeing them together after that day, but that wasn't unusual for Mac. She dated randomly in fits and starts. The guys never lasted long. I had a theory that she got bored with them—that they never measured up. None of these generic Davids or Toms or Noahs could hold her attention for long.

Before I could answer, the sardonic smile fell off her face, and she admitted woodenly, "I went home with him. And when I snuck out of his house later that night, I hated myself because I knew I didn't even like the guy that much. When he called me to ask me out again, I lied and told him we were in different places. I said I wasn't ready for anything serious instead of telling him the truth . . . that I fucked him to prove a point, one that didn't even matter."

I felt the color drain from my face and a hollow open up in my stomach. Suddenly, I was the one in danger of being sick. I thought—I thought—

"You know," Mac said sleepily, "I'm tired of making mistakes for everybody else. It's time I fucked up for myself for once."

The combination of shock and self-loathing and jealousy I didn't have any business feeling left me weak.

That day . . . we'd been bickering like always. Maybe I'd been feeling a spike of *something* at seeing her with another guy. I never imagined that my teasing would prompt such a reaction from Mac. If I had known—

"I'm sorry, MacKenzie," I whispered, aching to reach for her, to make her open her eyes to really see me and hear me. "I didn't mean it. I never—"

I cut myself off, unsure how to put it into words, ones that justified the pain I'd caused. *I thought we were on the same page. You gave as good as you got. I wanted you to notice me. I wanted to make sure you couldn't forget about me like you forget about the rest of them.*

Things between us had clearly gone too far. *I* had taken them too far. I'd hurt her, caused her to react the way she hated—in direct opposition to someone else. And in all that knowledge, I realized . . . I had the power to hurt her in the first place.

Before I could put any part of that into words or figure out a way to apologize again, Mac's mouth dropped open, and a broken snore filled the quiet. Her head drooped over and rested heavily against my shoulder. I stiffened, but she didn't wake. Mac had fallen asleep on me—trusting and unaware—and I hated myself a little more.

My mind wandered back through years of arguments and mocking. I didn't know how long I sat there with Mac's soft snore in my ear and her confession churning a maelstrom in my middle. But I blinked back into awareness sometime later when a pair of black combat boots came into my field of vision.

I glanced up to see Mac's cousin standing in front of us, eyes wide with obvious shock.

"Holy shit," Larry breathed in reverent amusement. "This is the best day of my life."

The pint-sized goth-pixie hurried to extract her phone from her jacket pocket and proceeded to snap photo after photo from multiple angles.

"Judd, I know she's my cousin, but would you like me to send you a copy of these? For posterity . . . or blackmail or whatever."

"No," I managed.

Larry paused, expression morphing to frowny confusion. "What? Why? I told her ass not to drink so much, but did she listen to me? No, siree."

I glanced down at Mac's sleeping face. Larry's gloating statement had me feeling suddenly protective, and I curved my body closer to the woman at my side.

I knew Larry didn't mean any harm, but the statement rubbed me wrong just the same. The two women had been close their whole lives, best friends as well as family. But what Larry had just said reinforced what Mac had admitted. Sleeping Beauty here had practically called it earlier. Larry had warned her she was going too hard and too fast, and, as a result, Mac had doubled down out of spite or rebellion or whatever you wanted to call it. An overreaction, an overcorrection, she'd said.

Staring at her now, passed out and dead to the world, I felt empathy for the woman who was always trying to prove people wrong.

And like a bucket of cold water to the face, I stiffened at the thought of my own role in Mac's decision-making.

Clearing my throat quietly, I looked back to Laramie. "Nah, I don't need a picture. She'll be in enough pain in the morning when she wakes up. Better not add insult to injury."

Larry looked at me like I was an idiot, but then she shrugged.

I wiggled my toes to try to get some feeling back. "Why don't you go start your car? I'll bring her over."

"Sure thing." With a jangle of keys, Larry and her combat boots drifted away, lit by the automatic floodlights on the side of the barn.

I made sure Mac wouldn't tip over onto the ground and got to my feet. Then I leaned down and carefully lifted her, one arm beneath her knees and the other cradling her back. I straightened and froze. Mac had slung her free arm over my shoulder and buried her freezing nose in my neck.

I waited a moment, but she didn't wake. So it was with cautious steps that I made my way to the little hatchback at the far end of the field. Larry opened the passenger door as I approached. But when I crouched low to place Mac on the seat, she clung to me and snuggled closer, mumbling, "Smells good," into the skin just below my ear.

Ignoring my burning cheeks and the recent memory of Mac calling me "Axe Body Spray," I forced my reluctant muscles to unlock and gently deposited my drunken charge onto the seat. With patience I absolutely didn't feel, I reached in and drew the seat belt across her, clicking it into place and then straightening out of the cramped vehicle, back to my full height.

I closed the door softly, willing Mac to stay asleep. I was not ready to deal with . . . whatever that had been. I didn't want to think about the way her body felt in my arms or the little moan that had vibrated against my neck when she'd said I smelled good. These were all things that I was not willing to unpack right this moment. After the earlier revelation that Mac had gone home with a guy she didn't even like because I'd given her shit over him, I literally could not process everything that was happening in my overactive brain. It was going a million miles an hour, and if Mac opened her eyes and looked up at me, I would probably panic and crawl under the car.

Fortunately, she didn't wake. But when I turned around, her nosy cousin was standing there with one perfectly manicured eyebrow raised and a shit-eating grin on her face.

I ignored all of that, too. "You'll stay with her? Make sure she's okay?"

A second dark brow rose to join the first. "Of course."

I swallowed uneasily and said, "Just tell her Abby carried her out here."

It would be better for everyone if Mac never remembered tonight—the things she'd said, her brutal, terrible honesty, the vulnerabilities she'd revealed. She'd hate it. And she'd hate me for it in an entirely different way. Mac would think I had something on her—that I'd use it against her.

Larry watched me for a long, uncomfortable moment, then nodded. "Like adding insult to injury, right?"

I took a step back, needing to put some distance between me and . . . everything. "Right," I finally agreed.

Then I made my way to my truck without going anywhere near the bonfire and took my dumb ass and my wayward thoughts home.

One week had passed and I hadn't seen Mac.

That in and of itself wasn't unusual. It wasn't like we texted or grabbed lunch between pranks and arguments. But, for some reason, her absence felt more intentional. Or maybe I was just noticing it more.

As I parked my truck in the field beside Abby's barn, a sense of small-town déjà vu hit me like a wrecking ball. I felt my heart speed up at the thought of running into her tonight. She didn't usually come out to the bonfire two weeks in a row, but maybe—

As I walked through the grass, my eyes passed over the corner of the building where we'd sat for over an hour last week. Thoughts burst rapid-fire in my mind, and I forced myself to take a deep breath and keep going.

I'd had all week to sift through what had happened last Friday, and I still didn't know what to do about it. I felt jittery and more distractible than normal—which was saying something for the ADHD kid who used to get detention because he couldn't just sit still.

My fingers fidgeted with the key chain in my vest pocket as my eyes scanned those assembled. I spotted Abby and Jase by the fire, both of them on their phones. There was a decent crowd tonight. My gaze snagged on Connor Pritchard. I hadn't seen the guy in a few years. His dad had been my assistant principal back in high school, and Connor had acted like he owned the place as a result. He'd played football and basketball and been pretty popular. He'd also dated Mac very briefly in eleventh grade before spreading a bunch of rumors about her and how she wouldn't put out.

My hand tightened around the cool metal of my key chain, and I forced my attention elsewhere.

After a thorough once-over of my surroundings, I didn't see Mac anywhere.

I felt equal parts relieved and disappointed. No, that was a lie. One emotion had a clear lead, and I didn't want to examine that too closely.

I made my way over to the coolers and grabbed an IPA. I popped the top on the side of the picnic table, and when I looked up, I nearly dropped the bottle in my hand. Mac was standing there in a low-cut green sweater dress over black tights, rooting through the cooler across from me. I stared in surprise, unsure how I'd missed her when I'd been looking so hard earlier.

She straightened with a bottle of water, and I wondered at her selection. Was she taking it easy because she'd gotten so drunk last week?

And why was she all dressed up? Mac's typical bonfire attire was casual—jeans and a flannel. I swallowed hard as I fought the instinct to check out her hemline, but she'd obviously made an extra effort tonight. Her hair looked soft and so did that dress. I couldn't help but wonder who she was trying to impress. Not that it was any of my business. And yet—

"What?" she said, after I'd been staring too long.

"Nothing," I practically barked before making my voice nice and even. You know, like a normal person. "How are you?"

I was waiting for her to say something about the other night. Maybe for her to issue a threat to keep my mouth shut about what she'd said—how much she'd revealed about her frustrations and her fears and her family. But it never came. She just kept watching me.

Eventually, she murmured, "I'm fine."

Mac's jacket was open over her dress, and my eyes dipped briefly to her cleavage before meeting her still-suspicious gaze.

An awkward silence descended while I made a conscious effort not to look at her in case my gaze drifted to her chest again because—holy shit—that dress looked really good on her. Of course, I'd noticed her breasts before. I was a heterosexual male. Mac was hot, but she was also a pain. I didn't want her to stab me for checking her out, so I typically kept my eyes to myself . . . for the most part.

"What's going on with you?" she asked warily. "You're being all squirrelly."

I forced myself to stare at her face and only her face. "Nothing. No, I'm not."

God, this was a disaster. Clearly she did not remember our conversation last week. She would have brought it up by now. I could just be normal. No, not normal. Normal led to teasing and then fighting. I didn't want things to devolve, and I didn't want to hurt Mac anymore.

"Did you share another wanted poster? Maybe take out an ad in the *Kirby Falls Chronicle*?" she accused.

I thought about the illustration still up on my fridge and cleared my throat. "No—no, I didn't. I wouldn't."

I could do this. I was determined to be nice to her, not rile her up or make her react. I didn't want that on my conscience. Even if I sounded like a stammering fool, I wouldn't be mean. I would be playful and funny. Laid-back and nice. Nothing hurtful. I would not tease her about dressing up for all us lowly peasants. I would not suggest she take an available seat on my lap. Jesus, I was a dick.

Her stormy gray eyes narrowed. "Did you let the air out of my tires?"

"No, that was you, senior year," I snapped, already ruining my attempt at nice. *Shit*.

I took a deep inhale to center myself, and that reminded me of the way Mac had been breathing last Friday.

"I did not prank, accost, demean, or defile you in any way," I clarified, and then mentally backtracked to noticing her nipples in that sweater dress and winced.

"I'm keeping my eye on you, Judd."

I grinned and saluted, aiming for charming and missing by a football field.

Mac raised a haughty brow and took her bottle of water back over to the bonfire to join her cousin.

I practically sagged against the cooler.

This was only weird and uncomfortable because we had so much history. Decades of learned behavior.

But I could change. I would.

Just treat her like you would anyone in town, I practically yelled at my racing mind.

She's not like everyone else, it whispered back.

It took two beers and about an hour for me to get my shit together and to start acting like a normal human. Eventually, I stopped being constantly aware of Mac in my periphery, waiting for the moment when she might approach and I'd have to ignore all my programming and figure out how to just *be* around her.

But it never happened. Mac didn't come over to chat because why would she? We were rivals. Enemies. The thorns in each other's sides. She never sought me out unless it was in retribution.

Abby and Jase asked what was up with me no less than six times, but I waved them off, saying I was just in a weird mood and it would wear off. And it did. By the time nine o'clock rolled around, I was laughing and joking and being my typical charming self.

But then my good mood took a nosedive when Connor Pritchard came over and slapped me on the back.

"Brady Judd. Good to see you, man."

Is it? I wanted to say. Instead, I pasted on a good-ole-boy grin and an aw-shucks attitude and said, "Connor Pritchard. How the hell are you?"

Abby shot me a look. He knew how I felt about the guy. Best friends with long memories were pesky like that.

But I was playing nice tonight, all around. I could shoot the shit with a former classmate. Even if that former classmate was a huge prick. But whatever, I wouldn't cause problems for Abby. Not again.

I'd picked a fight at a bonfire one similar night a few years back. Floyd Ellerby had shown up and gotten drunk and mouthy and called the cops. At one time, Floyd had been a teammate and good friend of mine. But things had gone downhill at the tail end of eleventh grade.

Thinking back to that time, my eyes drifted over to Mac across the bonfire. She was chatting with Emily Bates and Larry and looked like she was having a good time.

It was strange how so many of my experiences and memories led back to MacKenzie Clark. If you'd asked me two months ago if she was a big part of my daily existence, I would have said, *No, not really.* Mac was a constant, though, a regular in the story of my life.

But she was more than just a background player, hovering on the fringes. We'd crossed paths and come to blows more times than I could count. I had a memory of Mac at every age—from preschool to Bible study to soccer practice to this very field one week ago and a hundred times before.

Now, though, all those moments and realizations were stacking up in front of me, forming a wall I could hardly see over.

My interaction with Mac last Friday was the reason I could barely think straight tonight. Mac was why I thought Connor Pritchard was a dick and why I was biting my tongue at this very moment to keep from telling him so. And it was due to Mac that my friendship with Floyd ended junior year.

He'd randomly hooked up with her out at her family's farm. I'd been an asshole at the time and tried to talk him out of pursing anything with her. I'd had my reasons. Sure, they had been immature and selfish and stupid, but that was what had driven my seventeen-year-old self to keep Floyd away from her. I'd been an idiot and too cowardly to admit the actual motive behind my actions had been jealousy and attraction.

But Floyd hadn't listened. He screwed around with her in secret, too chickenshit to date her openly. And when she called him on it, he spread hateful rumors about how easy she was. Abby, Jase, and I had separated ourselves from Floyd after that. He'd quit the soccer team and avoided us too, taking up with guys like Connor and his lackeys. He'd lost his closest friends but gained the sort of drama-seeking bros who devalued and disrespected women for a chance at hot gossip and rising popularity.

Now Floyd worked down at Begley Auto with some other assholes.

When he'd shown up at the bonfire a few years after graduation, he tried to act like nothing had happened. Like he hadn't tried to ruin a young girl's reputation. Like we were all still good friends. I'd set him straight on that and caused a big scene in the process. I didn't regret it, but I knew how Abby felt about that sort of attention.

He was a respected business owner in town, and the last thing I wanted to do was make him regret our friendship. He put up with a lot from me. I was flaky and unreliable, loudmouthed and easily distracted. Abby had been the most constant presence in my life outside of my family. We'd been friends since kindergarten and roommates in college, and he was my brother in every way but blood.

So when Connor smiled his smarmy grin and bragged about the car dealership he managed over in Charlotte, I promised myself I would behave myself tonight.

And it worked for a little while.

Twenty minutes into reminiscing about his glory days, Connor nodded subtly over in Mac's direction and said, "Man, I wished I'd waited until senior year to get with Clark over there. Didn't realize she'd hit a growth spurt and have such nice tits. Back then, they didn't even fill up my palms."

His laughter died abruptly when I stood up and grabbed his expensive fleece jacket by the collar, dragging him with me. Dark spots clouded my vision as fury pulsed with every beat of my raging heart. All my wayward, misguided thoughts focused on the asshole in front of me and what I'd do to him for saying—

I clenched my free hand into a fist and opened my mouth, but Abby pushed between us in a hurry. "Brady, go calm down. Connor, you better watch your fucking mouth or you can get the hell out right now. Mac's a good friend, and you aren't a teenage idiot anymore. You've got no right saying shit like that about a woman—any woman."

Connor held up his hands in surrender and said obligingly, "Okay. You're right. My fault." His words were for Abby, but he was staring straight at me. "I take it back." Then he laughed lightly. "Didn't realize Kirby Falls had feminists all the way up in the mountains."

"Hell, we even got a Walmart now," I said amiably before making my voice hard with contempt. "We have all sorts of things you seem to have forgotten since moving away, Pritchard. Common decency and respect for women being chief among them."

I felt Jase rise from his seat to stand shoulder to shoulder with me. He had three younger sisters and had been raised by a single mom. We were on the same page here.

Connor laughed again, but it sounded strained this time. "I'm going to head out. Good night, gentlemen."

I watched him glance around nervously as he walked away.

It was quiet, the only sound was wood hissing and popping in the fire. I took in my surroundings, realizing conversation had halted as a result of the altercation. People—friends, former classmates, acquaintances—were all staring at me.

Against my will, my eyes found Mac. She was still across the way with Larry and Emily, but she was standing and looking between Connor and me.

My hand found the key ring in my pocket, and I swallowed uncomfortably at what she might have overheard.

I forced myself to take a steadying breath and face my friend. "Abby, I'm sorry for the trouble. I'm going to get out of your hair."

He sighed. "You don't have to leave, Brady. He was out of line. He deserved it. I was just trying to keep you out of jail. You know that asshat would have pressed charges."

I nodded. "And I was definitely going to punch him in the face."

My gaze flitted to Mac, who was still watching me.

"I'm taking off," I said abruptly and slapped Abby and Jase on the back. "I'll see y'all later."

Then, I ignored the way Mac started walking around the perimeter of the fire, and I bolted for my truck.

To avoid that dipshit Connor, I cut through the knee-high grass and took the long way around the barn. The whole way there, I replayed what had happened and why I'd reacted so violently. That led me back to the incident with Floyd years ago. We'd gotten in a little more back-and-forth shoving before Abby had stepped in that time. The reason was nebulous, floating in the ether, just waiting for me to reach for it.

Instead, I flung open the driver's-side door and threw myself into my truck, breathing hard and clutching the steering wheel in a death grip. I turned the ignition and cranked the heat up and stared unseeingly at the trees outside my window.

There had to be a logical explanation for why every single time I'd nearly come to blows with someone had been over the woman I couldn't even have a civil conversation with. Yes, Mac and I brought out the worst in each other. I liked getting a rise out of her. She got off on it, too.

But then my mind drifted again to last Friday, hearing her confession, feeling the weight of her in my arms, the way she'd burrowed against me and held on tight.

Of course, I was attracted to Mac. That was just . . . biological. She was beautiful. And, sure, back in high school, I'd wanted something different—something more. But I'd been too immature and stupid to make it happen. Maybe that was why I'd teased her so much. I'd wanted her attention, but I didn't know how to go about getting it in a healthy way—too afraid she'd laugh in my face.

And then the thing happened with Floyd junior year. It had been shitty, but it had taken the possibility of Mac hooking up with my friend to get me to open my eyes and try being nice to her. To understand that I, maybe, wanted her for myself. But it hadn't worked out, or it had been too little, too late. We'd devolved back into bickering and pranks, and from that point on, she seemed to hate me more than ever. I became the villain in a story that had gotten away from me. Where the character had overthrown the plot.

But that had been so long ago—over a decade. Sure, there had been times over the years when I'd gotten Mac good and riled and wondered what would happen if I kissed the hell out of her. I didn't usually let myself venture too far down that path, assuming it would end in a praying mantis-style mating ritual and I'd end up headless. I didn't have a head to spare—either one of them.

As my hands continued to tighten reflexively on the steering wheel of the truck, I pictured Mac's maniacal glee over a well-timed zinger, the way her gray eyes flashed when I hit the mark in return. I remembered her cold nose pressing into my neck and the throaty sound of her voice telling me how good I smelled.

A hazy, imprecise realization was taking shape, like the Ghost of Christmas Past becoming corporeal so he could smack down some knowledge on my ignorant self. I shook my head, unwilling and firmly in denial.

"No," I said out loud into the darkness.

But other images flashed behind my eyes. Mac cackling in the stands after she stole my soccer uniform freshman year, and I'd had to play the first half in a pair of her short shorts she'd shoved into my sports bag instead.

Or that time at senior prom when she'd brought a college sophomore with her. I'd caught up with them at the punch bowl and told her there'd been no need to pay a long-lost cousin to pose as her date. That had gotten her good and mad. Later, I'd watched from the sidelines as she'd danced in a very nonfamilial way with the mystery guy. My own date had gotten so pissed at being ignored that she gathered up her friends and took off with the limo I'd saved up all spring to rent.

It was Mac, over and over again. I couldn't stop the rush of information or the knowledge landing like a sledgehammer over my head.

The way her eyes lit up and her energy crackled when we sparred. How my stomach flipped over itself when she slid into the market booth next to me on a Saturday morning. Anticipation, bright and addictive. The craving for her attention, for any kernel of acknowledgement, a single glance, a vicious grin. And the absolute satisfaction I felt anytime I could make her crack and get a laugh out of her.

My eyes shot open and I panted into the quiet, "Oh shit. Oh *fuck*."

I dropped my head to the top of the steering wheel and practically wheezed, "I think I've been in love with MacKenzie Clark my whole life."

MAC

"What the hell was that?" I demanded when I reached Abby.

He sighed. "Just some toxic masculinity and unwelcome realizations."

I frowned. "Why did Brady go after Connor like that?" *And why did I get the feeling it involved me?*

Abby glanced at Jase, who shrugged before resuming his seat.

"Mac, I don't need another fight on my hands. I'd rather not tell you what was said."

I flung an arm in the direction Connor had gone. I was pretty sure I could see the taillights of his Mercedes bumping over every gopher hole in the field as he fled the scene. "Connor is gone. He hightailed it out of here. I'm not going to kill him."

This was the first time I'd seen the guy since we were teenagers. I'd avoided him tonight on purpose. I didn't want to end up in jail, either.

Back at Kirby Falls High, Connor Pritchard had been one of the popular crowd. At sixteen, I'd been shocked that he'd wanted anything to do with me. But I'd learned pretty quickly that he only wanted to get in my pants. When I'd asked him to slow down one night, he'd told the whole school I was a tease. The guy had made an enemy of me for life. And he'd made me feel like there was something wrong with me for not wanting to lose my virginity in his parents' basement with a neon Coors Light sign hanging over my head.

So, yeah, there was no love lost between us. I sure as hell wasn't pining for the idiot. I just wanted to know what had gone down on the other side of the bonfire. I was nosy, and I didn't like other people in my business if what had happened did, in fact, involve me somehow.

"And Brady's gone too," I said. "I won't be causing any trouble tonight. Come on, Abby. Tell me what happened."

Abby released a breath, clouding the air between us, before wincing and repeating what Connor said about my tits. I mean, he wasn't lying. I did have great boobs, but they hadn't joined the puberty party until I was almost eighteen. Connor was still a pig, though.

"And Brady reacted how Brady does. We told Connor to shut his mouth and grow up. He slunk away in embarrassment rather than face any sort of consequences or facilitate personal growth." Abby shrugged like *what can you do?*

I felt my brows narrow as I pieced the altercation together. "So Brady . . . like . . ."

"Defended your honor," Jase supplied helpfully without glancing up from his cell phone.

"Defended my honor," I repeated dumbly before meeting Abby's gaze. "But why?"

"I don't know, Mac. Why *would* Brady do that?" He raised his eyebrows expectantly, like the answer was obvious.

I swallowed awkwardly. Maybe it was because of last Friday. Maybe he felt sorry for me. That could explain why he'd been acting so weird when he first got here. I could tell he was waiting for me to bring up my drunken escapades from last weekend. But I wasn't about to give him the satisfaction.

There was also the fact that I couldn't really remember what *had* happened. That knowledge burned. I knew he'd found me out by the barn and that I'd nearly fallen over, but he'd helped me to the ground. Being on the receiving end of Brady's assistance chafed a little around the edges. Humiliation threatened, but I wasn't going to let him see that.

In my fuzzy memories, I thought he might have sat with me for a while until I fell asleep. I couldn't recall what our conversation had been about or if we'd even talked at all. Knowing Brady, there had been plenty of talking. I could vaguely remember the scent of Axe body spray. That was probably why I'd been so nauseous, not the six-pack I'd put away on my own in a relatively short amount of time.

Damn Larry for trying to parent me. At the time, it had seemed important to prove a point.

And I'd proven it all right. I was almost thirty years old, and I could not hang. My hangover had lasted two days. Hence, the water I'd been drinking tonight and for the foreseeable future.

I'd been fine abstaining. I'd actually been having a good time until that almost fight had broken out and made everything weird.

Because, apparently, Brady had stood up for me.

Stranger things had happened, but I sure as hell couldn't think of one right this minute.

My attention drifted to all the vehicles parked in the distance. I hadn't heard two leave. Maybe Brady was still here.

He needed to know that Mac Clark could take care of herself. I didn't need him, of all people, rushing to my aid. The idiot who thought I'd vandalized his property. The man who goaded me every chance he got. My nemesis since diapers.

I shook my head, fully intent on giving Brady Judd a piece of my mind.

"I don't know," I said, finally answering Abby's question about why Brady had done what he'd done.

Abby hung his head in response.

"But I'm going to find out."

His gaze snapped up. "That is a great idea."

I gave him a nod and a wave and headed in the direction of the field, but then I spun back around, remembering my manners. "Oh, and, Abby? Thanks for carrying me out of here last week. Sorry for getting so wasted."

He gave me a look that my grandmother pulled out sometimes. It very clearly said, *Bless your heart, you sweet little idiot.*

I scowled. "What?"

"I didn't carry you anywhere."

"But—Larry said—"

Abby smiled, his dark eyes sparkling with humor from beneath the bill of his Flyers hat.

"Then who . . ." I trailed off as the horrible realization swallowed me in increments like quicksand.

"You're getting there," Abby said happily. "I always knew that A/B honor roll would come in handy for you someday, Mac."

With a growl, I turned and stomped off toward the field. I could see headlights shining in the back row of parked trucks, illuminating the thick trees and undergrowth that surrounded the property.

There was no way Brady was going to get away with riding to my rescue twice in one week. Just who did he think he was?

I'd known Brady my whole life. He'd been my childhood tormentor. My prankster equivalent. The pain in my admittedly great ass. But I'd been all of those things right back.

He'd never once tried to take on this misguided role of gentleman protector. We didn't do the nice, polite thing. We were real with each other—our most unhinged selves. He was the one person I could count on to *not* go easy on me.

I relied on his ridiculous sense of humor, his consistent immaturity, and his dedication to revenge. We were supposed to be on the same page. He was not supposed to carry me to my car and make sure I got home okay. Nor was he supposed to stand up to bullies and defend me behind my back without even blackmailing me over it!

Brady had deviated from his role—from our expected outcomes. He'd entered uncharted territory, and I didn't like it. Not one bit.

Did I owe him now? How could I reciprocate all of . . . that?

And where had this knight in tarnished armor even come from? Just a few weeks ago, he was accusing me of destruction of property. And for the last twenty-five-odd years, he'd been taking every opportunity to get under my skin.

Frustration mounting, I shook off thoughts of the past as I tromped across the dying grass of autumn toward my target.

Brady doing something nice tonight didn't *really* matter. We had a history to contend with. And I was good at holding a grudge. Two good deeds didn't change things between us. It just turned down the volume. We were how we were. We played to win.

Except now, he was trying to change the rules of the game.

I marched right up to Brady's big truck and peered in the passenger-side window. What I saw had me pausing with my fist raised, prepared to knock and get his attention. But Brady was hunched over the steering wheel, hanging on for dear life and breathing like he'd just run a four-minute mile.

Stunned to high heaven, I remained motionless, watching him heave with panting breaths. He looked like he was on the verge of a panic attack. What the hell? Why would a run-in with Connor Pritchard make him react this way?

I made a split-second decision and hammered my fist on the glass to get his attention, figuring he'd be better off in the long run if I snapped him out of whatever was going on inside that brain of his.

Except Brady jumped a mile in surprise, smacking his head on the top of his truck.

Wincing, I opened the door and slipped inside. "What? You thought I was carjacking you?"

Brady stared at me incredulously. "What are you doing? Trying to give me a heart attack?"

You looked like you were already in the middle of one, I wanted to say, but kept that to myself. "Not specifically, but it was a nice side effect." I grinned.

He grimaced and looked away. "Please, MacKenzie. Not tonight."

Stunned, I turned in the seat to face him fully. He *never* used my full first name. It was always Mac Mac or Big Mac or MacBook Pro or Mac Daddy. Between this fact and the scene I'd walked in on, something was up. Sudden interest had my eyes narrowing. The urge to be nosy threatened, but I'd followed him out here for a reason.

"Listen, Brady, they told me what you did. What you said to Connor," I clarified. "And while I do not need a man to defend my honor—I can defend my own honor, thank you very much—I still appreciate the effort."

Brady wasn't giving me his attention, and I didn't like it. His focus was trained on the windshield in front of him. The blue glow from his dashboard highlighted the hard swallow he took.

What was going on here? Why was he so visibly rattled, and why had he bothered standing up to Connor in the first place?

Curiosity getting the better of me, I blurted, "So why did you? Do it, I mean. Why did you get in Connor's face and defend me like that?"

Finally, Brady's gaze swung to mine. His eyes looked troubled, and his face was tense in a way that was completely unnatural and unexpected. This guy could talk down an irate customer, charm tourists and locals alike, and diffuse nearly any situation. I'd watched him stop a bar fight at Mattie B's by juggling billiard balls and singing "Sweet Home Alabama" at the top of his lungs. Seeing him without a smile on his face was a rare occurrence. Even when we sparred, he always looked like he was enjoying it.

"I really can't do this right now, Mac." His tone was worryingly quiet.

"Do what?" I asked genuinely.

He huffed a quiet laugh that was completely devoid of humor. "Argue. Fight. Coexist in a confined space. Take your pick."

"I'm just talking."

Brady's look said, *Come on now.* "We never *just* talk."

I was sure we'd managed one or two civil conversations in our very long shared history. Probably. And there had been whatever we'd talked about last Friday when I was three sheets to the wind. I didn't remember fighting with him then. And apparently, he'd carried me to Larry's car. A fact I'd be discussing with my cousin very soon.

"We've talked before," I challenged. "There was the science project sophomore year."

"We got in a fight during the presentation in front of the whole class, and you broke the trifold presentation board over my head."

I winced. Right. I'd gotten a week of detention for that. We'd managed a B minus, though.

"Oh," I countered. "What about that spring league in middle school where we both had soccer practice at the same time at Tanner Park, and my mom drove us to the field twice a week?" I remembered sitting in the backseat talking about our favorite players and arguing whether the US women's team was better than the men's. His parents had been overworked with three kids and the orchard. My mother had offered to drive Brady to help them out. I'd grumped and eaten dinner in my room for a week when she'd told me.

Before he could question it, I went on, "And I drove you home a few weeks ago. We survived that car ride."

But he was already shaking his head. "I don't think I can manage it right now—trapped in a car or otherwise, okay?"

"Why? I don't understand."

Through gritted teeth, he said, "I'm having a revelation here, and I need a minute."

So I counted to sixty in my head. He went back to staring out the windshield and gripping the steering wheel like the lap bar of a roller coaster.

I felt like I was at the zoo, observing an animal I'd never seen before. This version of Brady Judd was just as mysterious and confusing as an albino giraffe.

When a full minute of silence passed, I said, "Well, how much longer?"

"Damn it, Mac!" Brady brought one hand to his face and pinched the bridge of his nose in obvious frustration before glaring at me. "I just realized I would have put Connor fucking Pritchard in the hospital. I would have done anything to shut his stupid ass up for talking shit about you. No one gets to talk about you like that."

"Except you, right?" I said on instinct and then regretted it immediately.

Brady deflated, looking stricken. His eyes lowered to the console between us and quiet descended, so thick and heavy I could feel it pressing me into my seat.

His strange admission about Connor made me feel things—inconvenient things like gratitude and satisfaction. I was a petty sort of person, and I liked the idea of that asshole getting what was coming to him. But having the potential hand of justice belong to my longtime nemesis gave me mixed feelings. Up was down. Day was night. What were Brady Judd's motivations anyway? Why the hell should he care about defending my honor?

I still wanted answers to those questions, but this alternate-reality version of Brady was incapable of providing them. Maybe he was disturbed by the near violence of what had happened. Perhaps he hadn't thought himself capable of hurting someone and was now struggling with the possibility.

But there had been that shoving match a few years back with Floyd Ellerby. Brady hadn't reacted like this back then. He'd joked around with the cops who'd showed up, and he and Abby had talked their way out of any citations or arrests.

My eyes narrowed as I watched Brady avoid my gaze and attempt to slow his breathing.

I wondered what it would take to get him to snap out of whatever spiral I was witnessing. If I thought teasing him would work, I'd do it. But something told me that was not the answer. That he was thirty seconds away from abandoning me in his own truck just to get away from my questions and my presence.

This was the first time—maybe in my whole life—that Brady Judd had ignored me, and I was shocked to realize I didn't fucking like it.

How could I get him to just talk to me, to tell me what was going on? To stop avoiding me?

Suddenly, Brady licked his lower lip and then sighed. My gaze followed the movement, and I straightened.

I wondered what he'd do if I leaned across the console and just . . . kissed him.

Maybe I'd thought about kissing him before—once or twice. He had nice lips when they weren't constantly yapping, full and soft looking. And he was, admittedly, a handsome guy. He had that Captain America thing going on. Tall but not imposing. The only thing brighter than his smile were his blue eyes. They were framed by dark lashes that were unfairly long. And there was *something* about that dimple in his right cheek.

There had been times, mid-argument, when I figured pushing up onto my toes and bringing my mouth to his might actually shock the life out of him. But typically those deeply traitorous thoughts were quickly replaced and became secondary to the urge to smack him upside the head.

But here and now, in the overly warm cab of Brady's truck, my eyes lingered. I took in the wide shape of his mouth, the plushness of his lower lip. That ridiculous mustache that didn't have a snowball's chance in hell of growing on his perpetual baby face. My phantom gaze slid to his cheek. I knew exactly where his dimple would appear if he'd just turn back into himself and stop being this weird, serious version who apparently didn't smile. Or look at me. Or answer my questions.

I swore this was the one time I actually needed his big mouth to talk.

Well, he'd never been particularly good at giving me what I wanted, but, honestly, that was part of the fun.

So I made a decision. One that was reckless and irresponsible and, frankly, desperate. I leaned forward, keeping my eyes on my target. With one hand, I braced myself on the center console, and with the other, I snagged the front of his ridiculous puffy vest, pulling him toward me.

Brady's head snapped up, and his confused expression was the last thing I saw before I closed my eyes and planted my lips firmly on his.

He made a sound of alarm, and I wondered briefly if he thought I was trying to attack him or suck his soul out or something. That had me smiling against his mouth, my lips separating as they widened in amusement.

But then I felt Brady's hands come up to gently cradle my face. His touch traced the length of my jaw before grasping my chin—a firm press into the divot below my bottom lip. The long fingers of his other hand pushed into my hair, and it was my turn to make a sound in the back of my throat. Brady's mouth opened with mine, and I felt our tongues meet in the middle, a tentative pass at first—more cautious and timid than I ever expected either one of us to be. However, with each stroke, we grew bolder.

It didn't take long. Foreign attraction surged through me, not unwelcome but sure as hell unexpected. I was hot all over. My initial goal had been distraction. We were well past that now, and I couldn't stop, didn't want to. We kept kissing and touching.

My fingers tightened into a fist, still trapped between us in the fabric of his vest so I could keep him close, exploring his mouth and sucking on his tongue.

One of his hands smoothed down the side of my neck. He was so warm, and I liked the weight of his rough hand and the pressure of his fingers wrapping around my nape, drawing me closer.

I must have been too far gone, drunk on this unforeseen detonation of lust and the way our kisses had turned frantic and sloppy, because I wasn't the least bit worried he'd shift his hold and strangle the daylights out of me. I was fully in the moment, groaning as he sucked my bottom lip into his mouth and gave it a firm bite.

I fully intended on doing that right back—grazing my teeth over the lush bottom curve of his mouth and making him squirm in return—but a moment later, an engine revved somewhere close by. We broke apart abruptly as the sound intruded. There were two more loud growls of a big redneck truck before someone else honked a horn and hollered.

Brady and I stared at one another, chests heaving, as the commotion carried on behind his vehicle. The bonfire was breaking up. People were leaving.

And I was in Brady Judd's front seat where I'd just kissed the hell out of him. *Oh my God.*

I watched as his eyes dropped to my lips, and some shameless hussy inside me shouted, *We should do that again! For science!*

But then his blue gaze met mine and widened. "What the hell was that?!"

"I don't know!" I shouted back, unprepared for his reaction.

Brady stared at me in bug-eyed astonishment.

I felt defensive all of a sudden. "I don't know," I snapped. "It got you to stop freaking out about Connor Pritchard, who is honestly not worth the effort." I noticed Brady's gaping mouth and inability to speak and amended, "But now you're freaking out about this, so I'm not sure it was the best decision."

He visibly made the effort to speak several times, but nothing came out.

"You look like a dying fish," I observed helpfully. "I never thought I'd see the day you were stunned into silence."

"Congratulations," he choked out.

My gaze strayed to his lips. "I know that mustache is still in its infancy, but it kind of tickles."

"I've been growing it for over a month," he replied flatly.

"Whoops. My bad." I grinned. This sort of teasing felt good. We were getting back on track. Back to normal . . . if you didn't count the making-out thing.

"Are we going to talk about this?" Brady said seriously, pulling us out of the familiar once again.

"About what?" I attempted.

I thought I might have pushed him too far because he gestured wildly between us. "Your face! My face!" Then he smooshed his hands together in a violent back-and-forth.

I snorted in amusement, and he glared.

Then I thought about the kiss, how it had been . . . good. Great, if I was being honest. Even with the fine hairs of his failed mustache. I remembered the sounds he'd made, needy and eager. His touch was gentle but determined, like I was delicate but he remembered at the last moment exactly who he was dealing with. There had been something desperate in his touch. It was as if he just couldn't help himself. The way we'd caught flame from a tiny spark. I could still feel his hand on the back of my neck urging me closer, the way he'd bitten my bottom lip and then soothed it with his tongue. He'd tasted like citrus, like the orange Tic Tacs he used to crunch all the time.

Suddenly, I didn't feel like laughing anymore.

"Mac," he said impatiently, and I got the sense it wasn't the first time he'd tried to get my attention.

I'd been too caught up in replaying what had happened.

Dear God, I wanted to do it again. I wanted to climb across the center console, straddle his lap, and have him make those hungry sounds all over again. I wanted to feel his hand stroke down my neck to other more interesting places.

With a jolt of gutting awareness and sudden panic, I straightened. "No. No, we are not going to talk about it. We shall never speak of it again!"

At my admittedly forceful declaration, something complicated happened to Brady's face. If I didn't know any better, I would have said he looked hurt or disappointed.

But then he nodded stiffly, just once. "Good to know. Now, if you don't mind, I'd like to go home."

Swallowing hard, I climbed out of his truck on unsteady legs. I left without my answers or another word, wondering what the hell I'd just done.

BRADY

The crowd in the main dining room of Carter Bistro was loud for a weeknight. Folks sat along the bar that curved through the center of the space. All the booths that lined the perimeter were full of people I didn't recognize. Servers dashed in and out, balancing glasses of wine and trays of pasta, steaks, and Southern staples with a twist.

The restaurant probably had reservations until closing time for the next two weeks. But that was prime tourist season for you. The leaves were nearly at their peak, so visitors to Kirby Falls would be plentiful for the next little stretch, eager to take in our famed foliage.

Abby had a front-of-house shift at Carter Bistro tonight, and he'd told me to stop by for a drink. I planned on at least begging an appetizer off him. His chef made the best hush puppies and served them with this amazing chipotle honey butter.

Carter Bistro was just one of Cole Abernathy's many business ventures. He had his hand in stuff all over town. But this restaurant was the first one he ever opened, and it probably meant the most. It had a prime location, smack-dab in the middle of Main Street, just across the way from the municipal courthouse. You could sit on the bistro's rooftop deck and watch the Orchard Festival parade, the annual Christmas tree lighting, or someone you went to high school with reporting for jury duty.

Tatum Willis, Abby's longtime manager and right hand here at Carter Bistro, waved me back as soon as she saw me elbowing my way through the leafers gathered in the restaurant's narrow foyer. Tatum was in her mid-forties and terrifyingly capable. She'd helped Abby open each new restaurant, trained the staff, and then came back to handle her domain here at the bistro.

If she was here, I wondered why Abby had needed to come in at all.

I said hi to a few more servers as I walked back toward the office.

Abby was seated behind his desk in the small space. He was typing on his laptop, but there were two beers and a plate of hush puppies already waiting next to his keyboard.

"You are a sight for sore eyes," I said as I shut the door and slid onto the only other available chair in the tiny room.

"Well, hello to you too," Abby murmured without taking his eyes off the computer screen.

"I was talking to the hush puppies, Abigail." I popped one of the delicious morsels into my mouth.

Abby snorted but finished up whatever he was typing and then closed the laptop. "Nice to know where I rank."

I grinned. "I saw Tatum out front. Why are you on the schedule tonight?"

He took a sip from the glass that was already half empty. "She has to leave in thirty for her daughter's dance recital. I told her I'd cover for her."

"Gotcha. I'm working late tomorrow, too. Candy is organizing this paint-and-sip event at the orchard after closing. People apparently pay to drink wine and paint pumpkins. I told her I'd stay and help her close up."

Abby nodded. "That's a good idea."

"Yeah. She's been a big help bringing in customers this season. All of her ideas have been a hit so far, and this thing is already sold out."

"You don't mind the extra work?" Abby asked, eyeing me curiously as he reached for a hush puppy.

My sister's plans for generating more profit at the farm had caused a bit of a stir. Joan had been grumpy about Candy's involvement, but I'd support the new stuff if it made our parents more money and took some of the pressure off them.

I typically coasted at work. I went where I was needed and did what was asked of me. I never minded because I liked all of it. I could work with Mom in the refreshment stand. I could pass out u-pick buckets to the tourists. Or I could go work in the fields with Mercer and Joan, picking apples and tending crops. I was easily adaptable.

"Nah," I finally answered. "It'll be good in the long run, and I'm glad to have my sister home."

"I guess it's probably smart that Candace doesn't have to close up alone. Especially since the vandal was never caught."

I glanced at my friend. There was an amused edge to his tone like he was baiting me, but I just dipped my fourth hush puppy in an obnoxious amount of butter and agreed with him. "Yeah, she shouldn't be there by herself at night."

Abby raised a brow and made his move. "And you still think Mac had something to do with all that?"

I shoved the fried cornbread into my mouth and chewed slowly. I didn't know what to think about Mac anymore.

She'd kissed me over two weeks ago. Kissed me. On the mouth. Like it was no big deal and then promptly flipped the fuck out and had been avoiding me ever since.

We had trivia the other night at Trailview Brewing, and she hadn't even argued or started a fight. My team had won, and she'd calmly stood and gathered her things while the trivia host played the closing music. Totally out-of-character, unhinged behavior.

I'd watched her like a hawk all night, waiting for a glance of acknowledgement, a telltale blush, a screech of outrage—hell, anything.

But she'd sat stoic and aloof at a nearby picnic table with her back to me through eight rounds of trivia. That had never happened before.

Now I knew she'd been serious about pretending the kiss had never happened, and she was trying to avoid me as a result.

That was fine. I'd give her some time.

I needed to sort through my own screwed-up epiphany. Realizing you'd been secretly in love with your lifelong nemesis was not something I'd recommend. It would have helped if I'd had more than five minutes to think on it before Mac had popped up outside my window like a serial killer.

The timing could not have been worse. And then the kissing thing happened, and I'd been even more confused as a result.

The kiss had been . . . a total surprise and a swift confirmation.

When Mac's red lips had touched mine, I hadn't even thought. I'd reacted. Instinct had taken over, and I would have done anything to get closer. My hands had reached for her before I'd given them permission. She'd smelled like cinnamon and woodsmoke, her cheeks cool beneath my palms.

If we hadn't been interrupted, I wasn't sure what would have happened. No part of me had wanted to stop, I knew that.

But her quick denial and refusal to discuss anything left me feeling heartsick.

I knew Mac, though, and the longer I thought about it, the more I realized she'd bolted because she was scared. I'd seen the flush on her cheeks and the way her hand trembled in her lap, how she'd slid unsteadily to the ground as she'd practically sprinted out of my truck. She'd been just as affected by that kiss as I was.

Mac was running scared.

And I'd let her go for now. She had a lead, but I had every intention of catching her.

"Hello. Earth to Brady." Abby's impatient words drew me out of my Mac-infused daydream.

"Sorry. Yeah. No. Maybe. I don't know," I finally settled on. "I don't know if Mac had anything to do with the vandalism, but I still wouldn't put it past her." I paused and then murmured, "She's probably looking to strike again right about now."

Abby frowned. "Why do you say that? She was pretty chill at trivia night."

I debated how much to say. While it would be nice to get someone's perspective, I wasn't ready to admit that my friend had been right all this time. Well, at least right about me. He'd been bugging me about MacKenzie Clark since we were preteens, so smug and sure Mac and I were destined to be together.

I still needed to figure out what my feelings meant. There was a ton of history between us—most of it *not* good—and I didn't know if pursuing her was even an option.

An image of her cherry-red, bee-stung lips flashed behind my eyes, and I thought I might not mind the challenge.

Either way, I knew Mac would be reluctant. She would ignore me and then lash out. It was likely she'd try to explain away what had happened between us as a freak accident that had no meaning to her.

She would basically move through the stages of grief as a result of kissing me. That did not instill confidence.

But, on the other hand, I could still hear the phantom groan of approval from when I'd sucked on her bottom lip.

"You are extra distracted tonight," Abby noted when I'd, once again, failed to answer him.

I noted he'd popped the final hush puppy in his mouth and I felt extra sad about it.

"Mac kissed me," I admitted.

Abby sucked in a startled breath, which was unfortunate because he had a mouth full of appetizer. His eyes widened, and he started choking and coughing while I calmly sipped my beer.

"You did that on purpose," he managed after he'd regained use of his lungs and his eyes had stopped watering.

I grinned. "Yes. Yes, I did."

He rolled his eyes. "She kissed you? When? What happened?"

It was my turn to roll my eyes. "Would you like me to braid your hair while I recount the story?"

"Sure. But be gentle. I'm tender headed."

I gave him a flat look but then confessed, "It was after the bonfire the other week. After the thing with that idiot Pritchard."

Abby actually rubbed his hands together like a Bond villain. "You should have seen her face when she realized you'd stood up for her."

I leaned forward without meaning to. Something very desperate and needy inside of me wanted him to describe her features in great detail, to leave absolutely nothing out.

Instead, Abby fist-pumped. "It's happening. I *knew* it."

"If you shout 'in your face' at me, I'm leaving."

He abruptly snapped his mouth closed.

I sighed. "She followed me to my truck and then shocked the hell out of me by planting one on me. Then, she looked like she'd rather die than discuss it. She said we should just pretend it never happened. Then she ran away and has avoided me ever since."

I wasn't going to mention that Mac claimed she was trying to snap me out of my near panic attack. Abby would just ask what I'd been freaking out over, and, if he was smug now, I'd never hear the end of it if he found out *that* particular truth.

"Man, I knew something was up when we won on Monday," he lamented.

"Yeah, well, I guess she was serious about never acknowledging it."

Abby leaned forward and lowered his voice even though the door was closed. "Was it good?"

I glared because that was none of his damn business. But then I went and ruined the effect by shifting in my seat as I remembered her spicy vanilla scent, her touch, her taste.

He hooted out a laugh. "Ohh, that's a yes. I fucking knew it. All this time."

"Not all this time," I argued. "She's hated me all our lives. She hates me right now. I don't know what the hell's going on. What makes you think this changes anything?"

"This is just step one. Rome wasn't built in a day."

I wanted to laugh at his optimism, but the part of me that was still smarting from Mac's immediate rejection dulled the urge.

"You know what you need to do," Abby said, oblivious to my conflicting emotions.

"Order another batch of hush puppies?"

He chucked a pad of Post-it notes at my head. "You need to try being nice to her. Just to see what happens. Test a hypothesis."

"What's the hypothesis?"

"If you treat Mac like she's any other girl instead of a demon plague, then she might want to kiss your sorry ass again."

Again, that voice inside my head made itself known. MacKenzie Clark would *never* be just another girl.

I swallowed with some effort. My throat was probably just dry from all the hush puppies. "Okay, so just treat her nice?"

Abby's eyes narrowed. "Don't tease her or give her shit. Don't try to trip her or accuse her of having back hair."

"That was one time! And I was twelve."

My friend shook his head in disappointment. "So when you see her again, maybe pay her a compliment. Tell her she looks nice or you like her outfit. Talk about the weather or other safe subjects. And for the love of God, don't mention the paintballing incident or accuse her of destruction of property."

I nodded. "Right. Okay. I can do that."

Abby didn't appear convinced.

"What? I can. I will," I amended, standing.

"Keep me posted," Abby said, opening his laptop. "And, Brady—" I turned from where I'd reached the door. "Good luck, man. You're gonna need it."

The following day, I got the chance to test the hypothesis, to put Operation Nice Guy into action.

It was funny because most people in Kirby Falls actually found me to be a pretty nice person. I was definitely the most popular Judd sibling. Though, that wasn't a hard contest to win. Joan—bless her heart—was not a ray of sunshine. My older sister just didn't have it in her. She was no-nonsense and too practical for her own good. She had high expectations for everyone around her, and generally, no one ever managed to measure up. Candace was nice enough, but before returning this summer, she'd been gone for over seven years. She was basically out of the running.

I was funny and approachable, and I got along with everyone. Well, everyone except for Mac.

But not tonight. Tonight, I would charm the pants off the ornery woman.

Great, now I was thinking about getting her pants off.

Clearing my throat, I made my way to where a bunch of ladies were gathered at the picnic tables at the orchard. The area had been decorated with white table-cloths, and a small pumpkin and paint supplies sat at each place setting. There was also a food table with bottles of wine and an elaborate charcuterie spread. Someone had dragged over and set up the outdoor heaters. Those would feel nice. Now that the sun was on its way down, the temperature would drop.

I'd spotted Mac when I'd parked my truck. Her Jeep was two spots over, alerting me to her presence tonight at Candy's paint-and-sip event. Plus, I could pick out Mac's dark hair and red lips anywhere—even across a field.

She was surrounded by what looked like friends, co-workers, and most of her family. I spotted Larry plus Mac's mother, Patty, and her aunt Maggie in among the group of ten or so women.

As I drew closer, sudden nerves took hold. I reached into the pocket of my vest and fiddled with the loop of my key chain.

Mac was talking to my sister, holding a corkscrew and opening a bottle of wine. Her hair was long and loose, curled in a way that looked effortless but probably took half an hour. She wore jeans, and her black jacket hid the rest of her.

I could be nice to Mac. I *would* be. I'd be on my very best behavior.

With Abby occupying one shoulder like an angelic reminder, I led an internal chant to compliment her, be attentive, and be charming. Then I took a deep breath to steady myself. *Say you like her outfit*, tiny Abby whispered in my ear.

But then, as I approached, the devil took over my mouth, and I blurted out, "Are you sure it's a good idea to arm her?"

Mac turned at the sound of my voice, and I saw fire in her eyes as she took me in. It was the first time she'd looked at me since that night in my truck. The first kernel of attention I'd had in two weeks. Her reaction stirred a familiar satisfaction, but there was something else too—a building heat, an awareness, the aching knowledge I now had that the skin of her neck was incredibly smooth.

Her stormy eyes narrowed, and I heard a low growl as she kept her attention on me.

Positive reinforcement at its finest.

So, like an idiot, I kept going. "And you're giving her wine?" I glanced at Candy. "Wow, sis. No self-preservation instinct in you at all. She's probably using her access tonight to case the joint."

I could hear the faint high-pitched sounds of distress coming from the direction of my shoulder. Tiny, imaginary Abby was likely having a conniption fit.

Mac glowered. "I've told you a hundred times, Brady Judd. I did not vandalize your property. It was probably someone else who finds you painfully annoying."

"Oh, yeah?" I asked, throwing in a smirk for good measure.

"Yeah. We have a club and everything," she stated matter-of-factly. "We meet on Tuesdays down at the library. Only room big enough to hold us all."

Our stares held. I knew I was grinning, and she was too.

This had always been the problem. Getting Mac's attention had usually been my aim, even at six years old. And the surest way to go about that was to get under her skin. Even now, at twenty-eight, it was too tempting. My blood was pumping in my veins like I was on the soccer field having just scored the game-winning goal. And this feeling was the closest to satisfaction I could possibly get outside the bedroom.

Unfortunately, I was fucking up Operation Nice Guy right out of the gate.

"What are you doing here, Brady?" My sister's words interrupted our heated stare-a-thon, and my brows lowered in annoyance.

Reluctantly, I dragged my attention over to Candy. "I'm working this event with you and closing tonight. I just got back from my dinner break."

She frowned. "I thought Mark was on the schedule. He was out here helping me for over an hour."

I could sense Mac drifting away, wine bottle in hand, so I told Candace, "Nah. He was off at five. I'm your backup tonight. And good thing since you have a violent delinquent in your midst."

That brought Mac's stony glare back around. She snapped, "I swear, Brady." But then her attention dropped down to my lips, and the sense of relief I felt nearly had my chest caving in.

I didn't want to be the only one carrying around this secret. The weight of it, the perfect memory playing on repeat at three a.m. when I couldn't sleep. I wouldn't be able to stand it if I was the only one thinking about the way we'd fit together, how we'd come apart. I needed some sign that she remembered too. That it had affected her at all.

But in the next instant, the moment—and this brief connection—was over. Larry called out, "Mac, can I get some of those orange Tic Tacs? I know you have them in your purse. You've been sucking on them all week."

For whatever reason, Mac's eyes widened in alarm. She placed the wine bottle on the table and started digging through her bag, but not before I caught a deep flush working its way onto her cheeks.

Before she could pass the tiny plastic box off to her cousin, I took a step closer and said, "Man, I love those. Can I have one too?"

Mac wheezed out a cough and then cleared her throat, tossing the candy to Larry over her shoulder. "No. No, you may not. Tic Tacs are for people who *don't* accuse me of vandalism."

I fought a wince but nodded instead. "That's fair."

Mac gave me one last glare and turned to join her companions.

I knew Abby would be disappointed in me for calling her a delinquent, but, truthfully, if I *had* walked right up to Mac and complimented her hair, she would have thought I was either up to something or suffering from a head injury. It was better to ease into the plan, to spread out the niceties. If she assumed things were getting back to normal—our version of normal, with teasing and bickering and whatnot—she might stop avoiding me and pretending the kiss never happened. We needed to talk about it, but I had a feeling that if I forced her hand or rushed her, Mac would shut down and that lip-lock would be a distant memory I pulled out at night to keep me warm.

The women were chatting and putting a sizeable dent in the cheese board. I looked around for my sister, but Candy was nowhere to be found.

Clapping my hands together, I announced, "Ladies, it looks like I'm in charge. I say we take some shots before Candace gets back and ruins our fun."

That got me some laughter from the crowd.

"Brady Judd, you're a troublemaker," Maggie Clark called with a twinkle in her eye. She was Mac's aunt and in charge of the bakery at Grandpappy's. I'd known her since I was a kid, and we'd always gotten along. She made the best yellow cake with old-fashioned chocolate icing.

"Yes, ma'am," I answered with a grin.

I had half a mind to go track down my sister, but everyone seemed content to eat, drink, and visit for the time being, so I told those gathered, "Y'all settle in and enjoy the wine and snacks. We'll get the painting portion of the event started in a bit."

For the next few minutes, I mingled and chatted with the women present. I'd known most of them my whole life, so it wasn't a hardship. My momma always said I could talk to a wall and be content. As a child, she'd often found me chatting with parents at the playground instead of the kids my age.

Mac and I circled one another. If I moved to speak with someone nearby, she'd find a reason to shift sideways, by either grabbing a cracker at the food table or refilling her wineglass. But she kept an eye on me, always aware and recalibrating her movements as a result. I wasn't discouraged in the least. I liked that she was off-balance and that I knew the probable reason behind it.

I eventually caught sight of Candy striding out of the Apple House. She looked happy and pink-cheeked. She must have given herself a pep talk in front of the mirror in her office. Poor kid.

Finally, she got things rolling with the event. Everyone sat and started painting their pumpkins. For the next half hour, I circulated and refilled drinks, striking up conversations as I went. The autumn air was cool, but the heaters kept everyone comfortable in their jackets and flannels.

With a bottle of Lonely Mountain rosé in one hand, I passed behind Mac. She stiffened as I checked out her pumpkin painting. Her careful strokes had created the silhouette of a cat in front of a giant moon. It looked real good. Mac had the neatest handwriting of anyone in our grade, and she'd always excelled in art class.

"That looks nice," I told her when I'd circled the picnic table.

Mac's gaze drifted briefly to mine before darting back to her pumpkin. "Thank you." Then she resumed painting, but I could tell she was being tentative, waiting for me to leave so she could finally take a deep breath.

Larry was seated across from Mac. I offered her a refill, and she held out her glass, grinning as she glanced between the two of us. The rest of the table's occupants had wandered off to go and look at the artwork nearby.

After a moment, Larry stood and stretched. "Well, I need more cheese to go with this wine. Y'all play nice."

Mac glared at her cousin like she'd been stabbed in the back, but I would take this opportunity and thank Laramie Burke in my prayers tonight.

Sliding onto the bench seat opposite, I placed the wine bottle on the table and was careful not to stick my elbows into any leftover paint or my foot in my mouth.

Gray eyes flicked to mine, and Mac's frown deepened. "Are you just going to sit there and watch me?"

I smiled. She was so defensive. This would be a good time to move forward with the plan. I'd just complimented her pumpkin. I could do this. Ease her into normal interactions. Shoulder Angel Abby practically shouted for me to talk about the weather.

But before I could remark on our mild October thus far, Mac said, with her attention still on her squash, "I see you finally shaved that sad excuse for a mustache off your face."

My natural inclination was to take offense and sling a zinger back in her direction, but then I thought about the last time she'd brought up my mustache. Two weeks ago, in the front seat of my truck, telling me it tickled.

Instead of returning her insult with one of my own, I raised my eyebrows meaningfully.

Realization dawned on her pretty face, and she rolled her eyes heavenward, but I caught her lips twitching as she focused back on her painting. That knowledge had a slow smile growing on my face. I could feel my dimple crinkling in my right cheek, knowing I'd scored a point. Another little reminder that said, *It happened. We did that. And you fucking loved it.*

A moment later, she reached for something at her side and tossed it over to me without a word. I caught the pack of Tic Tacs neatly against my chest.

"Thank you," I said genuinely.

"You're welcome." Her reply was prim. She was still attempting to keep her attention on her work. But I saw the cracks sneaking through. The way her eyes peeked over at me, how stiffly she held herself—straight-backed and so very aware. I wanted to pump a fist into the air.

However, my goal—for once—was not to rile Mac up. I didn't want her on edge. I wanted her at ease with me, comfortable in a way we'd rarely ever managed. Except when she'd had her tongue in my mouth and her fingers fisted in my clothes.

I reached one long arm forward and placed the candy back on the table in front of her. I made sure my tone was easy and affable, then said, "Yeah, I thought it was time to let the mustache go."

"Oh yeah?" she murmured.

"Yeah." I stretched out my legs and deliberately bumped her foot beneath the table. She stiffened momentarily but didn't move her boots. "I give good face. Seemed a shame to cover it up."

"*Mostly* cover it up," she countered, grin wicked and eyes sparkling. "In patches. Unevenly."

I shrugged, wearing a smug smile of my own. "Gotta give the ladies what they want."

Mac snorted. "The ladies, huh? I'm trying to recall the last time I saw you out with anyone, and I'm drawing a blank."

I considered that, feeling my chest heat beneath my flannel in embarrassment. It *had* been a while since I'd dated anyone. But I didn't want to dwell on that because, as I stared at Mac, I realized the reason was more than likely sitting directly across from me.

Suddenly uncomfortable and self-conscious, I wiped my sweaty palms down the length of my thighs and said with little forethought, "Well, some people get around more than others."

Mac froze, her paintbrush hovering in midair as she turned her glacial gray eyes my way. "Are you calling me easy?"

"What? No," I replied quickly. I hadn't meant it that way. I'd been flustered at the realization and embarrassed that I didn't have a clever answer for her regarding my sparse dating history as of late. So I'd spouted off the first thing I could think of. And, okay, yes. Replaying it in my head, I saw how my statement could easily be misconstrued as judgmental. But I hadn't been intentionally implying anything about Mac's dating life. Especially after what she'd confessed about David the dentist when she was drunk. I wouldn't do that. Not ever again.

"That's not what I meant," I said honestly, frustration pinching my features. I straightened on the bench, drawing my legs back to my own side.

But Mac didn't look like she believed me.

This was getting out of hand. I didn't want her to be angry with me—not in a way that touched on real insecurities. I needed to get us back on solid ground, not in this avalanche of misunderstanding. And I knew how to do that. I'd been doing it my whole life.

Operation Nice Guy was probably in the fail column for the night, but that was okay. I'd rather argue and bicker in a way that was comfortable and known to us than have Mac think I was insulting her as a living, breathing, dating woman in the twenty-first century.

So I put a smirk on my face and said, "Although, I do find it interesting that you've been keeping such close tabs on my love life."

"That is not—I could care less who you do or do not date."

I leaned forward. "It's *couldn't care less*." I emphasized the final three words.

"What?"

"The phrase is 'I *couldn't* care less' otherwise, you're admitting that thoughts of me and my imaginary paramours are keeping you up at night."

She scowled and pointed her dripping paintbrush in my direction. "I am not thinking about you at night or any other time."

Her heated gaze, her forceful denial . . . it brought me a familiar sense of accomplishment. It also put us firmly back into normal territory. I'd tried the nice thing again, and it had been going well until I'd gotten nervous and messed it all up. Falling back on my old antagonistic ways was easy and comfortable. And it was a hell of a lot better than getting tongue-tied and having Mac thinking I'd called her a slut.

This was alright. I could fix this. Maybe not tonight. But eventually, we'd have a conversation and figure out where things stood, talk about that kiss, and see if it meant anything to her. I wasn't good at being patient, but this felt too big, too important to rush.

For now, she could rail at me and threaten to paint my face like a jack-o'-lantern. Because it meant I still had her attention. I was still in this. Mac sure as hell wasn't ignoring me anymore.

Later that night, when I couldn't sleep and my chocolate chip protein muffins were baking in the oven, I pulled out my phone.

My gaze caught on the printout I still had on my fridge. The surly, embellished, and inaccurately illustrated version of Mac glared back at me.

Standing in my kitchen, I opened the Chatter app. In the compose box, I typed

. . .

@JuddsFamilyOrchard: @GrandpappysApples, I know my mustache tickled, but I barely noticed yours at all.

Then I chuckled quietly to myself and backspaced over the whole thing.

Swallowing, I started again.

@JuddsFamilyOrchard: @GrandpappysApples, That was the best kiss of my entire life, and I'm terrified I'll never get the chance to do it again.

With a sad smile, I made sure to hit the button that would save my draft rather than post it. I couldn't say any of that to Mac. She wasn't ready to hear it.

And, honestly, neither was I.

seven

MAC

I squeezed my cell phone to within an inch of its life and was pretty sure I heard some plastic cracking.

I was used to the snipes on the Chatter app. Brady and I battled it out on social media all the time. But sometimes that man was so annoying, I wanted to get him alone and wrap my hands around him and—

Abruptly, my mind took a mini vacation to the front seat of Brady's pickup truck. I'd wrapped my hands around him alright, but not in a violent sort of way. I thought of the sweetness of his kiss, the citrus on his tongue, and his thumb pressing the dimple in my chin.

I'd been doing my best to prevent any thoughts of that impromptu make-out session. Avoiding Brady had been at the top of the list. But then I'd seen a row of orange Tic Tacs by the register at the gas station, and my traitorous hand had reached for a pack.

The pumpkin-painting event at Judd's had been the first time I'd interacted with him since the kiss that shall not be named. I half expected him to announce it to all my family and friends. But what I expected even less was his attempt at a normal conversation. It had backfired, of course. We weren't conditioned for that sort of thing.

Now, nearly twenty-four hours later, sitting in the Grandpappy's pumpkin patch booth, I covered my face with my hands and fought a growl.

I didn't want to think about Brady Judd. I didn't want to know what his lips felt like (surprisingly soft). I didn't want to know the sounds he made when he was turned on (needy, desperate, admittedly hot). And I definitely didn't want to see his stupid social media posts when I was busy *not* thinking about him.

@JuddsFamilyOrchard: It's a fine day at the farmers' market. Nice and peaceful. Just letting the locals and tourists alike know it's safe to venture downtown. The harpy that usually haunts Main Street every third Saturday is on vacation.

I'd traded shifts specifically to avoid Brady today, and this was his super mature response. It was almost like he couldn't stand not having my attention. If I was going to skip out on our regular market interaction, then he was going to make sure he took a swipe at me in two hundred and eighty characters or less.

I shook my head and tucked my phone beneath the counter of the booth. I didn't want to see any more. It would just make me reply or force my blood pressure up . . . or both.

After another frustrated growl, I stepped out of the tiny shack that was big enough for one person, a stool, a heater, and a cash box. When folks picked out the pumpkins of their dreams, they brought them to me for pricing and payment.

Grandpappy's had closed ten minutes ago, and the stragglers were finally making their way toward the parking lot, purchases in hand. Thankfully, we only had another week until Halloween. But then this part of the farm turned into a Christmas tree lot, so it was just more of the same in a different season.

There were wheelbarrows and metal garden carts scattered around the enclosed area. Customers used them to transport their pumpkins. I needed to gather and lock them in the shed for the evening. As I moved around the space, I was grateful for the mild October weather. It was supposed to dip into the forties tonight, but it had been a gorgeous, sunny day.

I waved to Larry as she left her post at the corn maze and took off for the night. Mom and Dad stopped by after they locked up the General Store. They let me know that they had dinner plans and wouldn't see me later in case I stopped by the house. I fully intended to relax at home—well, Grandma and Grandpa's home—with a frozen pizza, a nice long bath, a new charcoal sheet mask, and a bottle of wine. With how busy we'd been, Saturdays on the farm were stressful, and as soon as I finished up here, I'd be on my way out.

I only had two carts left when Brady Judd came walking down the path from the main gate. I froze, debating darting behind the shed, but then realized I'd already been spotted. He had a huge grin on his face. I could see the dimple in his cheek from here.

My heart rate picked up. Yes, I'd been avoiding him, but my body was obviously confused by his proximity. I was probably just used to feeling the anticipation for our battles. That had to be it. I resisted pressing a hand to my sternum.

What was he even doing at Grandpappy's anyway?

When he veered into the pumpkin patch and approached, I called out, "Are you lost? Your farm is across the street."

His smile widened and he pushed his hands into the pockets of that damn puffy vest he always wore. "I knew I took a wrong turn somewhere."

I stared as he came to a stop in front of me.

His gaze moved all over my face, and I could feel myself going warm. Was he just going to stand there and . . . look at me?

Finally, he glanced down at the ground before meeting my impatient stare. "Joan called earlier and talked to William. He has a part she needs for the tractor."

"Ah." My uncle William was the head farmer. He and Brady's older sister got along remarkably well. They were both quiet, stubborn, and preferred the company of farm equipment to most people.

"But then I saw you and figured I'd say hi."

"Say hi?" I crossed my arms over my chest. Brady's attention briefly dropped to my cleavage, and I felt that warmth from earlier head due south. "I thought you were glad to be rid of me today?"

His bright blue eyes practically sparkled. "I don't remember saying that."

I wanted to pull my phone out and recite his stupid Chatter post word for word, but that would prove I cared about the things he said online. Plus, my cell was inside the booth.

I rolled my eyes.

"I *said*," he emphasized, "that it was peaceful. Not that I liked it."

"Oh." I frowned, suddenly feeling flustered. I didn't know what to do with that statement. God, he wasn't going to bring up the kiss, was he? I didn't think I could handle that right now. I still wasn't letting myself think about what it meant. And I definitely wasn't remembering how good it was.

In an effort to maintain some equilibrium, I grabbed the handle of the cart nearest to me and started towing it toward the shed. I heard the last remaining cart start bumping over the ground and figured Brady was following me.

"So did you have more fun here than at the farmers' market?" he asked casually.

I didn't turn around to answer. Just typed in the four-digit password on the keypad and opened the metal door. The rock I had it propped open with must not have been able to hold up. "My mom wanted to work the market. She asked to trade shifts."

Brady came up behind me, his Axe-body-spray scent washing over me and making me swallow hard. Hands brushing mine, he took the swinging shed door out of my grasp and held it wide. "Liar," he murmured against the shell of my ear.

I pulled back to glare at him.

But he only grinned harder. "Your momma said you were in a mood, and you begged her to take your shift. Said you'd even offered to wash her car for her tomorrow."

Betrayed, I gasped. "She did not."

"Oh, she did. I told her she should have held out for a wash *and* a wax."

I glared, then retreated inside the shed to park the cart among the others.

"You didn't have to trade shifts just to avoid me, Mac." Brady's smile was still firmly in place, but it looked purposeful, like it took some effort. And his voice was soft.

At his accusation, defensiveness mingled with guilt. The lie burst out of my mouth reflexively. "I didn't."

"You did," he argued. "But that's okay. I know why."

I had just a moment to wonder what he meant. Before I could tell him to stop, Brady stepped into the shadowed interior, pulling his wagon in with him and releasing the door.

"Wait," I called out just as the door snapped shut.

"I know you struggle with maintaining personal boundaries in confined spaces, but I'm not about to attack you, Mac Daddy."

"No, no, no," I murmured, rushing past Brady and pushing futilely on the door. "Shit," I said, giving it a final kick before I spun around to face the man responsible for locking us in the shed after hours.

He let go of the cart handle and straightened. "What?"

I gestured to the door. "We're trapped!"

This couldn't be happening. I patted the pockets of my jeans and my coat despite knowing damn well my phone was back in the booth where I'd stowed it after seeing Brady's stupid Chatter post.

My gaze locked on the reason for this ridiculous turn of events, and my breathing went decidedly dragon-like.

"Why would we be trapped? Who locks a shed from the outside?" Brady marched to my side of the building and pushed fruitlessly.

"We put the lock on after that incident with the naked family. Didn't you see me type in the code?" I gritted out.

My anger and annoyance were mixing with panic, but I forced myself to relax my jaw.

While Brady examined the latch, I blurted, "Your phone! Where's your phone? We can call for help."

"It's in my truck," he mumbled, still facing away from me.

Hope died a quick death. "Why would you leave it in your truck?"

He turned to look at me over his shoulder. "Because I knew I would be talking to William. I don't like to be distracted by my phone. I thought I'd be right back. What about you? Where's your phone?"

"I was *working*," I replied with a healthy dose of sass, even though I regularly checked my phone while I was on shift. Brady didn't need to know that. "It's in the booth."

Brady placed his hands on his lean hips and stared off like he was thinking hard. "Okay, so we'll make some noise. Someone is bound to hear us."

I was already shaking my head. "No, they won't. I watched everybody leave for the night. I was the last one here. No one knows to come looking for us. Unless Joan was expecting you back?"

Brady bit his lip, and my eyes tracked the movement. "No," he finally said. "She was going to come over in the morning. I thought I'd try to catch William before he left for the day. I didn't tell Joan I was picking the part up for her tonight."

That information made me pause. "Why would you do that?"

He started going through the storage shelves along the wall and replied over his shoulder, "I'm a good brother. I do stuff for my sisters all the time."

My gaze narrowed. He was being shifty, not looking my way, not cracking a joke or smiling. Why had he really come over to Grandpappy's tonight, unprompted and of his own volition?

Brady peeked at me over his shoulder before shuffling items in the overhead cabinet.

Holy shit. Did he—he wouldn't have shown up out of the blue on some fake errand for his sister just so he could see me . . . right?

Right?!

My mind spun with the possibility that I'd been the reason for this little visit. Yes, I'd been avoiding Brady. But I'd assumed we'd been in the same boat—the avoidance boat. Then I recalled the night of the pumpkin-painting event and how he'd approached me and talked to me.

Maybe he wasn't trying to forget what had happened between us, after all.

This wasn't really the time or place to be speculating about Brady Judd's motivations. We were, in all likelihood, trapped in this shed for the night—until someone showed up for their shift in the morning and came to get the garden carts. I couldn't start freaking out about this. We were stuck.

Shit.

I rubbed a hand over my face.

"What about your family?" Brady asked, and I looked up. "Won't someone notice you're missing?"

I shook my head once more. "No. My parents are having dinner with their friends. Larry has plans. Will's off with Becca the tourist."

"No date tonight?"

His question was casual, but something about it made me want to search his face for a hidden meaning.

"Not unless you count that bottle of wine I had waiting on me at home."

Brady didn't reply to that, but he did pluck an electric lantern off the shelf in front of him and switch it on, lighting up the dim space. We probably had an hour or so until the sun went down, and then we'd lose all the light bleeding in around the edges of the shed.

Once he had the lantern, Brady got real nosy. He poked through all the shelving and cabinets while I stood there trying to think of some way out of this—this mess where we were forced to spend an entire night together, practically outdoors. All my frustration and annoyance were brought on by Brady's presence and nearness. This was all his damn fault. And, honestly, I was starting to panic over the forced proximity. Intrusive kissing-related thoughts swam in the forefront of my mind. I did my best to control my breathing.

The shed contained mostly extras and supplies we didn't use regularly. All the good tools were in the barn, but I saw Brady pull out an extension cord, some twine we used for Christmas decorations, three rolls of fishing line, and a first aid kit that hadn't seen the light of day in a long time. There were some old moving blankets, the leftover supplies from when we'd had beehives on the property, and a storage tote of string lights that we'd bust out in two weeks for the Christmas tree lot.

Brady examined some old stakes and tomato cages in the corner behind the wheelbarrows.

Finally, I snapped out, "What are you going to do, MacGyver our way out of here?"

"No," he said while fiddling with an old combination lock. "But that is an excellent new nickname for you. I'm disappointed I didn't think of it sooner."

He flashed me a quick grin, and I scowled.

"I'm just seeing what we've got to work with," Brady added. "Those moving blankets are rough, but they're thick, and they'll keep us warm when the temperature drops tonight."

The sinking weight of reality had me releasing a heavy breath. This was really happening. We were trapped. We'd be spending the night in this twelve-by-twelve-foot shed with its dusty floors and metal walls. What if there was a rat? What if I needed to pee?

"Hey! A pack of cards," Brady announced excitedly.

I blinked.

"We can play War or Egyptian Ratscrew. Spoons will be a little harder with only two of us, but we could—"

"Did you do this on purpose?" I interrupted.

Brady frowned. "Do what?"

"Get us locked in here together."

It was his turn to blink. "How would I do that? I didn't know y'all locked up your wheelbarrows like it was Fort Knox."

My gaze narrowed, scrutinizing. "You just seem too"—I gestured broadly—"okay about this whole thing."

He emptied the deck of red-and-black cards into one palm. "I'm making the best of it. We have something to keep us entertained. We have a way to keep warm. And we have light. Only thing we're missing is pizza and a six-pack."

Despite his annoying ability to put a positive spin on nearly anything, I guess it would be pretty farfetched to think Brady had actually locked us in a storage shed on purpose. We'd only added the keypad recently. Last month, I'd stumbled upon a family of tourists making use of the shed to hide and disrobe. They'd wanted to create a ridiculous photo op with pumpkins from our patch. Why that involved putting a baby inside a pumpkin and then everyone taking their clothes off and holding squash in front of their private parts, I still didn't know. But I'd caught them, and we'd banned them from ever visiting Grandpappy's again. Will had also thought it would be a good idea to keep the shed locked to prevent folks from poking around in places they didn't belong.

I'd been stupid to walk in without propping the door again or disarming the lock fully. But, I'd been distracted by the puffy-vest-wearing idiot.

With a sigh, I made my way over to the shelf closest to the door. Shifting aside a sack of birdfeed, I retrieved a cellophane bag and held it out. "There. We won't starve."

Brady's eyes brightened. "Look at you. Champion hunter-gatherer right there."

Larry kept a stash of candy out here for when she had to work the tree farm. Luckily, Twizzlers didn't go bad for a long-ass time, and this bag hadn't been opened.

Brady ripped into it and stuck the end of a red licorice rope in his mouth, grinning around it. "You don't have a secret stockpile of orange Tic Tacs, do you? Those are my favorites."

Heat flooded my cheeks, and I screamed internally. Oh, I knew they were his favorites. There were a dozen memories in the background of my brain where Brady at various ages popped those little orange candies into his mouth.

Then there was the fact that I remembered the saccharine-sweet citrus flavor on his tongue.

Hurriedly, I glanced away and busied myself retrieving the moving blankets to spread out on the floor. I was grateful he couldn't read my mind, or else he'd know why I'd bought that pack of Tic Tacs in the first place.

Forcing myself to answer calmly, I said, "No, just the Twizzlers. Besides, it hasn't even been fifteen minutes. You can't be hungry already."

"I'm a growing boy, Mac Mac. I'm always hungry."

Stepping around me, Brady took the other end of the gray wool fabric and helped me lay it flat.

The ground wasn't too hard once we were seated. I imagined it would feel a lot like camping when we eventually settled down to sleep. *Oh, God.* Sleep. I had to sleep in this shed with Brady Judd.

But it was barely six o'clock, so we had a lot of time to kill between now and tomorrow morning. Hopefully, someone would be in by seven, at the latest.

I really hoped I wouldn't need to pee. It was probably lucky that I hadn't found any bottles of water along with the Twizzlers.

Brady placed the lantern off to the side and began shuffling the cards. "What do you want to play?"

I gave him a flat stare. "You seriously want to play cards?"

He quirked a brow. "Would you rather braid each other's hair and gossip all night long like we're at a sleepover? Or I suppose we could put these cards away and chat." His challenging gaze dropped to my lips very meaningfully, and I swallowed hard. "I bet I can think of some topics to keep us talking. I know I've been curious about a few—"

"Okay!" I practically yelled, snagging the deck of cards from his hands. "Cards it is. I'll deal."

Brady grinned like he'd taken the lead in a race, and, unfortunately, I had to agree.

Shit.

I don't know how many rounds of cards we played. We cycled through every game we could think of while bickering and eating Larry's bag of Twizzlers. Some games we'd played with our families or learned at summer camp.

At some point, we'd started putting cards up on our foreheads and trying to guess the suit we held.

Brady held a king of hearts to his forehead with one finger. It was facing out where I could see it, and he was trying to guess what card it was. He'd gotten pretty good at naming the suit, so once he'd correctly identified hearts, I'd told him to try to name the card in three guesses.

His blue eyes looked nearly silver in the strange glow from the electric lantern. They narrowed on me as if he could pull the answer out of my head by staring.

"Is it . . ." He searched my face, and I snorted a laugh. "A jack?"

"Nope."

Brady closed his eyes and hummed.

"Are you divining the answer?" I teased. "Consulting the great beyond?"

"Maybe," he replied without opening his eyes.

"Two guesses left. Hurry up."

"I'm thinking," he insisted. Then he said, "Twizzler me," and opened his mouth like a baby bird.

I rolled my eyes but grabbed the licorice stick and put it between his teeth. He was ridiculous. I could feel myself smiling. *Damn it.*

"Three of hearts," he said after he finished chewing.

"Nope. Last chance."

His eyes were still closed, so it felt safe to study him. His brown hair was longer on top and generally styled like that of a messy frat boy who'd just rolled out of bed. But with the playing card in the way, his hair was sticking up a little more than usual in the front, making me grin. Despite the time of day, there wasn't even a hint of stubble on that baby face. I bet he still got carded when he bought alcohol outside of Kirby Falls.

My gaze fell to his lips. They weren't chapped or rough. I knew from experience just how soft they were. His bottom lip was fuller than the top, and as I watched, they parted on an indrawn breath.

When my attention finally drifted back up, I jolted in surprise. Brady's eyes were open. He was watching me watch him.

My stomach flipped, and heat washed up and over my sternum, making a beeline for my neck and cheeks.

"King of hearts," he guessed quietly.

A beat of silence passed while I collected myself.

"You got it," I murmured. Embarrassment had me standing abruptly and turning away.

I was stiff from sitting too long as I started pacing the length of the space, but thankfully, the cold couldn't touch me. I was too wound up and flushed from—

from whatever that had been. I'd gotten caught staring like a middle schooler. But Brady wasn't teasing me for it. In fact, he hadn't said a word.

I kept up my pacing as he gathered the cards and returned them to the small box.

Ignoring me, Brady moved a bag of mulch under the blankets and used it to recline against. He leaned back and wiggled until the covered bag held a Brady-sized impression, and he got comfortable. Stretching, he extended his long, lean body as far as it would go. The fabric covering his stomach rode up as a sliver of pale, toned midsection became visible.

I swallowed and looked away, ignoring the trail of fine, dark hair that disappeared beneath his jeans.

A groan escaped his lips as he stretched. I definitely didn't compare it to the sound he'd made when I'd fisted his shirt in the front seat of his truck.

Crossing his hands behind his head, Brady watched me walk from one end of the shed to the other.

"Did you just develop claustrophobia all of a sudden?" he said around a yawn.

My watch told me it was after eleven. It was quiet, but I could hear night sounds outside—insects and the rustling of the grass, probably some small animals.

But I wasn't afraid of the relatively small space we were trapped in. I was uncomfortable, and I couldn't put a finger on why. I didn't like being alone with Brady when I didn't know what was going on with my body. Between the kiss weeks ago and the way I'd been lusting after his lips just now, I didn't want to admit that I was probably (definitely) attracted to the boy I'd hated all my life.

If we kept playing cards and getting along, then I'd keep getting my wires crossed. I'd embarrass myself again. And worse, I'd keep smiling and laughing and . . . having fun.

"No, I'm not claustrophobic," I finally answered. "I just want to move around. We've been sitting forever, and I'm all stiff."

"Yeah, you do look tense."

I glared and then pivoted in the other direction. Pacing didn't take me but a few steps before I had to turn around again. "Well, we can't all be laid-back frat bros."

He chuckled. "Would you prefer I freak out and complain the whole time? We're stuck. We can't do a damn thing about it. So I'm making the best of it."

"Making the best of it?" I practically shrieked, halting in my frantic walking.

"Sure, why not? We're not going to die. Someone will let us out in the morning, and we can go get some breakfast if you want."

I stared at him incredulously. "We are trapped. In the cold. We don't have food or water."

He held up the half-empty bag of candy.

"*Real* food, Brady. What if one of us needs medicine or a doctor? Or a damn bathroom?"

What if I'm having thoughts and I don't like those thoughts? What if I'm considering grabbing you by the puffy vest and kissing the hell out of you again?

"Do you need to pee?" he asked, oblivious to my internal freakout. "I can face the wall and hum. I think I saw a watering can somewhere."

"No," I said quickly when he started to rise, presumably to get a watering can for me to pee into. *Jesus Christ.* "I'd rather die. Thank you."

He laughed and lay back down on the makeshift pallet. "Okay, calm down."

I must have shot laser beams of rage out of my eyes because he quickly backtracked. "Shit. Sorry. I didn't mean that."

With hands raised in surrender, Brady sat up. "You can be as mad or worried or upset about this as you want. But I'm going to stay positive. As long as both of us don't panic at the same time, we'll be okay."

After a long moment, I nodded. That sort of made sense.

"Now—if you'd like—come sit down and get under a blanket."

I frowned, wondering why he'd said that.

As if in answer, Brady clarified, "You're rubbing your arms. You're cold."

I looked down to see that he was right. My hands were moving up and down the smooth fabric of my jacket. Now that I wasn't dying from embarrassment or full of furious anger, the cold had seeped in without me noticing.

Brady returned his hands behind his head and closed his eyes like he didn't care what I decided to do.

So I sat. Then I burrowed beneath the top layer of the blanket mound.

He cracked one lid open. "You know, we could snuggle for warmth."

"Oh my God," I growled.

"I'm just saying!" He closed his eye, but there was no hiding that grin.

———

Brady

It was an hour later, and I could hear her teeth chattering.

We'd dimmed the electric lantern, and it emitted only a faint circle of cool blue light. But I could see how stiffly Mac held herself.

The blankets were plentiful, but they were rough and thick and not very well insulated. It was like trying to cover up and keep warm with a scratchy suit jacket. The blankets might have been economical, but they weren't comfortable like a quilt or a fuzzy fleece.

Despite the cold, Mac had been hell-bent on ignoring me. I shouldn't have pushed. Obviously, I'd rattled her.

I was going to lose a thumbnail if I kept nervously fiddling with the key ring in my pocket, though.

"Will you please just come lie down with me?" I finally blurted. "Just for warmth. We do not have to talk about anything you don't want to talk about. But you are very clearly freezing."

"No," she said, shaking her head.

"I'll never tell anyone. It'll be our secret."

Her eyes locked on mine, and I just *knew* she was thinking about the other secret we shared.

So I hurriedly added, "I'm tired of listening to your teeth clickety-clacking. I'll never get my beauty rest if you're over there getting hypothermia."

Mac glared like I knew she would.

I flung back the blanket covering me and spread my arms wide.

She looked like a woman facing a firing squad, but she eventually crawled over to me. I swallowed hard and focused on not getting an erection at the sight of her on all fours.

Once she'd snuggled into my side, her head resting on my shoulder and her arms wrapping around my chest, we got the blankets situated on top of us. The only sound besides the crickets outside was our steady breathing.

I wrapped one arm around her back and pulled her close. We didn't talk, and all I could think about was how good she felt, how well we fit together, how nice it was to be close and quiet—even if we were trapped in an old shed.

After long moments, she finally murmured against my chest, "How are you this warm?" Her tired voice was a little muffled from the fabric of my vest.

"I've always run pretty hot." I grinned against the top of her head. Her dark hair was soft and cold beneath my lips. "Admit it, Macaroni. You think I'm hot."

She snorted. "Yeah. A hot mess."

"Nope. A smoke show."

"Like a dumpster fire."

I laughed into the darkness.

"Besides," she continued, "you're not really my type."

From our long history, I knew she was trying to get under my skin, but even with that knowledge, I couldn't ignore the sharp edge of hurt her words caused. Maybe I'd only realized it recently, but I *did* want to be MacKenzie Clark's type.

"Oh, really," I said, making sure my tone was even, casual as a Friday. "Because I'm not a loan officer or a dentist."

Mac held so still that I didn't think she was even breathing.

Maybe it was weird that I knew the occupations of the last two guys she'd dated. I probably shouldn't have said that.

Finally, she replied primly, "There's nothing wrong with being a loan officer or a dentist."

"I totally agree. Gum health is important."

That had her exhaling a short laugh.

But what I didn't say could fill up every wheelbarrow in this shed. Mac needed more than a safe guy with a steady career and a 401(k). She needed someone to challenge her, to call her on her bullshit. Mac didn't want to be taken care of by some buttoned-up nice guy.

As long as I'd known her, she'd been bold and fierce with a wild streak a mile wide. Now, she was a strong, independent woman—fearless and vulnerable in unexpected ways.

She always picked Kirby Falls transplants to date. Men who moved here in adulthood. They usually owned businesses or held down standard nine-to-five jobs.

Mac dated those men because there was a safety net beneath each one. But in reality, if she let them see who she really was, she'd eat them alive. Instead, she settled, and then she got bored. It didn't take a genius to figure out why. It was like she was forcing herself into a mold, and then when it got too uncomfortable, she bolted.

"But?" she prompted, jolting me out of my thoughts. "I know you want to say something. And not about gingivitis."

My heart thumped hard in my rib cage, and I wondered if she could feel it. This was getting close to the imaginary line we'd drawn. Who Mac dated skirted the border of things she wasn't ready to talk about . . . like kissing in front seats and how all those guys should have been me.

So, I hedged a little. "But . . . I think they're a little boring. For you."

She lifted up on her elbow to look at me. "For me? What does that mean?"

I couldn't look at her when she was this close. Not when I could feel her legs tangled with mine and her hand resting over my heart.

So I shifted, placing my hands behind my head and looking up at the dark ceiling of the shed. "It just means I think you date these safe, boring guys who don't hold your interest. I think you need someone who would be a good match. Someone who's a little wild. Someone who's going to be more than safe, where you're concerned."

It took everything in me to keep my gaze fixed on the roof over my head. I wanted to gauge her features in the dim lantern light. I wanted to watch her react to my words before her brain reminded her I was the one speaking them. But most of all, I wanted to kiss her again and make her *see* me.

Thirty seconds passed while I fought my instincts. I didn't fidget or squirm or reposition my body.

Mac settled back at my side but remained quiet. It wasn't like her. I was used to a Mac who reacted quickly and, at times, violently. This thoughtful, subtle creature nestled against me was an unknown.

Attempting to break the tension, I joked, "You're not going to bite me, are you?"

"Where did *that* come from?" she asked, incredulous.

I grinned and brought my arm back around her shoulders, my fingers sifting through her dark hair. I felt more content than I had any right to be lying on the floor of a cold shed. "I just remembered how mad you got that time in kindergarten when you bit Mrs. DeBusk. Annnnd you're pretty close to my jugular."

Mac laughed, her breath warm against the exposed skin of my neck. "I'm not going to bite you. Jesus. Why do you even remember that?"

"I remember everything, Macklemore."

Another moment passed. I felt her swallow before saying, "That's a new nickname."

Grinning, I rested my chin on top of her head. "I just thought of it."

MAC

The harsh sound of metal and rusty hinges woke me the following morning.

I squinted against the sunlight streaming in and tried to force my groggy brain to come online.

"Now, *this* is the best day of my life."

The voice came from my cousin Laramie, who was silhouetted in the doorway of the shed.

I groaned as the night before came rushing back. Being trapped. Playing cards. Snuggling for warmth.

Oh, God.

"Just five more minutes," the man beside me slurred as his arms tightened around my middle. Brady's cold nose burrowed into my neck, and something large and impossibly hard ground firmly against my thigh as he shifted closer. Suddenly I was wide the fuck awake.

I heard the manufactured shutter sound of a phone camera snapping away, and I turned an incredulous glare on Larry.

"What?" She grinned. "This should be documented. For posterity."

"You don't even know what that means," I hissed, extracting myself from the cocoon of uncomfortable blankets and the very prominent erection beneath them.

Larry wore a toboggan over her dark hair. Her perfectly lined eyes were wide with excitement as she held the door ajar and took in the situation.

Brady was still mumbling sleepily into the space I'd left behind.

"Have y'all been stuck in here all night?" Larry asked. "Hey! Are those my Twizzlers?"

I stood and slipped my socked feet back into my boots. "Yes, we got locked in, and your candy stash kept us alive."

We both watched as Brady slowly sat up, rubbing his eyes.

"Not a morning person, is he?" my cousin murmured. "That feels important to note. Guess you'll be the one making the coffee."

"Shut up," I whispered. Embarrassment was swiftly followed by defensiveness. I felt like I was in high school and I'd gotten busted for sneaking out. "It was an accident. The door closed, and everyone was gone. We didn't have our phones."

Larry's grin was amused. "And you needed to conserve body heat?"

I glared.

"You know," she said, "that works better when you're both naked."

"That's what I tried to tell her," Brady said, finally rising to his feet. His voice was rough from sleep, and now I knew how he sounded when he first woke up in the morning. *Oh, God.*

My gaze snapped to him, and, I'm not proud of this, my attention immediately lowered to his groin. But he was folding one of the moving blankets in front of him, and I couldn't see anything. Not that I *wanted* to see anything. But it had felt surprisingly enor—

"Thanks for the Twizzlers," Brady said, interrupting the horrifying thoughts running through my brain. "They kept us alive in our time of need. I'll buy you a new pack."

"Oh, not necessary," Larry said brightly. "Believe me, finding y'all has been payment enough. I'm just glad you and Mac didn't freeze to death."

For whatever reason—and there were many—I couldn't meet Brady's gaze. I kept my head down and made for fresh air and freedom.

Uncomfortable truths were swirling around inside me like a tornado of destruction. Like the way Brady must have worn a different cologne last night or something because he didn't smell like alpine yeti or whiskey-soaked machetes or whatever the hell Axe body spray was going for. When I'd snuggled against his side, he'd smelled like something warm and bright—a beach, complete with saltwater spray and glorious sunshine.

"Thanks for the rescue," I heard Brady say when I'd stepped out into the shining light of early morning.

"No problem," Larry replied as I rushed by her. I ignored the what-the-fuck look she was aiming my way. "This has been the second most exciting thing I've ever found in this shed."

The wind tunnel of realization whipped another helpful fact my way. I was still attracted to Brady. The kiss wasn't locked away and forgotten. It was a reminder, and every time I glanced at his lips, muscle memory had me leaning closer, seeking him out.

Brady's voice was distant as I hustled away in near panic. "Guess she doesn't want to grab breakfast."

The unhelpful thoughts spun faster. How we'd barely fought at all last night, and even when we had, it had been fun, entertaining bickering. The way he always noticed me, and how much history existed between us. How he'd read my past relationships like an open book, then highlighted, color coded, and annotated them for maximum impact.

I didn't want to think about the guy with a king of hearts pressed to his forehead. Or the fact that my nemesis couldn't settle down and go to sleep knowing I was shivering across from him.

As I breezed through the pumpkin patch toward the General Store, knowledge continued to assault me. A teasing grin and a dimple in his right cheek. A playful quip that had me fighting a smile. A gentle hand rubbing warmth into my freezing back. A strong thigh beneath mine and a soft place to land. Steady optimism to combat my overwhelmed frustration. And an accident turned adventure. One that I'd enjoyed more than any date I'd ever been on.

As I closed and leaned against the door to the restroom in the General Store, I covered my face with my hands.

It came then. The most unfortunate truth of all. One that had me sucking in lungfuls of air.

Maybe I didn't hate Brady Judd after all.

I didn't go to the Friday night bonfire at Abby's five days later. When Larry asked me with a knowing smirk what my big plans were instead, I gave her my best I-don't-know-what-you-mean stare and told her to have fun without me.

Then, the following day, I'd worked my mother's shift at the farmers' market. My gaze strayed to the adjacent booth more times than I wanted to admit, but it had only been Mercer and Candace working the table for Judd's.

The night in the shed had messed me up. It had shifted something out of alignment that no chiropractor could adjust. I was off-kilter and unsteady. Being aware of Brady—or attracted to him, whatever—had caused chaos to reign. I thought about him all the time. Replayed that illuminating and annoying conversation about the guys I'd dated not being enough for me. I wondered if he'd been genuine or if the real Brady was just playing some elaborate prank.

I'd been checking my Chatter app for notifications and new posts constantly. But so far, he'd been quiet. It was like he knew that being out of sight would drive me out of my fucking mind.

I wanted to see him, but I didn't trust myself. I was scared I'd expose something, inadvertently show my hand. I worried I wouldn't be able to keep my eyes to myself or, worse, my hands and lips. Deep down, I knew that something big had changed—bigger even than the kiss that was playing on a loop in my head.

What would it be like to declare a truce with Brady Judd? And was this just some weird attraction that would pass in time?

I had many questions and zero answers. Mostly because I was too chickenshit to come face-to-face with him.

But when trivia night rolled around on Monday evening, I gave myself a stern talking-to. I'd had over a week to be a coward. That wasn't who I was.

MacKenzie Clark didn't lose her mind over a man. Especially not one she'd seen eat his own boogers in preschool.

When I got to Trailview Brewing, the place was abuzz. Plastic vinyl panels enclosed the seating area to keep the cold out, and every picnic table was filled with people. A lot of them were locals, teams of folks I faced weekly for trivia. But the watering hole was also packed with tourists. The line at the bar had a dozen people. So I was grateful when I spotted Larry, Kayla, Bonnie, and Danny already seated with an extra beer waiting on me.

"I wondered if you'd show up," Larry called with a grin while I stripped off my jacket.

"Why wouldn't Mac show up?" Bonnie asked in confusion. My sister was a sweetheart, but I didn't want to get into this right now. Larry thought the shed incident was hilarious, but, strangely, she hadn't mentioned it to anyone. And I hadn't told a soul about getting locked in overnight with Brady.

Larry had always been convinced that Brady and I had the hots for each other, and I knew that was why she was giving me a hard time right now. That was partly why I was so reluctant to admit I was having . . . feelings.

I slid onto the bench next to my sister and kicked Larry under the table. "Of course I'm here," I said brightly. "Gotta lead this team to victory."

Bonnie wrapped her arm around me and squeezed.

Larry was rubbing her shin beneath the table, and Kayla passed over the extra beer. "Here you go, Mac."

"Thank you. I did not want to wait in that line."

"I'm going out to the car for a minute," Danny announced out of nowhere.

Bonnie frowned. "But—"

"I'll be back in a few," he interrupted, standing with his phone in hand and shuffling off through the crowd without a backward glance for his wife.

Danny and Bonnie had been together since high school. They'd been a unit. Their relationship a fixture in my life since I was twelve years old. Danny had been part of our family for a very long time, attending festivals, birthday parties, and holiday gatherings.

He'd taught me how to drive a stick shift and change a tire. But Danny had been acting off for a while now. Distant and aloof. On his phone all the time.

I eyed my sister and took a sip of my beer.

She watched her husband with a frown before noticing me out of the corner of her eye. Her brows unfurled themselves, and she forced a smile. "Probably just needs to make a call," she said quietly and then reached for her own glass.

Larry caught my eye, and we shared a brief look.

Bonnie was the peacemaker. She'd been an overachiever since birth. While her education and career had taken her away from the farm, she was still devoted to our family. Every dinner at Aunt Maggie's, Bonnie showed up with bells on. She served on committees and volunteered her time. She was a people-pleaser through and through.

My sister taught art down at the elementary school, and she was great at it. So talented and good with the kids. You couldn't go anywhere with her in Kirby Falls without running into her students or their parents. Everyone loved Bonnie. She'd been my playmate, my reliable older sister, and my confidant. There wasn't anything I wouldn't do for her.

And she sure as hell deserved better than Danny Jensen.

There was a part of me that saw my sister and her husband as a cautionary tale. They represented the dangers of falling for someone so young, someone you'd known your whole life and latched on to before you were old enough to know better—to realize there was more out there than some farm boy who hadn't done a damn thing to earn your heart besides exist in the same small town.

How could you meet the love of your life when you'd barely even lived it?

Bonnie cleared her throat, drawing my attention.

Larry and I went back to our drinks and kept our mouths shut. It was Kayla who spoke up. "Did y'all hear they had another scare over at Judd's?"

My attention snapped to her. "What?"

Kayla nodded. "Yeah, last night. I heard someone came onto the property and triggered the motion sensors. They just got a glimpse of them on the cameras, but it was too dark, and whoever it was had their face covered."

Dread slithered up my spine, and for the first time since I'd walked in the door, I let my eyes seek out Brady. He was seated several tables away with Abby and Jase. As if he could feel me looking, his eyes found mine, and I glanced quickly away.

What did it mean that someone had tried to vandalize their orchard again? And did he still suspect me?

"Were they trying to paintball the property again?" Larry asked.

"No, no one saw a paintball gun or anything on the camera footage," Kayla replied. "Or if they were planning on it, they got scared off before they had a chance to get their gear. There was no damage or anything. Brady got there real quick. He had the alerts set up on his phone. The sheriff's department came out too, but they didn't find anything."

"Man, that's weird," Larry murmured.

"I'm glad there wasn't any damage or anyone hurt," Bonnie said.

Suddenly, all three of my tablemates were looking at me expectantly.

"What?"

"Aren't you going to say something?" Larry asked.

I frowned. "What do you want me to say?"

"I don't know," she said. "That it's strange or bad luck or you're surprised it happened again."

"I mean, yeah. All of those things."

Kayla leaned in and whispered, "Where were you last night, Mac?"

I stared in shock before everyone else erupted in laughter.

"I can't believe you guys," I hissed.

Larry grinned, unrepentant. "We're just giving you shit."

"We know you didn't have anything to do with it," Bonnie added.

"But that mug shot of you in the town Facebook group *was* pretty hilarious." Kayla laughed.

My sister and cousin both joined in, chuckling.

I glared. Ugh, if my own friends and family were bringing this up, I could only imagine what Brady would do with the possibility. Did he actually think I was capable of trespassing on his family's property?

"Well, I was pretty proud of that one. Thank you, ladies," Brady said from out of nowhere.

I jolted in surprise and banged my knee on the underside of the table, cursing.

How could someone so damn tall sneak up on people?

"Are you coming over to get Mac's alibi, Brady?" Kayla teased, winking my way.

I scowled.

"Couldn't hurt," he replied with a grin.

"She was with me," both Larry and Bonnie said at the same time.

Brady's blue eyes sparkled as he looked between all of us. I was two seconds away from dropping my head in my hands.

"We were together," Bonnie hurried to add.

"The three of us," Larry confirmed.

It was then that Danny returned to the table and sat down on the other side of my sister. Without missing a beat, he said, "No, you weren't. We were at my parents' house last night."

Bonnie's cheeks flushed pink at being called out, but Brady didn't seem upset. He was still watching me calmly.

"Is that right?" he said, shifting to put his hand in the pocket of his vest. "So where were you last night, Mac Mac?"

"Busy," I replied evenly. Truthfully, I'd been bored at home, obsessing over his dumb ass. But no one needed to know that.

Our gazes held, and I could see that he was entertained.

"Didn't you have that date last night?" Larry called, breaking our weird staring contest.

All that easy amusement vanished. Brady's mouth tightened, and he glanced away.

I shot Larry a what-the-hell-are-you-doing look, but her bug-eyed response gave off "I'm helping!" vibes.

Sighing, I turned back to Brady. "I was at home last night, if you must know. Alone. So I don't have an alibi. Add that to your investigation."

"I wasn't—" he started, but Larry cut in, "Y'all should have a stakeout. Maybe the perp will come back and try again since their attempt was thwarted."

The perp? I mouthed. "Are you serious right now?"

"That's a good idea," Kayla agreed.

"And if Mac helps, it would prove once and for all that she didn't have anything to do with it," Bonnie stated determinedly.

"Y'all," I tried.

"That's not a bad plan," Brady said, nodding. "What do you say, Mac Attack? You up for a stakeout?"

My laughter was a touch unhinged. "No way. I do not need to play cops and robbers to prove my innocence. Come on, you guys. This is ridiculous. Of course I didn't have anything to do with this." I felt like I was the only sane person at this table—in this whole damn town.

"Well, you didn't have an alibi, sweetie," my sister said apologetically, rubbing a supportive hand on my back.

"And who knows?" Larry said enthusiastically. "Maybe y'all will catch the culprit."

I blinked several times, so baffled by this turn of events.

"How about this?" Brady said genially. "If my team wins trivia tonight, you'll do the stakeout. And if y'all take home first place, then I won't bother you about it again."

"A bet?" I asked, incredulously. "That's seriously how you want to handle this?"

I couldn't help but feel manipulated. Brady knew how competitive I was. But when it came right down to it, if I was involved, he was just as obsessed with winning.

Of course I was reluctant to spend more alone time with him. This attraction thing was weird and inconvenient and messy and—

"Come on," Larry encouraged. "We've got this."

My attention snapped to Brady, where he stood, gloating and arrogant with his ridiculously messy hair. His blue eyes held a challenge I was physically incapable of backing down from. My gaze narrowed, and his narrowed right back.

"What's wrong, Macklemore? Are you scared you'll lose?"

This whole thing was absurd, borderline preposterous. But at least the interaction was something I was used to. We were back to goading and glaring, pushing each other's buttons. That off-balance feeling I'd been wrestling with all week hadn't gone anywhere. I still couldn't look at Brady without thinking of lips and warmth and orange Tic Tacs. But this, at least, was familiar territory. We'd been trying to get the upper hand with one another for a long time.

And the illusion of power could make you do stupid, stupid things.

"Fine. I accept your terms," I taunted. "May the better team win."

I blamed Larry for flubbing the NBA question in the final round.

We'd finished just two points shy of Brady's team. And when they were announced as the winners, he'd strutted to the front and snagged the microphone, thanking a long list of people—me included—before accepting the winners' gift certificates to the Hogs Wild food truck.

I never should have agreed to the stupid bet. Now, I couldn't back out without looking like a sore loser.

So, the following night, I drove across the street to Judd's Family Orchard while the bitter sting of defeat rode shotgun. There was also a tiny bit of nervousness as I fretted over being alone with Brady once more.

He was waiting on me when I climbed out of my Jeep. Judd's was closed to the public until later in the week, and I wasn't on the schedule for the next day, so I could sleep off this ridiculous overnight stakeout.

The chances of "the perp" coming back on a random Tuesday night were next to zero. I anticipated being very bored and irritated. I hoped there would, at the very least, be snacks.

I eyed Brady suspiciously as I approached. He looked absurd in head-to-toe camouflage, but his blue eyes sparkled with mirth. I felt a tug in the center of my chest. One that made me want to be close to him and simultaneously run the other direction as fast as my feet could carry me. It was confusing and disorienting. But a bigger part of me was curious enough to go through with this plan. And like hell I'd back down from a challenge.

Was I still attracted to this bozo? Yes.

Did I still want to kiss him? Also, yes.

And the most infuriating part of all: I didn't know what that meant.

I felt like I was once again on the bow of a ship, getting tossed around by the waves, completely off-balance and out of my depth. And there stood Brady, calm and amused, looking as steady as an oak tree.

"You know camo doesn't actually make you invisible," I quipped as I came to stand before him.

He had a green-and-brown-patterned toboggan on his head, covering most of his hair. Camo pants and a camo jacket encased his tall body, and dark brown work boots completed the look.

"At least I'm prepared to be covert," he replied, unbothered. "You can probably see those fire-engine-red lips in the dark."

I scowled. "There is nothing wrong with my lipstick."

"I didn't say there was." His gaze dropped briefly to my mouth before he cleared his throat. "It looks good. It's just not very subtle, and we're supposed to be undercover."

My mind took a little journey—one that was unwelcome and horrifying— thinking of ways Brady could smudge my lipstick right off.

Thankfully, he interrupted my dirty, dirty mind and said, "Come on," before leading me out of the parking lot. We walked back up the gravel drive to the highway and quickly locked the chain across the path.

Then we made our way into the Apple House.

I noted the night was quiet except for a faint buzzing, like a fan blowing somewhere.

The whitewashed wooden Apple House was mostly an open-air building, wide and exposed to the elements on three sides with tables, pre-packaged produce for sale, a long counter for employees, and a closed office door beyond. I knew that Candace, Brady's younger sister, had been using the office since returning to town. She'd gone to school for marketing and sales and had come back home to help out here at Judd's. We got along well, and she and my sister, Bonnie, had been hanging out quite a bit.

It was dim beneath the covered area without the lights on, but I could make out the back of the Apple House where they kept the equipment for pressing. We had a pretty similar setup over at Grandpappy's. But when I peered beyond the tank and machinery and conveyors to the outside, I stopped in my tracks. The flood-lights illuminated the space behind the Apple House nicely. It looked like part of the area had been sectioned off for new plantings, but positioned around them were three wacky waving inflatable tube men. In red, orange, and turquoise, the three arm-flailing vinyl figures were the source of the low hum. Air filled their cylindrical bodies as they waved and flopped and snapped to and fro.

"What is that about?" I asked, pointing in the distance.

"Oh," Brady replied from my side. "That's Brad, Chad, and Jeff. Candy's idea. We started some raspberries and blackberries back there. They don't have any fruit yet, but the deer love to eat the leaves. The inflatables scare them off. Plus, the kids love it."

I smiled to myself as I watched the colorful men wobble and sway. "That's funny."

"Yeah, Candy is full of ideas. You want something to drink?"

"Diet Coke, if you have it."

"Sure." Brady slipped behind the counter and into Candace's office. The overhead light briefly illuminated the space, and I could see the cash register and work area behind the counter a little better.

Brady emerged with a plastic shopping bag from Winn-Dixie in one hand and a bottle of Diet Coke in the other.

"So, what's the plan?" I asked, rubbing my hands together. It was just after nine o'clock, and the late-October air was chilly and getting colder by the minute. "Are we just watching security monitors in the office or hanging out in our cars or what?"

My stomach did a weird little flip when I thought of conducting this farce of a stakeout from the front seat of Brady's truck. I pushed aside memories of a warm cab and even warmer hands.

"Nah," Brady replied easily, drawing my attention—thank God. "I've got us all set up."

"Outside?" I whined.

"Yes, outside. How else are we supposed to keep watch?"

"I don't know. This whole thing is a waste of time."

"We don't have a bank of security monitors," he explained. "The cameras and monitoring app connect to my phone." He gave me a challenging, superior look. "But if you really want to watch from the parking lot, my truck is right over there. After you."

I glared. I knew he was trying to get a rise out of me, and I hated how predictable I was. I also hated that a little part of me—the horny, confused part—wanted to climb back inside with him and see what happened.

Brady grinned knowingly. "Let's go, Macintosh."

With my Diet Coke held hostage, he made his way down the front stairs of the Apple House. I sighed and followed.

When I reached the bottom step, my breath puffed visibly in the crisp autumn air. "I'm too Southern for this kind of cold. The sweet tea will freeze in my veins."

Chuckling, Brady spun back to me. He thrust the plastic soda bottle my direction and used his free hands to pull off his camo winter hat. His light brown hair was a mess, sticking up in all directions, and for a moment, I had no idea what he was doing. Possibly attempting to smother me in order to stop my complaining.

But then he leaned forward and popped the toboggan on my head, drawing the warm fabric down over my cold ears.

"You lose eighty percent of your body heat through your head and feet," he said as he straightened the hat into place.

I forced a hard swallow and watched him. "Is that true?" My voice was embarrassing—rough and hushed at the same time. Brady was being sweet with me, and I didn't know how to act. But I liked the feeling of him fussing over me. And I didn't mind wearing something of his even if it smelled like . . . I pulled in an unsteady breath and registered that now-familiar scent of sun and sand and salt water, the gesture warming me in more ways than one.

Brady's smile widened. "Sure. I saw it on the internet."

I rolled my eyes, but I was grinning, too.

"Come on," he said. "I promise you won't freeze."

And true to his word, I didn't, because Brady had us set up on the temporary pumpkin patch. Most of the squash had been sold, only a few stragglers remained this close to Halloween. But the hay bales had been carefully arranged to form a wall that faced the entrance road. A few sections had been removed as covert peepholes for what I imagined Brady meant by "keep watch." There were bales arranged on the back side for seating, covered by thick blankets. And positioned behind everything was an outdoor heater. It looked like one of the ones they'd used for the pumpkin-painting event.

I stared in surprise as Brady got settled on one of the covered hay bales.

"This will be the best stakeout you've ever been on," he bragged.

As I made my way over to sit next to him, I thought he might just be right.

Then I inwardly rolled my eyes at myself because this was the only stakeout I'd ever been on or would ever be on, in all likelihood.

Brady started unloading items from his grocery sack. He pulled out a small container of Tic Tacs, and I fought valiantly against my blush. Then he tossed me a plastic-wrapped bag of candy.

I caught the Twizzlers in my lap.

"For old times' sake," he said with a wink.

I bit my lip to keep from grinning back, and his smile widened.

"I saw that," he teased. "I also have some cards in here, but I figure we'll be alright with our phones for a while. There's a mobile charger, too. Gotta stay charged in case we need to call the sheriff's office."

"You really think we're going to find someone out here?"

"I don't know. Maybe," he replied.

I opened the bag of Twizzlers and passed him one. "And you really think I had something to do with it?"

It was a fair question, one I'd let bother me beyond surface annoyance. Brady and I went too far sometimes. The Elmer's Glue Incident of 2009 came to mind. But the fact that he'd seemed to truly believe I was capable of trespassing and causing damage to his family's property had been a shock to the system. So my initial reaction to his accusation had been anger and disbelief.

Brady sighed and stared at the licorice rope in his hand. "At first, I thought you probably hated me enough to do something like that."

"I don't hate you," spilled out before I'd given it permission.

He met my gaze and raised one dark brow like he didn't believe me.

"I don't," I repeated. "You just—you're so—I don't know how to describe it. But hate is reserved for serial killers and billionaire CEOs. People who don't deserve your time or attention because they don't know how to care about anything besides themselves."

Brady's attention had drifted back down to his hands and the candy he held, so it was easier to admit the next part, especially in the dark with only the moon and stars overhead. "You're a good person, Brady. You drive me fucking crazy half the time, but you'd never intentionally or knowingly hurt me." *Except for that one time when you were a dumb teenager.* "And while I know we've given each other hell over the years, I hope you know I wouldn't vandalize your farm or hurt your family or your livelihood like that."

"I do know that," he admitted quietly. "It was easier to blame you and make it all part of the game we play. Otherwise, it becomes a real threat, something unknown that affects my family—my parents and my sister, who live on the property." Brady raised his head and finally met my gaze. "I know you think this is dumb and a waste of time, but I do want to know what's going on. If it's just a teenager being stupid and making poor life decisions, then I want to figure that out, too. But the sheriff's office hasn't made this a priority, and I do want to keep my family safe."

I nodded. "That makes sense. And the security cameras and the lights were good ideas. It might be enough to deter someone out looking for trouble."

"I hope so," Brady agreed. "But I want to be sure."

Suddenly, the thought of being out here all night in the cold didn't feel so ridiculous. I'd do anything for my family, too. Guilt and resentment twisted my insides when I thought about my cousin Will and how he assumed I half-assed everything on the farm and just cruised through life. I didn't know that I could live up to his expectations, but I could probably do more to show him I was a committed part of the Grandpappy's team. I could take some initiative, be more of a leader, ask for more responsibility, and stop holding myself to the same low standards as the high schoolers who worked for us part-time.

I pushed away those inconvenient thoughts and feelings and said, "So we'll have a stakeout, and who knows? Maybe we'll get lucky and some punk will show up and we can kick their ass."

Brady laughed. "Always so violent, Mac and Cheese. No, we'll find out who they are and where they live and haunt them until they get so scared they turn themselves in."

"Ah, yes." I nodded sagely. "We'll *Scooby-Doo* them onto the path of righteousness."

"Exactly."

We shared a grin, and for the first time, it felt like Brady and I were in on something together. Maybe what we'd needed all this time was a common enemy, a shared goal. My eyes drifted down to his lips, and some inner voice whispered that what we actually needed was a flat surface and a box of condoms.

I looked away and shoved a Twizzler in my mouth, chewing deliberately.

Awkward silence descended as we sat side by side. Well, it felt awkward to me, but that was probably because I was so in my own head, sorting through these revelations about Brady, this stakeout, and the awareness I now had for the man beside me.

Luckily, Brady seemed oblivious. He was playing some game on his phone while I powered through six more Twizzlers in an anxiety spiral.

Then, out of nowhere, Brady said, "Are we ever going to talk about the kiss, Mac?"

I choked, bits of licorice lodging themselves in my windpipe as my pulse skyrocketed. Brady patted my back helpfully, and I eventually managed to squawk out, "I thought we agreed it never happened."

He locked his phone and placed it down on the blanket next to him. "*We* didn't agree on anything. You declared it and then ran away like a scaredy cat."

I stared at Brady, heart pounding, knowing we'd reached the point of no return. I was standing on the precipice of something that I couldn't come back from, and as soon as it was out in the open, that would be it.

"I . . ." I hesitated. "I don't know, okay."

It was one of the very few times Brady had ever looked serious. His brows were lowered pensively, and he watched me like he was trying to solve a riddle. I noticed a key ring in his hand, his thumb fidgeting busily over the smooth leather strap and the metal ring.

When he noticed my attention stray, Brady shoved the key ring in his pocket. Was that why he always had his hand inside the pocket of his puffy vest? So he could distract himself and fidget with his key chain?

Back in school, Brady had always been a hyperactive kid. He used to get in trouble for being out of his seat or not paying attention. As we got older, he had teachers who helped him manage his restless energy better, to channel it into learning. As a child, he'd played every sport before finally settling on soccer in high school.

In second grade, probably around the time he got his ADHD diagnosis, Ms. Ogle sat Brady next to me in an effort to keep him on task. He'd been disruptive in her class, attention seeking. I could recall her berating him and calling him lazy in front of everyone. Something about it rankled. Even back then, when we were chasing each other at recess and daring each other to eat worms on the playground.

The teacher's shitty plan backfired since Brady and I fought so much. Our bickering led to her moving Brady again. This time, Jase Wilcox, a quiet kid who hardly ever spoke in class, achieved what I couldn't manage. He kept Brady in his seat and on task, helping him with his work and drawing pictures of anything and everything Brady asked for.

In the end, even though Mrs. Ogle obviously had no idea how to accommodate a kid with ADHD, she'd managed to do something right by sitting them next to one another. She'd solidified Brady and Jase's friendship, one they'd kept and nurtured to this day.

Brady was fun loving, charming, and well-liked—always had been. No one picked on him or teased him for his ADHD, at least not that I remembered. If anything, he'd been the lovable class clown, generally charming his teachers and volunteering for everything under the sun. His ADHD had just been a part of who he was, not something that defined him. Plus, he'd never been shy about his diagnosis. I remembered a time in sixth grade when he talked openly at the lunch table about the medicine he took.

To me, there were so many *other* pieces that made up Brady Judd.

The image of him fiddling with the key ring brought back the memory of us together in the shed. When I'd been snuggled up to his side keeping warm, he'd twirled my hair around his finger over and over. I'd felt the gentle tug and motion against my back for a long time that night. He hadn't even seemed aware he was doing it, and I hadn't stopped him . . . for reasons.

I wondered if, as an adult, Brady needed to keep his hands busy to stay focused or if he was currently feeling nervous and off-balance, like me.

Finally, he met my gaze, and something like resolve stole over his features. "Maybe we should do it again. Kiss, I mean."

My eyes widened.

"For clarification," he added, turning his body to face me.

"For clarification on what?" I asked, feeling myself lean closer, tugged by an invisible thread woven with curiosity and the warmth he radiated.

"Well," he murmured, licking his lips, "clarification for you since you're so freaked out about it."

My eyes dropped lower, and so did my voice. "Oh, and what about you? You're not freaking out?"

I watched as his shiny lips tugged up in a rueful smile. "Nah, I already know what I want."

I didn't have the appropriate amount of time to freak out about *that* statement because he was getting closer.

With careful movements, Brady leaned into my space. I had plenty of time to turn my head, hop up, or push him away, but I did none of those things. Instead, I met him halfway, closing the distance between us and searching for the clarification he'd promised. I didn't know if I'd find answers or more questions when our lips met, but when it happened, it felt like truth rushing through my veins.

Brady's hand cupped my cheek. His thumb, once again, came to rest on my chin. There was no surprise this time—no hesitation or playing catch-up. Our lips moved in sync, slotting together as I rested my hand on his thigh for balance.

Brady's hand shifted as he ran his fingers along my jaw before threading into my hair. Our mouths opened, deepening the kiss. Tongues tangled and breaths quickened while I sought balance in the storm. I brought my other hand to his chest, warm and solid. Brady's fingers covered mine, holding me in place and steadying me.

Suddenly, his lips were gone, leaving me gasping for air as his mouth dragged over my skin. He kissed a hot trail from my jaw to just below my ear before rasping, "I want you, Mac. Just like this."

My eyes flew open at his words, the ones breathed into my skin like a confession, like an oath.

Chin tilted up, I stared into the clear, cold night, an ocean of stars overhead. I couldn't think—not with his tongue tracing down my neck as he turned his attention to a sensitive spot there.

Brady Judd wanted me, and, God help me, I wanted him too. *Just like this.*

Before I knew it, I was pushing against his chest to make room and climbing across his lap. He didn't miss a beat as my knees straddled his strong thighs. Two hands came to rest on my ass as he continued his ministrations across my collarbone and over the hollow at the base of my throat.

I wound my fingers into his messy brown hair, gripping tight and keeping him close. If I was too rough, he didn't seem to mind. Instead, he let out a tortured sound and a warm breath.

I used the opportunity to bring his mouth to mine. Our kisses were hungry and a little wild now. Each of us eager and restless. A battle raging between us even in this. I wanted to laugh, to smile, to whisper, *I fucking knew it*, into his ear before biting down on the lobe.

But I didn't get the chance because Brady kneaded my ass, urging me closer. When I settled flush against his lap, his dick pushed right between my thighs, lined up perfectly with the seam on my jeans, and I stopped thinking altogether. He was so thick and hard, and the prospect of coming felt so good that I didn't even care how embarrassing it would be to get off while dry humping my nemesis on top of a hay bale.

I moved, grinding and seeking. *Just like this.*

Brady's breath shuddered out of him roughly, breaking our kiss and giving reality a moment to intrude. But then he groaned, "*Fuck.* Keep doing that. Holy shit, you feel good."

So we kept going, eyes closed, mouths grazing, bodies straining. I rode his erection and listened to this golden boy breathe out filthy words against my lips. Telling me how hard he was and how amazing I felt, how perfect I was *just like this*.

My orgasm broke over me like I was under a waterfall. One second, I was standing in a pool of water, wet and wanting, and the next, I was a gasping, drowning wreck getting tossed around beneath the force of it. I should have known nothing about being with Brady would be gentle or coaxing or delicate. The pleasure was as subtle as a battering ram, just like the man himself.

My lips dragged along his cheek on a soft moan. I wrapped my arms around his shoulders and held on as Brady cursed beneath me. But the sound of his voice was far away, above the water and out of my reach.

Our heavy breaths registered first, and I realized we'd stopped moving. Brady still held me tightly to him, and I was clutching him back just as fiercely. But the reason we'd stopped was because I had—very obviously—had an orgasm, fully clothed and fancy-free. I had one single perfect moment of utter panic before the sounds of tires spinning and gravel spitting interrupted.

Oh shit. The stakeout.

Rising quickly onto my knees, I peered over the hay-bale wall to see a car speeding out of the orchard's parking lot. Taillights flashed just before my vision did the same. Brady popped up to see what was going on, and the crown of his head connected soundly with my chin.

I winced and drew back, eyes squeezing shut. "Ow."

"Shit," Brady muttered, hands gently cupping my cheeks. "I'm sorry. Are you okay?"

I opened my eyes as he continued prodding my chin and jaw. "Yeah, I'm fine." I brushed his hands away, and he frowned. "Did you see the car?"

Brady turned to look in the direction the vehicle had taken off, and I knew by the way his shoulders fell that he hadn't seen a thing. He'd been too preoccupied by me.

We'd both been distracted.

And we had no one to blame but ourselves.

BRADY

I tried to keep my focus on my phone conversation with the sheriff's office, but I was too aware of Mac pacing nearby. And what we'd been doing before being interrupted.

"I'm sorry. What was that?" I asked the woman to repeat her question, forcing my eyes away from Mac's disheveled hair and smeared lipstick. She looked messy and untethered and fucking perfect.

"Are you in danger? Is the trespasser still on the property?" the dispatcher asked.

Clearing my throat, I replied, "No, ma'am. They've fled the scene."

I watched as Mac worked to piece herself back together, stacking her bricks and putting her walls back into place. But there was no way I could wipe away the memory of her coming on my lap. The heat of her, the spicy-sweet scent, the way her thighs had gripped my hips. *Jesus*.

I forced myself to look away again and finished up with the call a few minutes later. "They're sending someone out."

"Okay. Good." Mac wouldn't meet my gaze. Her cheeks were somewhere between rosy pink and violent red, and if I was a betting man, I'd say it wasn't the cold causing her flush.

"Do I need to stay for this part?" she asked.

I frowned. "Of course. They'll want your statement as a witness."

"Right." She blew out a breath.

"You might want to . . ." I gestured to my mouth. "Your lipstick is . . ."

"All over your face," she finished for me and then started using her thumb to wipe away the evidence.

But there was no wishing this away or pretending nothing happened. She could fight it all she wanted, but things had definitely escalated. Stakeout make-out for the win.

When I finished rubbing my hands over my mouth and chin, I eyed Mac's still-tense posture, the way she was avoiding me already. I didn't think I could do this every time something happened between us. It was one step forward, three steps back. At this rate, it would take her a year to admit she had feelings for me and another decade before we got married.

So, I did what I thought might speed things along. "Thinking of making a break for it?"

Mac's attention came to me, and I resisted a fist pump. "No," she snapped.

I chuckled, rocking back on my heels. "You sure? Because you look like you're ready to run." Her eyes narrowed, and I added smugly, "Again." I might as well have called her a coward and reminded her that running was exactly what she'd done after the first time we'd kissed.

"I'm not going anywhere. If the cops want to talk to me, then I'll tell them what happened."

"Well, we probably shouldn't tell them everything that happened."

She sucked in a breath as if she was shocked I'd bring it up.

"I'm fine to keep the stakeout make-out between you and me," I offered.

Mac groaned. "Please don't call it that."

Grinning, I said, "I can't help it. It has such a nice ring to it."

"Well, maybe you wouldn't be so smug about this whole thing if you'd been the one embarrassing yourself on top of a hay bale—"

"Technically, you were on top of *me*," I interrupted.

But she ignored me and kept right on talking. "—having an *orgasm*," she hissed, "without even taking your pants off."

I nodded seriously. "Well, it is cold out here. If I didn't have my pants on, I'd probably have a hard time, incidentally, rising to the occasion."

But Mac wasn't laughing at my joke. Hell, she wouldn't even look at me. For the first time, I realized she was more than a little embarrassed. She was dead serious.

"Mac," I said, making sure I had her attention. "I swear, if you are ashamed or humiliated right now, I will lose my mind. It was hot as hell. Feeling you come apart like that was . . ." I struggled to find the words. "Unbelievable. A fucking revelation. For the love of sweet tea and Dolly Parton, do not be embarrassed. If that car hadn't interrupted us, you wouldn't have been alone in the orgasm department. I would have been right behind you, coming in my pants like a teenager."

Mac's expression was surprised and a little shell-shocked. But then her gray eyes narrowed, shadows of mistrust and years of animosity sneaking out around the edges. "Are you fucking with me right now?"

I laughed incredulously and waved a hand in the general direction of my zipper, where I was still half hard and hopeful.

"Oh," she breathed, eyes trained on my pants. "Well, maybe—"

Before I got the chance to hear the end of *that* sentence, an SUV from the sheriff's department came down the drive with lights on but no sirens. It caught Mac's attention, and she turned away, whatever she'd been about to say forgotten.

I sighed, thinking what piss-poor timing we had and wondering what she'd had in mind. *Well, maybe . . . we could pick up where we left off? Maybe . . . now that I know how it could be with clothes on, we could try it without? Maybe . . . I could suck you off behind that hay bale?* Any of those would have been fantastic options.

Instead, I took the opportunity to quickly adjust myself in my jeans and followed Mac to the parking lot to meet the deputy climbing out of his vehicle. In the harsh automatic floodlights, I noticed they'd sent Jamie Matthews. He'd been a couple of years ahead of us in school and a star on the football team. He was still tall and muscular beneath his uniform, but I had a few inches on him now.

Jamie nodded stiffly in greeting when he reached us.

"The chain was down. They cut the lock on the gate with bolt cutters," the deputy said, eyes scanning the area, straight to business.

Damn. Last time, the gate had still been latched, and they'd walked onto the property. That made me wonder what they'd been planning to do if they'd needed a getaway car.

"Yeah, we latched it around nine," I said.

Jamie nodded. "What time would you say it was when you heard the vehicle?"

I pulled out my phone to look at my call log because I hadn't even thought to check the time right when it happened. But Mac answered, "It was 10:04. I checked my watch right after."

The deputy's eyes narrowed, and he glanced between us. "What were y'all doing out here?"

"Nothing," Mac replied at the same time I said, "Stargazing."

She looked at me with wide eyes, like I was crazy.

"What was that?" Jamie repeated, obviously confused.

Again, we spoke at the same time. "Stakeout," I answered truthfully while Mac said loudly over me, "Working."

"But don't you work across the street?" he asked her.

"Yes," she said, a touch belligerent.

"She's visiting," I offered.

"It's pretty late to be working," he said, pulling out a notebook and writing something down. "Or visiting."

"Busy season," Mac and I replied in unison.

Jamie took our statements, asking minimal questions. He looked at the bald spots in the gravel where the vehicle's tires had spun. I mentioned that the movement had been out of the range of the motion-sensor cameras because there'd been no evidence on video.

"And you don't have any idea about the make and model of the vehicle?" he asked, pen poised over his notepad.

"I didn't get a good look," Mac admitted. "But it might have been a sedan, not an SUV or a truck."

I stayed quiet, irritated with myself for being distracted. But it wasn't like I could admit I hadn't seen a thing because I'd accidentally head-butted Mac and was worried I'd hurt her. Not to mention the fact that there had been absolutely no blood in my brain at the time because it had all been in my dick.

"A sedan," he repeated. Jamie didn't look like he believed her, but he scribbled another note. "I'm just really surprised y'all didn't see or hear anything."

I wouldn't have heard a plane landing in the field behind us with Mac riding my lap, but after a glance in her direction, I figured I shouldn't say that part out loud. But holy shit, it had been good. So good. The sounds she'd made. The way she'd held on for—

I blinked back into the conversation after taking a bony elbow to the ribs. "Ow." Both Mac and the deputy were staring at me expectantly, and I figured I'd missed part of the discussion. That was fine because this joker wasn't taking us seriously anyway. Straightening, I asked, "Sorry, what was that?"

"I said," Jamie exaggerated just shy of an eye roll, "I'll be sure to add this incident to the file. Please get in touch if you think of anything else." His eyes lingered briefly on the hay bales and our makeshift stakeout station before he nodded and climbed back in his vehicle.

Mac and I watched him drive away in silence.

Finally, she turned to face me, and I wished I didn't know her as well as I did. I was losing her. I could feel the cold of the night and the distance between us like a tangible thing. The way she'd closed herself off to me, to us—to the possibility of it.

So, I panicked. I reached her in two strides and wrapped my arms around her, bringing my lips to hers. The kiss wasn't rough or frantic. It was soft and deliberate, a reminder that I was here—right here—if only she'd bother to notice me. She kissed me back, and I wanted to sigh out in relief.

I was tired of feeling like I had to talk her into this every time. I didn't want to take those three steps back. I wanted to stay right here, on the same page.

With shaking hands, I rubbed my palms up and down her back. I broke the kiss and rested my forehead against hers, keeping my eyes closed and lingering in this moment for a little longer. I needed to handle this right. I couldn't rush her and scare her off.

For one more maddening time tonight, we spoke at the same time.

"Can I take you out?" I asked right as she said, "We should have sex."

My brain short-circuited, and I pulled back, eyes snapping open. "What?"

"Wait, what did you say?" she wondered, her dark brows creased.

"What did *you* say?" I fired back, heart racing. I'd heard her, but I didn't understand. "We should have sex?"

Mac bit her lip and then nodded. "Yeah, I think we should. Clearly, we have something"—she gestured between us—"some attraction or whatever going on. We should just get it out of our systems."

She wanted to . . . *oh*.

I stared at her, mind reeling, and wondered how the hell I was going to handle this. I couldn't come right out and tell her I loved her and wanted to be with her. She wasn't ready for that.

Part of me thought I should just take her up on her offer. It felt shallow and wrong, not nearly enough. But maybe if she just had time to see how good we could be together, maybe—

What the hell was wrong with me? Why was I feeling disappointed by the possibility of sex?

Because, I thought, *you know one time won't ever be enough.*

"It doesn't have to be a big deal," she was saying. "It's just sex."

It wouldn't be *just* anything to me.

I laughed even though she'd unknowingly taken an ice pick to my heart. "Are you propositioning me, Mac Daddy?"

"No, Jesus. I just thought it would . . ." Mac's eyes scanned my face like the words she was searching for were hidden there. "I just thought it might fix whatever is happening here."

Fix. Like we were broken.

I cleared the roughness and disappointment from my throat. "And we'd just go back to normal after?"

Mac swallowed and retreated a step. "Listen, if you don't want to, that's fine by me."

I laughed again, nearly breathless with relief that she hadn't actually answered my question. There was no going back for me. "Look at you backpedaling," I teased. "You training for the Tour de France?"

She gritted her teeth, and I grinned.

This was the moment. I could tell her I wanted to date her and lose her for good, or I could go along with her stupid get-it-out-of-our-systems plan and have more time with her.

As if I'd ever be able to extricate her. I couldn't separate our histories or untangle all my memories. There was no going back for either of us. She just didn't know it yet.

I simply had to hope that when the time came, once wouldn't be enough for her either.

"Well, I just want you to know that I require a little more than that. I need to be wooed and romanced before I put out."

"What?" she laughed incredulously.

"I'm not that easy."

Mac blinked. "Well, you seemed pretty easy to me on that hay bale over there."

"Oh really? Because one of us got off on that hay bale over there, and it wasn't me." It almost was, though.

Mac glared at the reminder, but I pressed on, "I want a date first. Dinner or a movie. Something."

She hesitated.

"Is that so much to ask, Mac? Really?"

She watched me for a long moment as if she was weighing the pros and cons, like maybe getting naked with me might not be worth it if she was subjected to a meal beforehand.

Finally, her gaze drifted to my lips, and she said, "Fine. But I get to pick. And it's one night, Judd. One. Then we'll never speak of it again."

The following day, I got a text from an unknown number: *I'll pick you up Friday at 6:30.*

I grinned and updated the contact info.

Me: Is this one of those phishing scams? Are you, a stranger, trying to gain my trust so I'll buy your bitcoins or something?

*Miggity Miggity Mac: No, you idiot. It's Mac. I'll pick you up Friday for our date.**

Me: What's the asterisk for?

Miggity Miggity Mac: Because it's not a real date. More like terms and conditions.

Me: I think you meant it's like how fields marked with an asterisk are required, because if you want to get this hot bod into bed, it's a real date.

Miggity Miggity Mac: Did you just say "hot bod"?

Miggity Miggity Mac: I changed my mind. No sex.

Me: Where are you taking me?

Me: Wait. Don't tell me. I love surprises.

Miggity Miggity Mac: Be ready at 6:30. If you're late because you're fixing your hair, I will leave you.

Me: You can't just honk at the curb. You have to come to the door.

Miggity Miggity Mac: You cannot be serious.

Me: Oh, but I am. Prepare to wine and dine me. See above: hot bod.

Miggity Miggity Mac: 😬 6:30!

Two days later, I was staring out the windshield of Mac's Jeep as she shifted into park. "You brought us to a farm?"

I hadn't made her come to my door after all. I'd been waiting outside my building when she pulled up at 6:26 p.m. I'd spent the forty-five-minute drive north picking songs to make her laugh and teasing her over the playlists on her phone. My goal had been to put her at ease. With the way she was gripping the steering wheel and trying not to look at me when I first hopped in the vehicle, I was worried this night would be over before it even got anywhere near a bedroom.

"Well, yeah," Mac said now, giving me a funny look. "It's almost Halloween. I thought it would be fun."

I guess I was surprised to see she'd brought us to a tourist attraction for our date. That was sort of our everyday reality.

Halloween was tomorrow, and this place was packed. The Haunted Forest in Weaverville opened every October for a season of scaring. People paid to get chased through the woods by masked figures wielding chainless chainsaws and other props. I'd been a few times growing up.

I waited, suspicious of her motivations.

She blew out a breath. "And I didn't want to do this in town where people would see us, okay?"

Ah, there it was.

A humorless chuckle left my lips. "You ashamed of me, Maximus?"

"Brady," she groaned, exasperation evident, "do you really want to sit and have dinner down at Apollo's while everybody and their brother comes up to us wondering what the hell we're doing together?"

I frowned. "Well, I do like their garlic knots."

She gave me a flat stare. "You know how nosy our town is. It seemed better to, you know, keep this between us since it's temporary."

"One night," I murmured, feeling that ice pick chip off another piece of my heart. What would I do if Mac woke up tomorrow—after everything—and was content to go about her life . . . without me? Would she really be able to act like nothing had happened?

"That's right. One night," she agreed, but her eyes skittered away and she quickly climbed out of the Jeep.

I followed as we made our way to the ticket booth, where I had to practically wrestle Mac to the ground in order to pay for our admission. I reminded her that the date was my idea, and she argued with me for a solid three minutes while the line behind us got longer and more aggravated and a bored teenage employee looked on in annoyance.

"Will you hold my hand if I get scared?" I whispered in her ear as we waited with our group for our turn to go into the haunted forest.

She turned her head to look at me, and we were so close I could see that swirling gray storm in her eyes. I wanted to lean in and brush my nose against hers, kiss those red lips slow and deep, and hold her hand, too. But I didn't know where the lines were drawn. Did "just sex" mean to hell with everything else? Or was there freedom in our affections because we were away from Kirby Falls?

While I was busy overthinking it, Mac took the opportunity to bring her lips to my ear. She rose onto her tiptoes and steadied herself with a hand on my shoulder. My hands went to her waist, so eager to have her close.

"First one to scream has to buy the other one a hot chocolate." She pulled back and tilted her head in the direction of the haunted concession stand.

I grinned, happy to play along. "You've got yourself a deal."

As Mac lowered her heels to the ground, I reluctantly released my hold.

A moment later, a man named Harold, dressed in dirty overalls and carrying a baseball bat, called for our group's attention. The dozen or so paying customers gathered around while the Haunted Forest employee explained the rules. Basically, there were a series of paths. We could take whichever ones we wanted; they all ended up in the same place—an open field in the middle of the forest next to a small building. I knew from experience that our group would be ushered into the shed, where the workers would play out a scene meant to scare us. The man in the overalls made sure to note that we were not allowed to touch the employees. And they were prohibited from touching us in return.

Mac listened intently, and I wondered if she was taking notes for Grandpappy's. They already did special ticketed nights in October when their corn maze turned haunted. They hired high schoolers in hockey masks to chase people while loud music played and strobe lights flashed. It was one more shock-value entertainment that Grandpappy's provided that a smaller farm like Judd's couldn't compete with.

"Y'all ready to run for your lives?" Harold asked with a wicked gleam in his eye.

There was a chorus of yeahs from several folks in our group. We moved as one toward the main path, but our orderly line was quickly dispersed as a person in a *Scream* mask jumped out behind us, revving a chainsaw engine.

People took off, separating and darting down different paths. The jump scare startled a laugh out of Mac, but she kept up a leisurely pace. I stayed beside her as most of our group bolted through the trees, leaving us to bring up the rear.

"You know, I'm not sure this is my idea of romantic," I said after the *Scream*-mask person revved their chainsaw again and went after the teenagers who'd gone down the trail to the right.

Mac shot me a look. "Who said anything about romance?"

"I did. Very specifically, when you begged for a night in my bed."

She stopped and crossed her arms over her chest. "Hold up, lover boy. Begged? That is not what happened."

With a smirk, I replied, "Well, that's the way I remembered it."

Mac opened her mouth to argue, I was sure, but her eyes widened over my shoulder. "Oh shit."

I turned and did a double take when I saw a huge guy dressed in a scary clown costume—he had to be six and a half feet tall—with a deranged expression painted on his face in bright, garish stage makeup. Fake blood splatter was all over his colorful clown suit, and he stalked toward us with an ax held in one meaty fist.

"Ugh, not clowns," I heard Mac moan from behind me.

Grinning, I spun back and grabbed her hand. "Let's go, scaredy Mac."

"I'm not scared." But she definitely squeaked that last word out as the giant clown man growled and darted forward, raising his ax.

I laughed, pulling Mac down the central path as we ran over packed dirt and pine needles. The clown stayed with us—probably sent to herd the stragglers so they could keep our group moving. I heard a chainsaw off to the right, so I kept us running straight.

We slowed as we rounded a bend in the path, and a black light lit the immediate area. I started as a coffin propped beneath the light rattled and shook, shouts coming from within. Just as we passed by, someone dressed as a vampire jumped out and lunged for us.

Mac and I shuffled out of the way, laughing as we went. Out of the range of the black light, the trail grew darker. It widened considerably, and I thought we must be getting close to the shack that was our destination.

"The clown's back," Mac breathed, squeezing my hand.

"I think I see lights ahead for the shed," I told her, glancing over my shoulder to see the manic clown bearing down on us. "Let's run for it."

We took off, Mac's hand in mine, and I thought maybe her idea of a date wasn't so bad after all. But then, as we reached full speed, my foot hit the ground, and it felt all wrong. My knee buckled as the hard-packed dirt turned to something soft and unexpected. I went down, bracing for impact and then grateful when I fell flat out onto a springy surface. I had only a moment to appreciate that I hadn't busted my face on the ground before Mac landed fully on top of me.

I wheezed out a breath and tried to roll over, but we were all panic and limbs, and Mac was laughing so hard that she couldn't speak.

I glanced around, but the clown was nowhere to be found. We were lying on an old mattress that had been imbedded in the dirt, flush with the surrounding ground. Jesus, this place was lucky they hadn't broken someone's leg and gotten sued.

"Are you okay?" I asked once I finally maneuvered Mac down beside me.

She was still laughing. "Oh my God. I saw you go down, and I couldn't stop." Tears were leaking from the corners of her eyes.

I grinned over at her and teased, "I knew you wanted to get me in bed, but I didn't think it would be like this."

Mac cackled again.

I stood on shaky legs and stepped onto the dirt trail. Holding a hand out, I pulled her up to join me. "Come on, let's go before that demon clown comes back."

We made it to the shed and survived the fake slaughterhouse encounter there. The path to the exit was through a graveyard, and we didn't see our clown friend again. Mac and I jumped and shouted when we were startled, then we teased each other and laughed in between.

I had fun, and I knew I wasn't the only one. She smiled and joked and didn't even complain when I wrapped my hand around hers again. We warmed up around the fire pit back near the entrance.

As our time at the farm wound down, I wondered what would happen when we got back to my place. Nerves settled in the pit of my stomach as I thought about the end result of this date—the only purpose, really. Mac wanted to have sex to dispel whatever inconvenient attraction she'd been feeling. The one that made her kiss me in my truck weeks ago and climb onto my lap Tuesday night.

She thought this was all physical and problematic.

I watched her as we drove back to Kirby Falls, unsure if I could actually go through with this when our aims were so different.

She wanted tonight, and I wanted a chance.

I wasn't sure where that left us, but I had a feeling I shouldn't get my hopes up. Mac was stubborn and determined.

You couldn't make someone love you if they weren't ready. There was every chance I was setting myself up for disappointment. We could wake up tomorrow, and Mac might really be over it.

The thing about taking what you could get was that you didn't get to pitch a fit when it blew up in your face.

MAC

The drive back to Brady's apartment was . . . a little tense.

We didn't talk much. There was no playlist critique or Brady sing-alongs to make me laugh or "Name That Tune" with songs he picked.

I drove exactly six miles over the speed limit, and Brady, well, he watched me pensively from the passenger seat. He stared at me like I was a riddle again. A puzzle he hadn't quite figured out.

The date* had been fun. It was hard to explain. Brady was a fun-loving guy. A walking good time. But in all of our years of pranks and practical jokes and endless bickering, none of that good-timing had been directed at me. Or if it was, it was in a way that I perceived to be at my expense. A mocking joke or a well-timed zinger.

Finally being on the receiving end of Brady's charms had made our little outing at the Haunted Forest a fun experience. I liked his sweetness as much as his teasing. And I didn't know how I'd never realized it before, but Brady was affectionate. He liked being close—holding hands and touching. It turned out that I liked it, too.

Maybe the date had less of an asterisk beside it than I wanted to admit.

But the date wasn't what tonight was all about. It was a means to an end. A way to gather up all this wayward attraction and the unexpected pull I felt toward Brady and channel it into a solution.

If my dating history proved anything, long-term wasn't something I specialized in. One night of hot—or mediocre—sex with Brady Judd should get whatever was happening out of my system.

Hopefully.

Because how was I supposed to live my townie life with Brady around every turn? He was there every Monday for trivia and every Friday at the bonfire. And again at the farmers' markets downtown on Saturdays. Our families knew each other. We ended up at the same events, festivals, and church picnics. Kirby Falls was not a big place, and Brady and I were in the same line of work. Our paths crossed often.

I didn't want to feel like this every time he walked into a room. The constant buzz beneath my skin—the awareness. I couldn't look at him or hear his voice without remembering how it felt to be snuggled up against him in a freezing storage shed or grinding on top of him on a hay bale. I was off-balance and questioning myself, which wasn't like me at all. Plus, I couldn't even encounter an orange Tic Tac without blushing like a schoolgirl, for Christ's sake.

Tonight would fix all that. I *needed* it to.

Brady spoke for the first time in half an hour, directing me to a visitor's spot behind his building. It had the added benefit of keeping my Jeep off the street where anyone could spot it.

My heart was pounding as I followed him inside and up the stairs to his apartment. Nerves tangled in my belly, but I forced them down. This wasn't a big deal. Just like I'd told Brady, it was only sex.

He unlocked his front door and stepped inside, flipping on the light.

Brady took off his shoes and placed them in a closet off the entryway. I watched in a strange, disconnected way as he shrugged out of his jacket and hung it in the same closet. He held out a hand, and it took me a moment to realize he wanted me to pass him my coat, too.

I hurriedly peeled away the black fabric and handed it over while he looked on in amusement.

It was such a casual, domestic activity that my brain sort of locked up and misfired. Brady Judd had a closet for his jackets and took off his shoes when he came home. Had I ever seen his socked feet before?

I stood awkwardly just inside the threshold while Brady walked into the kitchen.

The whole apartment—that I could see—was spotless. Very little clutter on the coffee table and end tables in the living room, and a simple vase of flowers sat in the center of the kitchen island.

"Mac?" Brady's voice interrupted my perusal of the space.

"Yeah?" I replied distractedly.

He was standing there watching me, still poised near the cabinet, two glasses in hand. "I asked if you wanted something to drink. Some water? A beer?"

"Oh." That weird, nervous energy was back, churning in my midsection. "Sure. Water, please."

Brady stared a moment longer and then gave me his back as he moved toward the refrigerator.

This was dumb. I was being dumb. It was just sex, I chanted inwardly, willing my body to walk fully into the apartment and stop acting weird.

We'd do the deed and be done with this whole thing. We could go back to being archenemies, giving each other shit. Brady could keep up the social media snark, and we'd duke it out during trivia night. Or maybe things would be awkward.

Maybe we'd be *nothing* after this.

The thought had me taking an involuntary step back, where I bumped into the door at my back.

"You can come all the way in, you know," Brady called, back still turned.

Spurred into movement by low-level panic and my own cowardice, I slipped off my shoes and moved into the kitchen. I put my bag on the island while Brady filled our glasses from a pitcher.

"I think we should talk," he said as he replaced the pitcher.

I peeled off my socks and dropped them on the floor. "Talk? Why?" Then I released my belt and slid the leather through the loop in my jeans as my heartbeat climbed into my throat.

Brady turned in my periphery, and I heard the water glasses thunk abruptly onto the countertop. "What are you doing?"

Gripping my sweater, preparing to bring it up and over my head, I said, "Getting this show on the road."

"Mac," he protested and made his way around the island in record time.

Brady batted my hands away and smoothed my shirt back down, covering my midsection. "Stop it. I wanted to do that."

I laughed, somehow less manic with his hands on me. "You wanted to?" I asked, finally meeting his gaze.

All playfulness gone, Brady answered seriously, "Yes."

Then he circled behind me, hands on my hips.

"I just thought—" My voice faltered as I felt his fingers unbutton my jeans and lower the zipper. "I just thought we'd get down to business."

Brady left my pants unbound but didn't move to lower the denim and reveal the lacy thong I'd talked myself into earlier. He brought his hands to the hem of my sweater and toyed with it for a moment before slowly raising it over my head.

"I'm not a get-down-to-business kind of guy," he admitted, sweeping my long hair over one shoulder.

For some reason, I closed my eyes as his touch unfurled around me.

"I like to take my time," Brady continued. "Make a detour or two." I felt his soft lips against the nape of my neck, and I swallowed hard. "Take the long way around and maybe a back road every now and then."

I sucked in a trembling breath as he traced a knuckle up and down my spine for long moments. Finally, on the next downward pass, he stopped to unhook my bra, like we had all the time in the world instead of just one night.

He teased, "Haven't you ever heard of foreplay, Mac?"

With my eyelids clenched shut, I stood unmoving, hardly breathing as Brady's hands and lips traced abstract designs across my shoulder blades and back. He slid the straps of my bra gently down my arms. I heard the sound of the fabric hitting the floor, but Brady made no move to touch my breasts. I felt my nipples tighten and fought the urge to grab his hands and place them firmly on my chest, to end this needless seduction.

But the man was in no hurry at all. He kissed down the length of my arm, encouraging it to bend at the elbow, and then he placed a hot, open-mouthed kiss on my inner wrist. That was a sensitive spot, and I made an embarrassing sound as a result. I felt his lips smile against my skin.

Finally, his palm came to my stomach and urged me back. The bare skin of my back met the soft flannel covering his chest, and the warmth he radiated nearly made me sigh in relief. Lips worked their way up my neck to just behind my ear.

And then a rough whisper said, "Open your eyes."

When I did, I nearly jolted in surprise. We were facing a mirror I hadn't noticed. It hung near the hallway on the wall opposite, and it reflected our bodies wrapped up in one another. My upper half was fully on display, breasts heaving with every breath and a flush of pink painting my neck and cheeks. Brady was watching me in the mirror, blue eyes dark and heavy lidded as his gaze followed the path of his hand across the pale skin of my stomach, up to cup my breast. His arm banded across my chest and held me to him.

"You are so fucking sexy," he murmured, eyes fixed on our reflection. "And I'm not going to rush anything about tonight."

With one hand plumping my breast, he brought the other around my body and dipped into the opening of my jeans, beneath the fabric of my underwear.

I drew in a sharp breath as his fingers danced along my seam.

"So soft, Mac," he breathed against the shell of my ear. "You feel so good."

Brady's touch wasn't firm enough to get me off like this. I needed more. But somehow, I knew that wasn't his goal just yet. True to his word, he was taking his time, exploring and meandering as he built me up slow and steady.

I felt the hard length of him behind me and gave an experimental push with my ass. His eyes shot to mine in the mirror and one long finger slid inside my pussy like he was trying to distract me and slow me down once again. It worked. I groaned and clenched around his digit.

"You're wearing an awful lot of clothes," I managed as his finger moved slowly, in and out. "Do I get to undress you?"

Brady's grin was wicked. "Only if you're good." The heel of his hand ground down on my clit and a moan escaped me. "But not yet. Widen your feet."

For once in my life, I complied when Brady demanded. The space created gave him more access to fuck me with his fingers. My hips moved in time with his thrusts, the pressure on my clit almost perfect.

Brady's fingers toyed with my nipple, drawing my attention to the mirror and him. He kept his eyes on me with an intensity I wasn't used to, but I liked it. I liked the way he was watching me—watching us.

"I'm going to make you come, right here, where I can see. Then I'm going to prop you up on this counter and eat you out until you come again. And then you can take off my clothes, if you want. But I need you to talk to me, to tell me what you need. How to get you there. I wanna hear you, MacKenzie."

I stared at him in the mirror, transfixed as he took charge with his blatant honesty and dirty words. Like he'd thought about what he'd do to me if he ever got the chance, and now we were acting out the fantasy step-by-sexy-step.

"Okay?" he prompted.

I nodded, so rattled and turned on I wasn't sure I could speak. I could hear how wet I was as his fingers continued working me.

"So, what do you need, Mac? Another?" He pressed a second finger into me as he asked, and I nodded again. "I want to hear you," he reminded me.

"Yes," I gasped. "And harder, on my clit. More pressure."

Brady obeyed, bearing down, the heel of his hand firm and so, so good, right where I wanted it.

"Like this?" he asked.

I started to dip my chin in agreement but remembered in time, hissing out a desperate yes.

"You're perfect. God," he said raggedly. "So hot and tight. I want to feel you come around my fingers and against my tongue and on my dick. I want you every single way I can have you, Mac."

My breath came in shaky pants as Brady's filthy words worked to bring me closer to the edge. He was going to kill me if he kept talking with that dirty mouth.

Plus, I could still feel him behind me, impossibly big and hard, as our bodies moved together. Despite being on the verge of my own orgasm, I was eager for more, the next step. I wanted to strip him down and touch him in return. I ached to feel him inside me.

"I'm close," I whispered.

Brady's brilliant blue eyes came back to mine in the mirror, and I groaned long and loud as all my muscles tensed before releasing in wave after wave of perfect pleasure.

My eyelids drifted closed, and I heard Brady exhale a broken "Fuck" as I pulsed around his fingers. My body sagged against him, but he didn't falter, just clutched me tighter to him.

There wasn't time to feel embarrassed or awkward because Brady removed his hands from my underwear and spun me around, kissing me hard. It was needy and worshipful, and, I realized, a precursor to how he planned to use that dirty mouth.

He pushed down the fabric of my jeans, but then paused when his hands touched the bare skin of my ass cheeks. His lips broke away from mine, and he looked over my shoulder, presumably at my lacy thong.

"If I had known that's what your underwear looked like, I would have taken your pants off first thing."

I smiled a satisfied grin as I rested my forehead against his collarbone and laughed. "Want me to take them off?"

"Fuck, no," he replied swiftly. "Not yet."

Then he lowered himself to the wood floor, helping work the tight denim down my thighs before flinging my jeans somewhere over his shoulder into the living room.

I smiled down at him, thinking how good he looked on his knees for me. I gave in to the urge to run my fingers through his messy hair. As I sifted through the surprisingly soft strands, I was rewarded with a quiet moan as Brady leaned into my touch.

Rough palms smoothed over my backside, kneading and stroking. Then he rested his forehead against my stomach and groaned, the sound muffled by my skin. "This ass. Jesus."

It turned out that Brady Judd was good for the ego because I had never felt so comfortable (mostly) naked in my whole life.

I'd never felt other things too . . . so cherished and cared for and completely overwhelmed. I was turned on again and ready for more, which was also new. I'd never come twice with a partner before; usually I was too sensitive to bother trying, or the guy was more worried about his own turn.

Something told me Brady wasn't thinking about himself right now.

True to his word, he rose to his feet and lifted me onto the counter and ate my pussy like a starving man. There was no slow, careful seduction or playful teasing touches this time around. He pulled my underwear to the side and feasted, with eager lips and teeth and tongue.

If I was a less confident person, I might have been embarrassed by the sounds I made or how wet Brady's chin was. If I hadn't been so lost to the pleasure he drew out of me, I might have also been self-conscious about the way I'd gripped his hair in my fist and then shouted my release for God, Brady, and his neighbors two doors down to hear. But I didn't care.

When Brady helped me off the counter, he steadied my boneless legs, and I draped my arms around his shoulders, smiling the dopey, satiated smile of the recently well serviced.

"Want me to carry you to bed, Macklemore?"

"Yes," I murmured and then squealed when he bent low and threw me over his shoulder like a sack of flour.

"Brady!" I clung to his hips as he sauntered down the dark hallway.

He smacked my ass, and I yelped out a surprised laugh.

Brady set me down on a plush rug in the middle of a tidy bedroom. He steadied me until I had my feet under me, then stayed close.

The room was dim but not dark. There was light coming from the attached bathroom, and I could see well enough to make out Brady's features. I could have seen the specifics of the furniture or the décor as well, but I was too distracted—too aware of the man in front of me.

With efficient movements, he started unfastening his flannel. I went to work on his belt and button-fly jeans. It wasn't an elegant striptease by any means. We were both too anxious for what came next. But when I pushed his pants and underwear down his lean hips, I paused to take him in. I'd felt his size a couple of times—the morning we woke up together in the shed at Grandpappy's and then earlier in the kitchen—and he didn't let me down now.

I managed to get his clothes the rest of the way off, along with my thong.

Then I wrapped my hand around his hard length, and he made a rough sound in the back of his throat. It reminded me of that first kiss in the front seat of his truck. His eyes closed tight as I pumped up and down in a slow, steady rhythm.

Brady balanced himself with his hands on my waist, and I watched as a pained expression moved over his features. Then words poured out of his mouth in a rush. "When we wake up in the morning, I'll make you breakfast. Pancakes. Stuffed French toast. Bacon. Whatever you want."

I paused my movements, feeling amusement bubble up inside my chest. His eyes popped open as he regarded me solemnly.

"Brady, you're a twenty-eight-year-old man, and you have me naked in your bedroom. You want to talk about cooking breakfast and staying over to cuddle?"

He frowned. "You have a tragic view of masculinity."

I squeezed his very prevalent masculinity and made to resume my teasing motion, but Brady stopped me with a gentle touch on my wrist. "I have you for one night."

"One time," I corrected. Why was he bringing this up? I hadn't even been able to judge the thread count of his sheets yet, and he wanted to talk about *after*.

"One night," he insisted. "You said so yourself." His hand journeyed from my waist around to my ass where he gave a firm squeeze. Then he leaned his tall frame down and placed hot, wet kisses along my jaw. "You're so worried about getting this—getting me—out of your system."

His tongue grazed the sensitive skin below my ear, and I shuddered.

Voice soft and measured, he said between kisses, "But I'm only thinking about getting under your skin and staying there."

I swallowed hard, struggling to focus on his words. "This feels like a conversation we should be having when you aren't doing that with your tongue."

Brady shook his head and dragged his teeth down to my shoulder, making my eyes roll back in my head. "You're not ready for it," he whispered.

We fell into bed then, a tangle of limbs and searching hands and lips. I briefly noted a fluffy white duvet before I was distracted, pulling Brady over me. He stretched his long body out, reaching toward the bedside table.

A moment later, I watched him sit back on his heels, rip the condom wrapper, and start to roll it on, but I batted his hands away and gave him back the line he'd given me. "Stop it. I wanted to do that."

He grinned as I took over the job of protecting us both, but the cheeky smile faded quickly as I gave him a rough squeeze.

"You ready?" I asked, bending my knees as he settled between my thighs.

"Yeah," he gritted out. "You?"

At my nod, he slowly—and I mean slowly—eased inside me, one hand gripping the base of his shaft and the other wrapped around the outside of my thigh.

I breathed through it, adjusting to his size and girth, grateful I was slick enough to ease the way.

Halfway through, Brady shifted onto his elbows and bowed his head, resting it against my shoulder and letting out a string of curse words.

Finally, when he was completely seated and I was so full I thought I might split in half, Brady's breath whooshed out, and he laughed hoarsely. "I am never going to last. Holy shit."

I shifted my hips a little, and he groaned, causing me to grin.

On an experimental thrust, Brady's hips pulled back slowly and then pushed in again. I felt him everywhere. When he bottomed out, he ground down, his pubic bone hitting me in just the right spot. I reached around, gripping his ass, encouraging him without words to please, please do that again.

He did, over and over. Shallow, gasping thrusts that forced me higher on the mattress. I brought my trembling thighs over his hips, and he settled even deeper, making me cry out.

"You feel so good," he praised. "I want to fuck you all night. I don't want to come yet."

"I've had two orgasms, Brady. You don't need to hold out on my account."

Amused, I watched as he shook his head. Suddenly, we were moving, rolling across the mattress, still connected as he settled me on top of him. I took the change of scenery in stride and planted my hands on either side of his head, rolling my hips and shifting back and forth.

"Shit," he breathed, trying desperately to still my movements. "That did *not* help."

"It helped me," I laughed, rocking over him, loving the angle.

His eyes couldn't decide where to focus. Brady tracked my bouncing tits and then down to where we were joined before his lids shut tight and his jaw clenched.

"Talk to me, Mac," he encouraged. "Tell me what you need."

"Sit up and grab my ass," I panted.

Complying instantly, Brady jackknifed up, lean muscles flexing. I wrapped my arms around his shoulders, holding him close as I rode him. His hands smoothed down the globes of my ass before squeezing and urging me on.

Everything was lined up perfectly, and with Brady chanting in my ear, telling me how good this was and how he'd never recover, I came in a blinding flash. Pleasure radiated through my limbs and held me hostage in its grip.

I felt Brady bucking up into me in jerky movements until he stiffened and groaned, the intimate sound vibrating against my sternum and making me squeeze tighter around him.

With a groan of my own, I collapsed onto the bed, side by side with Brady, who lay panting on top of the covers.

He had an arm thrown over his eyes, but when he felt my noodle body settle next to him, he uncovered his face and turned his head to look at me. "Whenever you're ready, I'll take that hot chocolate. Because you were definitely the first one to scream."

I blinked as my brain caught up with our bet from the Haunted Forest, and then I laughed until I couldn't catch my breath.

Minutes later, Brady had gotten rid of the condom and we were back to being sweaty in bed and staring up at the ceiling. He cleared his throat. "Sorry, I know it wasn't very good, but the next time will be better."

My brain stuttered to a halt, and I frowned. I'd thought—I'd thought it was the best sexual experience of my entire life. That last time, I came so hard I thought I was going to pass out. I still couldn't feel my toes.

When I looked over at Brady to see if he'd possibly suffered a brain injury, he was already watching my reaction, grinning like the fool I must be.

"I can't believe I fell for that," I mumbled in disbelief.

"I mean, it wouldn't have killed you to argue with me," Brady said, his warm shoulder nudging mine. "I thought that was your favorite pastime anyhow."

Part of me worried I had a new favorite pastime, and it involved this bed and the man in it. Which was unfortunate because this was a one-time thing. I needed to get up and find wherever he'd flung my pants.

"And, you know, I would take a compliment," he added. "If you had one lying around."

Reaching blindly with my opposite hand, I gripped a pillow from his headboard and brought it around, whacking him in the face.

Brady laughed and tossed the pillow aside, wrapping me in his arms and hauling me on top of him once more. I stretched out, sliding a thigh between both of his and propping my head up on his chest. He was all warm skin and loose limbs, completely at ease, naked in bed with me.

It should have felt weird, considering how we'd spent the majority of our relationship over the years. But it wasn't, and that had a little kernel of concern twisting in the back of my mind.

Something must have registered on my face because Brady gripped me tighter. "Stay. I can probably improve upon perfection if you give me an hour or so."

I cleared the roughness from my throat. "Perfection, huh?"

He pinched my backside, making me laugh. "You know it was good, Mac. Fucking fantastic even. You'll be thinking about me all day tomorrow."

I felt like I'd swallowed a ping-pong ball, aware that he was probably right for more than one reason. I could detect that delicious soreness already, the stretch and awareness that only came from really good sex. I knew I'd feel him tomorrow. I'd probably be sexy sore for a couple of days. It had been a little while for me in the bedroom department, and Brady was definitely above average in size. And he knew what he was doing.

That knowledge made the uneasiness spread.

This was supposed to be the end of whatever this was so I could get out from under the weird attraction and move on with my life. I should not be thinking about *tomorrow* in any capacity where Brady Judd was concerned. Maybe I just needed to clean up and sleep on it. Take a shower and wash away the scent of him on my skin, his fingerprints on every inch of my body.

Brady turned so I was back on the mattress. Then he threw an arm across my middle and nuzzled his nose into my tangled hair.

I willed my breathing to slow as I stared up at the ceiling. This wasn't part of the plan. Cuddling and *tomorrow* and the rising tide of panic radiating throughout my limbs. Sex was supposed to be the answer. It was supposed to get it out of my system, not make me want more.

I needed to get out of here. Clearly, my initial instinct to avoid Brady had been the right one. I'd let my hormones and my body take the reins, and look where it had gotten me. Snuggled up to a dirty-talking golden boy.

It didn't take long. Soon, Brady's deep, even breathing warmed the side of my neck. I counted to three hundred in my head and then carefully slid out from beneath his arm.

Standing by the bedside for a moment, I took in Brady's ridiculously long body stretched diagonally across his king-size bed, sleeping soundly. Pressure behind my rib cage made me take a sudden step back, unwilling to consider the reason for it.

Then I grabbed the opposite corner of the duvet and draped it across him before I lost my nerve.

I looked around until I found my underwear. Next, I crept down the hallway, collecting articles of clothing as I went. When I was dressed and there was nothing left to do but retreat, I took one last look around the apartment, the comfortable, ultra-tidy place Brady called home.

Finally, I quietly shut the door, feeling like a coward and a liar all the same.

Brady

I knew she was gone before I even opened my eyes.

Rolling over beneath the edge of my comforter, I squinted at the clock on the bedside table. It was 2:48 a.m., and it seemed my brain wasn't going to let me drift back to sleep tonight. It was awake and replaying the evening with Mac and how all the possible scenarios where she snuck out ended in disaster.

With a sigh, I got up and threw on some basketball shorts and a tee shirt. I'd shower in the morning. I wasn't ready to scrub away what had happened. I wanted to hold on to the memory for a bit—it might be the only one I got.

Walking into the kitchen, I figured I could bake something to bring into work tomorrow. Cinnamon rolls seemed like a good option. They were high maintenance and needed time, and, well, I had plenty of that.

So I wiped down the counter while my mind recounted the way Mac had propped her feet on my shoulders and screamed her release. Then I mixed the dough and wondered where we went from here. Was she going to avoid me? Did she truly get me out of her system the way she'd wanted? Surely she felt it, how good we were together, how important this was, how right.

Mind wandering through the minefield of worst-case scenarios, I left the dough to rise and made myself some coffee. My eyes drifted to the empty spot on the refrigerator. Thank God I'd remembered to take down the mug shot. Now, though, I walked over to the drawer that held my dish towels and opened it, revealing the folded piece of paper. Smoothing it out, I popped it back onto the fridge, holding it in place with a magnet.

With my attention on my phone, I took a sip of coffee and pulled up the Chatter app. Nothing new from Mac and the Grandpappy's account. Not that I'd expected there to be.

I scrolled for a while, distracting myself, before tapping the icon to create a new post in Chatter.

The optimistic side of me was having a hard time rationalizing the way Mac had left. I couldn't find the silver lining or talk myself into a promising outcome. We'd had a good time tonight—a great time—from the asterisk date she didn't want to the life-altering sex. I knew she couldn't deny it, but she was stubborn enough to ignore it. Sex hadn't changed anything for me. I still wanted her. But it might have changed things for Mac. And maybe not in the way I'd hoped.

@JuddsFamilyOrchard: @GrandpappysApples, I can still smell you on my skin, warm and sweet. I know your scent will fade, but I just want to hang on to it—and you—a little longer.

Then, I saved the draft and exited the app before I did something stupid.

eleven

MAC

With the farmers' market season over, it was easier than I thought it'd be to avoid Brady. I just had to skip weekly trivia at Trailview Brewing, beg off attending Friday night bonfires with Larry, and wait ten minutes before I walked down the drive at Grandpappy's to latch the gate after closing.

Some things made ignoring him more difficult, though. His text messages, for example.

The first one had come through the morning I'd snuck out of his apartment with my underwear in my pocket and a sinking feeling in my gut. *Hey, Mac Attack. Want to grab a drink after trivia on Monday?*

The next one arrived Monday night after I'd skipped out on my team. *Can we talk?*

Finally, five days after the plan to get it out of my system had failed spectacularly, I got the last text. It was sitting on read in my message app, and for some masochistic reason, I kept making myself look at it.

Brady: Mac, please.

All this unexpected freedom from social engagements gave me plenty of time to catch up on all the travel blogs I followed. I'd planned out a hypothetical trip to

Thailand (two stops), started a new horror novel that was keeping me up at night, and cleaned out the pantry.

Brady had left me alone after that final text. There'd been no swipes on social media, no mentions or replies on Chatter. No impromptu appearances at Grandpappy's to pick up tools or anything else.

I should have been relieved. I'd made myself scarce, and Brady hadn't challenged me on it. But instead of relief, I felt unsteady. That same roiling-on-the-bow-of-a-ship feeling. A nagging disquiet that my world was off-kilter, everything shifted over a foot. Not quite sufficient to upend my life, but enough to have me jumping at shadows and stubbing my toes on what used to be there.

Yet, I persisted. I made it through Thanksgiving a month later, even when Larry pulled me aside and asked what the hell was going on. I'd given her the same bullshit excuse, saying I was fine, just busy, and not interested in socializing. I couldn't very well confess that I was miserable and it was my own doing. Will was being a grumpy asshole, too, since Becca the tourist had gone back to Detroit. My aunt Maggie had threatened to make the two of us eat our turkey and fixings at the kids' table by ourselves.

But I'd survived the event, and, eventually, Larry had given up on me and joined everyone else for dessert while I sat on the porch and contemplated what a big fucking chicken I was.

As painful as it was to admit, I missed Brady. For years, I'd had his undivided attention. And then briefly, his affection and his sweetness. Everything was all mixed up in my head. I wanted him to tease me and then kiss it better. But I didn't know how to make myself vulnerable and admit the truth to the one person I'd always had to guard myself against.

Instead, I let my bad mood carry me through. I went to work and I saw my family. I went through the motions, and I resisted the urge to show up somewhere I knew Brady would be, just to see his face.

However, six weeks after I had my first and last date* with Brady Judd, Larry and I were on shift together in the tree lot at Grandpappy's, and she cornered me. The farm was all decked out for the holidays. We decorated it every December to within an inch of its life, and the tourists ate it up. We transformed the General Store into a giant gingerbread house that had locals and leafers alike stopping by to take photos.

However, I was not particularly in the holiday spirit when my cousin made her way back to the booth after helping Trudy Caswell to her SUV with a six-foot Fraser fir in tow.

I'd just finished running the credit card payment for the customer waiting when Larry cleared her throat at my side.

I glanced over to see her looking pale.

"What's wrong? Did you hurt your back getting that tree up on the roof of Trudy's Suburban?"

Larry frowned. "No, I'm fine."

She was silent for a moment while I rang up another tree purchase, and then when we were finally alone again, she blurted out, "I need a favor."

My eyes narrowed. "What is it?"

Larry blew out a breath that reeked of reluctance before saying, "I know you're going through"—she waved her hands vaguely about my person—"something. But I really need you to come to the bonfire with me tonight."

Immediately, I opened my mouth to protest. The chances of running into Brady there were extremely high, and I was messed up enough.

But my cousin cut me off. "I don't ask for a lot, Mac. But I'm asking you to come with me. Kayla will be there, and she's bringing some guy she's been hooking up with."

I stared at Larry's face, trying to discern her meaning. She rarely looked unhappy or frustrated, but she was both of those things right now, visibly. And she was right. She didn't ask me for much.

Everybody should have someone they could ask to help bury a body. This girl would have showed up for me with a tarp and a shovel, no questions asked. Larry hadn't called on me for anything so criminal or dramatic, but this request felt just as serious for some reason.

"I'll come. Of course, I'll come if you need me," I said.

She sighed, but this time in relief. The lines on her pale forehead smoothed, but the tightness around her heavily made-up eyes remained. "Thank you."

"What's wrong?" I asked gently. "Do you not like the guy Kayla is bringing? Is he an asshole or something?"

"Or something," Larry murmured as she stood from her stool, already reaching for the door of the booth to step back out into the cloudy, cold December day. "I'll pick you up at seven."

And then she was off to help a woman and her three kids select the perfect tree.

I stared after my cousin for a moment, questioning what was going on and then figuring it was only fair that I had to wonder because I was hiding things from her, too.

Larry's secrets didn't reveal themselves during the drive to Abby's property later that evening. Nor was I able to deduce the reason behind her panicked invitation once we arrived. Everything seemed fine on her end. I, however, was a hot mess as I kept an eye out for Brady. Nerves made me fidgety and distracted. I told myself I didn't want to see him, but the truth had my heart rate climbing into my throat.

When Brady failed to materialize, I didn't bother with a sigh of relief. Instead, I tried to focus on running interference for Larry and playing the role of buffer. But for her part, Larry laughed and joked as she sipped her beer around the bonfire like she didn't have a care in the world. And like she hadn't begged me to be her backup here tonight. I was confused about why she needed me. She wore a smile for everyone—Kayla's new hookup included.

The guy had to be six five, and he was built like a tank. His name was Adam and he seemed nice. He followed Kayla around like a puppy and looked at her with stars in his eyes.

Maybe Larry was nervous for her friend. Kayla had been in a long-distance relationship with her high school boyfriend for many years. They broke up probably six months ago, and since then, it seemed like Kayla was making up for lost time, regularly bringing home guys from the tourist bar where she worked. Could be that Larry didn't want to see her friend get hurt again if things with Adam were progressing past the one-night-stand phase.

I wasn't sure why Larry wanted me by her side, but that was where I stayed. Even when Brady finally made an appearance. He caught sight of me and stumbled into the back of Jase Wilcox. I forced myself to look away and focus on whatever Kayla had been talking about.

Brady's bonfire attendance wasn't unexpected, but there hadn't really been a way to prepare myself for it. The temptation to look his way was strong, but I kept my gaze resolutely on my companions. I stiffened as the breeze carried snippets of his voice or his laughter my direction. Whatever gravitational force that had pulled us together in the first place was working its magic tonight, too. I was overly aware, waiting for the moment he appeared at my side with a teasing jibe or a challenging look.

But that moment never came.

With three ignored texts burning a hole in my pocket, Brady continued to give me the space I hadn't really asked for but had demanded all the same.

It was nearing eleven when Larry elbowed me and asked me to grab her another beer from the coolers.

"You sure?" I said quietly, still looking for any sign of distress.

Her eyes narrowed playfully, the winged liner sharp enough to sting, as she said, "Yes, Mother. I'm sure."

Kayla and Adam laughed, and Larry turned away from me.

Swallowing down my confusion, I stood and made my way toward the picnic tables beneath the awning.

In my distraction over my cousin and her strange behavior, I failed to check my surroundings. Brady was already digging through one of the coolers when I approached.

He glanced up and stilled momentarily before removing his hand from the ice and rubbing it dry on his jeans.

We watched each other for a long moment, and I fucking hated how I was acting —like I was scared or cautious, when I'd never been either of those things in my whole damn life. But more than that, I hated how Brady was being with me. This tentative version of himself. It was like watching him in his truck that time, in the grip of some unseen panic right before I'd kissed him to snap him out of it.

Brady felt distant, out of reach and miles away. Even when we'd hated each other—or I'd thought we did—he'd been someone I couldn't ignore. Present in a way that punched me in the gut. A firework in brilliant, sparkling colors that demanded my attention.

This version, here and now, was dull and hazy around the edges. And knowing I'd made him that way just compounded the distance between us and the shame squeezing my heart.

I didn't want things to be so *off*. I didn't want to feel this way. I liked routine and expectation, normalcy and comfort.

But what version of normal did I even want?

The one where we fought like cats and dogs, or the alternate timeline where Brady ate me out on his kitchen counter and I wanted to fall asleep in his arms.

"Hi," I finally managed, voice rough and uncertain, knowing I couldn't keep standing here just so I could look at him.

"Hey," he returned softly.

Suddenly, the image of that final text flashed before my eyes. *Mac, please.*

I could hear it now in his voice, see it all over his face, and I felt sick with regret as a result.

Brady shifted, his hands going into the pockets of his brown winter coat. "How've you been?"

"Busy," I replied automatically. The same answer I'd been peddling for over a month now anytime anyone asked.

He nodded slowly, expression closed off. "Well, glad you could make time for your neighbors tonight."

I couldn't decide if he was making fun of me or accusing me of something, but his narrowed gaze made me think it was a challenge all the same.

"No one cares if I'm here or not," I said truthfully. "The bonfires just keep on going no matter who shows up. Nothing ever changes."

Brady snorted. "Some things change."

My eyes sharpened, searching his face. I was taken aback by his tone. I'd done that, I thought. I put that wounded look on his face, that sharp edge in his voice when Brady Judd had never been cynical a day in his life.

The weight of my guilt sank deep in my chest. I didn't know what I wanted from Brady, but I knew it wasn't this. While I'd been wary and nervous to set eyes on him tonight, I couldn't ignore how good it felt to see him after going weeks without. How something had slotted neatly into place behind my ribs.

Abruptly, Brady took in a deep breath and gathered himself. A mask slipped over his features, jovial and light. And if I didn't have the reminder of a *Mac, please* text swallowing me whole, I probably would have bought the act.

Then he was grinning and saying, "Well, I heard Eloise Carter went vegan, so I guess not everything stays the same."

I frowned. Why was he talking about Eloise Carter? Why was he playing nice when he should have been telling me off?

I wanted him to be angry. That was what I deserved, and, at least, that would be real.

I wanted him to yell at me for sneaking out of his bedroom. To call me out for ignoring his texts and hiding from him like a coward for weeks.

"That's not what I meant," I managed.

His mask slipped. I could see a spark of indignation in his bright blue eyes, and I thought we were getting somewhere. "No? What did you mean, Mac? You want a new-and-improved Friday night activity to keep you entertained?"

"No, I just meant, it's always more of the same. These people, this place. Locals are born here, and they die here, and they never try anything different." I didn't know why we were talking about this or why I was voicing these thoughts aloud. I was angry with myself, yet *these* were the words crawling out of my mouth. It was like a trigger engaging or a switch being flipped. I'd gone from making painful conversation with someone who had recently seen me naked to whatever the hell this was.

Brady looked surprised momentarily before reining it in. "There's nothing wrong with staying in Kirby Falls. People are content here. It's home." He said it slowly, like he was testing out a theory he'd long suspected.

"Yeah, but how do they even know they're content if they never get out and do more?"

"Look at my sister," he countered immediately. "Candy left to go be successful or whatever in the big bad city, and now she's back, and I'm pretty sure she wished she'd never left. I went away to college. I traveled to other countries. And I came back because I wanted to."

I didn't know Brady had traveled anywhere. The part of me that was greedy for information wanted to ask where he'd been. I wanted him to describe it all, to leave nothing out. But I couldn't do that. I didn't have the right, and this wasn't the time.

Brady's eyes searched mine. "Everything just reinforced that this is where I want to be. Kirby Falls is where I belong. I don't need to be embarrassed about it. I'm happy here. And news flash, Clark, you're a townie, too. You were born and raised here. You're still here. Maybe you should stop being so judgy about the tourists who visit and find something about this place that they love. Maybe you should stop acting like Friday night bonfires are so beneath you."

"They're not," I argued, but Brady kept right on talking.

"Living in your hometown doesn't make you less than. It doesn't mean you've settled."

The word *settled* lodged itself in my windpipe. I thought of the farm and my work there. How my cousin Will thought I half-assed everything and barely trusted me with basic tasks. And how maybe I deserved that.

I *had* settled. I'd worked for my family since I was a teenager, and then I just kept right on, never asking for more or proving I deserved it. Doing just enough to get by and pay my bills. I'd never even considered going to college or doing anything different, like moving out on my own.

I wanted to criticize my hometown, but I was just like everyone else. A hundred tabs saved on my laptop for places I'd never visit.

"So you think I'm what? A loser?" Brady's words cut through the thoughts crowding around my head like an angry mob. "For coming back after college, working at the orchard. For being content with my life. Same friends, same job, same Friday nights."

"I didn't say that," I said softly, even though I'd implied it. I hated how defensive Brady sounded. "What kind of hypocrite would I be? Like you said, I'm a townie in the exact same boat."

"Yeah, but you're ashamed of it. Think it's embarrassing or weak or whatever the fuck you've convinced yourself you believe."

"I didn't mean it like that," I defended once more, but I could feel the heat in my cheeks and how my tongue stumbled clumsily over the words. This conversation was going down a path I hadn't intended.

Brady took a step toward me—just one—and my body leaned forward in answer. "I'm happy with my life, Mac. Maybe it's too small or too familiar for you, but it's just right for me. I like this town and these people. I love my family and working with them. Not everyone is meant for more."

I had to swallow twice before I could speak. "I know that." The words were a whispered confession filled with shame and self-loathing.

How did you explain to someone that the same choices could be wrong for one person and right for another? That I was happy Brady had a place he belonged while also feeling like I didn't quite fit. My life—the current shape of it—wasn't enough for me. Or maybe it wasn't what I'd thought it would be.

He watched me like he was waiting for me to say something—admit something. But I couldn't get any of the words out. Not about our hometown. Not about my life here. And certainly not about how I was so mixed up over my feelings for him.

Our shared history, so faded and yet somehow raw, wouldn't let me admit that I couldn't stop thinking about him. That I wanted his hands on me, his sweet affection, his teasing. Whatever argument we were in the middle of was a casualty of my own cowardice. It was easier to avoid the real issue—simpler to fight. We'd been doing that for years.

This current battle didn't make me forget, but it kept me from making a fool of myself. I'd agreed to one night with Brady, and I couldn't go back on that. It didn't matter that I'd been wrong and I still wanted more.

How did you turn your life upside down for someone you never saw coming? Brady had slipped past my defenses, and that only made me want to lash out. The simple truth was: I was scared. Terrified to tie myself further to this life and this place in one more quantifiable way. Fall for the boy who used to tease me on the playground. I was a walking Hallmark movie. A hometown cliché.

"I'll see you around, Mac." Brady brushed by me and went back to the fire. Abandoning me and the conversation, likely knowing it was a lost cause. I couldn't say I blamed him.

I closed my eyes and called myself every kind of idiot.

When I eventually made my way back to Larry, she didn't even question why I hadn't returned with any drinks. Kayla and her guy were gone, and my cousin was alone, staring moodily into the fire.

"Everything okay?" I asked.

"Yeah," she lied, without looking away.

"Want to talk about it?"

"No. Not right now."

I nodded, hoping she'd find it within her stubborn nature to seek me out when she was ready.

Distraction felt like the way to go, and I was rattled enough by the conversation with Brady that I actually wanted her opinion.

"Larry, do you think Will is right about me?"

She glanced at me and frowned. "What do you mean?"

"How he's always checking up on me, making sure my work gets done, assuming I'll half-ass everything."

Larry looked thoughtful, and I appreciated that she didn't immediately throw out some bullshit to pacify me. "Well, it's not like you really go out of your way to volunteer for things. I think he knows you don't want any more responsibility."

My mind went through a film reel of the past several years. Will asking me to trade shifts or stay late and cover for someone. How I never offered to set up early for the festivals or handle the committee meetings and represent our family or the farm. The way I contributed the bare minimum for the most part.

When I remained quiet, Larry rushed to add, "I don't think Will thinks he can't trust you. It's not that. He just knows you're not invested. It's just a job to you. Nine to five, you know?"

I nodded, knowing she was right. That *was* how I viewed things.

After dedicating his life to a sport and his subsequent injury, Will had been forced to come back to Kirby Falls, but he'd made the best of it. While I wasn't sure he was capable of being happy without baseball, he was doing what was important. He was intense and obsessed with being the best at everything all the time, but maybe I could use a little more of that in my life. Some motivation. A bigger role.

Like Brady had said, it didn't *have* to be settling. I could let myself be happy here.

Grandpappy's was my family's legacy. The Clarks were leaders in this town. I'd been content to keep right on keeping on. A selfish teenager turned aloof twentysomething. It was probably time I grew up and took some responsibility for my place in all this. And if it was Brady Judd's voice in the back of my mind urging me on, well, that was my own problem.

I got to work early the next day. And the next.

When I passed Will grabbing some coffee in front of the Bake Shop, I told him to put me down to work the Holiday Market. It was a weekend street fair that was part of Kirby Falls' annual Holiday Jamboree. There was a tree lighting and parade and everything. Similar to at the farmers' market, Grandpappy's had a booth on Main Street alongside other local businesses and artisans, selling items from the bakery. It was the second biggest tourist event, behind the autumn Orchard Festival.

My cousin gave me a funny look but nodded and said he'd add me to the schedule.

It felt like a step in the right direction.

Another opportunity arose the following day when Will called a staff meeting. It wasn't unusual to have everyone get together, but it didn't happen very often. Typically, only at the beginning of apple season when we were inundated with seasonal and part-time employees who needed information and training. But we were well into December now, and it was mostly family present along with some of our regular full-time employees who knew the lay of the land.

Will shifted uneasily in front of us. We were gathered at the picnic tables by the Bake Shop prior to opening. The outdoor heaters lined the perimeter, but it was still cold.

I rubbed my hands together and gave Larry a look, but she seemed just as confused as I was about the reason behind the meeting.

Finally, Will stood and cleared his throat before the small crowd. "I'll keep this short. I've already spoken with some of you, but I've decided to take a step back from the farm."

I nearly toppled off the bench seat in surprise.

"We'll be hiring a general manager for Grandpappy's to handle the day-to-day tasks I've absorbed over the years. Someone to run point, make the schedule, and handle issues that crop up. I'll mainly stay on in a support role and to manage the accounting."

"And," Aunt Maggie added loudly from the front, "he'll be working remotely for the most part."

Larry elbowed me sharply in the side, and we shared a *holy shit* look. Will had been miserable since Becca left. I didn't know precisely what had gone down between them, but I knew they weren't talking. Larry and I had kept in touch with Becca, texting often. She was our friend, after all. I definitely hoped this change—Will stepping back—meant good things for them in the future. It was long past time they figured their shit out and Becca made her move to North Carolina official.

When I glanced back to Will, I could tell he wanted to roll his eyes at his mother, but he knew better. "Right. So that's it. We'll post the new position and begin interviewing in a few weeks so that we can have someone in place by January first."

Will was so fucking stubborn. It ran in the family. I never thought I'd see the day he recognized his own happiness and put himself first.

Maybe things *could* change.

The meeting dispersed, and I could tell Larry wanted to break down everything that had just happened, but my heart pounded in my throat as I watched Will make his way back to his office.

I stood quickly. "Sorry, Larry. I'll catch up with you. I need to talk to him."

By the time I opened the door to Will's office, he was just settling down at his desk. His dog, Carl, ignored me in favor of his heated pet bed and a stuffed avocado squeaky toy he rested his head on.

Will's dark eyebrows jumped high on his forehead when he saw me. I might have actually slammed the office door behind me in my exuberance.

"I want the job," I blurted.

"Really?" My cousin frowned. It was a good frown, severe and effective. He'd practiced it a lot.

I swallowed my nerves and explained, "I want the manager position." Will still looked unconvinced, so I went on, "I'm ready for more responsibility here on the farm. And this would be a . . . different kind of challenge."

I felt like I was already interviewing, trying to throw around big words and make my weaknesses sound like strengths. I wished I was wearing a blazer or something instead of nervously sweating inside my winter coat.

Will regarded me skeptically. "A challenge?"

I nodded. "Yep. I mean, yes. One I'm ready to take on."

Will crossed his arms and leaned back in his chair. "But you hate the tourists."

"So do you," I accused on instinct. "But I wouldn't be dealing with them the same way, right?"

"I suppose," he agreed. "You'd be handling the complainers and the troublemakers, though. But you wouldn't have to see them every second of your shift like you do now. Do you still want to handle social media?"

"Yes!" I practically shouted. "I like that part."

"What brought all this on, Mac? I thought you didn't want to be here."

Shame felt like a knot in my chest, twisting me up and making it hard to breathe. I knew why Will assumed that, the way my actions had supported it.

I didn't want to tell him about the conversation with Brady. How I'd felt like a disgraceful chicken and criticized my neighbors and this town when I was really unhappy with myself.

I didn't know why it was so hard to admit that I'd allowed myself to be unfulfilled and figured it was easier to do nothing than to accept some responsibility for my actions.

"I'm ready for a change," I answered. It wasn't the whole truth, but it was honest nonetheless.

Will nodded like he, maybe, understood. "Me too."

After a long moment, he said, "Okay. But we're still holding interviews. You'll have to apply like anyone else. But I'll back you if this is what you want, Mac."

"It is," I assured him, feeling my heart rate gallop as if to confirm my words.

He leaned forward, gray flannel straining across his shoulders as he rested his forearms on the desk. "No more changing the prices by a penny."

"Right," I said, dipping my chin in shame-faced agreement. That had been dumb.

"I mean it. That shit is annoying. You and Judd need to grow up."

I swallowed hard, thinking he was probably right.

When I wandered out of Will's office a few minutes later with a spring in my step, I found Larry waiting on me with a coffee in one hand and one of Chloe's pastries in the other.

"Well," she said, eyes huge and expectant. "What the hell was that all about?"

We were on shift at the tree lot in ten minutes, so I tilted my head in that direction. "Let's walk and talk." Plus, I didn't want Will to overhear anything and change his mind about supporting me.

As my boots traveled over the worn path, past the fencing decorated with warm white lights, I admitted quietly, "I told Will I want to be considered for the general manager position."

"You did? Why?" my cousin asked, slightly horrified.

I frowned. "It seemed like it was time, you know, for me to step up and take on more. Stop acting like the high schoolers we hire for the summer."

Larry pulled me to a stop near the ticket booth. "Does this have something to do with the other night? When you asked me if I thought Will was right about you? The nine-to-five thing? I didn't mean to hurt your feelings."

I shook my head. "You didn't hurt my feelings. I asked you because I trust you to be honest with me. And, I think, I needed to hear that. It was the truth, but I didn't want it to be. I need *something* different. I don't know. I don't even have my own place. I still live with my grandparents, Larry. I need to grow up and stop coasting by."

"That feels like a gross oversimplification, but okay," she murmured, then took a huge bite of almond croissant. When she'd finished chewing, she said seriously, "But is taking over for Will—being general manager of the farm—something you actually want?"

I took a deep breath and considered her question. I did love the farm. And I loved working with Larry and seeing her every day. She was my cousin, but she was also my best friend. I think I'd done the easy thing for so long because it felt safe. Stepping into a new role would be scary, but in a good way.

"Yeah, I think it is," I finally replied.

Throughout my shift, I thought about what the future might look like. I let the giddy feeling of something new on the horizon fill me up. This could be a chance for me to put down roots instead of just hovering on the surface.

The excitement bubbled up in my chest the more I thought about it. I realized I wanted to tell Brady so I could get his opinion. Then I smiled to myself, thinking how he'd probably try to invent a manager position over at Judd's Orchard to even things up.

My smile faded just as quickly when I remembered the way he'd looked at me on Friday. I needed to talk to him. Sex clearly hadn't simplified anything. And it definitely hadn't made me want him any less. Maybe I could fix what I'd broken between us.

"Hey," Larry said later when we finally had a lull in foot traffic. "You think Will stepping back at the farm has anything to do with Becca? I am ready for him to get his head out of his ass and go get that girl."

"Me too." I grinned, considering once again, that stubbornness was a family trait, and I had some cranial extraction work of my own to do.

twelve

MAC

When I was eight, I accidentally stole my neighbor's dog.

Well, it wasn't an accident. Not really. I'd wanted her dog and thought I'd be a much better pet owner. So I'd taken him.

Mrs. Landrum's land bordered Grandpappy's. She was friendly with my family and attended service on Sunday at the same church. But I really felt like her chocolate Lab, Baker, needed more attention.

After school most days, Baker would come to visit me in the fields, and we'd run and play.

And one day, I just decided he should come home with me instead.

Oh, and I renamed him Brownie Sundae.

I managed to hide him in our barn for two days, bringing him food and water. But my dad heard him barking and caught me red-handed when I snuck out of the house with my pillow and a blanket to sleep in the barn so Brownie wouldn't be lonely.

Dad hadn't yelled or gotten angry. In sleep-rumpled pajama pants and a faded white tee shirt, he'd simply sat down on a hay bale and stroked the dog's ears while I gave a convincing argument and a laundry list of reasons why I should be able to keep Brownie for myself.

My father had then gently explained that what I'd done had been theft, and while my intentions might have been pure, Baker wasn't content to stay in our barn.

"There's a reason you had to trap him in here, MacKenzie," he'd said. "If you'd opened that door, he would have run on home."

He reminded me that because of my actions, Mrs. Landrum was probably very worried about Baker. And while she might not be able to play with the dog the way I played with him, she still loved him.

And so, at four in the morning, my father made me walk beside him through the corn field and across Mrs. Landrum's pasture to bring her dog home. He hadn't explained away my behavior. He'd expected me to own my mistakes and speak for myself.

I still remembered walking in frustrated silence, almost wishing my dad had yelled at me so I would have had an excuse to be angry at someone besides myself.

And that was exactly how I felt now, sitting in my Jeep, fighting angry nerves and willing myself to get out of my vehicle and go talk to Brady Judd—to own up to my bad behavior. Whether I was apologizing for animal thievery or being a remorseful ghoster, swallowing my pride never really got any easier. It still tasted like bitter regret.

I'd thought about just texting Brady. But the apologetic equivalent of a *you up?* text didn't seem like the most sincere course of action. And the simple fact was, he deserved better than that. I didn't want to be someone who made excuses for hurting people.

So, here I was, at Abby's on the Friday before Christmas, surrounded by more Kirby Falls High alumni than had attended my ten-year class reunion.

The holidays were always a busy time. Former classmates returned home to celebrate with their families and usually made their way here, to the bonfire, to visit old high school friends. Tonight was rowdier and louder than a normal bonfire, that was for sure.

But the last two weeks had been busy. This was my first real chance to get close to Brady. Grandpappy's had been inundated with tourists who wanted to go on tractor sleigh rides, visit Santa's workshop barn, drink hot cocoa, and eat peppermint bark from the Bake Shop.

I'd worked all three days of the Holiday Market downtown and had my inter-view for the general manager position as well. It had gone well, but they were waiting until after Christmas to select a candidate.

There'd also been a quick trip to Detroit with my family to pick up Becca and bring her back home. That was a whole different story, but it had been a frantic few days of travel with no time for sightseeing. I'd made Larry drive and kept my face plastered to the window, taking in the view while we'd been in the city.

Now, however, I was here, and I was determined to clear the air with Brady. See if he was open to another date, maybe? This time without the asterisk.

He needed to know that I was sorry for hurting him, and I wanted to earn his trust despite my shitty, selfish behavior.

I took a steadying breath and inhaled the smell of woodsmoke as I weaved my way through the parked cars overflowing the field. When I reached the barn, people were standing around in clusters everywhere. I stopped briefly and spoke to the folks who said hello, but I was too focused on finding Brady and making things right. So I promised to circle back around and catch up with them later, many of whom I hadn't seen in years.

As I made polite conversation and scooted my way through the crowd, I searched for Brady. I stayed alert, training my eyes to pick out his tall form or puffy vest among those gathered. It wasn't until I'd completed a pass around the bonfire and was on my way back toward the covered patio that I accidentally stepped into his path.

Brady pulled up short, and I smiled reflexively. "Hey."

"Hi," he replied.

"How are you?" I asked, giving myself a mental high five for managing normal conversation.

"I'm good," he said cautiously, like this might be a trap.

"That's good."

Then I noticed what he was wearing. His jacket was missing and so was his puffy vest. The green flannel he wore was tucked into dark-wash jeans. But the slightly dressy attire wasn't what gave me pause; it was the leather suspenders cresting the tops of his rounded shoulders before descending his lean torso.

"What's this?" I asked, reaching forward and snapping one of the straps.

"Excuse you," he scolded, leaning away.

"What are you wearing, Brady?" I couldn't get over them. He looked even taller somehow and just . . . rural fancy. He looked really good.

"They're suspenders, you heathen."

I grinned, following the material with my eyes. "I see that."

When my gaze finally made it to his face, Brady wore a satisfied smirk. "You like them."

"Yeah." I shrugged. "They'd be great to strangle you with."

He snorted out a laugh, and we stared at one another, amusement mirrored on both of our faces. This sort of teasing wasn't exactly normal—it was too benign for us—but it did put me at ease. The sharp edges were gone, and I felt like maybe there was a chance for me to say my piece and have it received. Not an angry confession mumbled into the ground beneath my shoes, but something genuine and honest.

Abruptly, before I lost my nerve, I blurted out, "Hey, can we talk? I need to say some things and—"

"Sure," Brady interrupted, eyes drifting over my shoulder briefly before returning. "But I need to get these drinks back."

Suddenly, I noticed his hands. All this time, I'd been so distracted I hadn't realized Brady had been standing there holding four beers, the necks clutched awkwardly between his fingers.

"Oh, sure. Of course."

"I'll catch up with you, yeah?"

I nodded quickly and stepped to the side.

As I watched, Brady returned to the bonfire. A small triangle of people opened up to welcome him, and he handed out beers to Abby and two women I didn't recognize. One of them leaned in and squeezed his arm, mouthing a thank-you.

Something hollow and achy settled in the pit of my stomach the longer I stood there staring. The four of them laughed and chatted, and Brady didn't look in my direction once.

The women were pretty. All glowing pale skin and long blond hair. They looked younger than us by a few years. I definitely would have remembered them from high school, but they were strangers, barging in on a local gathering . . . for locals. Who even invited them anyway?

My thoughts had a jealous, spiteful edge, and I forced myself to walk away and go find someone to talk to. It worked for a while, but I was distracted waiting for Brady to come back so I could apologize like I'd planned. And I was angry that I cared so much. We weren't in a relationship. We'd had sex one time. He could talk to whomever he wanted. It was none of my business.

But my eyes betrayed me. They sought him out, punishing me when I witnessed his carefree laughter over something one of the women had said. Twice, the person I was talking to had to repeat themselves because I'd gotten sidetracked when the girls had leaned in to take a selfie with Brady.

I was disgusted with myself and pretty sure I should just leave. Forget this whole stupid night. But then the foursome approached. I was under the awning talking to Benny Jameson, one of the bartenders over at Trailview Brewing.

"Oh my gosh," one of the women said suddenly. "You're here."

Benny's smile brightened. "Yeah. Glad you ladies could make it."

"Thank you so much for inviting us," the other blond said.

Ah, so Benny the bartender invited some pretty leafers to our bonfire in an effort to get laid. I resisted the urge to roll my eyes.

"We've been having the best time," the first blond added. She squeezed Brady's arm again as she said it, and I wondered briefly if he'd have a bruise there tomorrow from all the flirty manhandling.

"Hi, I'm Aerrin," the same woman said, turning to me.

"Oh, hi," I said once I realized she was introducing herself. "I'm—"

"That's A-e-r-r-i-n," she interrupted. "I know people your age are used to the more traditional spelling."

I felt my eyes widen comically. "People my age?" I asked as Brady snorted into his beer.

Aerrin, not Erin—the traditional spelling, I guess, what the fuck—laughed like I'd told the funniest joke.

"And I'm Beckleigh," the other woman said. "Soooo nice to meet you."

"Sure," I murmured, irritated for a million reasons, none of them feminist or anything I'd be proud of in the light of day.

I stood in the strange conversation circle while Aerrin and Beckleigh told stories about their own high school friends, who lived in Arizona, apparently. I cut Benny a glare for inviting tourists, but he was too busy staring at Beckleigh's lips wrapped around a beer bottle to notice.

When I risked a glance in Brady's direction, he seemed totally at ease, listening and laughing, joining in with a funny anecdote, hitting it off with the outsiders.

Eventually, Benny meandered away when it was clear the women weren't interested in him. Feeling like an awkward fifth wheel, I excused myself, but no one seemed to notice. I made my way inside the barn to where Abby had renovated and added bathrooms about five years ago. Just as I was finishing up in the stall, I heard the door open.

"I get to take the lead this time, okay?" Aerrin said, and I froze.

"Yeah, that's fair," Beckleigh replied before smacking her lips together a few times. "We deserve a good time after that guy the other night just wanted to watch."

"Right?" Aerrin said. "I am ready for some fun."

"And I think these bonfire boys look like *lots* of fun," Beckleigh added with a giggle.

My heart was beating hard, and no matter how much I reminded myself that Brady wasn't mine, I couldn't help the sudden urge to be sick.

I stayed completely still, making sure my shoes didn't scuff on the concrete floor.

A moment later, the door opened again, and the two women left.

I counted to forty-five, hoping they'd all be gone by the time I exited the barn. I didn't want to see the before part of whatever good time they were planning on having.

I was *such* an idiot. I'd naively come here tonight to apologize and work things out. But of course Brady had other options. He was a friendly, good-looking guy. And now I knew he was good in bed. I shook my head and stepped out of the dark interior of the barn.

Stopping abruptly, I realized I should have counted to sixty because Aerrin and Beckleigh were just now disappearing around the side of the barn and into the field where all the cars were parked. Maybe Brady was warming up his truck. That sounded like something he'd do.

Cursing myself and my own stupidity, I spun around to return to the bonfire. I'd seen Hazel Bradford with a bag full of s'mores supplies. I would go and eat my feelings and then head home.

But before I could take a step in that direction, there was Brady, casually leaning against the awning post, watching me. He had a smirk on his face, dimple threatening in his right cheek. I realized suddenly that he'd seen me staring after his new pals, probably looking like the last kid picked for dodgeball in PE class.

"What?" I snapped reflexively, feeling my cheeks heat from mortified embarrassment.

He straightened and held up his hands in surrender, grin still perfectly in place. "Nothing at all."

My eyes narrowed and I couldn't help the accusation in my voice. "Aren't you missing out on your threesome?"

Brady took a step in my direction. "Nah. Abby's going to join those nice ladies and have an interesting night."

I wouldn't admit it to anyone, but something loosened in my stomach. Probably the anxious, jealous knot that I'd spent the evening twisting and tying off.

"Why not you?" I asked. "You seemed to hit it off."

"Oh, they offered," he said easily, managing another step closer. He was so close, I could have reached out and tugged on his suspenders again if I'd wanted to—which I did not. "Not my thing. Too many feet."

That surprised a laugh out of me despite my irritation.

Brady stepped right into my space, one hand coming to rest on my waist as he dipped his head close to my ear. Then he whispered, making the fine hairs along my neck shiver, "I prefer to give a woman—singular—all my attention. And when I'm touching someone like that, I want them to know it's me."

His lips grazed the shell of my ear as desire made me unsteady. I rested my hands on the hard planes of his chest as his grip on my waist tightened.

"And," he went on, voice low and deep, "I don't like to share."

I swallowed hard and closed my eyes.

"You were jealous," he teased, nipping my earlobe.

"I was not," I lied, finally finding my voice amid the upheaval in my mind and body.

"You were," he insisted, nudging me to take a few steps back into the barn.

"You shouldn't play games like that, Brady."

"I was just being friendly," he said, walking me back another step.

"Friendly?" My tone was disbelieving. I wanted to pull back and see his face, but I liked being close. It was easier to be honest that way. He'd maneuvered us into the shadowed corner of the barn, the side opposite the restrooms and out of sight from the bonfire-goers.

"Yeah. Friendly," Brady insisted. "Things look very different when I want to be more than that."

My hands drifted, finding the straps of his leather suspenders. I gave them a sharp tug, and that was all the invitation Brady needed. He reached down and grabbed my ass, pulling me against him, mouth meeting mine in a frenzied kiss.

The weeks and distance fell away. He was here, and I was right back where I started—unable to get enough of him and unwilling to come up for air.

I couldn't get close enough, and maybe he felt the same because a moment later, Brady gripped the outside of my thighs and lifted. I wrapped my legs around his hips and hung on to his shoulders as he straightened to his full height, taking me with him. His hands came back to my backside, keeping me supported and lining us up in a way that had me moaning into the kiss. He was thick and hard against me, and I didn't want to stop.

"We're going to get caught," he managed between kisses that were all enthusiasm and zero subtlety.

"I don't care," I said, dragging my nails along his scalp.

"Liar." He chuckled, pressing his hot mouth along my jaw before sucking on the sensitive skin of my neck. "I thought you wanted to talk anyway."

"I do," I gasped as his teeth scraped below my ear.

"Well, what did you want to tell me?"

My fingers gripped the suspenders once more. "That these are really doing it for me."

I felt his smile bloom against my skin, warm and pleased.

"It's true," I insisted. "You should wear them all the time." Then, my naughty thoughts took a detour to those suspenders in my bedroom and Brady tied up and at my mercy.

My thoughts were officially in the gutter. No, lower than the gutter. All my dirty imaginings might as well have been in the ditch that floods in the west field. I couldn't think beyond his hands on my ass, his ragged voice in my ear, and the hard ridge of his dick right where I wanted it.

"Then I'll wear them all the time," he replied, softly. "Just for you." With a final kiss to my jaw, Brady pulled back to look at me. "Tell me what you wanted to say. Before."

"Oh," I breathed, having trouble switching gears between full-speed impending orgasm and the steady idle of real talk.

Our little corner was shadowed, but I could make out his earnest gaze, equal parts wary and curious.

"I shouldn't have ignored your texts and avoided you," I confessed. "It was a shitty thing to do, and I'm sorry for it. I was wrong."

He nodded, just a small dip of his chin. "So, did it work?"

I frowned. "Did what work?"

"Am I out of your system? Did you get what you wanted?"

With my thighs still wrapped around him, I hugged his hips as if to say, *What do you think?* Then I sighed. "About that . . ."

"Oh yeah?" And if I wasn't mistaken, there was some amusement there, hidden in the dark.

I snapped one suspender in retribution and he squeezed my ass.

"I would be open to maybe continuing our arrangement," I offered.

"*Arrangement*? Are we in a historical romance novel? Or are you trying to *Pretty Woman* me?"

"Brady," I groaned, face-planting into his collarbone as I fought my laughter. He smelled like sand and sunshine and I loved it.

"My affections can't be bought, Maximus."

"You know what I mean. We could do more of this," I said, tightening my thighs once again. Date, hook up, amorous congress, bam-bam in the ham-ham—whatever he wanted to call it.

Brady was quiet for long enough that despite the hardness I still felt between my legs, I began to worry that he might not want more.

"What are you thinking?" I whispered, hoping I didn't sound too eager or desperate.

"Okay," he finally replied. "I'm in. But I want to keep this thing between us. Nobody else."

Shock had my mouth dropping open. I wasn't opposed. I was just . . . surprised. "You want us to be a secret?"

"Yeah, can you handle that?"

I snorted, despite the weird feeling I couldn't name. "I can handle it. Can you?" Brady wasn't known for being subtle. Also, he had a big mouth.

"Sure," he replied confidently. "Sounds like fun. We can sneak around. Be covert. I'll get my camo back out."

I laughed, and I liked that his arms tightened around me when I did.

"But, Mac." Brady hesitated.

"Yeah?"

"The next time you get scared, don't run away, okay? You can't keep doing that."

My hackles were mid-rise at the accusation, but shame was climbing just as swiftly alongside it. Because Brady was right. I *had* avoided him after the kiss, and again after sex, because I was scared and overwhelmed.

"Just . . . stay, okay?" he said. "Stay and talk. We'll figure it out. Or we'll fight it out—we're good at that. But don't hide from me."

"Alright," I said softly, forcing away the righteous indignation that had come close to bubbling up to the surface.

Brady leaned forward and gave me a soft kiss for my trouble.

When he pulled back, I asked, "Can I come home with you?"

He winced, the movement barely noticeable in the dim light. "I told Abby I'd stay and shut everything down tonight. Wait for everyone to leave and make sure they get where they're going. Put out the fire. What about tomorrow?"

"We have the Christmas party at Grandpappy's. I promised to help."

Brady's lips twisted into a grin, white teeth flashing. "I'm invited to that, you know?"

"Oh really?" A spark of anticipation burned away the disappointment from a moment ago.

"Yeah, maybe I'll see you there."

"Maybe you will."

He patted my backside and slowly lowered me to my feet. "And maybe we can do some undercover work."

"Okay, but start an argument or something so no one gets suspicious."

Brady nodded emphatically. "Yeah, and make sure to call me an idiot."

With my hands still wrapped around his suspenders, we grinned at each other, proud of our plan.

The unsteadiness that had plagued me receded. The imaginary waves settled, and I felt like I was on solid ground for the first time in weeks.

The scent of woodsmoke and ocean breeze followed me home.

"Mac," Will called, his head hanging out of his office door. "You got a minute?"

"Yeah. Let me drop these tablecloths off, and I'll be right there."

I'd spent the day helping my mother, Chloe, Bonnie, and Aunt Maggie in the Bake Shop. We were prepping treats for the Christmas party this afternoon. After I'd finished decorating the last batch of sugar cookies, Mom had asked me to head over to the barn to pull the event linens out of storage. We had about two hours until the party started, and our friends and neighbors would be arriving soon.

The Judd family would be attending, as well as some of the other small business owners in Kirby Falls. Even our part-time and seasonal employees were invited along with their families. We were expecting a big turnout.

And Brady was coming too. The thought put an extra spring in my step as I unloaded my items and made my way around the back side of the bakery to Will's adjoining office.

I rapped a knock before going inside.

The room was warm from the electric heater in the corner. Will's desk was plain and mostly bare.

For once, his dog wasn't fast asleep in his bed. The reason why was perched in the only other chair in the room. Becca smiled at me as she stroked Carl's ears. She passed him a hunk of string cheese before standing. "Hey, Mac."

I smiled back, so glad she'd returned to Kirby Falls where she belonged. She was good for Will, and I was happy for them. "Hi, Becca."

"I'm going to head out and help Maggie and Chloe set up." She squeezed my arm as she passed. "You two have fun." Then she winked, and I wondered what that was all about.

Will gave Becca a small smile and followed her out with his eyes. Carl trailed after her, nearly as besotted as my grumpy cousin.

"What's up?" I asked, taking the seat Becca had vacated.

Will's face morphed into a serious one. "We were going to wait until next week, but I talked with my parents and your parents, and they thought it was best to go ahead. So it wasn't hanging over you during the holidays."

I straightened as sudden nerves clenched my belly tight. Was he about to tell me I hadn't gotten the manager position? Were they going with one of the other candidates? I knew they'd interviewed Ethel Jennings. She was a transplant, but she'd been in Kirby Falls for a few years now. Her background was in sales. She'd retired early and moved from Florida because she and her husband had fallen in love with our town after visiting every autumn for nearly a decade.

Ethel was capable and smart. She served on a number of committees and even volunteered at the library with Mrs. Crandall. I bet they were picking her. She was older and more polished and about a million other things I wasn't.

I took a deep breath to settle myself. "Okay. Lay it on me."

Will paused dramatically, and I almost reached across the desk and punched him on the arm. "We would like to formally offer you the position of general manager."

"Really?" I squeaked as some big, nameless emotion swelled in my chest.

My cousin fought a smile. "Yes. Really. You've stepped it up in the last few weeks."

"Thanks, Will."

"And since you're family, you'll be really easy to fire if you fuck up."

I glared as he chuckled at his own joke.

With a smile still lingering, Will offered, "Congratulations, Mac. I'm proud of you."

"Thanks, Will," I repeated, but this time emotion made my voice rough.

Something pride adjacent warmed me from the inside out. I knew it wasn't some huge accomplishment when everyone on the hiring committee shared your DNA.

But I'd gotten the job. From now on, I was determined to do more with my townie existence than just scrape by.

Clearing my throat, I let my gaze roam the small office. "So when do I get to redecorate?"

Will's stare was baleful. "We'll start training next week. And January first, it's all yours."

"I can't wait." I grinned.

When I stepped out of my future office, Will came with me. He said he was off to help Becca and our moms finish setting up for the party.

I carefully pulled the door shut with a quiet snick. It was at odds with the loud excitement coursing through my veins. I'd found a goal and set out to accomplish it. And it felt good to have succeeded. I couldn't remember the last time I'd actually been working toward something instead of openly avoiding it. Probably high school, honestly, with my teammates on the soccer team.

As I walked slowly across the wooden decking to the front of the building, I pulled out my phone, eager to share my good news.

And I knew just the person to tell.

Me: Guess who's the new Manager of Farm Operations and Social Media Director?

It didn't take long for the reply to come through, and I rolled my eyes affectionately when I read it.

Grandma Nola: Is it Larry? No, wait, did they offer it to Becca? I haven't met her yet, but she sounds like a peach.

Me: Ha. Ha.

Grandma Nola: I'm just pulling your leg. Congratulations, MacKenzie Eloise. I knew you had it in you.

The recognition from my favorite person in the world had me clutching my phone a little tighter, suddenly grateful we were texting and not on a video call.

Me: Thanks, Grandma.

Grandma Nola: We're in the RV. Should be in Kirby Falls by Monday morning. Can't wait to see you, sugar.

I smiled, excited to have her and my grandfather home for the holidays.

Me: Drive safe. See you soon.

I was just returning my phone to the back pocket of my jeans when I heard a low "Psst!" from behind me.

Spinning around, I caught sight of Brady peeking around the corner of the building. "Hey," he whispered.

"Hey," I whispered back, crooking my finger and urging him closer.

He looked good. Brown hair messily styled to within an inch of its life, blue eyes dancing with mischief, puffy vest in place over a bright yellow flannel.

"No suspenders?" I pouted when he came to stand before me.

His grin widened. "I knew how they affected you. Couldn't have you mauling me in front of our family and friends on our first covert operation."

I gave him a flat stare, but it was ruined by the fizzy happiness bubbling inside me, spilling out alongside a smile I couldn't contain.

I scanned the area around us. We were on the back side of the Bake Shop with only a plowed winter field for company. I checked my watch and figured we had time.

Reaching out, I snagged Brady's hand and towed him inside Will's office. *My office*, I mentally corrected.

The blinds on the lone window were already closed, but I locked the door in case Will or Becca wandered back over.

"Ohhh, another stakeout?" Brady asked, clearly enjoying sneaking around.

I urged him to sit on the desk and then stepped between his legs, unbuttoning his flannel as I went. "Only if you prefer a stakeout without pants on."

Brady stilled my hands, which had just latched on to the waistband of his jeans. His gaze searched mine, but I could see the excitement there, too. It mirrored mine.

I was giddy with the prospect of this new . . . thing between us. I still didn't understand it, but now I was free to look and touch and taste. And I wanted to do that right now.

"I don't have a condom," he finally said.

I nodded. "That's okay. Change of plans." And then I dropped to my knees, unzipping his jeans as I went.

"Shit," he breathed above me, a little tortured and a lot desperate.

I worked on shimmying his pants partway down his lean hips while Brady focused on getting his shirt and vest all the way off.

He kept up a steady stream of chatter while we got him indecent. "Should we really be in here? Will is so grumpy. I don't want him to kill me for desecrating his office."

As I leaned in to playfully bite the edge of his hip bone, I fought the urge to tell him it would be my office in another week or so. But it felt too soon. I wanted to wait until it was real to tell Brady. This wasn't the same as texting my grandmother out of sheer excitement. If I shared my news with someone outside the family, then it would be out there. And Will still had to train me. He could easily fire me out of annoyance, thinking I wasn't mature enough or smart enough to take over for him.

"It's fine," I said.

"Are you sure?" he whispered, fingers clasping the elastic of his underwear, halting my progress.

"Yes, I'm sure. Now let go." I batted his hands away.

He stayed propped and white-knuckled against the desk while I took him out of his boxer briefs. Given our one night together, I hadn't really gotten the chance to explore him in the light of day.

After I'd looked my fill, I gazed up the length of Brady's long, lean body and smirked. "I thought you'd be . . ."

"If you say bigger, I'm leaving right now."

I laughed. "No," I managed, still amused and impatient and deeply turned on. He was plenty big enough. I squirmed a little at the memory of him inside me—

thick and insistent. "I was going to say I thought you'd be more agreeable. You seem very worried about getting caught. Unless you're trying to stall for some reason. Or maybe you don't want my mouth on you."

Brady swallowed, and I watched the movement of his Adam's apple. "It's not that I don't want you to. It's just that . . . a blow job requires trust. You can't ask some hookup or one-night stand to suck your dick."

"Plenty of people do," I argued lightly, still entertained.

"Yeah, not me."

I reached out and wrapped my fist around his length, and Brady sucked in a sharp breath.

Perhaps it was the memory of those blond leafers, but something curious and a little spiteful made me ask, "So you do that often? The one-night-stand thing?"

"Well, no. But that's beside the point."

I smothered my laugh against his hip, where I placed another biting kiss. Then I remembered weeks ago, accusing him of not dating much. Now, to hear him tell it, he didn't hook up either. Suddenly, I wondered what Brady Judd was waiting on.

Leaning back, I looked up at him once more. His eyes were clenched shut, jaw tense as I pumped his length slow and steady. "Is it okay if I get back to what I was doing?"

His lids fluttered open, and he regarded me warily.

I laughed again. "Brady, come on. Let me use my mouth. No teeth, I swear. It'll be good. Do you need references?"

He frowned, eyes narrowed. And if I wasn't mistaken, he sounded a little jealous when he snapped out, "No, smartass. I don't want to hear about the guys you've been with."

I grinned. "How about a sales pitch?" I touched my tongue to the very tip of him, a barely there caress that made his nostrils flare. "Need me to tell you all the things I'll do to you?" A long, slow lick this time, up the full length of his erection. "Or would you rather my mouth be nice and full?"

Brady made a pained grunt in the affirmative before dropping his head back to stare at the ceiling.

I took that as a binding agreement and swallowed him down.

Whispered curses flew up and over my head. When I risked another glance up, I saw that Brady's attention was focused back on me, on the way I was moving, bobbing up and down at a steady pace, taking as much of him as I could until he tapped the back of my throat.

It didn't take long to figure out what he liked—messy and a little rough. I worked him over while he groaned and fought for control. But I didn't want a calm and collected Brady. I wanted him desperate, wild, and reckless . . . over me.

When his hands hovered in the air like he couldn't decide what to do with them, I guided one toward my ponytail. He made a relieved sound as he wrapped the length around his fist, as if he needed an anchor in this storm as much as I did.

As I increased my pace, I kept my gaze trained on his. With desire blazing in his blue eyes, he clenched his jaw tight and nodded roughly, a helpless groan escaping in what I assumed was a warning.

But I kept doing what I was doing, content to see this through to the end. When he came a moment later, hips bucking in inelegant little thrusts, I swallowed every last drop.

With panting breaths, Brady released his hold on my hair, gently smoothing it across my shoulder. I watched, amused, as he fought to gather his composure.

"Did that meet your approval?" I teased.

He gave me a look that loudly conveyed, *Yes, you idiot*, but then said, "God, yes. I will never look at your red lips without seeing my cock disappearing between them."

The casual, filthy way he said that had me squirming where I knelt, disappointed anew that neither one of us had a condom.

I forced myself to check my watch. "We need to get out there before someone notices. I'm supposed to go round up any tourists and clear the property before the party. You could head down to the gazebo to help Bonnie and Danny with the tables. Our paths won't cross, and no one should suspect anything."

Brady nodded, still looking a little dazed. Twisting at the hips, he leaned back to reach for the shirt he'd flung onto the desk behind him.

I was still eye-level with his middle, and when he turned, I could see part of his backside where his lowered jeans didn't cover. A shocked gasp left my mouth, and I grabbed his ass to keep him from pivoting back.

"What the hell is that?!"

He froze and then sighed. "Fuck."

Unrepentant glee threatened to unhinge me. My eyes traced the lines of the small tattoo—my fingers too. "Do you have a Big Mac tattooed on your ass, Brayden Howell Judd?"

"Jesus," he groaned, trying to dislodge my hold and pull up his pants at the same time. He eventually wrestled them away from me amid much squealing and squawking on my behalf. "Stop it. I'll tell you." Then he tugged me to my feet.

With a serious expression, he regarded me as his hands quickly buttoned up his shirt. I could hardly keep my smile from cracking my face wide open so that satisfied delight could spill out.

"My sophomore year at UT, I got shit-faced at some party. There may have been a bet, but I was drunk enough that it seemed like a good idea to go and get a tattoo from some disreputable place that would tattoo a wasted nineteen-year-old."

When he didn't say more, I prompted giddily, "And it's a Big Mac because . . .?"

Another sigh escaped, but I could see the curl of his lips and the threat of his dimple when he said, "You know why. Abby gave me shit constantly about you. He was just as drunk as I was and thought it would be a great idea to immortalize our rivalry with your name tattooed on my ass. Something got mixed up in my inebriated communication with the artist, and when I woke up the next morning, sore and hungover and confused, I had two all-beef patties, special sauce, lettuce, cheese, pickles, and onions on a sesame-seed bun . . . on my ass."

I giggled like a schoolgirl, and I wasn't even embarrassed. "This is the best day of my life."

Brady shook his head ruefully but was still smiling. "Mine too, Big Mac."

My stomach pitched like I was driving and had hit a dip in the road. The amusement I'd gotten over the secret tattoo discovery morphed into something else—sudden awareness and bone-deep affection. Realization elbowed its way in, letting me know that even with so much history between us, this man could still surprise me.

To ease the pressure building in my chest, I teased, "Of course it's the best day of your life. That was a top-notch blow job."

Brady laughed and hugged me to him, pressing a kiss to my temple. His cologne, body spray, whatever, wrapped me up in warm sunshine and salt air. "Come over tonight."

I leaned back so I could see his face. "You want more?"

"Yes," he replied earnestly before giving me a devious grin. "And I want to return the favor."

"Okay," I agreed, easily for once. Unable to deny that I wanted him too.

Later that night, after an eventful Christmas party, Brady did return the favor. Twice.

But when I woke up at 3:22 a.m., warm and confused with his body wrapped around mine like a vine, it was easier to tell myself this was just a fling, a temporary physical relationship that would burn itself out—the way all my relationships did.

Brady didn't wake when I extracted myself from his sleepy hold. He just grumbled softly and pushed the side of his face into the pillow where my hair had been.

Sitting on the edge of the bed, I watched as he relaxed into a contented sleep once more. The corner of his mouth twisted up into a wry smile, and I wondered what he was dreaming about. Though, that was more than likely just Brady, so friendly and affable, he even smiled in his sleep.

With my cell phone, I snapped a quick picture of his face and then stood on unsteady legs and made my way home.

BRADY

The holidays put my secret meetups with Mac on hold for a little while.

She'd only managed to sneak over twice in the last two weeks. I knew her grandparents were in town and she lived with them. So I told myself that was why she'd yet to stay the night at my apartment.

Abby and I were at the gym early one cold January morning when a text came through from Mac. Given the time, I figured she'd just woken up to get ready for work, and I liked the idea that she'd reached for her phone with me on her mind.

I paused the music streaming through my earbuds so I could focus on her message. The clink of weights and the hum of cardio machines faded into the background as I read.

MacKenzie: I thought it was an anomaly, but you do it every time. You actually smile in your sleep.

Then a picture attachment came through. It was of me. My eyes were closed, and my head was on my pillow. She'd snapped the photo from beside me in bed, and, true to her word, my lips were tilted up even as I slept soundly.

MacKenzie: Does your friendliness know no bounds? Are you charming folks in your dreams, Mr. Popular?

Me: I can't help I'm charming, Big Mac.

MacKenzie: You know who else is charming? Cult leaders.

I snorted a laugh.

If she thought her teasing was going to bother me, she'd played this one all wrong. The woman who didn't do long-term and couldn't figure out her feelings had taken a picture of me sleeping. I was ignoring the part where she'd snapped the photo as she snuck out of my apartment. But despite that, something had compelled her to stop before she left. Maybe she had been amused by the fact that I was smiling in my sleep. But maybe she sat there staring for a while. Thinking. Feeling. Maybe the impulse to take a sneaky picture had been motivated by something more than the casual hookup vibes she put off.

Either way, I liked knowing she had that image of me on her phone. I liked even more that she knew what I looked like when I slept. How it brought me peace to wrap my arms around her and hold her close. To have her warm cinnamon-sugar scent linger on my pillow.

Me: If you think you're giving me shit right now, you are sorely mistaken. You paparazzi'd me in my sleep, Clark. Why are you so obsessed with me?

MacKenzie: Omg. The ego on you.

Me: Is that what we're calling it?

MacKenzie: LOL

MacKenzie: Besides, this coming from the guy who basically has my name tattooed on his ass. Talk about obsessed.

I snorted again. If she only knew.

Then I typed out, *Oh, I just really like burgers. Did you think that was in some way related to you?*

MacKenzie: Nice try.

Me: Wait, did you save this picture of me so you could make another voodoo doll?

MacKenzie: God, that was such a good prank.

Me: Fifteen-year-old Mac was creative. Is that why my knee hurts sometimes?

MacKenzie: Yes. I think I left the pin in your leg, wherever that doll ended up.

Me: Well, if you could track it down, that would be great.

"What are you smiling about?"

Abby's voice made me blink. I glanced over to find my friend perched on the weight bench, staring at me. It was an effort, but I forced myself to stow my phone and focus on the workout we were in the middle of.

"Nothing," I said and then swallowed down the uncomfortable feeling of lying to my oldest friend.

Abby's dark eyes narrowed. "Come spot me."

"Sure."

Moments later, I felt my phone buzz in my pocket and fought all my instincts to check it, instead keeping my attention on Abby and the bar's steady progress up and down over his chest.

Abby blew out a breath after the final rep and said, "You're being weird. What's going on?"

The urge to tell him about Mac was admittedly strong, but it had been my idea to keep things a secret, and I needed to stick to that. It would be safer in the long run.

Plus, I already knew how Abby felt about Mac and me. He'd be excited and supportive until he found out about the casual, secretive aspect of our relationship. Then he'd worry that I was going to get my heart broken.

Honestly, he was right to worry. I was half convinced that was the way things were going to go if Mac couldn't own up to her feelings or if she got bored with me. But that was the whole point of keeping things just between the two of us.

It took the pressure off. I'd known Mac too long, and I'd witnessed every relationship she'd ever had fail for a variety of reasons. But it was never because the guys broke up with *her*.

I hoped that by keeping this thing between us under wraps, we could avoid pressure from the town. I fought a shudder as I imagined the posts in the Kirby Falls

Facebook group. There was every chance a friend or family member or neighbor would get in Mac's head about dating the guy she'd spent the last twenty years hating. The memory of our date to the Haunted Forest validated my decision. She hadn't wanted anyone to see us together then. It seemed safer to keep it that way now.

Rationally, I knew we couldn't stay a secret forever—I wouldn't want us to, anyway. But I'd really like to have a chance at something more with her before things went public.

It was obvious that Mac wasn't ready to defend what we meant to each other when she hadn't even figured it out for herself. I couldn't expect her to be where I was—not yet, anyway. She needed time to fall, and I could wait. It wasn't a strength of mine, but I could be patient. She was worth it, and our chance for a future together was worth it, too.

"I'm not being weird," I answered defensively as Abby finished racking his weights. My response had the distinctly argumentative tone of *I know you are, but what am I*, and I felt embarrassingly childish as a result.

My friend's raised eyebrow said he'd heard it too.

"What?" I challenged.

He brushed a hand through his dark hair and then shook his head. "Nothing. You're a shit liar but I'm not going to force it out of you. You'll tell me when you're ready."

Guilt and remorse nearly had me opening my mouth as Abby turned away.

He called back over his shoulder, "I'm doing cardio. I'll see you later."

"See you," I said weakly.

With a sigh, I went to the locker room and gathered my stuff. Abby was right. I was worthless today. No point in hanging around.

When I made it outside, a cold drizzle fell, the sky dark and moody as the early-morning sun struggled to rise. I waited until I'd started my truck and cranked up the heat before pulling out my phone.

The unread message was waiting . . .

MacKenzie: If you can get away for lunch today, you could meet me at the tiny house. It's on the farm, behind the big barn. There's a private lane to the left of the main entrance. Just follow the gravel drive until you get to the little A-frame. You can't miss it.

Five hours later, I didn't even have time to knock before Mac opened the door to the small cottage and yanked me inside.

Her lips fastened to mine, and her eager fingers went to work on my belt.

I awkwardly held the bag of sandwiches I'd picked up at Montell's to one side as I shuffled into the space.

Ah, so this was going to be *that* kind of lunch.

Mac didn't stop until the brown paper bag impeded her from getting my vest all the way down my arms.

She pulled back, red lips plump and tempting. "What's this?"

I smiled tightly. "Lunch?"

Realization dawned. "Oh." Then she brightened. "Good, we'll need to refuel after."

A surprised laugh made its way out of me despite the disappointment gnawing subtly at my belly.

And then Mac was tugging the bag out of my hand and placing it on the counter. She returned and kissed me slowly this time, quieting the whispers of surprise and confusion and the distress I couldn't place. The urgency fell away. Her hands were still eager but less careless and rushed. Her touch lingered as she undressed me, and I returned the favor.

It was easy to forget all the *more* I wanted when her hands were on me, making me think this was enough. It was enough to have her time and her attention. Enough to gather up her smiles and her laughter and keep them for myself. Enough to bend her over the couch and take her the way she wanted, her voice a desperate chant in my ears. I had to be a greedy bastard to want more than her body in my arms, lost to pleasure and clenching desperately around me.

For now, it had to be enough.

By the time our panting breaths quieted and the sweat had cooled on our skin, I wasn't even thinking about the fact that she'd meant this to be an afternoon quickie instead of a real lunch date. It was just a chance to see her, to be with her in the confines I'd established myself.

Later, I was unwrapping the sandwiches while she grabbed plates and drinks.

"What is this place?" I asked. "Does anyone live here?"

Mac shook her head. Her red lipstick was smeared a little, and I figured the evidence was spread somewhere on my skin. "No. Becca was staying here before she moved in with Will. And Chloe lived here briefly before that. But the tiny house was just something we had as a rental property at one time."

I could see that being profitable, but also a huge hassle since it was on Grandpappy's property.

As if reading my mind, Mac continued, "But it ended up being more trouble than it was worth. So we stopped renting it out to tourists and just kept it for ourselves. Will used to crash here a lot. Back when he overworked himself."

I passed her half of an Italian sub before asking, "But Will's not overworking himself anymore?"

She hesitated for just a moment, but then her gray eyes settled on me, and a small, shy smile graced her lips. "Yeah, he's taken a step back from the farm. Actually, you're looking at the new Manager of Farm Operations and Social Media Director."

I straightened on my stool, surprised and pleased and happy for her. Mac had only ever worked at Grandpappy's, as far as I knew, but it had always seemed like something she did to pass the time. Like it was more her family's legacy than hers, and she was just in it for an easy paycheck and to have co-workers she liked.

But I could see from the way she was watching me that my reaction was important. And, if I had to guess, I'd say the shyness and reserve on her pretty face— so surprising and rare—was because she was tentatively pleased with her new role, and not in the smug way I would have expected.

I didn't want to say the wrong thing. Somehow, I knew I couldn't praise her accomplishment or she'd brush it off. I couldn't admit I was proud of her for stepping up and taking something for herself. I knew Mac well enough to know it would make her downplay her position and lash out as a result.

So I gave her an appraising look and said, "Are you telling me I'm banging management? Oh, can you maybe wear a little skirt suit next time? I think I could be into that."

Mac laughed and reached across the kitchen counter to punch me on the arm and then steal my pickle spear. But I could see the relief in her grin, the way her shoulders relaxed from their tense, bracing set.

I grinned and snatched my pickle back. "I wonder if I can wrangle a title for myself at the orchard."

"Oh my God. I knew you'd try to do that." But she was still smiling as she took her first bite.

We ate and chatted for the next twenty minutes. She told me about the tasks she was taking off of Will's plate and handling herself. It sounded like she was eager for the responsibility and happy with the change.

"So, my grandparents are staying another week," Mac said as we finished cleaning up our lunch.

"Oh, yeah?"

"I thought maybe we could meet up here at the tiny house if you wanted. It's close to both of our farms. Nobody will notice." Her voice was tentative, as if she'd shared a secret with me and was waiting to see what I'd do with it.

Did I love the idea of a hookup spot for sneaking around? No, not really. But I had no one to blame but myself. If staying here made it easier for Mac and allowed her to sleep in my arms a little longer before returning home, then I wasn't going to argue. I'd meet her here as often as she'd let me.

"Sounds good," I managed evenly, sliding my vest back on.

She nodded, eyes bright and pleased. "Okay. See you tonight, then?"

"We have trivia tonight," I reminded her.

"Oh, right."

I brought my arms around her and pressed a kiss to her forehead, sneaking in affection as much as we were sneaking behind the backs of everyone in town. "I'm thinking we fight during the third round. That way, we can get booted early, and I can come back here and make you dinner."

She grinned. "I like the way you think. What do you want to argue about?"

I shrugged, ignoring the coiling tension in my shoulder blades. "We'll figure it out as we go." Then I pressed one last kiss to her lips before stepping away. "We always do."

I added staged public fights to our secret arrangement portfolio, alongside a clandestine meeting place in the woods. It was all just another brick laid to build our deception.

Who was I to complain? I thought sullenly. I'd gotten exactly what I'd asked for.

I woke in a panic, gasping in a foreign room while cold sweat dampened my forehead. My eyes searched the low light of the small bedroom until I found Mac curled up beside me.

I breathed out a sigh of relief, unsure what I'd been dreaming of or why I'd snapped awake so violently. But everything was okay. We were at the tiny house, and Mac was still here. She hadn't left yet.

Reaching for the end table, I snagged my cell phone and checked the time. It was only 12:36 a.m., barely morning.

We'd left trivia around seven thirty and stopped by the store to pick up supplies. Then I'd made us a quick dinner of baked lemon dill salmon with rice and a Brussels sprout salad. Unlike earlier in the day, we'd made it to the bedroom before we got each other's clothes off and had fallen asleep not long ago.

I knew Mac had an alarm set to get herself back home around four. But she'd slipped me a key when we'd arrived tonight and told me to stay as long as I wanted.

I looked down at her, breathing deep and even. Her long, dark hair was piled on top of her head in a messy bun, and the red lipstick she favored had faded from her mouth with every brush of my lips. I knew beneath those covers she wore only underwear and an oversized tee shirt because her bare legs had been tangled with mine.

Mac had this tiny little vee between her eyebrows. I grinned to myself as the last of the panic abandoned my system. It was fitting that if I smiled in my sleep, she would frown in hers.

My phone was still in my hand, so I brought up my camera app. The room was dark, but moonlight streamed in from the window that faced the field behind the tiny house. She had a picture of me. It only seemed fair that I take one in return.

I stared at the image of Mac on my screen. The difference was, she'd use my photo to tease me, whereas I'd probably pull up this picture of her and look at it every night before I went to sleep. A portrait in an invisible locket, the weight of it pressing warm and solid against my chest.

I was just about to put my phone back on the bedside table when an alert came through. I straightened as the notification indicated there was motion on the farm that had triggered the floodlights to turn on and the camera to start recording. The settings weren't so sensitive that a bug or even a small animal could cause an alert like that to go out.

Swiping over to the app, I pulled up the live feed. Damn. Right there in the top corner of the video was the blur of a foot in motion. A black-and-red sneaker hustled across the grass on the edge of my screen.

"What is it?"

My eyes found a sleepy Mac rising onto her elbows.

"Someone is at the orchard. The motion sensors were triggered, and the app notified me."

She sat bolt upright. "Well, let's go get them." I opened my mouth to protest, but she cut me off. "And if you say something stupid about me staying here where I'll be safe, I will one hundred percent punch you in the junk."

I thought about arguing, but we were low on time. It was maybe a two-minute drive across the road to my family's property, but the intruder could leave any moment.

We could approach cautiously and call the sheriff's office for backup. I wouldn't let anything happen to Mac.

So I grinned and stood, pulling her to her feet. "Well, we wouldn't want that. You need my junk for stuff."

She gave me a quick smile, but then we were a flurry of motion, pulling on clothes and shoes and scrambling out the door.

Mac hustled to the driver's side of her Jeep.

"What are you doing?" I hissed.

"Driving," she whisper-shouted back.

"Your bright yellow vehicle is pretty conspicuous. Let's take mine."

She thought about it for two seconds before grumbling under her breath and hopping into the passenger side of my truck instead. I tossed her my phone and shifted into gear.

"Can you keep an eye on the live feed and see if you notice anything?"

"Yep," she replied, eyes glued to the screen.

I maneuvered us along the gravel drive back toward the highway. Then, I cut the lights and headed down the private road toward my parents' house. This way, we wouldn't have to get out to unlock the gate at the highway and could approach stealthily from the direction of the main house.

"The chain's still on, and I don't see any getaway cars," Mac observed.

"Yeah," I agreed. "You think they parked down the highway and walked onto the property?"

"That would make the most sense. Want me to call the sheriff yet?"

I hesitated. It would be the smart thing to do, but if the intruder was already gone, it would be one more incident with zero evidence or outcome. The deputy assigned to the case already thought I was an idiot.

"Let's hold off. See what we see."

The truck bumped along the unpaved trail between the house and the orchard. Rows of dormant apple trees lined the right side of the road, which was no more than a worn truck path with two ruts in the grass. The moon was bright enough that I could see where I was going, but I'd been traveling this path for as long as I could remember. I could probably manage it with my eyes closed.

Finally, the Apple House came into view. The floodlights on the eastern side were still blazing and guided us like a lighthouse on a rocky shore. I slowed the truck to a crawl, on the lookout for any movement in the dark surrounding the building.

"There!" Mac shouted, throwing an arm out and pointing to the back of the Apple House where the new berry bushes were planted.

I hit the brakes and threw the truck into park before jumping out and taking off. The figure was dressed head to toe in black and made a startled sound when they caught sight of me. They fell back, scrambling on hands and feet before I was on them, tackling them flat to the ground.

I could hear Mac racing up to where I held a squirming body face down in the grass. They landed a sharp elbow to my midsection that had me grunting out a curse, but once Mac turned a flashlight on us, they quit struggling.

"Call the cops, Mac," I gritted out.

At my announcement, gangly limbs started moving again as the body—much smaller than mine—attempted to buck me off once more.

"Stop! Don't call the police," said a voice that sounded painfully young.

I froze. "Stop wiggling a minute."

Their body complied.

I met Mac's wide-eyed gaze briefly before heaving a sigh. "Okay, I'm going to get off you, but if you try to run, I will tackle you again AND call the cops."

"Okay," they said, breathing hard.

I sat back on my heels. Keeping one arm in my grasp, I urged the trespasser to roll over.

"Shit," Mac whispered from above us. She had the flashlight shining down onto the face of a boy, probably no more than fourteen or fifteen years old. "Aren't you a little short for a burglar?"

The boy glared.

"What are you doing out here, kid?" I asked in frustration. This was someone who should have been in bed on a Monday night, getting ready for school the next day. Not breaking and entering.

"Nothing," he spat. His features were hard and belligerent, but his dark eyes slid behind Mac briefly.

She followed the motion with her flashlight over to where the steady hum of fans sounded louder than normal.

My mouth dropped open at the destruction she'd revealed—strips of nylon, tattered and strewn across the muddy ground. "You killed Brad and Chad!"

The kid tried to yank his arm out of my hold, but I held tight.

"Jeff's still standing, though," Mac said helpfully, turning her light back on the undersized intruder, making him wince.

"Yeah, I guess we surprised you before you had a chance to cut up all of the inflatable tube men."

"Why do you even have those?" the little delinquent asked.

"To keep away the deer," Mac and I answered in unison.

"And why are you out here trespassing and damaging our property?" I asked. "You the paintball perpetrator too, little man?"

"I'm eighteen," he lied indignantly.

"You better hope not, short stuff," Mac said. "Then you'll get tried as an adult."

Even in the warm glare from the flashlight, he visibly paled. "Listen, it was a stupid dare, okay. I barely hurt anything. I'll pay you back. Just don't call the cops."

Mac and I shared a look.

"Who dared you?" I asked.

"Just . . . some kids. My friends," he amended quickly.

"You need some better friends, half-pint," Mac said flatly.

Now, the boy's cheeks flooded with heat, and I felt a small pang—really small, mind you—when I remembered how hard it was to be a teenager. I'd always had good friends, though. I'd been popular and well-liked and hadn't needed to impress anyone overmuch or try to elbow my way into a friend group by committing petty crime.

"What's your name?" I asked.

He hesitated, and Mac shook her phone at him for emphasis. "Amos."

"Amos what?"

"Amos Coates."

Mac and I shared another look, this one longer, with undertones of *ah, fuck*.

I only knew one Coates in Kirby Falls, and it was Rhonda. She was a bartender over at Firefly Cider. She worked for Jordan Rockford and had a lot on her plate. A single mother with no nearby family to speak of. If this was her kid, then there was no way I was letting Mac connect that call to the sheriff's office.

With a sigh, I kept one hand wrapped around the scrawny arm beside me and got us both to our feet.

"This is what's going to happen, Amos Coates," I said sternly. At least, I hoped I was stern. It wasn't something I attempted very often. "You're going to get in that truck, and I'm going to drive you home, where I will speak to your mother about your nighttime activities. You will report here after school tomorrow to start working off the damage you caused."

He made an abbreviated sound of protest, cut off when Mac shined the flashlight in his eyes again briefly.

"And you will work here as long as it takes—with your mother's permission—if you don't want me to let my friends down at the sheriff's department know exactly what you've been up to."

I could feel Mac's attention on me as I spoke.

The kid kept his eyes downcast on his muddy black-and-red sneakers before nodding jerkily.

We all made our way to the truck, the flashlight bobbing across the ground and illuminating ragged shreds of red and blue nylon every so often.

The cab was silent as I drove back across the street to drop Mac off at the tiny house, where her car was parked.

She lingered outside my window, eyeing the surly teenager in my backseat. "Are you sure you don't want me to come with you?" she whispered. "I'm good backup."

I smiled. "Oh, I know. You killed it at bad cop out there tonight."

Mac's lips stretched wide as she took a few steps backward. "Good night, Brady."

"'Night, John Mac-Lane."

Her quiet laughter filled the space between us, making me wish I was following her back inside instead of dealing with the mess I was currently knee-deep in.

My gaze drifted to the rearview mirror and found the kid watching me before he quickly glanced away. I couldn't help but wonder for the hundredth time if I was doing the right thing.

<hr>

I didn't sleep after I left Rhonda Coates's house early this morning. She lived in a small two-bedroom duplex near Tanner Park. Amos had a little sister who was six, and I'd had to keep my voice low to avoid waking her up while Rhonda and I discussed what to do about her son.

Rhonda had been deeply apologetic and mortified to hear about what Amos had been up to. The kid was fourteen and a freshman at Kirby Falls High School. She'd said he had trouble making friends and spent a lot of time playing video games while she was at work. The neighbor on the other side of the duplex babysat for Rhonda in the afternoons and evenings while she worked her shifts at Firefly.

After Amos had stomped off to his bedroom, his mother and I worked out an arrangement to deal with the vandalism and destruction of property. One that didn't involve the sheriff's office or Rhonda attempting to empty her savings account.

I remembered what it was like to be a dumb kid with too much time and energy on my hands. I'd been a troublemaker at a young age before leveling up to class clown during my teenage years. The difference was I had been well-liked, and I'd charmed my teachers and administrators while I was at it.

However, I wasn't blind to the concept of being bored enough to find trouble. I'd just had better influences like Cole Abernathy and a voice of reason in Jase Wilcox. I'd burned off energy playing sports and genuinely enjoyed being part of a team. And I'd had a strong support system in my siblings and parents. Plus, the idea of purposefully damaging someone's property never would have crossed my mind—even on a dare from older kids.

Though, now, staring at the bits of brightly colored nylon that Amos had hacked up behind the Apple House, I was cursing my benevolence.

It was just after seven in the morning. This day was going to be a long one.

"Rest in peace, Brad and Chad," I mumbled as I got to work cleaning up.

It wasn't long before I heard an engine coming down the path between my parents' house and the orchard. Glancing up, I did a double take when I saw a bright yellow Jeep.

Mac hopped out and made her way over to me. She was in worn jeans and a fleecy pullover. Her messy bun was still in place, but the faded lipstick had been replaced with a fresh layer that drew my attention to her mouth. She looked so fucking pretty walking toward me in the cloudy January morning that I had to force a rough swallow before I could speak.

"Hey," I said, confusion evident in my tone.

She gave me a small smile. "I figured you'd been here, cleaning up. Thought I'd come help." I opened my mouth to object, but she shook her head. "It's my day off. I can spend it however I want."

I watched her for a long moment, wondering if she knew that secret hookups who were only in it for the sex didn't really offer to help someone clean up a mess at the crack of dawn. I tried not to read too much into the fact that she was here when she could have been warm in bed without me. But there was a traitorous tightness in my chest that said I wasn't managing it all that well.

"Thank you," I said roughly as she reached into my back pocket for the roll of trash bags I'd stashed there.

She pulled a couple off for herself and then returned the remainder of the roll to my jeans, smacking my ass and grinning on her way to where Chad littered the ground.

When I got to work near her, Mac asked, "So what did Rhonda say? Did y'all decide on a punishment?"

I crouched and grabbed a handful of blue nylon. "Amos is going to help me here after school two days a week for six weeks."

"Did you get a chance to talk to your family?"

"Yeah, I came out here early and had coffee with Mom and Dad, then caught Candy and Joan when they started their run. Everyone was okay with it. Mercer too. Mom insists on feeding Amos an afternoon snack before he starts work, though." I rolled my eyes.

Mac laughed. "Oh, Amy. She's a good one."

Smiling, I agreed, "Yep." My mother was pretty great. She'd put up with me being an overactive pain in the ass often enough; a sullen teenager would probably be a walk in the park.

I still worried I'd taken advantage of my family's generosity. Amos had been young and dumb and reckless, but he'd also snuck onto our property multiple times and caused some destruction—albeit minor. Between the paintballing and the inflatable tube men, it was damage, nonetheless. What if his second attempt hadn't been thwarted by Mac and me? What if he'd smashed all the pumpkins on the farm or burned down apple trees because his idiot friends in the getaway car thought it would be fun to watch our livelihoods go up in flames?

Part of me worried I should have just called the sheriff and let them handle it. That the right path for that boy would be some tough love instead of a second chance to hurt my family again.

"Do you think I made the right decision?" I asked Mac without looking at her. "Handling it myself like that? It was the heat of the moment last night, and maybe I acted without thinking. Too impulsive or—"

"Brady," Mac said quietly, stilling the rambling thoughts pouring directly out of my mouth. Her gray eyes were soft with understanding. "I think you gave that kid and his mother a gift. Amos just doesn't know it yet."

I nodded, still unsure but happy to have Mac's support.

When the scraps of the two inflatable tube men had been picked up, Mac and I stood side by side watching Jeff wave sadly in the cold morning air.

"Brad and Chad Junior will be here by Friday," I offered.

"Oh, thank God," she replied genuinely. "Jeff looked so lonely and pitiful."

We shared a smile.

"Did you think it was hot when I did that flying tackle last night?" I asked, my eyebrows bouncing.

Mac tapped her chin. "You mean when you carelessly launched yourself at an intruder?"

"Well, it sounds less hot when you say it like—"

"Or did you mean when you tackled a fourteen-year-old child to the muddy ground?"

"Okay, never mind." I pressed a hand to my side. "I think I pulled something anyway."

Mac laughed. An honest-to-God giggle that had me swaying closer to her, ready to plant a kiss on her grinning lips.

But then a bright "Hey, y'all!" sounded from behind us, and we stepped away from one another.

We turned to find my sister Candace approaching cheerfully, still in her running gear with her long brown hair in a sweaty ponytail.

"Do I have to separate you two?" Candy teased, reminding me that everyone in town still thought Mac and I hated each other.

I laughed half-heartedly as Mac said, "You know us," in a perky tone that was as artificial as a banana Popsicle.

My sister looked at the two of us, a little wrinkle forming between her brow. "What are you up to this morning, Mac?"

Mac shifted on her feet, and I could tell that she was nervous about getting caught with me. "Oh, you know. I just heard about the incident last night and wanted to clear my name." She gave an awkward chuckle. "Provide an alibi and all that."

Candace laughed like Mac had told a funny joke. "Brady knows it's not you. Actually, he caught the person last night. Just a kid being a kid. So you're off the hook!"

"That's great," Mac managed.

Candy's lips twitched, and she gave us both another curious look. "I was coming down to grab Brady for breakfast. Mom and Mercer are making biscuits and gravy. You should join us, Mac."

"Oh, I wouldn't want to intrude."

"Nonsense. You're my friend. It won't be weird at all."

I stood very still, like I was being stalked by an animal that could sense fear. And in a lot of ways, that was what a nosy sister was.

Candace tugged Mac in the direction of the house amid her protests, and eventually, I followed, equal parts reluctant and eager to see how this played out. If I was being honest, the curious part was winning, pleased at the possibility of having Mac in my family home among the people closest to me.

"Look who I found," Candy announced proudly to everyone gathered in the kitchen.

My mother and father greeted Mac warmly. Between school and sports and the local business community, we'd been in each other's orbits for so long that my family had known Mac since she was a little girl. She was commonly referred to as "the spitfire across the street who gave Brady a run for his money."

Mac was polite, if a little stiff. It looked like she didn't know what to do with her hands. After her second attempt to help with breakfast, my mom led her out of the kitchen to "get her opinion on something."

"What are you making me?" I asked Mercer, who was dutifully stirring something on the stovetop.

The big man didn't take his eyes off the pan of bubbling liquid. "Amy's teaching me to make her gravy."

I smiled. My parents loved Mark Mercer. He was a model employee here on the farm, and now that he was dating Candace, I thought Mom and Dad both hoped he'd officially be family sooner rather than later. It was no secret that they'd considered him a son well before Candy came back home and started seeing him.

Joan was sitting at the breakfast nook, drinking coffee and reading the newspaper. I didn't even know people under forty read the newspaper, but there my grouchy sister sat, still in her running gear, gaze scanning the newsprint.

In general, I liked to joke around and give Joan a hard time. It was good for her. At six years my senior, she was too serious and uptight for her own good.

"Good morning, Joanie." I slid into the seat across from her.

Her blue eyes—the same pale shade as my own—stayed on the paper. "Did you get the inflatables cleaned up?"

"Yep," I answered, popping the final letter obnoxiously. "Mac showed up and lent a hand."

She smoothly turned the page, still focused on her reading. "That was nice of her, considering she was over late helping catch the burglar."

The smile slipped from my face as sinking awareness took hold. I could hear Mac, Candace, and my parents chatting in the living room, but I couldn't make out the words because my heart rate had tripled and blood pounded in my ears. What did my sister know about Mac and me?

I swallowed, attempting nonchalance. "What was that?"

Finally, Joan gave me her attention. "I have that security app on my phone, too, baby brother. And the camera feed works just fine." Then my grumpy-ass sister smirked and went back to her newspaper.

So she knew that Mac had been with me last night. It wasn't like we'd made out in sight of the cameras . . . that time. Whatever Joan thought she knew, I knew I could bluff my way out of any trouble. It would be fine.

"Joanie," I said evenly. "Whatever you're thinking—"

"I *think*," she interrupted firmly, "that it's none of my business."

I wanted to argue or explain, but just then, everyone returned to the kitchen. Mom took over for Mercer at the stove while he and Candace grabbed plates and utensils to set the table in the dining room.

Joan didn't spare me a word or a glance as we all got seated and served ourselves. Mac sat beside me and became much more at ease as the meal progressed, which only seemed fair since I was the one all bent out of shape over my sister's subtle accusation.

My focus had been entirely inward for the first part of breakfast. I'd eaten two gravy biscuits and three pieces of bacon before I felt a foot nudge me beneath the table.

I glanced up to find Mac watching me with obvious concern. *You okay?* she mouthed.

Nodding quickly, I flashed her a smile.

I didn't know why I was so bothered. Joan had implied something was going on between Mac and me. It wasn't the end of the world, but it might be the end of us if Mac got spooked by someone finding out. Yes, the secrecy thing had been my idea, but by now I could tell that Mac liked it. She enjoyed sneaking around. If that was how I had to hold her interest and keep her in this with me, then that's what I would do. But I didn't want harmless teasing from my older sister to impact that.

"Remember when Brady was, like, eight and refused to wear a shirt?" Candace said with a light in her eyes that indicated feral sibling torture was forthcoming.

"Is that why most of his photos on that shelf in the living room are of him topless?" Mac asked, looking amused and earning several laughs.

"It did last for a while," my dad confirmed. "But I had a little man-to-man talk with him and broke the habit."

I snorted at that. "No, you didn't. Mom paid me a dollar after school every day that I kept my shirt on and the teacher didn't have to call home."

My father looked scandalized and betrayed. "Amy, is that true?"

"Yep," my mother replied without remorse.

"So the lesson is," Mac began, "if you want Brady to do something, you have to give him a dollar?"

My family laughed, and I joined them.

When the conversation turned to the other end of the table, I leaned close to Mac and whispered, "That doesn't work anymore. I'm an adult and prudently invested. I now require sexual favors."

Mac choked on her orange juice, and a little dripped down her chin. I passed her a napkin, chuckling.

But when I glanced across the table and caught Joan watching us, I didn't feel like laughing anymore.

MAC

Our February book club meeting was bustling when I arrived. Becca was hosting at the homestead that overlooked Clark land and Grandpappy's below.

The house had originally been my great-grandfather William's. When he'd moved to an assisted-living facility after a difficult dementia diagnosis, he'd asked my cousin Will to take over the responsibility and upkeep of the house. Will had done some renovations here and there throughout the years, and even more now that Becca was in the picture.

The kitchen had been updated months ago, and that was where everyone was now, gathered around the large central island where Becca had arranged a giant charcuterie spread directly onto the surface. It looked like a work of art, with small dishes of jams, dips, and spreads nestled in among fruit, slices of cheese, neatly arranged crackers, and flowers made out of salami and prosciutto. It was honestly too beautiful to eat, but everyone looked to be giving it their best effort.

I greeted Becca with a big hug, then said hello to Chloe and her friend Andie. Magdaline was there from Apollo's restaurant, along with my sister, Bonnie. Candace and Joan Judd were passing out mimosas to everyone. My eyes snagged on Larry sitting at the end of the island on a tall stool. She was a slash of dark in an otherwise bright kitchen, and her mood matched her goth-pixie attire.

Larry had been off for the last couple of weeks. We still saw each other at work, but my tasks kept me mostly in the office. We were officially in the off-season now. There was no corn maze or pumpkin patch or tree lot to staff. But Grandpappy's was still open to the public for hayrides and apple-cannon shooting, and for any visitors to the General Store or the Bake Shop.

Larry and I saw less and less of each other these days. It probably didn't help that I'd been spending most of my free time with Brady. But when my cousin and I did manage to hang out at family dinners at Aunt Maggie's or trivia night, she'd been reserved, not her usual sassy self.

Things had been different since that bonfire last month, and I wasn't sure what was going on. She'd yet to open up about whatever was troubling her. The shift in her mood had me concerned. Larry hadn't confided in me, and the longer she kept dealing with whatever it was on her own, the more worried I became.

I made my way to her now, dragging over a nearby stool and plucking the cracker out of her outstretched hand. "Hey, cousin."

"Hi, Mac," Larry said, tone flat. "You're late."

"I wanted to run home and get changed after closing," I said without meeting her eyes. Brady had stopped by my office after work, and things had gotten a little, ah, messy. Good messy. But I'd needed to run home for a new shirt. And underwear. I bit down on my grin, thinking about how I'd see him later when we finished up our girl dinner and monthly book discussion.

Candace reached between us, passing Laramie a champagne flute. "Hey, Mac, would you like a mimosa? We've got orange, cranberry, and apple."

I smiled, genuinely happy to see Brady's sister. "Hi, Candace. Yeah, apple would be great."

She called over her shoulder. "Joanie, another apple pie mimosa."

"Coming up," Joan replied, then turned to make my drink. I watched as she confidently went to work mixing sparkling wine and fresh-pressed apple cider before draping a curling apple peel on the side of the glass and carefully grating a cinnamon stick with a piece of kitchen equipment I'd never used before.

Brady's sisters were an interesting pair. Candace was bubbly and fun, while Joan was stoic and reserved. Joan was only six years older than me, but somehow she'd always seemed like the adultiest adult in any room. She didn't smile often and laughed even less. But she was one hell of a farmer and would do anything for her family. I'd watched her represent Judd's Orchard over the years and answer any call put out into the community for volunteers or donations.

It was funny to hear Candace call her "Joanie." Joan didn't have the sort of attitude or facial expressions that invited nicknames, but she was here interacting with all of us nonetheless. She kept quiet during book club for the most part, but she was polite and seemed to really listen when people talked. I'd caught her nodding along when Bonnie made a good point or when Becca noted a touching quote from whatever we were reading.

Joan wasn't the sort of person you could just win over with baseless charm. For some reason, I wanted to earn her respect. Hell, I thought I might want to *be* her when I grew up.

"Here you go," Candace said brightly, placing the drink at my elbow.

"Thank you," I said. "Both of you."

Candace smiled and moved down to Magdaline to get her order. Joan nodded at me and tucked a strand of hair behind her ear. It was brown, shot through with a healthy amount of silver. She'd started going gray in her twenties, and I loved that she'd embraced it. It suited her.

Ten minutes later, once the charcuterie spread was demolished, we moved the meeting to the living room. There was more furniture now than there had been the last time I'd visited, and a large area rug really pulled the room together.

We discussed this month's book for the next hour, but I noticed Larry stayed quiet at my side, wedged into the corner of the large sectional sofa. She was usually the first to voice her opinion or call out the miscommunication trope or an unnecessary third-act breakup. But today she mostly nodded along to what everyone else said. Becca tried several times to draw her into the conversation but eventually gave up when Larry persisted in one-word replies.

My worry grew as the evening progressed, and when everyone stood to gather their jackets and bags, I hung back, hoping I could get my cousin alone so we could talk.

I hugged my sister goodbye and promised to grab dinner with her sometime this week, and as I turned back to find Larry, I saw her lingering in the living room with Becca.

The typically cheerful woman wore a serious face as she spoke, and Larry nodded along to whatever she was saying. Then Becca wrapped her in a tight hug.

When they finally broke apart, Becca met my gaze and approached. She didn't say anything, just smiled and squeezed my arm as she passed to say her good-byes to the remainder of her guests.

The concern that had been developing became fully formed after I witnessed their exchange. What did Becca know about my cousin? And why weren't they telling me?

I beelined straight for Larry, wide-eyed and a little frantic. "Are you sick? Are you dying? What is going on?"

Larry's sullen expression turned to one of surprise. "What? No, I'm not dying. What the hell? Why would you think that?"

"Because," I accused, "you've been off for a while. Not talking to me and not being yourself. You're too quiet. Too reserved. And then I see Becca over here comforting you. If I were dying, I'd want Becca to hug me too."

"Oh, Jesus," Larry muttered with an eye roll, completely ignoring my panic. "Come on. Let's go talk in the Jeep."

We grabbed our coats and made our way to my vehicle. I watched my cousin warily while I turned on the engine and cranked up the heat.

"Well?" I prompted, annoyed with how high my voice came out but too worried to care.

Larry rubbed her hands together in front of the vent before sighing. "I'm not dying, Mac. I'm perfectly healthy. I've just been going through some things."

"What things?"

"I . . ." She paused, searching the windshield and the trees beyond for words or courage, I didn't know what. "I'm bi."

I blinked, waiting for her to finish her sentence. When she didn't, I asked, "Bi what?"

Finally, she turned to look at me. "Bisexual, Mac. I am bisexual. I am attracted to both men and women."

My mind went fuzzy like static between stations. I thought about Larry dating Edgar Matthews in the eighth grade and losing her virginity senior year to Justin Crabtree. I thought about the numerous dick jokes over the years and the way she was obsessed with Henry Cavill and his muscles.

"Oh," I managed. Then I thought about how Larry had been acting recently, how she'd been awkward with Kayla and needed backup for the bonfire when her friend had brought a guy with her. "*Oh*," I repeated.

"Yeah," Larry breathed, looking away.

"Wait." I hurried to reassure her. "I don't care about that, Larry. I mean, I do care, but not, like, to judge you or something. You can love whoever you want to love, and I'm going to keep right on loving you. I just mean, what happened to make you so unhappy lately? Did something go down with Kayla?"

I wasn't lying or just trying to tell Larry what she wanted to hear. She was my family, my best friend. All I wanted was for her to be happy. Was I surprised? Sure. Did it change the way I loved my cousin? Not in the least. I was more curious than anything. *And*, a small but peevish part of me whispered, *disappointed she hadn't told me sooner.*

Larry sighed with such force that the windshield fogged. "No. Kayla doesn't know."

"You've never thought about telling her?"

She flopped back against the headrest. "I have thought about it. I want to. I'm just scared. I don't want to lose my best friend because I accidentally fell in love with her."

"What if she feels the same?"

Head still tipped back, she looked over at me. "She doesn't. Or she wouldn't be hooking up with randoms at Magnolia every week."

I pivoted in my seat to face my cousin. "Maybe it's like a multiple-choice test, and Kayla thinks she has to pick A, B, or C without knowing that you're even an option. Maybe she just hasn't considered it because she doesn't know this part of you. Because you've been hiding it your whole life." I worked hard to keep the petty accusation out of my tone, but Larry caught it and gave me a pained look.

"Fuck," I muttered, voice tight. "I'm sorry. I didn't mean that. This is not about me. I just"—sudden emotion made my nose sting—"hate the thought of you going through this alone."

"Mac—"

"I would have been there for you. I love you, okay? All I want is for you to be happy. If that's with a man or a woman or Kayla or whoever. I want it for you."

Larry smiled, watery and barely there, then she reached for my hand. "I'd like to tell you I have it all figured out. That I'm confident and know exactly who I am. But I don't."

I nodded because that made sense. I figured most people didn't know what the fuck they were doing. I sure didn't have my life figured out.

After a long moment, I squeezed her hand and asked quietly, "What's it like? Being with a woman."

Larry did something I didn't think I'd seen since our third-grade talent show when her skirt had gotten stuck in her underwear on stage. She blushed a violent red that I could see even in the cool glow of the dashboard lights. "I don't know," she eventually mumbled.

I frowned. "What do you mean you don't know?"

"I've never been with one. I just know I'm attracted to them. We live in this tiny-ass town. And there's only ever been the way I feel about . . ."

"Oh. Well, maybe you should go out and see what it's all about. We could go to Asheville or Charlotte, even. You could try to meet someone. I could be your wingwoman."

Larry smiled. "I appreciate you offering. But I don't think I'm ready for that."

"Okay," I assured her. "It's up to you, but I'm here for you whenever you're ready."

"Thanks, Mac. And for the record, I wasn't scared to tell you because I thought you wouldn't support me. I just—I didn't know how. Becca found out by accident. I was drunk and rambling, and she guessed. Anyway, I just wanted you to know."

I nodded, the petty, shameful part of me slightly relieved to know that she hadn't intended to reveal the truth to Becca. "Thank you for telling me. And I won't say anything to anyone. This is your decision—when and who you let know you."

"I love you, MacKenzie Eloise."

Smiling, I said, "I love you too, Laramie Annabeth."

Time passed quick and easy from the chill of February into the dampness of March, the way anything comfortable does. Like floating warm and lazy in the middle of the lake, time drifted away from me.

One minute, Brady and I were rushing to get each other's clothes off, and then we were wading into calmer waters. He cooked dinner for me and left notes on the windshield of the Jeep. He texted me throughout the day, making me laugh, and showed up at my office in the afternoon, making me smile in a variety of ways.

If we didn't have the benefit of secrecy keeping us in a tidy box, I would have said I was in a relationship, dating the boy next door. But all I had to do was recall the agreement we'd made, how Brady had required we keep this thing to ourselves. It was easier then to remember we were just having fun, fooling around and playing out some covert mission to the tune of our inexplicable attraction and lust-addled bodies.

When the end of March brought my birthday, Brady showed up on my doorstep one Friday evening with two sacks full of groceries and a gift bag with sparkly tissue paper.

"What are you doing?" I asked in surprise as he shuffled by me and into the kitchen.

"Making your birthday dinner," he replied easily while divesting himself of his burdens.

My stomach fluttered, but it was probably just in anticipation of Brady's cooking. He really knew his way around the kitchen. I ignored the swoopy sensation in my middle and said, "I didn't tell you it was my birthday."

Brady just rolled his eyes. "I've known you since preschool, MacGyver. Of course I know when your birthday is. I've had so many of Maggie's cupcakes during classroom celebrations that I can practically taste them in my sleep."

"It wasn't that many. I'm only twenty-eight, you jackass."

"Twenty-nine," he corrected with a dimple-popping grin.

Then he snagged the gift bag off the counter and said, "Close your eyes."

"Why?" I narrowed them instead.

"Good girls have to follow directions if they want their presents."

"I think we both know I'm not a good girl."

He bit his lip briefly, distracting me, before replying, "Oh, sometimes you are a very good girl."

Heat blazed a path through my middle, and I cursed the way my body still seemed unsure how to handle this inconvenient attraction. In all these months, it hadn't worn away or gotten easier to ignore. But I closed my eyes like he asked rather than jump him in the kitchen.

I heard the tissue paper rustle and smiled to myself, realizing he was opening my own damn present. Something soft and warm settled around my shoulders before Brady gently scooped my hair out of the way and wrapped it around my neck.

"Okay, you can open them."

I blinked, finding him watching me, more serious-faced than usual.

Looking down, I saw that there was a red knitted scarf draped around me. The yarn was variegated and soft between my fingers, and the scarf was long enough to loop around my neck twice.

"Do you like it?" Brady asked shyly, hands worrying the tasseled ends.

I nodded, touched by his thoughtful gesture. This wasn't the same as him grabbing lunch and surprising me in my office or leaving a candy bar in my Jeep because he knew I was on my period and craved chocolate like crazy.

This was something else.

"Thank you," I said, meaning it. Then I smirked. "Bet you've been dying to do this."

"What? Ensure you dress weather appropriate?"

I shook my head. "No, strangle me and dispose of the body."

He laughed, bright and happy—and if I had to guess, a touch relieved. Then he used the ends of the scarf to tug me forward, off-balance and into his arms.

I hugged him hard, laughing too. "Thank you. I love it," I repeated.

"Happy birthday," he murmured into the sensitive skin below my ear, making me shiver.

When we separated, Brady went back to his grocery bags, unloading ingredients for what would be an undoubtedly tasty dinner.

I examined the scarf more closely, noting the tidy knitted rows. "This is really pretty. Did your mom knit this?"

"Nope," he said absently, grabbing a pot out of a cabinet and moving to fill it with water.

That weird hollowed-out feeling in my gut returned as my fingers smoothed over the soft yarn. "Brady, did you knit this scarf?"

He grinned at me over his shoulder.

I straightened, alarmed. "Shut up. You did not."

"I did," he confirmed easily, rooting around until he found a box of pasta in the mess of items on the countertop.

"You can't be serious." He'd *made* this for *me*? "Am I being *Punk'd*?"

"Pretty sure no one has been *Punk'd* since 2007."

I stepped around the center island and stood next to him, eager for his attention. "You knit? *You* are a knitter? One who traffics in handknits?"

He shrugged like it was no big deal and not the single greatest revelation of my life, besides the butt-tattoo thing. "Yeah. My mom taught me. We started with crochet, and then once I got that down, we switched to knitting. I was always a busy kid, couldn't sit still and caused trouble when I got bored. On nice days, I'd go outside and kick a soccer ball because that was what I liked doing. But when it was cold or rainy, I'd knit. I liked the repetition, the sense of producing something and seeing the quantifiable results."

Brady said all this easy enough, like it wasn't an admission. Like it was just something to chat about while he gathered and prepped vegetables for the saucepan. He and I were so different. If I had revealed something so personal about myself, I would have been snapping and snarling like a distrustful mutt, afraid someone would use my vulnerability against me.

But I could remember a young Brady in elementary school, how he'd been a troublemaker early on before he'd eventually embraced his class clown persona. Oftentimes, he'd been hyper and unable to sit still. Some teachers had been better than others at managing his energy and keeping his attention.

In third grade, our teacher had let him stand up and walk around if he needed to, not requiring him to stay seated while he listened. There'd been Mrs. Ostler in sixth grade who'd given him a fidget block that he kept in his desk. But early on, there had also been educators who'd made him sit out in the hall when he talked too much or called him out in front of the class when he hadn't paid attention.

Something I'd noticed over the years was that if Brady liked something and was engaged in it—like soccer or geography and maps—he could stay focused, no problem. But if it was fourth-period biology that basically had us regurgitating the textbook, then he had trouble. He'd skipped that class a lot junior year.

Brady was never on the honor roll, and he hadn't received any academic awards on banquet night, but he'd utilized his athleticism and his personality. He was a charmer, and teachers liked him. In high school, he came in early and stayed late. It was obvious he didn't like reading our biology assignments, but he helped Mr. Ammons set up experiments and participated in extra-credit events at the local wildlife center to bring his grade up.

Hearing Brady speak so casually about his ADHD made me wonder how he managed the specifics of it now. Then I thought more about the way he could focus easily on the things he cared about and how his attention on me had never wavered.

I swallowed and wrapped the scarf more snugly around me. "You're a man of many talents, Brady Judd."

He gave me a pleased grin, then went back to chopping onions.

"So how's it going with Amos lately?" I asked, suddenly eager to change the subject.

It had been nearly two months since the kid had gotten caught and been put to work. Brady had mentioned him a few times but didn't say if his punishment was over yet. At first, it had been pretty rocky. Amos had a typical teenage attitude. The little punk hadn't realized he'd been lucky in the long run.

"Good," Brady offered. "His six weeks were up a while back, but he kept showing up. I've been setting aside wages for his mom, figured it was the right thing to do. He's been helping me prune, and we'll have pest control to manage soon. The kid has actually taken to Joan. Follows her around like a puppy, asking questions."

The teen with the chip on his shoulder and the grumpy farmer. The image made me smile. "And she actually answers him?"

"Oh, yeah. She's way more patient with him than she is with me." Brady laughed.

Eventually, Brady didn't let me get away with just standing and watching. Despite my protests and evidence of being horrible in the kitchen, he was pretty determined to teach me a thing or two. We made it through meal prep with minimal incident and enjoyed a casual dinner together in the sunroom.

After I'd shoveled in the last bite of my individual-sized chocolate-peanut-butter lava cake, I heard a sound from outside.

"What's that?" Brady said, setting his plate aside and rising to his feet.

I joined him at the back door as we watched a shaggy black bear wrap its paws around the hanging birdfeeder.

I sighed. "That's my grandmother's bear."

"What?" he asked, incredulous.

"See her left ear?"

Brady's breath fogged the glass as he peered out into the dark.

"She comes around every now and then and breaks the birdfeeder," I explained. "My grandma Nola loves her."

"Well, don't worry," Brady said, opening the door. "I'll protect you."

I rolled my eyes. "She's just hungry and probably couldn't find a full trash can anywhere. And I don't need protecting," I shouted over the sound of Brady loudly clapping his hands, trying to get the bear to move along.

As expected, the bear ignored Brady's efforts. But then movement off to the side of the porch caught my eye. Two smaller furry bodies were sniffing eagerly along the flower bed. The bear cubs looked young and adorable. However, their presence just complicated matters. Black bears weren't really aggressive unless they felt like their offspring might be threatened.

"Brady," I hissed right as the bear raised her head and abruptly abandoned the birdfeeder, attention focused on her cubs and their proximity to the two dumb humans.

Reaching forward into the chilly night, I snagged Brady by the back of the shirt and yanked. "Get inside!"

The momma bear was already on the move.

"Shit," Brady said, scrambling back as he finally caught sight of the two cubs and their enraged mother. We hurriedly slammed the glass door as she charged across the yard.

The two little cubs kept up their perusal, totally oblivious. And I breathed a sigh of relief when the momma bear veered in their direction, pace slowing.

Brady and I retreated further into the room as we watched the bear family through the glass doors of the sunroom. Eventually, the babies made it over to the birdfeeder, and then all three bears went to work dismantling it and eating the contents.

"Damn," I muttered. "That's the fourth feeder she's busted this year."

Then I snapped a picture for my grandmother.

"They are really cute," Brady said with a big smile on his face, like a four-hundred-pound bear hadn't just herded him back indoors.

Eventually, we cleaned up and made our way to my bedroom, where Brady peeled off my clothes and gave me another present for my birthday. He was focused only on me and my pleasure until we collapsed boneless and spent. He asked if he could stay the night, and while it wasn't something I ever let myself do at his place, I found myself saying yes easily enough.

Brady borrowed some toothpaste and climbed under the covers naked, making himself right at home.

It wasn't until later, when Brady was wrapped around me like a weed, that I wondered about him showing up here tonight, eager to spend my birthday with me—something a boyfriend might do.

He hadn't asked why I was home tonight or why I wasn't out celebrating with Larry or Becca or anyone else. Truth be told, there was going to be a party for me tomorrow at my parents' house, and most of my family would be there.

For a wild moment, I realized I wanted to invite him. I wanted him with me. In front of God and everyone.

But as he breathed evenly into the side of my neck and my fingers carded through the soft hair at his nape, I reminded myself that Brady wasn't my boyfriend—he wasn't mine in truth. And I should just keep my mouth shut and not get too comfortable.

The next morning, I awoke to the sound of the garage door opening and sat up in alarm.

Brady grumbled something and pressed his face into my pillow, one ass cheek hanging out from beneath the covers, a double cheeseburger on full display.

I stood, grabbing the first article of clothing I could find—Brady's hoodie—and ran to the window. Shoving the curtains aside in a panic, I peered down to see my grandparents' RV backing into the driveway. "Oh shit," I breathed.

What were they doing here? I mean, technically, this was their house, but they were supposed to be in Florida until Easter. I grabbed my phone off my bedside table and checked the time—7:02 a.m.—and then cursed when my calendar app didn't reveal the answer to my question. Easter was still a week away.

Why were they here early?

With frantic movements, I grabbed the closest pair of pants—Brady's joggers—and sat down on the edge of the bed to slide them on. A tanned forearm snagged me around the waist and attempted to drag me back to bed.

"No," I whispered. "We can't go back to sleep. You have to get up."

Brady tugged me closer, his face burrowing into my messy hair. "Uh-uh," he complained.

"My grandparents are here," I hissed, trying to free myself from his hold so I could go downstairs and run some interference.

A door slammed somewhere, and I froze.

Brady's eyes popped open. "Okay, I'm up."

I wriggled out of bed. "Stay here. I'll go distract them."

He opened his mouth to say something, but I was already rushing out my bedroom door and closing it gently behind me.

I reached the kitchen just as my grandparents came through the front door with what looked like their second load of luggage.

"Mac!" they said in unison when I came into view.

"Hi, guys," I returned.

"Sorry if we woke you, honey," Grandma offered.

"It's okay," I said, walking over and giving them both a hug.

Grandma took in my appearance, forehead lines crinkling. "You don't have any clothes that fit?"

I swallowed uncomfortably, noting that Brady's rec league softball hoodie was definitely two sizes too big and his joggers dragged the ground while being snug through my hips. "I, uh, need to do laundry."

She nodded like she understood. "Me too, sugar. We took the long way and have been cooped up in that RV for two days. I can't wait to take a long, hot bath."

"What are you doing here?" I asked.

Grandma smiled. "We came home for you, birthday girl. Your mother invited us to your party tonight. We wouldn't miss it."

"Oh," I breathed, surprised they'd returned to Kirby Falls early, just for me.

"I'm going to get the rest of the food out of the RV," my grandfather said quietly before letting himself back out the front door.

Once he was gone, Grandma Nola narrowed her eyes and said, "Okay, spill, MacKenzie Eloise."

"What?" I nearly choked.

"Who do you have upstairs in your bedroom, young lady?"

"Grandma!" I hissed and then lowered my voice. "I am a grown woman." And I'd never once brought a man home. There were limits to the humiliation of living with my grandparents. I loved them, but I was not about to parade some hookup or casual fling in front of them. And, Brady, well . . . he was something else entirely. But that didn't matter. I hadn't known they'd be rolling in this morning at the ass crack of dawn.

"I'm aware," she replied, unbothered. "I took you to get your first bra. Remember?"

"Oh my God," I moaned, wishing she wasn't so damn sassy. "Can we not?"

"Whose car is in the garage? And when can I meet him? Bring him down. I'll make eggs."

She was way too delighted by the prospect. And, truthfully, if Brady and my grandma met, they would probably be best friends, texting each other memes and cooking together on the weekends. *Jesus*.

I gave up. "You can meet him the next time you visit. Not right now. It's not a good time."

"Because he's naked?" she asked seriously.

I could feel the blush creeping up to my hairline.

"Wow," she murmured. "Your face is really red."

A hysterical laugh burst out of me. "Grandma! Stop it."

"Okay, fine." She grinned. "I'll go out and keep your grandfather busy. I'll tell him I heard the RV making a weird sound. You go smuggle your man friend—"

"Don't call him that," I groaned.

"—out the back. Tell him I look forward to meeting him next time."

I nodded. "Thank you for covering for me with Grandpa."

"Honey, neither one of you is ready for that conversation."

While I hurried up the stairs to my bedroom, I couldn't help but think about the next time my grandparents would be in town. Grandma Nola wasn't going to forget this. It would probably be Memorial Day before they returned. They threw a big party at Lake Archer every year.

I wondered how much longer Brady and I would be able to keep this up.

My steps slowed as my chest grew inexplicably tight.

Would we still be sleeping together by the summer?

The uncomfortable ache over my sternum only worsened. *Sleeping together*. I hated how that sounded. But what else were we really doing? We weren't dating. We were secrets and lies. Rivals to the outside world, sniping on social media, starting fake arguments at trivia night, and bickering for fun at bonfires, while we stole glances and touches where we could find them.

We were something *else* behind closed doors. Something that had become soft and comfortable without me noticing. The longest non-relationship I'd ever managed.

I was frustrated and overthinking when I opened the door to my bedroom.

Brady spun around from his place by the window and made a sound I would have gladly teased him about if I hadn't been suddenly bitter and angry for no damn reason I could pinpoint.

He was still naked, with a pillow in front of his middle.

"Why didn't you get dressed while I was gone?" I said.

Brady blinked like I was an idiot and then motioned in my direction with his free hand. "Did you want me to grab something out of your closet?"

"Oh, right." I was wearing all of his clothes.

We did a frantic clothing swap while I explained that we had only a few minutes to get him out the back door and to my Jeep while my grandparents were occupied. I told him we could switch cars later. I failed to mention that my grandmother was in on everything. I figured Brady would vote for an introduction and eggs if he had that tidbit of information.

We managed to sneak down the stairs and out through the sunroom. Pausing briefly, we took in the bears' destruction from the previous night. It was unapologetic in the light of day, bits of plastic birdfeeder scattered and the iron pole that once held it bent to an unnatural angle.

"Damn," Brady said.

"I'll pick up another one this weekend," I said with a sigh. "Let's go."

We hurried to where my Jeep was parked near the side of the house. I pushed the keys into his hand as his lips pressed against my forehead.

"I'll text you later," he said before sliding into the Jeep. "Look at us. Doing covert spy shit."

I chuckled and shook my head, the irritation from earlier draining away as I watched him grin from behind the wheel of my car.

"I'll see you later, you maniac."

It wasn't until that afternoon when I got home from work that my grandmother was able to corner me.

I'd planned to slink up to my room and get ready for my birthday party, but she popped out from the half bath on the first-floor hallway and scared the shit out of me.

"Jesus," I gasped, grabbing my chest.

"Good. You're home." She grinned, white teeth flashing. She looked so innocent with a sleek gray bob, pleated trousers, and a cardigan set. But I knew better.

"You're a menace," I said, walking into the kitchen.

"I know. I want to show you something."

I eyed my grandmother warily as she led me toward the sunroom. Then it clicked. The birdfeeder. The damage from the bear last night.

"Sorry, I forgot to tell you," I said, still following her. "Your little friend stopped by with two babies in tow and destroyed your . . ." My words trailed off as the backyard came into view. The broken pieces that had been scattered around were gone. In their place stood a brand-new pole—sturdier-looking than the previous one—with a replacement birdfeeder on top. Three starlings were gathered around, pecking at the new offerings while a squirrel hopped beneath, content to grab what the birds dropped.

"A nice boy brought that by and left it on the front porch," Grandma said.

I cut my gaze to hers, eyes wide.

She smirked. "He looked very familiar. In fact, I'm pretty sure he was the Judd boy from across the street. The one who accused you of vandalizing their property."

My heart was beating very fast all of a sudden. "You should have your eyes checked," I managed, pretty proud of myself.

Grandma just cackled, utterly entertained. "I stopped him before he could leave and introduced myself. He said he was delivering for Burke's Hardware. He gave me a fake name that I'm relatively sure was a character in a James Bond film."

I groaned, and she laughed again.

"He stayed and put the birdfeeder in for me. We chatted for a bit."

A moment passed while I watched the birds enjoying their supper, not sure what to say, even less sure how to explain.

Eventually, my grandmother asked quietly, "Why didn't you want him to meet us?"

"It's complicated." My voice was sandpaper rough and barely above a whisper. But the answer in my head—the one I couldn't say—was loud, a vicious reminder. *We're a secret. He doesn't want anyone to know.*

"What's complicated about it? Are you embarrassed of us?"

I quickly turned to face her. "No, Grandma. Of course not. We're—we're keeping it a secret. It's complicated for the reason you just said. He's the boy from across the street. He's a Judd. And he accused me of vandalism, among many other things over the years. We've fought like cats and dogs our whole lives. Everyone in this town knows who we are to each other."

"No," she replied, blue eyes gentle. "They might know who you've *been* to each other. But only the two of you know the truth."

When I didn't respond, my grandmother smiled, the laugh lines around her eyes and mouth deepening. "I like him."

That made me chuckle despite my mood. "Everyone likes him." *Even me*, I thought wearily.

"Even you," she said, reading my mind like a damn television infomercial psychic.

I swallowed.

She laughed again. "Sometimes, the way we feel changes, Mac. And that's okay. Maybe you *did* fight like cats and dogs. Maybe you did hate him." *No, I didn't*, my heart protested. "But it's not admitting defeat now because your point of view shifted. I've known your grandfather for almost fifty years. Don't you think we've changed? How you care about someone changes with you. Love isn't a true-or-false statement. It's a spectrum, and it sounds like you've experienced both ends."

My nose was stinging and I didn't think I could answer her. I couldn't bring myself to argue and say Brady and I were just fooling around. That it wasn't anything serious. My mouth wouldn't have formed the words if I tried.

"It's okay to be happy, Mac. Even if you didn't expect to be."

She sounded hopeful, but I didn't know if what she'd said was true. Expectations were weighty, cruel things. They pinned you in place and held you hostage, if you let them. Like butterfly wings on a board.

Finally, she said, "You should have invited him to your party tonight, sweet pea."

With a knowing smile and a squeeze to my hand, my grandmother turned and walked back into the kitchen.

I listened to her footsteps fade, and when I was sure she couldn't hear me, I whispered to myself, "I know."

BRADY

The door swung open, and Mac said, "'Bout time."

I stepped inside and toed off my shoes. "Sorry, Your Majesty. Some of us don't get to sit in an office all day. I wanted to shower and change."

"You could have showered here with me." Her grin was sharp, a challenge.

I wrapped my arms around her and hauled her close, rasping into her neck, "We both know I wouldn't have gotten clean that way."

Mac's giggle broke off as my lips worked their way down the column of her throat. "Yes," she groaned. "Keep doing that."

It had been nearly two weeks since I'd been over to her place and vice versa. Her grandparents had stayed through Easter. The RV had pulled out earlier today en route to Florida once more. For some reason, Mac hadn't been open to sneaking out or using the tiny house like we had in the past. We'd still texted, and I'd visited her office at Grandpappy's, but she'd made her excuses about spending our evenings together.

However, earlier today, I'd gotten a message announcing Nola and Junior's departure, saying we were in the clear and the house was ours if I was free. I'd let the text sit there for all of twelve seconds before replying. Of course I'd be there.

I'd missed her, missed this.

As my hands drifted beneath the hem of her shirt, teasing and slow, I could feel her trying to rush us. Her fingers were at my waistband doing terrible, distracting things. For as much as I was eager for her touch, I wouldn't be hurried along. This was the first time I'd had her all to myself in weeks, and I didn't plan on racing to the finish line.

In a surprise move, I released her and bent low, lifting her over my shoulder.

Mac made a strangled sound and swatted my backside. "I hate when you do that. Give me a warning next time."

I landed a solid smack to her jeans-covered ass, grinning as she yelped. Then I made my way up the stairs to her bedroom. It reminded me of our first time together. She'd been eager then, too. Hell-bent on getting me out of her system and shoving me from her mind.

We'd come a long way in six months, but not nearly far enough.

Mac laughed as I tossed her down on top of the bed, dark hair fanned out like a siren. I crawled over her, unwilling to have any more space between us.

For long minutes, we just made out, lips eager and hands skimming over each other's bodies. I could feel her impatience in nails scored along my sides and the tug of her teeth on my bottom lip. But I still wasn't ready to strip her down and sink into her, no matter how good I knew it would feel.

To appease her restlessness, I lifted her shirt and shifted my attention to her breasts. Pushing down the cups of her lacy bra, I licked and sucked and nibbled her pale flesh, only running my tongue across her pebbled nipples when I felt her hands slip into my hair. I loved how soft Mac was here, a contrast to all the sharp edges she presented to the world. But I knew that somewhere inside lurked a tender heart, fierce for her loved ones but capable of softness too.

I trailed kisses down her stomach, noting that her jeans were already unbuttoned and unzipped, ready and waiting.

Well, she'd have to wait for what she really wanted a little longer. I tugged her pants and underwear down her thighs, and then I settled between them, enjoying another one of her soft places.

"Yes," she moaned, fingers moving frantically along my scalp, reaching for purchase as I licked her pussy deep and slow. I wanted her to be patient, to enjoy the ride. I wanted her attention and her focus, to really feel the connection between us.

Sex had never been like this for me—not with anyone else. Mac was special, and what we had was important. I just needed her to see it, to feel it, too.

I pushed two fingers slowly inside, relishing the tightness and the moan she let out. Her hips started moving, asking for more. So I gave it to her, suddenly desperate to be the person who met all of her needs.

My focus never wavered. Her pleasure had every bit of my attention as awareness seeped in. All her urgent little sounds, the way her body moved as she climbed higher and higher.

Finally, her limbs tensed, hands tightening in my hair. Then she was coming hard against my tongue, rhythmic pulses around my thrusting fingers. I gentled my touch and finally pulled away, resting my head on her thigh and gazing up the length of her body.

Mac was breathing hard, her face flushed pink in the warm light of her bedroom. And her eyes were on me. I pressed a wet kiss to her inner thigh and smiled.

She smiled back. "Get up here."

So I did, suddenly helpless to resist whatever Mac wanted.

When I'd undressed and settled on top of her, she grabbed my face and kissed me deeply. I groaned, knowing she was tasting herself on my tongue.

My dick was cradled against her pussy. She was hot and wet and insanely inviting.

Mac gave a tiny roll of her hips and then paused. "I'm on birth control. And I'm healthy. If you wanted to skip the condom."

I swallowed hard, wanting that and trying hard not to show how much. To feel her bare, with nothing between us.

Instead, I nodded solemnly and said, "If you're sure?"

"I haven't done that before, but I wouldn't have mentioned it if I wasn't sure."

I was immensely grateful that she trusted me in this moment and willed her to see that this wasn't just some hookup. It was more.

We were more.

Her gray eyes held a challenge, and as I watched, her hips shifted again, rubbing my length through her center.

I held her gaze as I took myself in hand, guiding the head of my shaft to her entrance. Then I pushed slowly inside.

I could feel the tendons of my neck straining against the pleasure of it as I held myself tightly in check. Trust Mac to get her way—to hurry things along and let her impatience win. Because I was not going to last long in the viselike grip of her sex, in the all-consuming heat, the vital intimacy that had me bowing my head against her shoulder and cursing every bit of how good she felt.

She clenched around me as she laughed. "Did I break you?"

I shook my head. Words weren't going to happen. My thoughts were fractured into sentence fragments and broken exhalations. *Too good* and *Jesus, fuck*. Then *Please, please keep me*.

My movements were tentative at first as I strove to feel everything and commit it to memory. The overwhelming pressure and the generous warmth. The way her red lips shaped my name on a ragged gasp. But then my instincts took over, and my thrusts grew faster and deeper. I ground myself against her, the way I knew she liked, and her legs wrapped around me in answer.

It didn't take long for both of us to spiral over the edge, coming in a rush of sweaty limbs and greedy touches.

Chest heaving, I rolled to the side so I didn't crush her. My shoulder pressed against hers, and I felt her leg hook over mine, keeping us close and connected.

"Jesus," I exhaled, as I stared unseeing eyes at the smooth ceiling overhead.

"I know," Mac agreed heavily from my side.

The longer we lay side by side, unmoving, the more my thoughts intruded, drawing me out and away from the moment. I worried Mac would push me away or make light of what had happened between us—what *kept* happening between us.

So I started talking, a desperate need to keep us right here, in this together. "What's your favorite prank we ever pulled on each other?"

That startled a laugh out of her. "Oh, God. I don't know if I can pick." Then after a moment, "Remember when you signed me up to run for homecoming, and I actually placed and got a spot on the court?"

I grinned. That had been fun. "You just like that it backfired on me."

"Well, yeah." But I could hear the smile in her voice, though I was suddenly too chicken to turn my head and confirm. "What's your favorite?" she asked.

"In fifth grade, when you won the contest to name the road the new library was on." My lips tugged up on the corners. "Brady Buttface Boulevard was legendary. Ten out of ten. No notes."

Mac cackled delightedly and buried her face in my arm. When she'd recovered, she admitted, "I spent every minute that summer reading so I could log the most hours and win."

"You were dedicated," I admired. "Like a sociopath."

She laughed again and rolled to face me. I turned, too, propping an elbow up and resting my chin in my hand.

Mac's expression was warm with the levity of our shared history. But there was so much more to it than that. Moments that were tainted with regret and shame— at least on my part.

"I used to go to Tanner Park with a soccer ball. Just hoping to run into you," I confessed.

Her smile changed, lips parting in surprise as her gray eyes softened. "You did?"

I nodded. "I said I was just going out to shoot, but I knew you went with your friends sometimes. Twelve-year-old Brady wasn't very enlightened."

She poked a finger into my bare chest. "I'm not so sure that twenty-eight-year-old Brady is all that enlightened," she teased.

I grabbed her finger and placed a kiss against the pad of it before twining our hands together. And instead of looking at her face, I stared at our fingers woven around one another when I admitted, "I had a crush on you. And like a lot of stupid little boys, I went about it all wrong. I teased you and picked on you, looking to get your attention even if it was with some nasty comment or stupid prank. I think after a while, the negative parts stuck."

The confession pressed a heavy hand around my heart, squeezing until I felt my pulse pound like a drum. I risked a glance at Mac, and she looked dumbfounded.

Maybe it had been stupid to tell her that. There was a helpless and vulnerable voice in my head, calling me every inch a fool. Too much altogether and more than she was willing to hear.

But then her gaze softened, amusement curling her faded red lips. "I don't know that chopping off my pigtail was the best way to go about making your feelings known, Brady Buttface."

I smiled, grateful for her response. "You're still bitter about that one, huh?"

"No six-year-old looks good with an asymmetrical cut. I looked like I was going to ask to speak to the manager."

We both laughed at the thought of a first-grade Mac with an emergency haircut and the image it provoked. Mine undoubtedly faded and timeworn tender while Mac's was probably sharper and bolder, like a drawing you'd traced over and over, committing it to vengeful memory.

So much of my youthful stupidity had come about with the intent of keeping and holding Mac's attention. As we'd grown older, my goals had remained the same. I'd watched dates and hookups come and go, losing her interest. Men that had been forgotten or discarded after a week, a month.

I'd chosen to make myself interesting instead. My methods hadn't been the best, but I hadn't been able to stand the thought of her forgetting me. I'd wanted to be memorable, a constant in her life, separate from her family but no less important. To be her last thought before she went to sleep.

Sure, good thoughts would have been nice, too, but I'd taken annoyance and irritation because it meant I was still hanging on, still relevant to the girl who'd occupied my own thoughts so desperately.

And now, after everything, I wanted to burrow down so deep that she'd never be able to get me out.

When our laughter faded, I squeezed her hand and said, "This is where you say you also liked me and just tortured me because you were trapped in the mindset of a second grader with a fruitless crush, too."

Mac grinned. "Nice try. No, I genuinely wanted to torture you."

"Really?"

"Yes, really. Although"—she paused dramatically—"when I was in high school, I definitely thought you were hot."

"Thank you."

She chuckled. "But I guess I stayed mad enough over the pranks you pulled and the things you said that the idea of not torturing you seemed a lot like losing. And I knew you could take it, whatever I dished out. You weren't going to tattle or whine about it. You were going to give it to me right back. I liked that you were never careful with me. As messed up as it was, we gave each other shit, but it was . . . fun. I wanted to strangle you half the time, but I also had to keep myself from smiling, if that makes any sense."

It did. It made so much sense. Our brains must have been warped in the same way.

I stayed quiet a moment, parsing through the memories and the immaturity that had driven her farther and farther away from me over time.

Eventually, Mac cleared her throat. "Since we're making decades-old confessions, I guess I should tell you that I overheard you and your friends." I frowned. "Junior year. Floyd was running his mouth about feeling me up, and you told him not to even bother. That I wasn't worth it, something like that. It's not important, but that was why I was so mean to you afterward and during senior year."

Mac's attention skittered away from my face, and I figured she remembered more than she was letting on.

An awful awareness left me stunned. I hadn't even considered that she might have overheard that conversation. I remembered it well. Probably because I regretted it so much. There had been the panic at hearing that Floyd was interested in her. The terrible, untrue things I'd said to warn him away. I'd told him she wasn't worth the effort. That nobody even wanted her, and she wasn't even pretty. When in reality I'd been an immature asshat, too scared to go after her myself and desperate to keep my friend from dating her.

"Mac," I sighed. I untangled our hands and cupped her jaw, drawing her gaze back to me, hoping she could see every ounce of shame I felt. "I'm so sorry I said those things. It was shitty of me. I was young and stupid, but that's no excuse. When I realized that my friend was thinking about going after you, I was jealous and misguided. I wish you'd told me. Or confronted me. Or punched me in the damn mouth."

She laughed a little at that. "I wanted to, but I think I was too stunned to manage it at the time. When you're seventeen, you didn't just keep walking when you heard three boys gossiping about you on the high school bleachers. You lurked, and you listened. And then you got even. You know what they say about eaves-droppers anyway."

My chest squeezed with regret. "I didn't mean it. I thought you were beautiful and funny and so smart-mouthed and sassy. There has never been a time when I've been able to ignore you."

"So you didn't want me, but you didn't want anyone else to have me either?"

"No," I admitted. "I wanted you. I just wasn't brave enough to make it happen. I'd thought we had too much history between us, and then after that conversa-tion, I tried being nice, thinking it might make a difference—that it might give me a chance. But you'd been angrier than ever, rebuffing any effort I made to talk to you. And I don't blame you," I hurried to add. "I didn't deserve another chance. Eventually, I fell back into what was easy between us—petty arguments and pranks."

"Is that why you stopped being friends with Floyd?" she asked quietly, brows furrowed. "Because he went after me?"

"No. I hated what happened and the way he'd gossiped and badmouthed you afterward, spreading those rumors. That was why he lost my friendship."

"Did you—that night at Abby's . . ." Her voice trailed off, but the question was loud and clear.

"Yeah, that's why we got into it that night at the bonfire," I confessed, feeling flayed open, a beating heart that had her name stamped all over it.

"So you've defended me twice now?" She brought her hand up to cover mine, her thumb brushing gently over my knuckles.

I thought about the shoving match with Floyd Ellerby and the standoff with Connor Pritchard, and I shook my head. "Not because you needed me to. I know you're more than capable of taking care of yourself. But because those two assholes are cowards. The only way they're brave enough to talk shit about you is behind your back, and *that* is what I couldn't allow. It had nothing to do with your pride, Mac, and everything to do with standing up for what's right."

"Thank you," she said finally. "For doing what's right."

Eventually, Mac rose to a sitting position. "I'm going to go clean up. You'll stay?"

I made sure my voice was casual when I replied, "If that's okay."

When she settled back into bed with an oversized tee shirt, I'd already pulled on my boxers and gotten beneath the covers. Mac turned off the light from the bedside table and rolled onto her side.

I spooned behind her, my body outlining hers as I breathed in the spicy-sweet scent I loved. I draped an arm across her middle as she wiggled tighter against me.

My thoughts were loud, urging me to talk to Mac about the way I felt. My honesty and vulnerability from earlier hadn't scared her off, and so the optimistic part of me considered telling her I wanted to date for real. No more of this sneaking around. I wanted to be together out in the open, go on a date without the asterisk. I thought maybe she was ready.

So I said, "Are you happy with how things are?"

I was close enough to feel her body tense and her breathing pause. I wondered if she could detect the rapid beat of my heart against her back.

When she stayed quiet, all my hopefulness evaporated like woodsmoke on a summer night. I quickly backpedaled, "You know, with your new position at the farm? You're liking it?"

Her breath whooshed out of her, the relief of it tangible and heartbreaking. "Yeah, for sure. I actually really like the responsibility. I've learned a lot by handling the vendors. And, of course, it's nice not to have to deal with the leafers all the damn time."

I swallowed hard, forcing the tightness out of my voice. "Poor baby," I teased. "Can't stand the tourists at your tourist attraction."

"Hey, you know exactly how they are. Entitled and bossy and unappreciative of our land and home."

Despite the turn the conversation had taken and my resulting disappointment, I felt amusement at just how grouchy this woman was. I chuckled a little and said, "Bless your heart."

She immediately rolled to face me, staring in incredulous shock. "Did you just *bless my heart*?

I laughed harder. "Yeah. So?"

"Everyone knows that is little-old-lady speak for 'fuck all the way off.'"

My shoulders were shaking, and I barely managed to say, "No, I meant it the nice way."

She scoffed like there was no such thing, but she wrapped an arm around me and tangled her legs with mine.

And I thought I'd do a lot more than bless her heart, if only she'd let me.

"Do you have work tomorrow?" she asked, her voice soft from sleepiness.

I thought about it, then reached one long arm to her bedside table to retrieve my phone. I scrolled to the list app I used—one that, for some reason, worked better to keep me organized than a calendar.

I was grateful Mac had asked because I'd completely forgotten to set my alarm for the morning. "No work," I replied distractedly, scrolling to make sure I hadn't missed anything else. "But I do play Frisbee in the morning."

"Frisbee?" she asked, sounding suddenly more alert.

I set the alarm and replaced my phone before I was able to answer her. "Yeah, Ultimate Frisbee."

"Oh my God. You are such a walking frat-boy stereotype."

"I was also in a frat," I said, pinching her side.

"Oh, I know." She pinched me back.

"It's just pickup with some folks in South Asheville. And it's a good way to stay in shape and meet people," I added, a touch defensively.

I could see her watching me, even in the dimness of her bedroom, infinitely amused.

"Do you want to come watch?" I asked.

"Hell yes, I do."

"You're just going to heckle me in front of strangers, aren't you?" I asked flatly, ensuring I kept the excitement out of my voice.

"They'll be quality heckles," she replied happily.

"Great. I can't wait." Then I remembered. "Oh, Amos plays too. I have to pick him up in the morning. Is that okay?"

"Sure. I can't wait to see the little punk again."

Then she snuggled into my chest and tightened her arms around me. I smiled into the dark.

The following morning, we woke up early and headed downtown to grab caffeine and breakfast burritos to go from Cubhouse Coffee Shop. I picked up one for Amos and a box of pastries for his mom and sister. I parked down the block, and Mac waited for me in the truck to avoid nosy neighbors and prying eyes.

Amos didn't seem to mind Mac's presence. In between bites of burrito, they fought over the music selection for most of the twenty-minute drive to the field.

When we arrived, Amos trotted off in his cleats to warm up with a few of the other teenagers who came out on Saturday mornings.

I'd changed back at Mac's house with the extra clothes I kept in my workout bag in my truck. Once I'd gotten her set up with a camp chair on the sideline, I tossed her one of my extra hoodies, knowing she'd probably get cold in the chilly morning.

Later, when I looked over to see her wearing it, I immediately dropped a pass and turned the disc over to the other team. But I couldn't find it within myself to be too upset about it. Not when she looked warm in the April air, wearing something of mine.

It was proprietary caveman bullshit, but there it was. I blamed science.

I kept sneaking glances at her while I played, staying distracted by her presence. As much as Mac claimed she wanted to come so she could give me shit, I mostly heard cheers and whistles from the sideline. I was happy she was here, I realized. Glad to have her in another part of my life.

When Amos and I were sweaty and worn out and Mac's cheeks were windburned and pink, we loaded up and headed back to Kirby Falls. I dropped Amos off first, even though it was out of the way. Then I took Mac home so she could get ready for a late lunch with her sister, Bonnie.

"I'll text you later," she said and then pulled me in for a kiss. "Or you can stay over again. If you want."

"I want," I confirmed and then leaned back over the console to kiss her again.

The smile stayed on her face all the way up the porch steps.

When I got to the end of the gravel drive, I shifted into park and grabbed my phone.

With the Chatter app open, I drafted a new post, letting my thoughts run away with me. It seemed safer this way. Like, if I let them out in a controlled environment, then I wouldn't blurt out how much I loved her to her face.

@JuddsFamilyOrchard: @GrandpappysApples, There's a place for you in every part of my life. In every corner of my heart. The sidelines, the front seats, east to west, north to south. You don't even need to ask. There's a reserved sign with your name on it.

That particular draft went into the vault with the other imaginings of a heartsick bastard.

What I actually posted was pretty simple, but I knew it would make her smile.

@JuddsFamilyOrchard: @GrandpappysApples, bless your heart.

MAC

The following weekend, my day off aligned with Brady's once again. He'd mentioned a band playing at one of the clubs in Asheville and asked if I wanted to go.

It must have seemed safer for him to openly spend time together fifteen miles north of our hometown. He seemed to enjoy the sneaking around and secrecy. And despite the smidge of bitterness I'd felt at the invitation, I'd readily agreed.

After months of keeping up appearances in public—the trivia night fights, the social media snipes—it was a relief to hold Brady's hand on a sidewalk in a city where we were unlikely to see anyone we knew. It made me think dangerous thoughts and wonder what it would be like to do this all the time, wherever we wanted.

But there was no sense in rocking the boat. Things were good. Better than good, actually. This was the longest non-relationship relationship I'd ever had. Maybe the secrecy was why it was working. Who was I to complain?

Either way, I'd enjoy the reprieve we had tonight in a town that wasn't home.

The club was busy when we arrived. People sat at high-top tables, and others danced while house music played. The stage at the front of the venue was pretty small, and staff milled around, plugging in amps, setting up microphone stands, and hauling things.

We made our way to the bar, and Brady ordered a beer for himself and a Jack and Coke for me. I thought he might balk at dancing, but I should have known better. We finished our drinks, and then Brady followed me out onto the dance floor, perfectly content to move to the thumping beat.

He grinned in the low light, pleased by my surprise. We danced together, limbs grazing and bodies touching in torturous ways. His gray henley was soft beneath my fingertips. I liked being so close. There was freedom in being able to take his hands and place them on my hips as we moved together.

Whenever we needed a break, we'd return to the bar. Brady switched to water at some point, but I kept drinking, the liquor warming my chest, determined to enjoy my night off and the freedom I had with the man at my side. I got looser and happier, less able to keep it contained. Brady and I danced closer, his laughter in my ear even over the loud music.

Finally, the opening band came on. I was delightfully tipsy by that point, everything soft around the edges. The crowd seemed to swell as people pushed to the floor, eager to get close to the stage. Brady planted his big, tall form at my back and kept the surge of bodies and the threat of elbows away from me.

After the opener finished up their short set, we made our way to the bar once more.

"Do you want a water?" Brady asked, lips right against my ear to be heard over the crush.

Grinning, I shook my head. "Grab me a shot."

His lips flattened, and I laughed, the sound swallowed by the voices around me. "I promise I won't puke in your truck. Get me a shot, and then I'll switch to water."

Because the bartender had enjoyed Brady's tips all night, he thought he was doing us a favor by bringing two tequila shots with lime wedges perched on the rims.

Before Brady could object, I threw them both back, grinning around the lime wedge in my mouth.

He shook his head at me and mouthed, *You're a bad girl.*

That had me laughing. I placed the lime back in the glass and pushed up onto my toes. "You like it when I'm bad," I said against the shell of his ear. "Order me a water. I'm going to the bathroom. I'll be right back." Then I smacked his ass and turned to go.

But Brady snagged my hand and reeled me back to him. Steadying my increasingly unsteady feet, he said, "Be careful, okay? I'll wait for you right here."

I nodded like a good girl, then made my way through the crowd to the bathroom, feeling buoyant and light—carefree in a way I hardly ever managed.

In contrast to the rest of the venue, the restroom was brightly lit by overhead fluorescents. There were several women gathered in front of the long, trough-like sink, adjusting their makeup or typing on their phones.

I found an empty stall, and when I finished up, I approached the sink to wash my hands. There was a woman next to me who was about my age, with long blond hair and a smear of mascara beneath her eyes that said she'd been dancing and sweating as much as I had. She dug through her tiny bag and then gave a frustrated huff.

"Do you need a tampon?" I asked, apparently friendly now that I was feeling the effects of those shots.

"No," she said, lifting her curls off her neck. "A hair thingie."

"Oh, here you go." I held out the black elastic band I kept on my left wrist.

"Oh my God. Thank you!" She threw her arms around me to show her drunken appreciation before accepting the hair tie.

I smiled back. "No problem."

Drunk girls in bathrooms gave off the energy we should all strive for. The world would be a much better place if we all made connections like we did when we'd been drinking and dancing all night. So much hope and sisterhood.

"Are you here for the band?" I asked as she twisted the strands of her hair into a giant bun on the top of her head.

"Yeah, my boyfriend likes them. What about you?"

I wetted my finger and then went to work on my smudged eye makeup. "Yeah. It seemed like a good time. The guy I'm with doesn't know them, but he knew I did."

I admitted that before I even meant to. The wonders of tequila.

"That is the sweetest," she cooed.

"Yeah, he's pretty great," I confessed some more. "He's like the friendliest guy ever. He gets along with everyone. I just left him at the bar for a minute, and he'll probably be best man in someone's wedding by the time I get back."

The other woman laughed, meeting my gaze in the mirror. "Right? I know exactly what you mean. My boyfriend is the same way. He makes friends on airplanes and usually ends up holding someone's baby."

We were still giggling when a gorgeous Black woman with a short floral dress burst into the restroom, stumbling a little. She appeared a little younger than me, maybe in her early twenties. Her cheeks were flushed, and her facial features radiated abject mortification.

"Oh my gosh, you guys," she rushed out, like she'd known us her whole life and we weren't just bathroom strangers. "I just crashed and burned so hard, and I'm not even mad about it."

"What happened?" asked the blond woman beside me, and I had to admit, I was pretty invested too.

The newcomer approached the sink and looked between us before answering solemnly, "I came up to a guy at the bar and asked him to dance. He turned me down in the nicest way possible. He said I seemed like a sweet girl, but he'd finally tricked the love of his life into going out with him tonight, and he's here with her."

"Oh. Em. Geee," squealed my new hair-tie friend. "That is adorable. Was he hot?"

"Yes," she gushed, cheeks still a little flushed. "Crazy tall. Like six four. Nice brown hair. Bright blue eyes. A gray henley that did amazing things for his shoulders."

I straightened as the tequila in my belly gave an unhelpful flip.

"The most gorgeous smile," she continued. "He just seemed really friendly, you know. A good guy."

Surely, she couldn't mean . . .

"I could tell," she finished with a dreamy sigh.

"Sounds like she's a lucky girl, the love of his life. Whoever she is," the other woman commented, sounding equally swoony.

I breathed deliberately through my nose in case I was about to puke, but the feeling in my stomach was not nausea. It was something else.

The blond finally noticed me in the mirror, brows creased in concern. "You okay, girl?"

"Yep," I lied quickly. "Uh-huh."

But my belly was still swirling, and my heart was beating fast. There was no way that had been Brady. But her description . . . the gray henley. He wouldn't just call me—

The blond hugged me one more time and thanked me again for the hairband. Then the women finally left.

I stayed in front of the mirror alone, trying to catch my breath.

I couldn't even think the words in my internal screeching panic, so I whispered them to myself instead. "The love of his life."

Why would he say that? Was he drunker than I thought? Could he have been lying to get that girl to leave him alone?

I knew he was attracted to me, and we had fun together. But Brady had asked—no, demanded—to keep our relationship a secret. And, sure, we'd been seeing one another for months now. But did he really feel that way?

When my thoughts had run themselves ragged, my vision refocused, and I looked at myself in the mirror, sure I'd see pale, wild-eyed horror—a cornered animal on the verge of fight or flight.

So imagine my surprise when the face staring back at me was flushed and smiling softly.

Suddenly feeling much more sober than when I entered, I gathered my courage and stepped out into the darkness and the vibration of the club. Brady immediately pushed off the opposite wall and came to me, worry etched into every line of his features.

"Are you sick?" He passed me a bottle of water. "You were gone so long, I got worried."

I searched his face, looking for the truth like I might find it in his eyes or his dimple or the strong line of his jaw.

When I failed to answer, Brady cupped my cheeks. "Mac, honey, are you okay?"

No, I thought desperately. *How could I be? I'm the love of your life.*

Instead, I nodded quickly, reaching up to clasp one hand and give it a reassuring squeeze, feeling soft over his concern. "Let's go listen."

The band had already started, the drumbeat pounding in my chest. Or maybe that was my heart. I couldn't separate the two.

Brady still looked worried, so I gave him a smile and then took a long drink from the water bottle to soothe him.

We moved toward the back of the crowd and listened to the music.

I ignored the steadfast warmth of Brady at my back. I ignored how he wasn't drunk at all and how I knew he wouldn't be since he was driving us home. I ignored how everything felt so right, like stars aligning.

Without meaning to, I fell asleep on the drive home, Brady's sweatshirt balled beneath my face as my forehead pressed soothingly against the cool glass. I came awake when he shifted into park behind his building.

"I'll drive you home if you want," he said quietly. "But will you stay?"

"Yeah," I croaked, warm and drowsy.

I hadn't stayed overnight at Brady's apartment yet. It felt a little like crossing a line and probably why I'd avoided it all this time. From that very first night together back in October when he'd wanted to make me breakfast the next morning, I'd been uneasy about staying. It seemed like an admission of something I hadn't been ready to hear at the time.

But, now, looking at him in the pale glow of the dashboard, the tentative slouch of his shoulders, the way his hand lay in his lap, open and waiting for me . . . I couldn't remember why I'd wanted to deny myself so badly.

Once inside the apartment—still as fastidiously tidy as every other time I'd seen it—I drank another glass of water over the kitchen sink. Brady gave me a spare toothbrush, a tee shirt, and a washcloth, then steered me into the bathroom.

I washed my face and got ready for bed, sliding his shirt over my skin, liking how it skimmed my bare thighs.

When I made my way into his dark bedroom, Brady peeled back the covers, and I slipped in next to him. I turned to face the open doorway so he could spoon me the way I liked. His face burrowed into my hair, the tip of his nose brushing the shell of my ear.

Like a big dumb idiot, I asked something I'd been thinking about for a long time now. "Why haven't you dated anyone in a while, Brady?"

He didn't freeze like he'd been caught in some lie. His breath remained even against my back, and his hand continued around my waist, tucking itself beneath my rib cage. "No reason. Just hadn't met anyone I was interested in dating."

"Tell me you weren't waiting for me," I said, voice as unsteady as I expected him to be.

But, once again, he surprised me. He drew his lips confidently along my neck, kissing the sensitive spot just below my ear, weaponizing my desire. I closed my eyes rather than moan the way I wanted to.

"Then I won't tell you," he finally whispered. "Don't make this weird," he murmured just before his tongue touched my nape.

"Me?" I practically wheezed as his fingers grazed along my stomach to grip my hip.

"You're so dramatic," he accused, and I could hear the amusement in his voice.

I rolled to face him, suddenly desperate to see the smile on his face and equally as determined to kiss it off. My lips started urgent and reckless, but he gentled the kiss by degrees, making long sweeping strokes with his hand up and down my bare back and pausing to kiss the corners of my lips and the tip of my nose.

Brady made love to me, and he made sure I knew it. Every reverent touch, every ragged breath, every ounce of pleasure he wrang from my willing body was imprinted with his adoration. For once, I didn't try to rush things or even the score. I just let him love me. I didn't question his motives or whether or not I deserved them. I allowed myself to be swept away and swept under.

Afterward, when I finally drifted off to sleep, it was with my head on Brady's chest and his steady heartbeat calling me home.

I awoke the next morning when a pan clanged down the hall, followed by a hushed, "Damn it."

I smiled into Brady's pillow before blindly reaching for his tee shirt on the floor. I pulled it over my head and breathed in the fresh scent of sun and sand. This was better than going into Brady's shower and huffing his bodywash like a lunatic. If he caught me, I'd never live it down.

The events from the previous night came rushing back. The giddy sort of joy at being out together in public followed by the revelation with the drunk girls in the bathroom. I thought about Brady calling me the love of his life, searching for anger or fear or righteous indignation, but, just like the night before, it never materialized.

Instead, I felt safe and warm, buoyed by his affections.

I was twenty-nine-years old, and I'd been dating since I was fifteen. And never once had I found myself in love. Nothing more than attraction or mild infatuation. Monogamous relationships that hadn't lasted beyond a few months, but more accurately, a few weeks. I thought starkly, *I should have fallen in love by now*.

Except for a few teenage dirtbags, it wasn't like there had been anything wrong with the men I'd dated. They just hadn't been for me. *Safe*, Brady had called them all those months ago. And he'd been right. People who hadn't known me as the outspoken Clark, the permanent fixture on her family's land and in this town. Transplants who could draw their own conclusions and accept the version of myself I presented as the unflinching truth.

So much of my hometown was tied up in knots inside me, tangled with expectation and shame and disappointment. But that had more to do with me and my own convoluted feelings than my neighbors.

Another metallic scrape drew my attention and urged me from the bedroom. I crept quietly, peeking around the corner and jolting in surprise. I fought my laughter as I watched Brady in the sunny space for a long moment.

All the years blurred along with the faces of the men I'd dated. The whys and wonderings of how none of them ever stuck swirled around the fact that I'd never loved a single one of them.

Some part of me worried that the man moving around this kitchen, wearing an apron and boxer briefs and nothing else, might be the biggest, sweetest, most ridiculous reason why.

"Hey," Brady said when he finally turned and found me lurking. His smile was bright and infectious, and I found myself grinning back. "You feeling okay? Want some pain reliever?"

Stepping more fully into the kitchen, I shook my head, noting his mussed hair and all the dirty dishes littering the countertops. "No, I'm good. What are you making me?"

"Well, I've got a breakfast casserole with baked eggs, some fresh strawberries, and lemon lavender scones in the oven."

I swallowed. That sounded amazing. And he'd made it for me. Been *waiting* to make it for me. "Scones," I teased. "Those are just high-maintenance biscuits."

Brady laughed. His blue eyes, warm and pleased, stayed on me until a timer went off, and he went to retrieve the fancy scones from the oven.

I watched in amused awe as he expertly drizzled a pale glaze over the tops before delicately sprinkling bits of dried lavender.

The scones were good, all said and done. Everything was delicious. We sat next to one another on tall stools at the central island while I ate every crumb on my plate.

"How'd you get so good at cooking and baking?" I asked once I'd taken the final bite of my casserole, the eggs so fluffy and tender I wanted to die.

Brady finished chewing before replying. "I liked helping my momma when I was a kid. She'd walk me through making brownies or chocolate chip cookies, and it just sort of stuck. Following directions and working one step at a time appealed to me. I kept it up in college, cooking once a week for my teammates. Usually easy stuff like pasta—nothing fancy. But it was something I enjoyed."

"I actually really like these online videos," he added shyly while I polished off another scone. "The channel is called *Not Your Aunt Linda's Kitchen*, and the baker is real personable and fun to watch. Sometimes, I watch those at night or bake something when I have trouble sleeping."

"You have trouble sleeping?" I asked, surprised. He's always slept soundly next to me.

Brady nodded before scooping up another bite of egg layered with bacon, cheese, and flaky croissant. "Sometimes."

We finished up and washed the dishes together. I knew Brady had dinner plans with his family tonight, so I'd texted Bonnie to see if she was up for a sisters' night in with me.

Brady hadn't said a word when I'd pulled my jacket on over his tee shirt I still wore. He'd just watched me with a pleased sparkle in his pretty blue eyes, which was good because he wasn't getting it back.

We'd said our goodbyes, knowing we'd be texting most of the day and seeing each other again tomorrow. I resisted the urge to throw my arms around his waist and tell him I was sorry I'd waited so long to stay for breakfast. I settled on a long, slow kiss in his doorway. Then forced myself to go.

Dinner with Bonnie was Indian takeout from a new restaurant downtown. We were currently stuffing our faces in the living room of Grandma Nola and Grandpa Junior's house. Open to-go containers littered the coffee table while *North and South* played in the background.

My sister and I both loved Richard Armitage, so we'd seen the British miniseries plenty of times. We felt comfortable eating and chatting throughout, but we definitely made sure to tune in for the "Look back at me" scene.

"What's Danny doing tonight?" I asked as I grabbed another samosa.

"Oh, um," Bonnie mused distractedly, "I'm not sure. He hadn't gotten home yet, and I just left a note saying I was having dinner with you."

That was . . . weird. The garage where Danny worked closed at five on Saturdays. Bonnie hadn't arrived with our takeout until almost eight.

"I see," I lied. "Well, I'm sure he'll text or something when he gets home."

She forked up some chicken tikka and shrugged. "Maybe."

I eyed Bonnie as she chewed and focused her attention on the television over the fireplace. She was in her weekend clothes—baggy black sweats and a college hoodie from where she'd attended—with a little blond topknot on the crown of her head.

As an elementary school art teacher, she wore flowy dresses throughout the workweek. She said they were professional but easy to move around in. So when she had downtime, like on the weekends, she entered her self-proclaimed "panda mode," where she lazed about in comfort. I supported that wholeheartedly.

My older sister deserved a break. She took care of everyone. I knew she loved her job and was close with our parents and other family members, but it had to be difficult to try to please so many people all the damn time. She and Danny spent a lot of time with his family, too. I knew they joined the Jensens for dinner several nights a week, with Bonnie usually doing the cooking.

While my sister had worked in the General Store during high school, farming had never been her thing. I admired her for going off to college and finding something just for her. But Kirby Falls had always been home. There had never been a question that she'd come back to start her life. Danny was here, after all.

I watched as another funeral took place on the screen, then asked, "How did you know you loved Danny? That he was the one?"

Bonnie looked at me in surprise, eyes wide. "Where in the world did that come from?"

I could remember her and Danny as fresh-faced teenagers, coming and going, watching movies in the basement at my parents' house, and attending holidays and birthday parties together. Joined at the hip from the time they were fourteen.

"I don't know. I was just curious, I guess." I loved my sister, but I wasn't about to tell her about Brady. I'd barely begun to acknowledge the swirling nebulous notion that I had some serious feelings for him . . . and him for me.

She seemed to think for a long moment before finally replying, "I don't believe in 'the one.'" I could hear the air quotes she'd put around the words. "I think there are any number of people you're compatible with or attracted to. Loving someone is a choice. It's hard work and dedication, not some sweet-smelling romantic breeze that ruffles your hair and guides you to your one true love."

That . . . was not what I expected my sister who'd married her high school boyfriend to say. "Oh."

Then Bonnie blinked like she was coming out of a trance. Her eyes met mine, and she smiled. "But, of course, Danny and I met young. So I was lucky enough to find my person early, you know? We grew up together."

That was what I was worried about. There was so much history to influence your feelings and perceptions. How did you know what was real and what was duty or obligation or nostalgia?

"If my life was a pie chart, Danny would have the biggest slice," my sister said simply, then went back to her chicken tikka masala and Mr. Thornton.

I frowned, thinking that didn't sound right. Or maybe it was supposed to be romantic, like a Hallmark card and grocery store roses on Valentine's Day. But instead, it made me think of missed anniversaries and candles burned down to nubs. The painful act of hanging your hopes on someone who didn't deserve them. A drain on your resources, an inconsiderate leech who only left you a tiny corner of the pie pan.

My relationship with Brady was nothing like that. He was generous and open, accepting the bits and pieces of myself I offered and never demanding more than I was comfortable with. He was patient and thoughtful. In the last four months, he'd done nothing but make *me* a priority.

I watched my sister, suddenly feeling helpless and raw. She'd always been the shining example of maturity and success in my life. Someone who'd gone after what she wanted and had a marriage that seemed happy from the outside.

Now, I wondered if she felt loved at all.

seventeen

BRADY

Mac didn't have to lock the gate in the evenings.

Now that she was management, she could delegate the task to someone else.

So, she didn't really *need* to walk down the path to where it met the highway and drag the metal rungs across the pavement. But she still did it.

"Hi," I called with a grin when she came into view.

Her hair was in a thick braid over one shoulder, and she wore a navy cardigan to ward off the spring chill.

She smiled. "Hey."

I crossed the highway and met her at the end of the drive. I wrapped my arms around her as I lifted her off her feet. Mac laughed as my lips met hers, and I didn't think I'd ever been this happy in my whole life.

The sound of an engine coming down the road had me placing her back on her feet and shoving my hands in the pockets of my jeans.

"You busy?" she asked. "You want to come up?"

It was a Sunday, and Grandpappy's closed at five. We hadn't made plans for the night, but we generally always ended up together in one way or another at the end of the day.

"I could be persuaded."

She gave me an amused shove as she went to retrieve the chain, but I beat her to it.

"What'd you have in mind?" I asked once the entrance to Grandpappy's had been closed off.

"I have to close up the office, but then I wanted to plant the sunflower field. Uncle William already plowed it, so it's ready to go. And I know Will planned to come down and do it after the last freeze, but I just thought I'd help out."

"Yeah, count me in."

So we made our way up the drive, chatting about our days. I told her about how Amos went to another Dungeons and Dragons event at the library downtown. And she told me that Bonnie wanted to start a team for the bowling league down at the Lucky Strike on Thursdays.

Everyone was gone by the time our boots brought us to the Bake Shop. It felt like we had the whole farm to ourselves.

When we approached the door to Mac's office, I noticed the shiny brass nameplate on the front and raised my eyebrows.

MANAGER OF FARM OPERATIONS AND SOCIAL MEDIA DIRECTOR

Mac appeared bashful but pleased. "My grandma Nola had it made and sent it to me."

I grinned. "Authority looks good on you, Clark."

"Thanks," she mumbled, turning the handle and opening the door.

I'd been in Mac's office a lot in the last few months. We ate lunch here together at least three days a week. I'd had her bent over the desk last Thursday, and she'd repeated her Christmas party blow job performance several times since the office had become hers.

I wasn't a stranger to her space, but I always found new additions. Local artwork on the wall. A family photo in a frame on the bookcase. Postcards tentatively added to a corkboard one by one. It was as if she was too afraid to decorate all in one go. Like the idea of settling into the office and making it hers was something she had to get used to. Dipping cold toes into the shallow end rather than cannonballing into deep waters.

The postcards were the most interesting. Most of them had been sent from her grandparents as they traveled the country in their RV. Places they'd been and sights they'd seen.

It could have been that Mac simply treasured the mementos from her family—people she loved. But I'd seen the stack of travel magazines in the sunroom at her house. I'd watched her pore over my photos from my summer in Europe. She'd lingered on the smallest details, and I'd answered all her questions about the food and the people and the places I'd visited.

I'd seen her on her phone, checking prices for imaginary flights. And then quickly hiding her screen like she didn't want me to know. Like her desire to get away was secret or shameful.

From what I could recall, Mac had never been outside the country or even very far from home. For someone who'd stared in awe at my photograph of the basilica in Florence and traced all the lines of architecture while I'd spoken about it, Mac didn't have a lot of travel experience of her own.

As she clicked around on her computer, I stood in front of her corkboard and took in the rectangles of lives lived outside our small community. "Did your grandparents like to travel when you were young? Did they ever take you anywhere?"

Mac's movements stilled on her keyboard behind me. "No, they were too busy with the farm when I was a kid. They didn't start traveling until they retired and passed things on to my dad and uncle."

My eyes skated over a postcard from the Grand Canyon. Then I carefully asked, "Where would you go? If you could go anywhere. Pretend money is no object. Where would you want to escape to?"

Another long pause came from the desk at my back.

I desperately wanted to turn and see her face, read her expression. To see if she was as uncomfortable as I imagined her to be. To witness the naked longing on her face that I knew in my heart would be there.

"Italy," she finally replied. "I'd go to Italy. I'd go to Venice and Rome. I'd see the Vatican and the Trevi Fountain. I'd take a train to the countryside. I'd drink wine and eat pasta and gelato and drive a Vespa."

I smiled at the image. Then I did turn, taking in the way Mac's sharp features had softened with want. A dream left in a shoebox under a bed.

"You should do it," I said, probably a touch too emphatically.

Her face transformed. Confusion and suspicion replaced the hunger and longing in an instant. "What?"

I took two big steps in her direction, joining her behind her desk. "Ask for the time. The farm could spare you for two weeks in the off-season. Get on a plane and go."

She laughed humorlessly, and I hated the resignation in it, wishing I could give her what she wanted and not understanding why she wouldn't take it for herself.

Then Mac turned her attention to the screen, shutting her computer down and pushing in her chair. "It was just a hypothetical, Brady. You're the one who said to pretend."

"I know. But I still think you could make it happen." Fear that she'd push me away or get angry had me reaching for the easy humor that I always kept close at hand. "Hell, I'll go with you. I could use a vacation. And I like gelato too."

Smiling my way, Mac stepped around her desk and grabbed her jacket off the coatrack by the door. "You're a nut."

With her preoccupied, I reached down and pried a letter off the old keyboard on the desktop. We might have been in the middle of a truce, but I still liked to keep her on her toes. And if I kept up this conversation and pushed her harder, she was liable to reject the idea of traveling on principle.

I slipped the letter in my pocket and followed her to the door. "Let's go plant some sunflowers."

The area for the sunflower garden was past the corn maze on the right. I could make out the top of the big red barn across the main path and the rows of Fraser firs planted in the distance. They went all the way to the mountain that overlooked the property. From here, the big house I knew was the original Clark homestead was barely visible through the newly budding trees.

"We'll go about six inches apart and three feet between the rows," Mac said, passing me a small sack of sunflower seeds.

We worked side by side for a time. I thought about this sunflower patch and how my sister Candace would probably like one over at the orchard. She'd already prepped the rear of the property for lavender, and it should be blooming in June or July. Her plan was to have it available for local florists and artisans—the soap makers and candlemakers and others who could extract the essential oils. We were planning on opening the orchard in July rather than August as a result. A pick-your-own sunflower and wildflower field might be a nice addition, too. We had the space, and it was pretty low maintenance. I'd talk to my sisters about it—

"Hey, where'd you go?" Mac's voice drew my attention. She was standing a few rows over, smiling at me.

"Sorry, just thinking about doing something like this over at Judd's. Talking to Candy and Joanie about it."

"You should," she said. "It's easy to manage. And while it's not a super popular attraction—"

"Not when you have an actual apple cannon," I cut in.

Mac laughed. "Yeah, but it's easy and good for photo ops and social media. Plus, it's Becca's favorite place on the farm, so I imagine Grandpappy's won't be getting rid of our sunflower patch anytime soon."

I nodded. The tourist-turned-resident seemed to be pretty well accepted among the Clark bunch. Becca was friendly, and everyone in town loved her, too.

Mac stood and stretched after she reached the end of the last row. "This looks good. I'll ask someone to come over and water it tomorrow."

The last bit of her statement was drowned out by the sound of an approaching engine. I glanced behind Mac's shoulder to see a baby-blue side-by-side coming up the path.

"Shit," Mac breathed from beside me. "Just, um, say you were here to—"

But we didn't get the chance to get our story straight because Maggie Clark was skidding to a stop in front of us, a big smile on her face. Her dark hair with a prominent silver stripe was hardly even disheveled from her very obvious mad dash over here.

"Fancy meeting y'all here." She beamed.

"Hi, Ms. Maggie," I greeted.

"Hi, Aunt Maggie," Mac said less enthusiastically.

"That was awful nice of you to work late, MacKenzie Eloise. But Larry said you weren't planning on coming to family dinner tonight because you had something to do." Maggie's keen gaze landed pointedly on me, and I could feel my ears getting hot.

"Oh, right," Mac said confidently. "I'm supposed to actually—"

"Good!" Maggie crowed, ignoring her niece completely. "So glad you can find the time to join us. And, Brady, honey, we'd love to have you come too. The more, the merrier." Her grin was wide and pleased and completely unhinged. All teeth.

I swallowed. I had a Southern momma, too. So I knew a threat when I heard one. It might have been wrapped in *honeys* and dinner invitations, but there was a very clear expectation here. And despite Mac's intent to avoid going, I had no desire of getting on Maggie Clark's bad side.

"Yes, ma'am. That sounds wonderful. I can't wait."

Mac shot me a disappointed glare.

"Perfect. See y'all up at the house." Then she was gone in a cloud of dust and Aqua Net hairspray.

"Shit," Mac muttered, staring after her aunt.

"It'll be fine," I assured her. This would be a good trial run for when everyone found out about us anyway.

But then Mac blew out a frustrated breath and said, "We'll just say you were spying on the farm for competition purposes and I caught you."

I frowned. "That is ridiculous."

She made a rude sound. "Yeah, but it's believable."

"Why don't we just tell them—" I cut myself off at her sharp glance. *The truth* stayed glued to the inside of my mouth.

"What? Do you have a better idea?" she snapped.

My brain practically shouted: *Yeah, just tell them we're together. That I fucking love you. That we've been banging for months behind their backs.*

Maybe not that last part.

I swallowed uncomfortably and kept my thoughts to myself, saying instead, "Maybe it won't come up."

Mac gave me an incredulous look.

"I don't want to lie, okay?" I confessed. "Let's just go to dinner before she comes back and drags us there by our ears."

"Fine," Mac said and started walking toward her Jeep.

I followed, feeling like I was marching to the front lines.

<hr>

It wasn't going . . . great.

But it could have been worse.

Everyone was gathered in the kitchen when we arrived. I could see Maggie stirring something at the stove while Mac's mom, Patty, stood nearby. Will Clark was next to the fridge, glass in hand. Becca and Larry were at the center island, counting silverware and placemats. And Mac's father, Robert, and his brother, William, were carrying in a cooler with ice.

I was all for helping out. If God or Maggie Clark would grant me something to do that was not just standing in the doorway being stared at, I would have really appreciated it.

When Laramie caught sight of me, she straightened on her stool at the counter and grinned so wide and hard that I checked behind me to make sure Dolly Parton or a Hemsworth brother hadn't strolled in.

"Stop it," Mac hissed at her cousin. "You look deranged."

Becca linked her arm through Larry's and said just loud enough to be heard, "It's finally happening."

"What?" Mac replied.

But no one answered because Will, who had been filling up water glasses at the refrigerator dispenser, continued staring at me and Mac in stunned confusion while liquid overflowed onto the floor. Becca nudged him gently with an elbow behind her, and Will snapped to attention, cursing and moving the glass from beneath the flow of water.

Without batting an eye, Maggie turned from her place by the stove and tossed a dish towel to her son, whacking him in the side of the head as he bent to clean up his mess.

"Oh, Jesus. Let's just do this," Mac breathed. "Everyone!" she shouted. "You know Brady Judd. He's joining us for dinner. Get over it."

It was coordinated chaos that had reached an awkward silence, and then suddenly everyone was rushing to say hello and welcome me.

I smiled and greeted them because I'd had twenty-eight years of experience charming folks, and just because Mac was as ornery as a raccoon caught in a tree, it didn't mean I couldn't have a nice time.

I shook hands with her dad and uncle, both of whom I'd met many times. Patty Clark gave me a warm welcome and said she was happy to see Mac and I were getting along. Daughter had then given her mother a severely betrayed look.

Will had approached slowly under Mac's watchful gaze. He gave me an uncomfortable nod and pointed to my Carolina Panthers sweatshirt. "How's your, um, team doing?"

I grinned. "Not in season, but nice try."

Becca laughed and patted Will sweetly before reaching out and snagging my arm. "Come on, Brady. Help me finish up the salad."

"Yeah, Mac," Larry called. "I need your help getting some potatoes from the basement. You can help peel them too."

Mac groaned, undoubtedly resistant to the inquisition that was about to go down.

I found myself grinning as Becca tugged me over to wash my hands before placing some cutting boards and vegetables on the countertop.

"I hate chopping tomatoes," she confided, like it was a secret she was deeply ashamed of. "They feel so awful. Like you're digging around in someone's intestines."

"Do you have experience with that?" I asked, deadpan.

She laughed like it was the funniest thing she'd ever heard, and I liked her even more.

We spent the next twenty minutes chopping vegetables next to one another, and I was grateful to have something to do with my hands. The repetition helped ease the discomfort of feeling like a zoo animal in an unfamiliar enclosure. Becca was sweet, and we chatted easily. And I was glad to not be standing awkwardly next to Mac. I didn't think I was very good at hiding my feelings. So it was probably safer that she was on the other side of the kitchen, aggressively peeling potatoes and fielding inappropriate questions from her cousin.

The meal came together around us, everyone chipping in to make it happen. It reminded me a little of dinners at my parents' house. But our group was smaller and less animated. Here, with the Clarks, there was always someone laughing or talking over someone else. A television was on in the other room while country music played in the kitchen. Maggie hummed along and shot me a wink whenever I caught her eye.

I felt welcomed even if Mac hadn't wanted me here.

What I didn't expect to feel was cowardly, like a fraud. I was dragging my feet on talking to Mac about us. I had been for a while now. The truth was buried beneath an effort to keep the peace and the threat of losing her.

Standing in her family's home where Mac was loved and accepted, I knew I wanted to be invited back. I wanted a place here with these people. And I didn't know how she'd feel about that. Uncertainty pressed down on me now, heavy and oppressive.

"You okay?" Becca asked gently, drawing my attention as she touched the back of my hand—the one frozen on my knife handle while I thought of all the ways I'd messed this thing up with Mac by trying to keep us hidden away.

Becca's blue eyes were earnest and concerned. "I know Maggie tricked you both here tonight," she whispered. "But she means well. We all do."

"I know," I said, and I smiled so she knew I meant it.

Mac and I ended up walking into the dining room at the same time.

Her elbow jostled mine, and I realized we had an audience. Her family members were watching us as they got settled at the table.

"You call those cucumbers equally diced?" she said smugly.

I shot her an incredulous look and mouthed, *What the hell?*

"Sorry, I couldn't think of a good burn," she whispered.

Mac roughly deposited the bowl of mashed potatoes on the oak tabletop and hustled back to the kitchen. I rolled my eyes and followed.

As soon as I was through the doorway, she snagged my hand and pulled me down the hall and into the laundry room.

I took in her wide, frantic gaze and tried not to feel disappointed over how uncomfortable she was to have me in her space.

"Mac," I said softly, cupping her face in my hands. "You have to stop freaking out. Everything is okay. You don't need to put on a show. This isn't trivia night fighting for the town's benefit. This is your family. They love you. We can just go in there and eat. You're the one making this weird."

She winced. "I know. I can't help it."

"Do you need an orgasm to calm down?"

A surprised laugh burst out of her. Then her shoulders relaxed by degrees until they were no longer up around her ears. She smiled at me—a real one, red-stained lips stretched wide. "I'm sorry. I don't like being surprised. Or ganged up on."

I placed a kiss on the tip of her nose. "I know. But we've got this."

We returned to the dining room and joined the others just as Patty and Becca placed the last of the dishes on the table. Maggie said grace, and then the chaos resumed. Conversations and clinking silverware, dishes passed from hand to hand.

I had a full plate and Mac at my side, her knee a comforting weight against mine beneath the table.

"I wouldn't do that if I were you," Larry said abruptly from across the table.

I paused with a mashed-potato-loaded fork in midair.

"Mac made those spuds, and she probably poisoned them, knowing you'd dig right in," Larry lamented.

Grinning, I said, "Well, thanks for trying to keep me alive."

"I don't have the energy to bury a body tonight," she deadpanned. "My sciatica's been acting up."

Everyone laughed, Mac included. After that, I could see the remaining tension ease out of her. Her cousin's teasing had restored order, returned everything to its rightful place. If they all were reminded that we hated each other, then we were back on comfortable ground.

Briefly and bitterly, I wondered what they'd all do if I kissed the hell out of Mac right in front of them. I was pretty sure Becca would cheer.

I shouldn't feel disappointed. Things were going well. Everyone was laughing and talking. Mac was enjoying herself now.

But as good as the food was, my stomach felt sour with the weight of my lies. I was tired of hiding the truth. With my awareness came my inability to ignore the way I felt. I wanted to drag Mac outside and confess. Tell her I loved her and I wanted to come to dinner here every Sunday for the rest of our lives.

However, I made myself focus. I listened to the conversations and joined in when I could. I didn't think about Mac's knee pressed against mine beneath the table, a silent *everything's okay, they don't know* tapped out in unspoken code.

With my hand in my hoodie pocket, I toyed with the keyboard letter I'd stolen earlier in the day. And I worked out what I would say when it was time to bury the secrets and lies.

Later that night, after I thanked Maggie for dinner and said my goodbyes, I turned down Mac's offer to drive me back to the orchard.

Instead, my thoughts kept me company as I walked through the Clarks' property and back down across the highway to my truck.

I could tell Mac was confused and disappointed. We did typically spend most nights together. But I didn't want to lose my nerve. If I followed her home or saw her asleep in my bed, I'd do anything to keep her there. Even keep playing these games.

Part of me thought she wasn't ready. Her reaction tonight at potential discovery had peeled back a particularly revealing layer. And this was her family—the people who loved her best. What did it mean that she'd been so fearful of their reactions?

But I was going to talk to her and soon. She needed to know I loved her and I wanted to do this for real.

I'd woken just before five in the morning, unable to get back to sleep. Especially when there wasn't a reason to keep me in bed, like a smart-mouthed brunette.

It was nearing seven when I finished up a batch of shortbread bars as a thank-you for Maggie's hospitality. The kitchen smelled like butter and sugar, and it eased some of the restlessness in me.

My phone buzzed on the counter, and I abandoned the sink and the dirty dishes there when I saw the notification.

MacKenzie: Did you seriously steal the letter D from my keyboard?

I laughed out loud into the quiet apartment, thinking about the small, pale square sitting on my bedside table right this minute.

Me:

MacKenzie: You are an infant.

Me: Nah. A toddler, at least.

I watched as three dots appeared, indicating she was typing. They stopped and started twice more.

Me: You laughed. Admit it.

MacKenzie: I will do no such thing.

MacKenzie: Give me the D, Brady.

Me: Anytime, honey. Just say the word.

MacKenzie: Jesus. You stole that letter just so you could make that joke.

Me: I have a commitment to comedy, Macintosh. Don't be jelly.

MacKenzie: Maybe this calls for a hostage situation. Perhaps I'll steal something from you. Get ready for payback.

Oh, she'd already stolen something, alright.

I typed, *I can't wait.*

I could feel the edges of my smile as I stared down at the phone in my hand. I was glad we still had this. The surprises, the silliness, the fun, the competition.

I thought, hopefully, I could spend a lifetime giving her hell and making her like it—making her love it.

As I eagerly awaited whatever retaliation was coming my way, I opened the Chatter app and drafted another fruitless post that would never see the light of day. Maybe this was like therapy for me—a way to express myself in a healthy way without fear or judgment.

Ah, well, whatever it was, I was doing it.

@JuddsFamilyOrchard: @GrandpappysApples, Hostage negotiations are open. I have a slightly used, decent condition keyboard letter in exchange for your fierce and equally tender heart. You've already stolen mine. Don't think you need two.

MAC

"I can't believe I missed Brady Judd at family dinner," my sister pouted at my side.

I took a sip of my beer and continued to ignore the conversation.

Bonnie and Danny hadn't been able to make it to Aunt Maggie's last night. Although I didn't see my ridiculous aunt chasing them down in her side-by-side, but whatever.

We were at Monday night trivia at Trailview, and Larry was giving my sister a complete play-by-play of yesterday's eventful dinner with Brady in attendance.

Danny was suspiciously absent from the table, but so was Kayla. We'd drafted Becca to come and join us from her normal team. Now, the four of us were ready. If only the emcee would get this show on the road so everyone at my table would stop obsessing over Brady.

"It was something to behold," Larry said, nodding sagely. "I thought Mac was going to have an aneurysm. But that Brady, he was cool as a cucumber."

"A natural charmer," Becca added sweetly.

I caught my eye roll mid-rotation and drained the rest of my IPA.

"It's not a big deal, y'all," I insisted. "Maggie happened upon us *fighting*," I emphasized, "while I was busy planting your sunflower field, Becca Marie."

The blond's cheerful features turned sheepish. "Sorry."

"You're all making a mountain out of a molehill." I stood. "I'm going to get another beer since they're running late tonight, apparently."

Voices called out as I made my way to the bar.

"Don't be like that," Larry said.

"Come on, Mac," Bonnie urged.

"I'm sorry!" Becca chirped.

I ignored them. The sooner they got over this obsession with me and Brady Judd, the sooner things could get back to normal.

If Brady wanted to be a secret, I wasn't going to be the one to out us.

Sure, I'd been off-balance last night. Mostly, because I knew my family would make a big deal about him being there, but I also knew they'd welcome him with open arms. I didn't want Brady to feel pressured by them. If he wanted casual, then meeting the family wasn't really the best way to go about that.

I thought back to the breakfast I'd shared at his parents' house and tried to compare the two. I'd been there as Candace's friend, for the most part. No one had assumed anything about Brady and me. There'd been way less expectation accompanying those biscuits and gravy.

My family, on the other hand, had zero chill. I was sure every single one of them suspected something was going on, but the girls were right. Brady had been laid-back and easygoing about it all. He hadn't been bothered by the questions or the stares or my cousin's insinuations.

That was just Brady. A charming charmer.

I didn't want sudden notice from my branch of the family to complicate things between us. It was almost May, and we'd been happy with our arrangement for months now. Something told me that having the secret out—even to people I trusted—would screw everything up.

But there was an insistent little voice in my head wondering how long we could possibly keep this up. What happened if we were found out? Would Brady end things rather than admit the truth?

Maybe it made me weak or a coward, but I didn't want this thing to end. I was happy. Happier than I'd been in a long time. Between our relationship and my new position at the farm, I felt good—or close to it.

As I passed by Brady's table on my way to the bar, I caught his eye. He winked, and I made sure my face was nice and even when I held up two fingers discreetly in front of my chest.

We'd worked out a system and pre-arranged our trivia night fights to keep up appearances. Mostly because it was fun. However, tonight I was really not in the mood for the nosy women at my table, so getting out of here within the next twenty minutes greatly appealed to me.

But Brady must not have gotten the message because when the second round started, he didn't take the bait of my shouted insult. He calmly sipped his beer and didn't even make eye contact.

Instead, we played on to the end. Neither one of our teams won. The bird-watching group got every question right, and Becca cheered loudly for them when their team was announced as the first-place finisher.

Larry, Becca, and Bonnie were staying on to hang out, but I told them I'd see them later and made for the parking lot.

I hurried to the end of the asphalt where Brady's truck sat and waited.

It didn't take long. He approached a few minutes later, his tall shadow stretching across the pavement in the glow of the area lights.

"Hey, did you not see my signal earlier?" I said by way of greeting.

"Guess I missed it." He turned to unlock the driver's side. "You want to follow me to my place?"

Something was up. He'd been quiet all night, and now he would hardly look at me. Sudden worry about the disaster dinner last night intruded, and I wondered if it had been too much, after all. We'd texted today. He'd teased me about the damn letter from my keyboard. But maybe he was overwhelmed and wanted space. Though surely, he wouldn't be inviting me over if that was the case.

I hated feeling so uncertain. This was not my default. I was a direct person who didn't rely on other people to influence the way I felt.

When I'd remained quiet too long, Brady finally glanced my way. His eyes were wary and secretive—an expression I'd never once seen on his face. "Will you come over? I thought we could talk."

It took all my effort to keep my face passive. "Sure," I said finally, voice flat.

If he wanted to break things off, he could do it right now, as far as I was concerned. And if he couldn't handle one little dinner with the most important people in my life, then he didn't deserve my insane but well-meaning family.

Brady scanned the parking lot over my head before leaning in and pressing a kiss to my cheek. "I'll see you over there."

Worry and confusion and irritation swirled around inside me in a bitter combination. I didn't even remember walking to my Jeep and climbing inside.

I followed Brady's taillights out of the parking lot and onto Main Street.

He'd been fine over text this morning. Chatty and sweet. Funny and teasing. What could have changed between then and now?

Brady approached the four-way stop at the intersection of Main and Sixth. My headlights shone in his rearview mirror, and I met his gaze briefly before he checked the empty intersection and pulled ahead slowly.

What was I going to say when he ended things? That was obviously where this was headed. Asking to talk was never a good sign. How was I going to—?

As I sat idling at the stop sign, an oncoming engine revved sharply from my left. I watched in horror as a late-model truck sped into the intersection and slammed into the side of Brady's truck. Metal crushed and scraped as the collision pushed Brady's vehicle up onto the sidewalk and pinned it against the telephone pole.

I was out of my Jeep with my phone in my hand before the incoming truck had fully rocked to a stop.

"Brady!" I shouted, running to circle the mass of metal.

My thumb fumbled to type 9-1-1 as I caught sight of Brady's brown hair resting on the driver's-side window.

"Brady," I called again, my voice distant over the sound of blood and panic coursing through my system.

The flat front end of the older truck was trapping Brady. His vehicle was crumpled around the intruding metal, all sharp angles.

I climbed on the hood of the green truck with the white stripe along the side and tapped on Brady's window. Vaguely, I was aware of sounds coming from the phone in my hand.

"Brady," I repeated. "Can you hear me?"

He was starting to rouse. I caught a grimace of pain on his profile before seeing a slash of bright red along his hairline.

I hit the speakerphone button on my cell and shouted that there'd been an accident on Main and Sixth and to send an ambulance. Then I ignored the operator's questions and shoved my phone in my pocket, trying to get Brady to meet my gaze.

His head kept lolling, and he couldn't seem to focus on where my voice was coming from.

Hurriedly, I climbed down off the hood of the truck that had T-boned him and ran to the passenger side of Brady's vehicle. But the hinge of the door was pressed against the telephone pole. I could pull on the handle, but couldn't get enough leverage or room to tug it open.

Instead, I stood up on the running boards and peered inside. I could see him better from this angle, and his gaze finally found mine through the glass. He tried straightening in his seat, but he was moving slowly, gingerly.

"Just stay still. The paramedics will be here in a minute." I scrubbed a tear off my chin and tried to smile. "They'll get you out."

Brady nodded and then winced. His head drooped back against his headrest, and I called out again. He blinked back into awareness, but he was sluggish and dazed.

I kept talking, telling him he'd be fine and not to worry, but I wasn't sure if he heard me through whatever head injury he'd sustained. I furiously swiped another tear off my cheek.

The sirens were getting louder now, but no sense of relief came.

I heard the squeak and strain of an old door opening.

Until that moment, I hadn't given a shit about the other driver. I'd recognized that truck the moment it had crashed through the intersection. But now I was stepping off the running boards and rounding the front of Brady's ruined truck.

Glassy-eyed and red-faced, Buck Adams was staggering off the bench seat and out onto the street. The smell of cheap alcohol accompanied the middle-aged man, and suddenly, all my useless fear from the last five minutes had a target.

"What the fuck are you doing, Buck? Look at what you did," I shouted over the sound of approaching sirens, furious and untethered—a snarling, angry dog freed from its chain.

The man caught sight of me and reeled back, intent on escaping back into his truck. He got the door closed, but his window was half down. I climbed up and reached through, desperate to keep him from leaving. I grappled and fumbled for the ignition, trying to reach the keys so I could toss them across the fucking street. But Buck beat me there and turned the truck over. It took a moment to catch as I clawed at his arms and yanked on the wheel.

Suddenly, I was weightless, kicking and shouting as an arm banded around my waist and pulled me backward.

"Jesus, Mac," the voice attached to the arm grunted. "Your elbow got me below my vest."

Hair whipped across my face as I watched another uniformed deputy drag Buck out of his vehicle.

The person holding me—Jamie Matthews, I could recognize him now—set me down on my feet. "You good?"

I nodded, content now that the no-good drunk wasn't going to get away. Buck had lived in Kirby Falls his whole life. His wife, Jolly, had finally divorced his ass a few years ago, and the town had thrown her a party. He'd caused scenes and had been drunk at every bar in the county. Jolly had used all her money trying to put him through rehab multiple times, but it never stuck. Up until now, he'd been a cautionary tale and sob story in my hometown. I knew the man needed help, but I couldn't see it right now. Not when he'd been driving drunk and had endangered the man I—

"Brady," I breathed, spinning out of Jamie's hold.

"They're getting him now."

And the deputy was right. I watched as the firemen used some kind of crowbar to wedge the passenger door open. The metal groaned, but they made enough space to get inside to Brady.

"You wanna tell me what happened, Mac?"

Without looking away from what was going on in the cab's interior, I told Jamie exactly what I'd witnessed. Brady moving through the intersection. Buck coming out of nowhere and slamming into him.

While Jamie asked me questions and confirmed details, the ambulance arrived. I could see Brady moving and talking, but the clawing fear in my belly hadn't gone anywhere.

He was out of the truck now, loaded onto a backboard. They weren't letting him walk. Thank Christ. Because his movements were all wrong. Something must have been broken or hurt.

Jamie passed me a tissue, and I swallowed painfully.

The sirens were off, but blue and red lights flashed everywhere. A tow truck waited patiently behind my Jeep, where it sat, still running, with the door flung open.

The firefighters were still gathered nearby while the two EMTs worked to secure Brady. I saw his lips move, and then everyone standing around laughed. Because, of course, the idiot had almost died and was cracking jokes.

I left Deputy Matthews when they'd loaded Brady in the back of the ambulance, approaching a woman in a navy-blue uniform.

"Louisa," I hissed as she started to shut the doors.

Brady looked pale through the opening, his eyes closed.

"Mac," she greeted. "You okay? Were you involved?"

I shook my head. "I'm fine. Is he— Is Brady okay?"

Her dark eyes took me in. "Yeah. Rattled his cage a little. Probably a mild concussion, but we'll bring him in and have him evaluated."

"Can I—can I ride with him?"

Louisa sighed. "No, I'm sorry. You're not family. And we need to get going."

"Please, Lou," I tried. And then I decided to fight dirty. "Remember that time junior year? You went to that college party and had me cover for you? I swear I will call your mother right this minute and tell her you didn't actually stay at my house that weekend."

"Mac, come on," she groaned. "You cannot seriously be trying to blackmail me right now."

I'd known Louisa Hernandez Cortez since she moved to Kirby Falls in fourth grade. We'd played soccer together and been good friends since we were little girls. She came out to Abby's bonfire at least once a month, and I ate at her parents' restaurant all the time. But I was not above using our history and friendship to get in the back of that ambulance with Brady.

"I'll do it," I warned.

"Let's go, Lou!" came a shout from the side of the vehicle.

"Listen," she said quickly, "drive to the hospital and meet us there. He's going to need someone to bring him home after he's checked out. He'll probably need concussion protocol and someone to stay with him for twelve to twenty-four hours. Meet us at the doors to the ER, and I'll make sure you get inside with him."

"Fine," I gritted out.

Before I could turn, Louisa gripped my arm. "He's going to be okay."

I nodded and fled when I felt another tear stupidly well up in my right eye.

I probably shouldn't have driven. I couldn't recall the path we took to the hospital, which was just over a mile away. I simply followed the flashing lights ahead of me.

As they worked to unload Brady at the bay doors, I found a parking spot and hustled over to where Louisa waited for me. She said we'd need to hold on for a bit while he was examined. Then she would take me back.

I could see Lou's confusion and her curiosity, but I wasn't in the right state to give her some bullshit answer about why I cared so much about Brady Judd and the accident I'd witnessed. The only thing that wanted to come out of my mouth was the truth. One that was likely already written all over my face.

She tried to be kind and talk to me while we waited for the nurses to get Brady settled, but I couldn't manage it. My thoughts were swallowed up by the sights and sounds of the ER around me. I was reliving the startling moment when Buck's truck collided with Brady, the way he hadn't been moving when I'd called his name.

True to her word, Louisa smuggled me back into the temporary room Brady occupied in the emergency department.

He was asleep when I got there. I didn't know if that was safe or not. I thought I'd read something about keeping people awake who'd sustained a head injury. But if the doctors and nurses weren't worried, then I guessed it was okay.

The cut above his eyebrow had already been taken care of, a barely there red line that had been closed with a butterfly bandage. The skin was slightly swollen and would likely be bruised by the morning.

My fingers hovered above the wound as I took in the rest of Brady. I didn't see any splints or slings or anything to indicate he'd broken or dislocated something.

"Mac," he breathed, startling me.

Brady wore a dopey grin, like he'd had one too many at a frat party.

I swallowed and clutched his hand without meaning to. "Are you okay?"

"Yeah, I'm alright. Just tired and a little dizzy. They want to do a scan just to make sure everything's fine." His eyes closed. "But said I should be able to go home after that."

"A scan of what?" I asked quickly, worried he'd drift back to sleep without answering.

"My giant brain," he said, lips quirking up at the corners.

A breath rushed out of me that might have been relief or amusement, but it was enough to have his eyes opening again.

"Hey," he said, squeezing my hand. "MacKenzie, I'm fine. Don't cry, honey."

"I'm not crying," I replied reflexively, but my nose was burning, and the room was going blurry.

Brady tried to rise up out of the bed but winced.

"Stop," I said, urging him back and pulling myself together. "You're going to hurt yourself. Just rest, Brady. I'll be here. I'll take you home when they let you go."

He settled after that, closing his eyes once more.

A nurse or technician in pale gray scrubs came in a short while later to take Brady for a CT scan. The man was in his fifties and gave me a kind smile as he wheeled Brady down the hallway. He told me to wait there, that it wouldn't take long.

They made it back twenty minutes later, just as it was nearing 11:00 p.m.

I'd tried calling Candace to let her know about her brother, but she hadn't answered. I didn't want to leave a message or text her and scare the hell out of her. I'd call again once I knew when they planned on releasing him.

Brady was sleeping when a Black man in slacks and a white coat entered the room just before midnight.

He smiled warmly. "I'm Dr. Owens. You must be the fiancée."

I fought to keep a straight face at the doctor's pronouncement, barely panicking over how much I didn't hate the sound of that. Apparently, that was how Louisa had managed to get me into Brady's room.

"That's me," I said evenly, noting that Brady's eyes stayed closed and his breathing even. "Is he going to be okay?"

The thirtysomething physician smiled again. I could tell it was meant to put me at ease, but I was still all twisted up. "His scan looked good. No trouble there. We'll send him home with you shortly. You'll need to monitor him for the next twelve hours. He'll want to sleep, but you'll need to wake him every two hours and ask him a few questions. Easy ones. His name. His birthday. Things like that. Give him over-the-counter acetaminophen for any pain. No work for the next few days. Reduced screen time."

I nodded, grateful to have something to do.

"He may be irritable or have headaches, but bring him back in if things worsen instead of improving."

"Thank you," I managed, my voice a little choked.

The doctor dipped his chin. "We'll get you out of here soon. Sit tight."

After another two unanswered calls to Candace, a nurse came in with discharge paperwork. She passed me a bag and then went to rouse Brady to have him sign some things.

I looked inside the bag to find his cell phone, keys, and wallet. And, in the corner, nestled in among a handful of pocket change, was the letter D from my keyboard.

My hands shook as I closed the bag and held it to my chest.

Brady was smiling at the nurse, and they were laughing over something. I couldn't make it out over the beating of my heart.

Finally, the woman met my gaze. "Want to pull your car around, and I'll meet you out there?"

"Yes, ma'am," I replied and stood on shaky feet.

Brady lowered himself into the wheelchair without complaint. He looked tired and sore but kept up the charm for the nurse's benefit.

We got him settled into my passenger seat. He seemed much steadier as he buckled himself in.

We didn't speak on the short drive to his apartment. I peeked at him every two seconds to make sure he was breathing, but I couldn't find any words to say. There were too many bouncing around in my head. Most notable were *I was so fucking scared* and *How dare you get yourself hurt*, closely followed by *This isn't fair* and *I didn't know it would feel like this*.

Brady was quietly amused as I insisted on supporting him up the stairs. And he looked on as I removed his keys from his bag of personal effects and unlocked his front door.

He took two acetaminophen and drank half a glass of water under my careful supervision. Then, I set an alarm on my phone for every two hours. Not that I imagined I would sleep anytime soon. But just in case the adrenaline wore off and I found myself inadvertently passed out in Brady's apartment, I wanted to make sure I did my duty to check on him throughout the night.

Brady changed into a fresh tee shirt and sleep pants, and I draped the covers over his body.

He gave me a drowsy grin and snagged my hand before I could pull away. "Thank you for taking care of me, Macklemore."

"You're welcome," I said, giving in to the urge to brush his hair back from his forehead.

"Anytime you want to break out the naughty nurse uniform, that's fine by me."

A surprised laugh shot out of me. His smile widened even as his eyes drifted closed and his body relaxed into the mattress.

My amusement quickly morphed into something else—something desperate and relieved as my brain catalogued the variety of emotions I'd cycled through in the last few hours like a children's flipbook.

My throat closed up, and I had to put my hand over my mouth and leave the room before Brady heard me sob noisily into my palm.

I paced his apartment, examining the pictures on the wall and the books on his shelf. I flipped through his photo album from his summer abroad, the images familiar by now. I traced the edges of his smile as he stood in front of the *Nike of Samothrace* or took a selfie with the *Mona Lisa*.

By the time my phone vibrated in my pocket around two a.m., I'd probably peeked in on Brady thirty-five times.

I woke him gently by rubbing circles between his shoulder blades. I asked him his name and his favorite ice cream.

"You just wanted to make fun of my love for pistachio ice cream," he grumbled into his pillow. And I smiled into the dark.

I spent the next two hours on what had become my side of the bed. But I didn't sleep. With my legs stretched out in front of me, I sat up against the wooden headboard and watched the slow rise and fall of Brady's chest. At one point, he rolled over and draped his arm over my thighs, snuggling his face against my hip.

When I woke him again, I asked him to confirm his birthdate and the name of our high school.

He blinked slowly up at me, and worry had me straightening. Was he getting worse? Did he not remember?

Then he said, "November 22, 1995."

But instead of answering the second question, he closed his eyes and gave me another loopy grin. "You had these jean shorts. These little cutoffs with the fringe on the bottom."

"Uh, yeah." The fear I'd been feeling intensified. I grabbed my phone from the bedside table, ready to search worsening concussion symptoms and when to return to the hospital.

But then Brady continued, voice slurred and sleepy, "They used to drive me crazy. I had dreams about them, Mac. Horrible, wonderful dreams. Teenage Brady lived in torment anytime you wore those shorts."

My eyes drifted from my screen to scan his features. "Does your head hurt? Can you rate your pain on a scale of one to ten?"

He laughed like I was silly. "Remember that time I got an erection in PE freshman year?"

I winced. "Yeah, Brady. Everyone remembers that."

I'd been an office worker at the time, running an errand in the gymnasium. I'd emerged from the locker room after delivering a message to the girls' PE teacher, Coach Yates. I'd seen the girls gathered on the volleyball court, giggling. And Brady was attempting to dribble a basketball on the other end of the gym while his athletic shorts did little to hide the situation at hand.

It had been all over the school by lunchtime. But in true Brady fashion, he'd laughed it off and made fun of himself along with everyone else. And the incident passed with little impact on his popularity. Two seniors got in a fight the next day and everyone moved on to the next thing, like typical teenagers.

"It was you and those fucking shorts. You came down from the office, and I took one look at you, and that was all she wrote."

Shock had me squeezing the phone in my hand. "What?"

"Yep. Even then." He sighed. "I know. I was so stupid. I think I put that hissing cockroach in your locker that same week."

I shook my head in disbelief, having no idea what to say. But the screen of my phone lit up with a list of symptoms, and I remembered myself. I needed to make sure Brady was okay. He was vulnerable and concussed. He probably wouldn't be sharing this stuff if he was in his right mind.

"Brady—"

"Kirby Falls High School," he interrupted, then shifted closer and pressed his cheek to the top of my thigh, arms tightening around my legs as he did so.

My breathing picked up as his settled.

This wasn't supposed to happen.

We were just having fun.

I wasn't supposed to be losing my mind at the thought of losing him.

I'd lived a fortunate life up until this point. I had both sets of grandparents, and I'd never had to mourn anyone I'd been close with. My great-grandmother had died before I was even born.

Rationally, I knew that Brady was going to be fine. He'd make a full recovery, big brain and all. But whenever I closed my eyes, I saw his truck skidding across the pavement, the sound of metal crunching. I heard my own voice shouting his name in panicked stereo as his head rested, still and unresponsive against the driver's-side window.

I'd been afraid. Really afraid. Completely blindsided by terror and unable to function in the face of his potential injury. I didn't like feeling so beholden to someone else. It made me feel weak and untethered—completely irrational.

Who wanted to let someone else dictate their life? Who wanted to live at the mercy of something so fragile and unpredictable? What kind of person voluntarily signed up for that?

Someone in love, my brain supplied readily enough.

Someone like you, my heart whispered back.

We'd been sneaking around for months, but I could imagine what Brady and I looked like from the outside. A couple. People who texted each other, shared meals, and spent their nights together. He had a toothbrush in my bathroom. I had two hoodies I'd stolen, sitting in my hamper at this very moment. I knew how he took his coffee, and he brought me Twizzlers whenever he knew I was having a shitty day.

I was one big heart-eyes emoji. I could taste orange Tic Tacs and smell sand and salt and sea air whenever I closed my eyes. He was a visage of my past and the future I'd been inadvertently barreling toward.

I worried there was an impression on my heart. Some stupid, tender part of me warned that if I bothered to check, it would be the depth of that dimple in Brady's right cheek or the perfect pressure of his thumb in the divot on my chin.

With effort, I forced my breathing to match his—slow and even.

I waited until 5:15 and texted Abby. I stayed put until I got a response.

Then I put on my jacket, slid on my shoes, and shut the front door quietly behind me.

BRADY

I woke up with a splitting headache and a very anxious-looking Cole Abernathy standing over my bed.

"Wha—" I sat up, wincing. The rest of my sentence failed to materialize.

The clock on my bedside table read 6:29 a.m., and the sky outside my bedroom window was just starting to lighten.

"I was just about to wake you up," Abby said. "For your concussion check-in thing. Are you okay? How are you feeling?"

I gave up on trying to get out of bed and just slumped against my pillows. "You're supposed to ask me my name or something I can answer. Those are too open-ended."

Abby glared at me.

Squinting up at him, I grinned. "I'm okay, man. I'm sore like I got hit by a truck." I waited, but there was no laugh. Tough crowd. "And my head is killing me. Would you mind—?"

But he was already out of the room.

Fourteen seconds later, he was back with two oblong white pills and a glass of water. "Mac said only Tylenol."

I was wondering when he'd bring her up. Obviously, she was the reason he was here. I was honestly a little surprised that I hadn't woken up to my mother or sisters beating down the door. Maybe Mac had to get to work or something.

There was a tiny flicker of disappointment that she hadn't stayed, but I quashed it. She'd done enough. More than enough.

"Yep," I replied noncommittally, but it would only be a matter of time before Abby wanted the full story on Mac. I snagged the pills and downed them, drinking deeply from the glass.

I managed to sit on the side of the bed without feeling dizzy. So I took it a step further and shuffled across the hall toward the bathroom. Abby hovered anxiously, like he might need to catch me.

"I swear, I'm okay," I assured him.

"Okay." He nodded. "Just leave it unlocked in case you fall or something."

I did as he asked, but everything was fine. I used the bathroom and washed my hands, wincing a little as I took in the bandage and bruising on my face. There was some faint discoloration from

where my head and cheekbone smacked into the driver's-side window. But, all in all, I was in pretty good shape.

A brief memory of Mac crying over me in the ER surfaced, and I realized it must have been pretty fucking scary to watch something like that unfold before your eyes. If our places had been reversed and I'd seen her get T-boned by another vehicle—no matter how minimal the damage—I would have panicked.

Abby was waiting in the hallway like a creeper, but I forgave him because he said, "You feel like eating? I brought stuff to make breakfast burritos."

I groaned. "That is the best thing I've ever heard."

We slowly made our way to the kitchen, Abby walking behind me like he was a new mother and I was a baby taking my first steps. I had half a mind to see if he'd carry me bridal-style just so I could give him shit over it for the rest of our lives.

Instead, I settled at the island on a high-backed padded stool as he went to work prepping our breakfast. A few moments later, he pushed a mug of green tea in front of me.

I eyed it warily.

"No coffee," he said sternly. "Caffeine is bad for people recovering from head injuries."

"Can you not call it that?"

He frowned. "What the hell else would I call it? You injured your head. It's a head injury."

"Just say concussion," I argued.

He rolled his eyes and turned his back to pull out a carton of eggs.

"Have you heard anything about my truck?" I asked as I sipped the green tea. It tasted good. He'd put honey in it.

"Jackie towed it over to her shop," he replied as he whisked.

"Totaled?"

Abby stiffened and looked at me over one shoulder. "Yeah, probably. I can take you over there later if you feel up to it."

"Thanks." I sighed. This was going to be a pain in the ass.

"Your stuff is on the coffee table in the living room," he let me know as he dropped some cubed potatoes into a hot skillet. "From the hospital. Your wallet and phone and stuff. I put your keys over there, too."

"Where'd you get the keys?" I was curious how the shift change went and what Mac had said to him. And if he was going to come right out and ask why Mac had been here in the first place. I wasn't going to lie to him. If Buck Adams hadn't run that stop sign last night, I'd have been done with all the secrets. I'd wanted Mac to come over so we could talk and figure out how to be together for real.

"They were under the mat."

I frowned at that. "Under the mat?"

Abby placed a lid on the pan and adjusted the temperature before giving me his full attention. "Yeah. Outside your door. Mac texted me early this morning. She told me about the accident and said she couldn't reach Candace. She didn't have Joan's number and didn't want to call the house and scare your parents. So she asked me to come over and wake you up at six thirty for a wellness check or whatever. She left the key under your front mat, and I let myself in ten minutes after she texted me."

Oh.

Thoughts crowded for positioning as my friend explained what went down this morning. I hadn't realized that Mac had tried to reach my sister and had been unable to get through. Maybe she hadn't actually meant to stay at the hospital—

But then she could have called Abby last night.

Maybe she felt bad or something. I didn't know. Something seemed off.

"I got in touch with your momma, by the way," Abby said.

"Thank you. I should call her."

"They'll be over in a bit," Abby said when I started to rise. "Are you going to tell me why Mac drove you home from the hospital?"

"She was behind me during the accident," I replied simply. It was the easiest answer, especially when I was growing less sure of her motivations by the minute.

"And why was she following you, Brady?"

I swallowed.

He leaned forward, resting his forearms on the island, staring at me expectantly. "Because a witness posted something very interesting in the Kirby Falls Facebook group this morning."

My already-uneasy stomach turned over.

"The witness said Mac almost got arrested."

"What?" I demanded.

Abby nodded sagely. "Yeah. Apparently, they had to pull her off of Buck Adams in the middle of Main Street. He tried to take off after the wreck, and she went after him. Elbowed Deputy Matthews in the stomach for his trouble."

I didn't recall any of that. There were some pretty hazy memories of her talking to me through the glass, and then she'd been in the ER when I'd woken up.

The thought of her losing it on Buck was . . . I didn't know what. Typical hellcat Mac, for sure. But the fact that she'd done that in defense of me was something else entirely. It was violent and irrational. So I didn't know what it said about me that it also made my chest feel warm.

"Why would she . . ."

"Why do you think?" Abby managed to catch my eye as I processed too much all at once. "You ready to tell me what's been going on?"

So, I did. I told my friend the truth. That Mac and I had been seeing each other in secret for months. That her failed experiment to get it out of our systems turned into a relationship—a secret relationship.

He was plating the burritos by the time I finished speaking. Then he just stared at me for a long moment, face impassive.

"You don't seem surprised," I said.

"Of course I'm not surprised, Brady. Jesus. I'm not an idiot. I've seen you three or four times a week my entire life. But the last few months, you've been a ghost. Obviously, I assumed a woman was occupying your time. Did I think it was Mac? Of fucking course I did. She is literally the only person you'd implode your life for."

I rolled my eyes. "My life is just fine."

He raised accusatory eyebrows. "Is it? Because normal people don't keep whole-ass relationships a secret from their families and friends. Not unless they're doing something they're ashamed of."

"Listen, I'm sorry I didn't tell you, okay? But I'm not ashamed or whatever you're making this out to be. I just needed it to stay under wraps for a while. I needed time."

Abby's eyes bulged. "The secrecy was *your* idea?"

"Yeah," I admitted.

"Who even are you right now?"

I reluctantly set my burrito down and sighed. "I needed time to make her fall in love with me, okay? Time to see that we're right for each other. Without distractions. Without expectations. Without reminders of our history and our past getting in the way. Without this town and the fucking Facebook group reminding her how much she's always hated me."

I knew without seeing the look on my best friend's face that this hadn't been my smartest move. And I was plenty aware that I'd been dragging my feet on being honest with Mac about what I wanted. But the truth, plain and simple, was . . . I was afraid of losing her. I didn't want to be added to the list of men who couldn't hold MacKenzie Clark's attention—who couldn't earn her love.

"Trying to surround your relationship in Bubble Wrap is completely unrealistic," Abby finally replied. "Love doesn't exist in a vacuum. And it's been months. Does she love you back?"

"Man, why are you pushing this?" I could hear the irritation in my tone as uncertainty twisted my stomach in knots. I'd thought Mac and I were getting somewhere. I'd thought—

Abby must have noticed my mounting frustration, too, because he sighed and said, "I don't want you to get hurt."

I shook my head in exasperated disbelief. "You've been giving me shit about Mac since I was thirteen years old. You finally got your wish. I realized I was in love with her."

"But is she in love with you?"

I hesitated.

I'd been tallying up proof in an imaginary ledger all this time. Every kiss, every text, every step forward. But in the face of my friend's question, I could only think of the deficit column. Her reaction at the family dinner at Maggie's. The way she'd smuggled me out of her house rather than introduce me to her grandparents. The way she'd taken off this morning without a word.

With doubts swirling and my head pounding, I ignored the question. "I'm going to talk to her about going public, being together for real."

Abby gave me a look I'd seen many times over the years. It was the you-are-so-full-of-shit staredown he'd perfected at age eleven.

"Damn, I will, okay?" I insisted. "It was my stupid idea anyway. I'll fix it."

"I hope it works out the way you want it to, Brady. I really do. But secrets and lies are . . ." He took a deep breath, and for the first time in my life, I wondered what secrets Abby was keeping. "This is the definition of fuck around and find out. All I'm saying is, be careful. You can't hide away from the world forever."

I picked up my burrito again and grumbled, "It's not the whole world, Abigail. Just Kirby Falls."

Abby nodded, the hint of a smile twisting his lips. "Well, for some of us, it's the same thing."

We ate in awkward silence until my family arrived a few minutes later. Abby made a pot of coffee while my parents and sisters and Mercer crowded me and loved me in the way only a family with boundary issues could. I was grateful for it. Glad to have people who cared.

While my mom loaded my favorite foods into my refrigerator and my dad and Joan and Mercer chatted with Abby in the kitchen, Candace pulled me aside.

"So, uh," she began uncertainly, "I'm prepping for that garden party event at the orchard, you know?"

I nodded, a little confused why she was bringing up promotional events and whispering about them.

"I scheduled some social media posts to announce it," she said anxiously.

Uhhh.

"And while I was on Chatter . . ."

Shit.

"I noticed some drafted posts." Candace winced.

I sat down hard on the couch and ran a palm down my face, mortified and slightly nauseous that my baby sister had read my pathetic inner monologue and secret feelings.

"Brady." She patted my back. "What's going on with you and Mac?"

Mac

I turned off the Jeep and sat motionless in the parking lot while the engine ticked like a countdown to certain doom.

My phone buzzed from my cup holder, and I jolted from the sound.

I tapped my forehead against the steering wheel a few times and then got up the courage to look.

Candace: He's doing well. He napped a little while Mercer and I were there. But he kicked us out after dinner. Said he was a grown-ass man and he'd be just fine 🙄

Me: Thanks for letting me know. Glad to hear your brother is doing well after the accident.

Candace hadn't really questioned it when I'd texted her throughout the day asking for updates on Brady. I figured I'd have had to explain my interest away, but maybe, in her eyes, knowing I'd witnessed the accident gave me permission for details.

I'd tried Abby first, of course. But his one and only response this morning had given me pause.

Cole Abernathy: You're both idiots. Check on him yourself.

But I couldn't very well check on Brady. I'd been at work, and he was supposed to steer clear of screen time to alleviate his concussion symptoms. Plus, I was actively avoiding my feelings and trying to figure out the best way out of this fucking mess I was in.

I watched the bouncing dots beside Candace's name for a long moment before a surprising reply came through.

Candace: If you need to talk, I'm here for you, Mac. I hope you know that.

I turned off the screen and placed the phone back in my cup holder, unsure what to make of her message. It didn't matter. I didn't have the emotional bandwidth to handle her sincerity, not when it was taking everything in me to wrangle my own fears and inadequacies.

I walked slowly up the stairs and gave a quiet knock on Brady's front door, willing my nerves to settle and my breathing to slow.

"I said I was fine!" he called, voice muffled through the door.

But it swung open a moment later. His very obvious irritation transformed when he saw me, and I almost turned around and walked right back down the stairs.

"Hey," he said. "Sorry, I thought you were another member of my family come to check on me."

The bruising was darker on his face, and he looked tired, his hair messy in a way that made me want to comb my fingers through it.

I clenched my hand into a fist and stepped inside but didn't remove my coat or shoes. "They were worried about you."

Some wariness was starting to enter Brady's features as I stood awkwardly in the small foyer.

I swallowed hard. "How are you feeling?"

"Better than the last time you saw me." He shoved his hands into the front pockets of his joggers. "Want to come in?"

I shook my head, still desperately sifting through words, knowing that none of them were right.

Brady's sudden, bitter laugh had my attention snapping his way. "Well, at least you aren't running and hiding this time." He nodded. "This here, ladies and gentlemen, is what we call personal growth."

"Brady," I tried.

His blue eyes were cool. "Nah, go ahead. Let's hear it."

My mouth was so dry I could hardly swallow. "I just think that things, maybe, went too far. Got out of hand. And we should, uh, take a step back."

He nodded again, as if considering, and then sought to clarify, "A step back where, exactly? Back to getting it out of our systems—which worked wonders, by the way. Or were you thinking a step farther, back to when you hated me?"

I hadn't expected this—this role reversal. I thought I'd be the belligerent, angry one, rushing out my words in an attempt to just get it over with. To break things off and simplify my life once again.

But, Brady—he was bitter and cold, and, suddenly I wanted to cry and run away.

"I don't know, Brady. I just can't keep doing this. It wasn't going to last forever."

"Why not?" he snapped.

I frowned in confusion. "You wanted to stay in a secret relationship forever? How exactly were we supposed to manage that?"

He sighed. "Forget the secret thing. That was—"

"Forget it?" I asked incredulously. "You were the one who said it had to be that way."

"And why do you think I did that, Mac?"

Frustrated anger was a little easier to pick out now in the mass of emotions swirling around my gut. "How should I know?" I practically shouted.

"I did it for you! To take the pressure off of you and this town and all your hang-ups about Kirby Falls. You don't date townies; almost like it means settling, instead of settling down. You would have gotten in your own head about our past and our history. I thought if we kept it a secret—kept it between us—then you might not get scared off."

I stared at Brady like I'd never seen him before. He'd—he'd planned this? In order to manage me? To what end?

"I made a mistake," he admitted, voice low and urgent. He visibly collected himself and took a step toward me. I retreated, my back bumping into the door. "It was a mistake. But, at the time, I thought it was the only way. I thought you'd get tired of me. That if the town kept reminding you of who we were to each other, I wouldn't be worth the whispers and the knowing looks. I didn't want everyone to get in your head. I wanted a chance, Mac. A real chance."

"A chance for what?" I breathed, not understanding. Not getting it.

He looked down at the floor briefly before meeting my gaze. The freeze had thawed, and his blue eyes were pleading. "A chance for you to fall in love with me. For you to get where I'm at. Hell, where I've *been*."

My mouth fell open in surprise, despite all the signs along the way. Not ignorant but perhaps unwilling to see what was right in front of me all this time.

"I love you," he confessed, voice desperate and raw. "I've been so careful, the most careful I've ever been in my life, just trying to hold on to you. To not frighten you away or give you a reason to run. I hid how I felt." He huffed a humorless laugh. "Not very well. But I love you, Mac. I'm *in* love with you, and I always have been. I was just too stupid and stubborn to do anything about it before."

My heart was beating so hard. I wanted to shut my eyes and cover my ears like a child. I also wanted to beg him to say it again, over and over, until it sunk in.

"But I'm telling you now," Brady said, taking a step forward and reaching out for my shaking hand. "I love you. And you love me too. You're just scared to accept it. Too terrified that everything you want is right here in this tiny town." He pressed my hand to his chest, right over his heart, and I wanted to die. "You think people who stay don't deserve to be happy. You're so fucking determined to resent it."

It hurt—these accusations he was slinging at me in his calm, confident tone. Hurt worse because they were true. But he didn't get to pass judgment on me. He didn't know what it was like. Brady Judd, the golden boy with the soccer scholarship and the one-way ticket out of town. But he'd come back. He'd *chosen* this place. And I didn't know how to reconcile that in the twisted ideologies in my head.

"This wasn't how it was supposed to be," I snapped, jerking my hand away. "It wasn't supposed to be like this."

"Like what, Mac? You weren't supposed to fall in love with someone like me? You were supposed to keep dating boring insurance salesmen until you found one you could stomach long enough to settle down and have two point five kids with?"

"That's not—"

The bitterness was back. Brady's jaw clenched before he interrupted, "Or were you supposed to move on and move away and do great, big things? Meet someone who doesn't know you like I do? Is that how it was *supposed* to go?"

I stayed silent and seething. I didn't understand how he could read me so well. And how saying it all out loud like that could make me feel so small and ashamed.

All of a sudden, the anger stringing his body tight loosened its hold. He took a step back, eyes drifting away from me.

"I think you resent me for leaving," he said quietly to the floor between us, "and for coming back. For choosing to make Kirby Falls my home. It's your hometown too, Mac, not your prison. You want to travel? You're dying to see the world? So fucking go. Get on a plane, take a trip, and live your life. Stop acting like we're holding you hostage—like *I'm* holding you back."

"It's not that easy," I gritted out, stripped bare and seen through once again.

But he ignored me. "I thought if I had enough time, you'd realize how right we were for each other. I really thought there was a chance. But now I realize you're never going to be ready. I already had two strikes against me for being born in this town and being happy here. You're going to strike me out because I've known you your whole life and love you just the way you are."

I finally gave in to the urge to close my eyes, but I couldn't shut out his words.

"We would have been happy, and you know it." He sighed. "Instead, you'd rather break both of our hearts just to prove a point. That you don't need Kirby Falls or anything in it—even me."

His thumbs brushed the tears off my cheeks, and I opened my eyes. Brady looked at me like he felt sorry for me. In that moment, I wished his anger would come roaring back. I'd take the righteous indignation over the pity any day.

Finally, his hands lowered to his sides. "Everything between us has been a competition—since we were kids. Well, here you go, Mac. You finally got what you wanted. You won."

My hand found the knob at my back. I turned without meeting his gaze and fled. Pride and hurt and fear kept my feet moving down the hall and toward the stairs.

As furious tears found their way down my cheeks, I had the bitter satisfaction of knowing Brady was wrong.

Because I knew without a doubt, I hadn't won anything at all.

MAC

The good thing about having a secret relationship was that when you went through a breakup, well, that was a secret, too. There wasn't anybody to try to make you feel better or to shit-talk your ex. My friends and family just assumed I was my ornery self or experiencing a monthlong bad mood, which was, frankly, not unheard of.

Larry was still pining over Kayla, so she wasn't one to pass judgment. Her moods were just as unpredictable as mine.

When I'd walked out of Brady's apartment three weeks ago, I'd given myself one day to wallow. I didn't deserve a pity party or to drown my sorrows in ice cream and sad movies. It had been my idea to break things off. I was the one who'd gotten scared by my own feelings for someone I was never supposed to feel those types of things for in the first place. And when I thought about how Brady had tried to handle the situation and manage me, it just made me feel that much more manipulated by forces outside my control.

So far, I'd avoided the places we both frequented. Now that the farmers' market was back in season, I casually checked in with Candace to find out who was working the Judd's booth and tailored my schedule accordingly. I didn't go to bonfires at Abby's anymore. Nor did I attend trivia nights at Trailview. My life was smaller than I liked it, but it felt like a fair trade-off. At least, until I could see Brady in public again without wanting to simultaneously burst into tears and strangle his neck.

He'd stopped posting on Chatter. All the content there was curated for promotion at the orchard.

It was probably wrong of me to wonder how he was or what he was doing. I didn't have the right. But I'd heard through the grapevine that Brady had gotten a new truck and a clean bill of health. And Buck Adams had gotten his license revoked.

The fight with Brady kept me up at night sometimes. It was stupid to dwell on it and why his words had struck such a blow. But as I struggled to sleep, I often replayed the things he'd accused me of. I didn't think I hated my hometown or wanted to move away. Not really. Yet I couldn't reconcile the ideas I'd had in my youth and adolescence. That getting out was the escape route to something more, something better. Rationally, I knew that my parents weren't losers. I didn't see Larry as a disappointment or Abby or anyone else who'd stayed.

Sometimes, the qualities we admire in others only look like weaknesses in ourselves.

There was probably some complicated psychological reason our brains did that—found shortcomings and underlined them in bright red permanent marker—but all I knew was it made me feel like a failure.

Maybe it was because I'd never even tried to leave. I'd never entertained the idea of living elsewhere or working somewhere new. Even as a teenager, I hadn't applied for college. I'd watched my peers write essays and fret over volunteer work to beef up their applications. I'd always known the farm was my future.

It was like Brady had seen all my hypocrisy and self-loathing and thrown it in my face. He was my opposite in so many ways. He'd seen the world and chosen home. I'd been too apathetic—too complacent—to even do that much.

The postcards and the travel magazines and all my browser tabs of hypothetical travel destinations mocked me, highlighting how truly disappointing I was. I'd created some fantasy version of myself and hidden her away. The horrible irony was that who I really wanted to be was a tourist—same as the ones I barely tolerated on a daily basis.

What did it say about me that I resented the people who found something to love about my hometown when I couldn't find it within myself to do the same? I'd always told myself that the leafers didn't appreciate the land and the residents and our livelihood, the simplicity of it, the value in it. But truthfully, I didn't understand how the thousands of tourists we entertained on the farm every year chose to make their way here—a tiny, podunk town in the mountains of North Carolina—when there was a big, wide world out there to be explored.

"Are you coming in or what?" Larry shouted from the porch of Will and Becca's house, jolting me out of the punishing thoughts currently running on a painful loop.

It was our May book club meeting, and I didn't want to be here. No disrespect to Becca, but I just wasn't in the mood for socializing. I hadn't even read the book. I'd made it to chapter two, where the hero had been described as having messy brown hair and piercing blue eyes, and had slammed the book shut, unwilling to read any more.

But Larry stayed on the porch until I exited the Jeep and made my way up the steps.

"It's a small crowd," my cousin offered, probably to help get me in the door. Or maybe to indicate there would be less casualties for my shitty mood. "Becca made lime punch," Larry added helpfully.

I nodded and reached for the doorknob.

"Mac . . ."

I finally faced my cousin when her voice trailed off.

"Did something happen?" she asked quietly. "Are you okay?"

"Yeah, I'm fine."

Larry scrutinized me, and I knew what she saw. Dark circles beneath my eyes from lack of sleep. A messy bun on top of my head from lack of motivation. And a blank expression on my face from a lack of anything more to offer.

"What about you?" I said. "Did you talk to Kayla yet?"

It was a low blow, but it did the job. Larry winced and looked away. "No."

Then I felt like shit for bringing it up, even as a distraction.

I reached out and pulled Larry into a hug, squeezing her hard. "I'm sorry," I mumbled into her shoulder.

After a moment, she returned the embrace, hands below my shoulder blades.

"I gave you a chance," she said softly before releasing me and stepping back.

"What?"

"Nothing!" Then she opened the door and went inside. "Let's get in there before Candace eats all the pizza rolls."

Confused and disoriented, I followed.

Larry had been right. It was a small group gathered for our monthly meeting. Only Becca, Chloe, Larry, Bonnie, Candace, and Joan were in attendance.

I felt a little weird being around Brady's sisters. But it wasn't like they knew about us. Plus, maybe they'd mention him, and then I'd—

Never mind. I needed to stop that train of thought before it derailed and killed all the passengers.

There were approximately six pepperoni pizza rolls left, and Larry and I split them. We settled next to each other on the small patterned loveseat in Will and Becca's living room just off the kitchen.

The ladies talked about the book. I stayed quiet since I didn't have anything helpful to add. It was a little difficult to do, seeing as there were only seven of us, but Becca was good at directing the conversation, and Candace had big feelings about this one, so she talked a lot.

"I think it's really interesting," she was saying, "how irresponsible the hero comes across. Even at the end of the book, it was like his character arc hadn't really changed. He was the same good-time guy who didn't take responsibility for his own actions and forgot things and meant well, bless his heart."

"I agree." Chloe nodded. "You can be as charming as you want, but there has to be something behind it. Something meaningful or the effort is hollow."

"And he was super immature," Joan added dispassionately.

"Yes!"

"Oh my God. So immature!"

"Definitely."

The chorus of responses had Candace giggling. "You know, he actually reminds me of Brady."

I shifted a little in my seat.

Joan whacked her sister on the arm. "God, you're right. Just the general air of doesn't-give-a-fuck. The selfishness and the way he lets everyone do everything for him."

I could feel my brows drawing together. *Wait, just a minute.*

"Exactly! That." Candace nodded emphatically and then reached for her drink. "I mean, he's not a billionaire like the guy in the book, but other than that, identical."

I couldn't believe what I was hearing. Glancing around the seating area, I was shocked to see Becca, Chloe, and Bonnie nodding along.

"That's a little harsh," I blurted without meaning to.

Candace paused, the punch cup halfway to her face. "What's that, Mac?"

I swallowed, feeling my face heat. "I just think that comparing Jeremy—"

"Gerald," Larry corrected from my side.

"Right, Gerald." I blinked, aware that everyone was now staring at me, waiting for me to elaborate. "I don't think Brady is how you described that guy . . . Gerald. I disagree."

"Oh?" Becca asked. "How would you describe him, Mac?"

"Well," I licked my lips, "he's not selfish at all. He's actually very thoughtful." There'd been the random texts throughout the day to check on me and see how work was going. One time, after we'd talked about Italy and how I wanted to go there, he'd sent me an article about the best must-see underrated tourist spots on the Amalfi Coast. And then another time, he'd brought breakfast to my office because I'd told him I'd slept through my alarm and had been running too late to eat.

"And the charm thing isn't an act or for show. He's genuinely a nice person who likes people," I added.

Becca's eyes widened, but she nodded encouragingly. "Go on."

I would because Brady's sisters needed to hear this and appreciate him, damn it. He loved them and talked about them all the time. "It's wrong to say he doesn't care or want to take responsibility. He was so worried about the orchard when the vandalism was happening, before he knew it was Amos. He installed all those cameras and the security system, and he didn't let Candace work a single closing shift by herself. And—and Amos!"

I was on a roll now. "He gave that little shit a second chance. He didn't want Amos to have a juvenile record, and I know he worried that he'd made the wrong decision. But Amos's mother was so grateful. He's basically mentoring that kid and guiding him down the right path, giving him a great male role model when Amos doesn't have that in his life."

I was breathing hard, and I wasn't sure why. Everyone was still staring at me, but I forced myself to take a stabilizing inhale and address Candace and Joan, where they sat beside one another. "Your brother does mean well. He's a really good person. He cares about you both and your parents so much. And the orchard, too. He—he loves his life working with y'all. And I think it's shitty to sit here and criticize him and compare him to that asshole Jeremy—"

"Gerald," Larry corrected again.

I shot her a glare. "Gerald. Whatever."

Candace was wide-eyed, her long brown ponytail bobbing in time with every nod of her head. Joan watched me with a little smile on her face that made me suddenly very uneasy.

I glanced around the room, taking in the other pleased expressions before landing on Becca, who grinned broadly.

"Thank you for that, Mac," she said, pleased as lime punch. "But I meant, how would you describe Gerald? The hero? You know, from the story we all read and have been discussing for the last forty minutes. If you'd rather talk about Brady Judd, we can do that too, I suppose." Her smile somehow got even brighter. "I'm not opposed."

Realization dawned as heat rushed to my cheeks. The urge to run right out of here with a pocket full of pizza rolls was admittedly strong.

Larry must have noted the tensing of my muscles for flight because she placed a staying hand on my knee. "I think you'd better tell us what's going on, Mac."

My eyes darted between the gathered women, specifically the ones who were Brady's blood relatives. "I—it's complicated."

"Mac," Becca said gently. "Try. It might help."

Instead of laying out everything that had happened with Brady, another truth forced its way from between my lips. "I think I'm scared. I think . . . I'm scared to let myself be happy here. That maybe I'm stuck, and I don't know what to do."

"What do you mean by 'here'?" Joan asked, face impassive but tone patient and curious.

My eyes scanned the space, unsure how to put all my tangled feelings about my life into words that made any sort of sense. My attention caught on the far wall, on the pictures of my family going back generations. My great-grandfather William, riding a tractor. The great-grandmother I'd never met, standing on the front porch of this very house, holding a teacup and saucer. A similar picture but of my cousin Will, his arm draped around Becca's shoulders as she laughed in the frame. A shot of Grandma Nola and Grandpa Junior on their wedding day. My parents behind the counter in the General Store. A childhood photo of me and Larry and Will sitting in front of a honeysuckle bush, covered in dirt and sticky from nectar.

"Home," I answered finally. "I feel like I failed some sort of test, ending up in Kirby Falls. Never leaving. Never applying myself. I realized a while ago that I was just coasting along, content to put in my time and then clock out and go home. But our farm—our life—is so much more than that. I just didn't see it, or, maybe, I didn't feel like I was a part of it until recently."

I looked at these women who had all ended up in Kirby Falls one way or another, and guilt twisted my insides.

"Are you ashamed, Mac?" my sister asked. Bonnie was a woman who'd married her high school sweetheart and taught at the same elementary school she'd attended.

"No," I answered reflexively, not intending to offend or belittle anyone in the room. "I don't know."

And I didn't know, not really. I had good neighbors, and I liked living out in the country. I wouldn't have made it in a big city. I needed the mountain air and the fields and the scope and range of the life I led. I liked trivia night and bowling league and book club and listening to bands at local breweries. My life wasn't small by any means. But I didn't know whose standard I was living by.

"You know," Candace said, "I think there's a stigma surrounding small towns. People think they automatically equate to small-mindedness. That people who've been raised on farms aren't educated. It's in the media and, honestly, it's part of growing up. I went to college with people who thought they were better than me. Had professors who were surprised to learn I was from a tiny town in Western North Carolina. I hid my accent and other things that would out me as a person from a rural area for a long time. Not because I was ashamed of where I was from, but because they were."

I nodded because I understood that. I thought of the tourists who came through and said our town was "quaint" or the ones you'd overhear calling us hillbillies. Both comments were offensive in different ways.

"But," Candace continued, "after a while, I realized it didn't matter. I wasn't really going to change anyone's mind about me by being confrontational or defensive. I couldn't change their worldview for them. It would only make them cling to those beliefs even harder. They could believe whatever stereotype they wanted. Because where I wanted to be—where I was meant to be—was right here."

"There are any number of reasons why people stay in their hometown," Joan offered. "Some just fit better there than anywhere else."

"Some get married too young and never have the means or the backbone to leave," Chloe said solemnly.

Larry squeezed my knee again. "Some folks have everyone they love right there with them and never have any desire to move away."

"Some can't stay away no matter how hard they try," Candace said with a smile.

"Some people aren't able to envision any other future for themselves," Bonnie said, her face unbearably honest and open. I felt my throat go tight.

"Some make a home for themselves with the family they choose," Becca added, blue eyes wet with unshed tears.

"And none of it is right or wrong," Joan concluded. "Sometimes, it's just the way things work out. But don't fall under the impression that those of us who stay aren't living rich, fulfilled lives. We all have our own stories to tell, wisdom to impart, and a legacy to uphold. Even you, Mac."

The things they shared reached deep inside me and tugged hard. I was so very fortunate to have these women in my life. To have a family who loved and supported me. Friends who accepted me. A community I belonged to.

"Are you happy?" Larry asked earnestly. "Would you be happier somewhere else? Because that's okay if that's the way you feel, Mac. You wouldn't lose us or—"

"No," I interrupted, feeling the truth of it in my bones. "This is my home. It's where I want to live my life, with the people I love." And I knew who that included, whether I'd planned for him or not.

"Then give yourself permission to be happy here," Candace said, smiling gently.

"I'd like to travel more," I admitted.

"Then fucking travel more," Larry said emphatically. "And take that Brady Judd with you."

I met her challenging gaze. "He hates me."

"We know. We know." She rolled her eyes. "You guys *hate* each other."

"No," I confessed. "Now he really *does* hate me. We were . . . seeing each other. Secretly, for months, but then I—I got scared. I broke his heart, I think." *Broke mine too*, I didn't add.

As I searched the faces of everyone in the room, it was telling that no one really seemed all that surprised.

"Then, maybe," Larry said, "it's time to say you're sorry."

Five other women nodded along before Becca piped up, "And a grand gesture couldn't hurt."

Brady

.   .   .

"Candace, I really don't want to be here," I said from the backseat of Mercer's truck, where I'd been kidnapped and was being held against my will.

"Well, too bad, big brother. Nola and Junior invited our whole family, and we're going."

Mercer met my eyes in the rearview mirror. He winced and focused back on the road.

It was Memorial Day weekend, and the Clarks were throwing their annual party out on Lake Archer.

But I didn't have it in me. I had no desire to play cornhole or ride Jet Skis. I didn't want to grill hamburgers or eat Maggie Clark's tortellini pasta salad, which was saying something. And I definitely didn't want to see Mac.

It had been just over three weeks since we'd spoken. I didn't know what was left to say. She'd wanted to break things off, so I needed to let her. Seeing her today would be torture.

You didn't stop loving someone just because you were angry and hurt. I knew Mac was hurting, too, and that was, maybe, the worst part of all. Because I knew she loved me back.

Still, I couldn't be the one who tried to fix this. She had to reach her own conclusions and, ultimately, live her own life, with or without me.

If you chased someone long enough, all you'd do was eventually wear them down. And where was the love in that?

So when Candace and Mercer had practically wrestled me into the truck today, I'd been quietly panicking and loudly protesting. I'd even tried the door handle at a stoplight and they'd put the damn child locks on.

"Stop pouting," Candace called as she slipped her sunglasses on.

"I liked it better when you lived in a different state, butthead."

She tossed a grin over her shoulder. "No, you didn't, buttface."

"Jesus," I heard Mercer mutter. Then we turned onto a bumpy gravel road that would take us out to the Clarks' private property overlooking the lake.

To add insult to injury, the day was beautiful. May in Western North Carolina could be unpredictable, but the sun was shining bright on the water, and Mercer's windows were down, letting in the lakeside breeze.

Nola and Junior's property sat well above the shoreline. Their house was positioned on an overlook, but there was a trail with several switchbacks that led down to their private dock. The party wasn't being held at the house, though. They'd built a large pavilion nearby for entertaining, a big covered open-air structure that housed a dozen picnic tables. It also held hammocks and swings that faced the water. There was a fully functional kitchen attached as well as a renovated bathhouse next door.

I knew the matriarch and patriarch of the Clark bunch spent a good deal of time out here during the summer months, and it was a beautiful place.

As I reluctantly climbed from the backseat of the truck, I took in the rolling mountains in the distance, the dark water shimmering in the sunlight, and the tiny islands that dotted the landscape. I could see how it would be a peaceful place, meditative even. That was, if there weren't seventy-five neighbors making a ruckus as they drank and played yard games.

I could hear the buzz of Jet Skis, and I watched as pontoon boats trawled and speedboats zipped across the surface of the water.

"Here," Candace said, pushing a covered dish into my chest. "Carry that."

"You know, had I planned on attending, I would have prepared my own dish," I sniped. "Not whatever you threw together."

"That is strawberry yum yum pie," she said pointedly, as if I should be so lucky to carry it into a potluck. "And Mark made it."

"Oh, good. At least it'll be edible."

My sister glared at me. "Let's go find our hosts and say hello."

Pie plate in hand, I stopped walking, remembering suddenly the day I'd panicked and installed a birdfeeder rather than tell Nola Clark I was dating her granddaughter.

Mercer and Candace turned to face me.

"I, uh, I'm going to take this to the kitchen. Y'all go say hello. I'll catch up."

Then I speed-walked by them, my shoes eating up the gravel as I made my way beneath the covered patio. People were milling about everywhere, talking and eating. Plastic tablecloths flapped in the breeze, held down by plates of delicious-looking food. Kids I didn't recognize stacked giant Jenga blocks on the lawn beside the pavilion.

Despite my mood, I nodded to folks who greeted me. A few people asked how I was feeling.

I assumed they meant my mostly healed head injury, and not my still-broken heart.

I caught sight of Will Clark and his best friend, Jordan Rockford, manning a pair of grills, and wondered if I could hide out with them all afternoon. Will leaned back from the heat as the flames hissed and jumped. Jordan wore a ridiculous apron that made it look like he was dressed in a hula skirt and a coconut bra.

I'd heard that Jordan and his girlfriend, Chloe, had gotten engaged a few weeks ago. And as if summoned by my thoughts, Chloe dropped off a platter of veggie burgers on the worktable next to the grills. The redhead grinned and pinched Jordan's backside on her way back to the kitchen. Her fiancé called out to her, something that made her throw her head back and laugh even as she scurried off.

I felt like a jealous, pathetic loser as I watched the lovey-dovey exchange. I wouldn't be hiding out with those two, in any case.

Sighing, I kept moving toward the kitchen. When I was about ten feet away, Mac breezed through the open doorway, a platter of fried chicken in her hands.

I took a step back on instinct, certain I'd step on the pieces of my shattered heart, expecting to feel the crunch of them beneath my feet.

She turned without seeing me, making her way to the long buffet table while I stood staring like an idiot. She looked—she looked gorgeous. Her long, dark hair was up in a sleek ponytail. She had on a bright yellow button-up that was thin and gauzy. It was tucked into—I swallowed hard—cutoff jean shorts.

If there was heartbreak or unhappiness on her face, I couldn't find it. No dark circles beneath her eyes or any overarching misery. She was smiling at Lettie Louise Walker as she dished up some macaroni and cheese for the older woman.

"Brady."

I jumped, nearly fumbling the pie in my grasp.

"Oh, Lord," Maggie Clark said as she reached out to grab the covered dish. "Let me take that, sugar."

I felt my cheeks heat, relatively sure Mac's aunt had just caught me staring at her niece like a creeper.

She smiled. "Actually, why don't you come with me?"

I cleared my throat. "Yes, ma'am."

I was put on cornhole duty, and honestly, I was grateful for the task. Maggie set me up at a table with a list and an envelope for money. People were buying in for doubles tournament play for five bucks each. The winnings would go to the top two teams. Pairs would be chosen at random, and a bracket would be made by Maggie herself. I was just supposed to sit there and take the money and write down the names.

Fifteen minutes into my appointment, Patty, Mac's mom, brought me a huge plate of food. "Sorry you got put to work, Brady. I can take over for you if you'd like."

I smiled, genuinely this time. Patty was a sweet one—must be where Bonnie got it from. "No, ma'am. I like staying busy. It keeps me out of trouble."

She patted my shoulder. "I'll be back with dessert for you."

Before I could stop her, off she went.

As I sat alone at the table with my clipboard, I didn't catch sight of Mac again.

Eventually, Maggie made her way back to me. "Oh, shoot," she said, eyeing the sign-up list. "We have an odd number. You'll play, won't you, Brady?"

Damn it, I did not want to play cornhole. I was hoping Candace and Mark were ready to go. But when I did a quick search of the area, I found my sister over at the beer pong table chugging away.

Resisting a pained groan, I replied, "Uh, sure. I can do that."

Maggie smiled at me and patted my cheek. "Thanks, sweet pea. I owe you one."

Well, it turned out Maggie Clark owed me more than one. She owed me an explanation for the knife in my back, because when she announced the pairs for the cornhole tournament ten minutes later, my name was right next to Mac's.

I stood staring at the neat lettering on the chalkboard and tried to figure out how the hell I was going to get out of this.

"Maggie," I said.

She gave me a distracted "Hmm?" from where she sat, handing out beanbags and organizing the chaos.

The giant Jenga blocks and the bocce- and ladder-ball equipment on the side lawn had been moved to make room for the eight pairs of wooden boards facing one another with some twenty-odd feet in between.

"Maggie," I tried again. "I don't think this is a good idea. I don't think I can play after all. Can you find a replacement for me?"

She checked off something on her clipboard before smiling sweetly at me. "No."

I blinked in surprise.

She was already back to handing out beanbags as people shuffled in and around me.

I opened my mouth to respond, sure I'd misunderstood her, when a voice came from behind me.

"What's the matter, Judd? Afraid you don't have what it takes?"

My jaw clenched, and I turned to find Mac casually tossing a red beanbag in one hand. Her grin was all challenge, and, for the life of me, I couldn't figure out why she wasn't trying to get out of this forced partnership too.

"No," I said reflexively. Old habits die hard, apparently.

"Good. Because I always make it to the final. Let's do this." She threw the bag and spun on her heel.

I probably would have caught the damn thing if I hadn't been staring at her ass in those shorts. Instead, it bounced off my chest and hit the ground.

Sighing, I retrieved the bag and followed her to our assigned lane, dread and misgiving keeping me company.

How could she be fine with this? Did she really think we could go back to the way we were? I didn't want to bicker and fight. Hell, it was hard enough to look at her. I figured if I tried to carry on a conversation, or God forbid, trash-talk, then I'd probably lose all my resolve and beg her to give me another chance.

Our opponents were already waiting for us.

"Hi, honey!" My mom waved from beside the far board facing the lake.

I approached, and she gave me a tight hug around the waist. "Mom, have you ever even played cornhole?"

She grinned. "Nope. But Patty made it sound like fun."

I glanced across to the other board and saw Mac standing next to her own mother, who gave me a wide smile.

I waved woodenly and then sighed again. Random assignments, my ass.

Well, there was one way out of this mess. I'd just throw the game. It wouldn't be my finest moment, but it would get me away from Mac. That worked for me.

"Can we take a few practice tosses?" Mom asked.

"Sure," I said. "Why not?"

Then I watched as my mother tossed a one-pound blue beanbag about six feet wide of the board. Her second attempt wasn't much better. It went well over the target. Mac actually had to dart out of the way to avoid being hit.

God, throwing this game was going to be harder than I thought.

We skipped the coin toss and just picked our lanes. I had no problem with Mac and Patty taking the board opposite me, alternating tosses to try to get them in the hole of the board near my feet.

Patty only managed to get one on the board. Mac landed two in the hole and two on top, giving our team a score of seven right out of the gate.

I went next and missed the board on all four tosses.

Brushing the dust off my hands, I made a *yikes* face. "Guess I should have taken some practice tosses too."

Mac's gaze narrowed on me before watching my mother land two points for Team Mom.

The next turn had our score climbing to sixteen, thanks to Mac, and Mac alone.

When I flubbed another three tosses, Mac held up her hands. "Time-out!"

"There's no time-out in cornhole," I argued.

"Well, excuse me if I don't trust your knowledge of the sport. You clearly have no idea how to play," she said, striding across the lawn separating us.

"That's okay!" Patty called happily. "I need another drink."

"Oh, me too!" Mom declared and hurried off.

"What are you doing?" Mac said when she stood toe to toe with me.

Ignoring her angry eyes and her legs in those shorts, I crossed my arms and looked down my nose at her. "I don't know what you mean."

"I mean, you are throwing this game on purpose, and it's really fucking obvious because our moms are terrible."

I tapped my chin thoughtfully. "Funny how our moms got paired up and we got partnered together too. I'm starting to think Maggie didn't pick these names out of a hat after all."

Mac blinked, then scowled. "It doesn't matter. Just stop cheating."

I leaned down to scowl back. "I am not cheating. Maybe I'm rusty, okay?" My eyes narrowed further, daring her to call me on it. "Maybe something is affecting my performance."

She tilted her pointed chin and rose onto her tiptoes. "I've never known your performance to be affected."

My mouth dropped open. Was she—? Did she just—?

"Alright, kids!"

My mom's voice had us springing apart from where Mac and I had gravitated toward one another.

My teammate shot me one more vicious look before marching back over to her side of the lawn.

I had one last toss to complete my turn.

There was a big part of me that wanted to tank this match and be done with this whole damn day. It was practically my adolescent pastime to try to mess with Mac and keep her from getting what she wanted. If she was going to get in my face and sling insults, my natural inclination was to get back at her, though. Then, there was the competitive idiot who lived inside me. He wanted to get her goat and give it a tug.

So I hefted the beanbag in my right hand, kept my eyes on hers, and sank it into the hole on the opposite board without even looking.

Her victorious little smirk made something flicker to life in my chest. Something that had been cold and dark since she'd walked out three weeks ago. I worried there'd always be some part of me that craved her attention, yearned for it.

Mac wrapped the game up on the next turn, hitting twenty-one points easily. The moms gave us hugs and wished us luck in the tournament. Then they ambled off together to grab more drinks with umbrellas in them.

In the next round, we faced off against Mason Gentry and the tourist-turned-resident Becca Kernsy. Her whole face lit up when she saw the two of us.

Mason was a high school junior and a pretty good baseball player. He was also staring at Becca like she was a Disney princess.

Despite playing against her friend, Mac had her game face on. When it was my turn to toss, I swung my arm back, took a step forward, and heard her call out, "Foot fault!"

I stared at Mac incredulously. "I'm on your team!"

She winced. "Right. Shit, sorry." Then louder, "His foot was fine!"

Becca shrugged and grinned. "Today is the first time I've ever played. I have no idea where your feet are even supposed to go."

Mason didn't object when I resumed my turn because, again, he was mooning over the blond opposite him.

Mac and I won the round easily.

Becca hugged me hard afterward. "Good luck. I'm pulling for you."

I patted her back awkwardly as Mason glared at me over her shoulder.

We had a few minutes until the next round of the tournament started. There was a low stone wall around the perimeter of the lawn. I sat down and stared out at the water, feeling confused and wrung out.

The sun was setting, turning the sky shades of pink and orange. Café lights strung over the lawn clicked on right as Mac climbed over the wall. She passed me a bottle of beer and sat down next to me. Not so close that our shoulders brushed, but not so far that I couldn't remember how it felt when they did.

"The next game will be tough," she said, then sipped from her own bottle.

Mac looked soft and warm in this light, her cheeks and the bridge of her nose a little pink from being out in the sun this afternoon.

As difficult as it was to be around her like this, I relished it. After weeks of silence, here she was, right beside me. She'd been egging me on and teasing me, smiling my way. We were having fun, and I had to admit that when forced to choose between nothing and something . . . I'd pick something every time.

I cleared my throat. "Oh, yeah? Who are we up against?"

"Mattie and Seth." She pointed over my shoulder. "They're just finishing up."

Turning, I followed where she'd indicated. The game must have just wrapped because the two players were high-fiving one another.

Mattie was Matilda Bartholomew, the owner of Mattie B's downtown. She was a badass behind the bar who didn't take shit from anyone. We locals had managed to keep Mattie B's a hometown secret by review bombing on social media. The leafers mostly hit Magnolia Bar as a result, and that worked for all of us.

Mattie was also a regular star on the rec league softball circuit. And her current cornhole partner was just as good. Seth Rockford was Jordan's teenage brother. He'd played baseball since he was a toddler, so he'd likely have a good arm and aim.

I slowly spun back to face Mac. "How do you want to play it?"

She swallowed and looked out at the water. "Come out swinging. They only need a few turns to put it away. We keep it as close as we can."

I nodded and decided I wanted her attention back on me. "I think you should play across from Seth and unbutton the top two buttons on your shirt."

Her attention snapped to my face, gray eyes flashing. "I'm not doing that. He's seventeen years old."

I grinned and let my eyes dip purposefully to her chest. "Exactly."

Mac shook her head and whacked me in the stomach with the back of her hand, but when she stood and climbed back over the low wall, she was smiling.

Somehow, we eked out the win. Even without the distraction of Mac's cleavage. And when she walked over to me after the game wearing a huge grin, I didn't hesitate to pull her in for a hug.

All the remaining partygoers crowded around to watch the final match. People cheered and chatted. Neighbors sat on the low wall surrounding the lawn and spectated.

I sort of always felt like I lived in a Hallmark movie, what with our picturesque tourist town and small community. Looking around at everyone gathered, I wondered how Mac felt, if she resented the close-knit group. How she could probably name nearly everyone in the crowd just like I could.

Before the game resumed, I stared at her across twenty feet of grass. She was smiling at whoever had her attention. Another person called out to her, and she ran over and gave a high five. She didn't look unhappy. She looked like she fit.

I swallowed hard and picked up four red beanbags.

Unfortunately, we got our asses handed to us in the final round by our seventy-year-old former high school biology teacher, Mr. Ammons, and my sister Joan, of all people.

We shook hands with the winners, and I was surprised when Joan pulled me in for a hug. She gave me a rare smile before she headed off into the crowd.

"Well," Mac said, coming to stand next to me. "Good game."

I nodded. "Yeah, good game."

A wave of sadness washed over me. I didn't know where Mac and I went from here. So I turned and started walking to the parking lot.

My heart felt tender and bruised. I realized I didn't want to have fun with her. I didn't want to revert back to our long-standing history. And more than anything, I didn't want to forget the last six months. It felt like trading one for the other, and I was ready to let go.

I'd force myself to be mature about it someday, when it didn't hurt so much just to be near her.

Mac found me five minutes later, standing in the spot where Mercer's truck had been parked eight hours ago.

I had my hands on my hips, staring at the gravel as if it had betrayed me.

"Hey!" she called. "You forgot your winnings."

I saw the cash she held out in my periphery, but I didn't turn. "Just keep it."

After a moment, she said, "Candace and Mercer left a while ago."

I didn't respond because of fucking course they did.

"I'll give you a ride," she offered.

I closed my eyes. "Fine."

It felt weird to climb into her Jeep. I fumbled with the seat belt, unsure where to look or what to do with my hands. In all my years of knowing Mac, I couldn't remember feeling this uncomfortable around her.

She turned on the headlights and bumped along the gravel, but we didn't make it far. As soon as her grandparents' lake house came into view at the top of the hill, she pulled into the driveway that wound around the side, out of view of the pavilion, and parked.

"What are you doing?" I asked.

She pivoted in her seat to face me. "I wanted to talk, Brady."

I released a humorless laugh. "I've already been kidnapped once today. I'm not really in the mood."

"I know. I'm sorry."

I frowned over at her. "You know?"

But she ignored me. "Brady, I'm sorry. I'm so fucking sorry I ended things that way. When you got in the accident—" Her voice broke, and she covered her mouth with her hand.

I had to resist the urge to reach for her, to comfort her when what she'd done had hurt me worse than the front end of Buck Adams's truck.

Mac sniffed and composed herself. "After the accident, I got scared. So scared. I'll never forget looking through the glass and seeing you unmoving and bleeding. And knowing that I loved you so fucking much, I didn't know what I'd do if something happened to you."

I watched her struggle through the admission, knowing she meant it. Her loving me wasn't a surprise. Hearing her admit it was, though. But it didn't bring me satisfaction to know she'd been scared or confused. I didn't feel vindicated. I just wanted her to be happy. I wanted us both to be happy.

"But you were right." She nodded. "About everything. I never anticipated falling for you, and I did what I always do when I'm insecure or off-balance. I lashed out and rejected those emotions. Pushed them away by force, and you right along with them."

This was what I'd hoped for. Her admission. Her self-awareness. But I told the foolish heart vibrating wildly in my chest not to get ahead of itself. "So what changed?"

She took a breath. "I realized I have unhealthy expectations for myself. And it turns out, some of my very favorite people were born and raised and still live in this town. I'm sorry I punished you for something that's broken in me."

I gave in and reached for her hand. "You're not broken, Mac. Do you want to move away? Do you think that would make you happier?" I hated that it might be true, but I knew I'd go with her if she asked.

She was already shaking her head, though. "No. Kirby Falls is home. I like my job at the farm. I feel good about where I'm at. I love my family and my friends. And I love you. I'm sorry I hurt you. If you don't think you can forgive me or if you don't want to be—"

I cut her off by closing the distance between us and pressing my lips to hers.

She made a sound, one of relief tinged with desperation, and a moment later, I felt her warm tears against my cheek.

I rested my forehead against hers. "I can forgive you. It's okay, Mac."

She pulled back and opened her eyes. They glistened silver in the low light of the Jeep's interior.

I swiped the moisture from her face and smiled. "You admitted you love me."

Mac laughed, a surprised, happy sound. "I do. I love you. I want to go on a date without an asterisk. I want to get a tattoo of your name on *my* butt. I want you to call me stupid nicknames for the rest of my life. I don't want to be without you. Somehow, someway, you're my best friend and my worst enemy, and I never want that to change. We can fight forever if you want, Brady. Just promise you'll love me too."

I kissed her again and then pulled back suddenly when my brain caught on something.

"Wait, was all this—today—your plan? Did you *grand gesture* me?"

"Yes," she admitted sheepishly.

"Have you *ever* read a romance novel?" I asked incredulously.

She straightened away from me. "Yes. Have you?"

"Of course I have. So your idea of a grand gesture was to fight with me about cornhole and wear teeny-tiny shorts to torture me?"

Mac tucked a wayward strand of hair behind one ear. "The shorts were Becca's idea."

I shook my head, thinking back to her tight hug and her whispered *I'm pulling for you*. She hadn't been talking about cornhole at all. "God, she looks so sweet and innocent. Diabolical."

Then my mouth dropped open. "So, this whole thing? My sister and Mercer?"

"I had to get you here. And also strand you here."

"And Maggie needing one more player? And assigning teams?"

Mac grinned.

"Wow. Just wow," I said, amazed by the level of deviousness and oddly endeared by it.

She threaded her fingers through mine, serious-faced now. "I just figured, you fell in love with me back then, before. Through all the pranks and arguments and bickering. I thought this"—she gestured around us to the lake, the day, the plan, everything—"felt more like us. That it would mean more than showing up at your door with an apology and my heart in my hands. I wanted you to remember who we've always been to each other. How integral. How vital. I know you wanted to keep us a secret—"

"I'm sorry," I interrupted. "That was a mistake. I was never ashamed of you. I don't actually want to hide us from anyone."

"I know." Mac squeezed my hand. "I know that now. But it's okay to remember how we got here. It's okay if people bring up our history, like how we tried to kill each other with Elmer's glue fifteen years ago. It'll just make a good story for the grandkids someday."

My happiness was too big to be enclosed in such a small space. I could feel how wide my smile was, the dimple creasing my cheek. "We have lots of good stories."

"Yeah, we really do."

BRADY

Family dinner at Maggie's was different this time around.

No one was awkward or surprised by my appearance. There was still teasing from Larry. And Becca and I prepped the salad again.

But Mac and I were together, and everyone knew it.

I could reach for her hand beneath the table. Or lean over and kiss her if I wanted.

Which I did now, distracting Mac and swiping the bowl of peach cobbler her grandmother had just placed in front of her.

Nola and Junior knew I was dating their granddaughter, too. I didn't sneak out of their house anymore, but mostly because Mac was at my place every night. Nola still gave me shit about the birdfeeder thing, but I figured that was a sign of love because she and Mac were relentless with one another. And I knew Nola loved her granddaughter something fierce.

Once Mac had pinched my ribs and recovered her cobbler, she glanced down at her phone for the fourth time.

"What's wrong?" I asked.

"Nothing," she said. "It's just that Bonnie told me she was coming tonight."

Our eyes found the two empty place settings at the end of the long dining room table.

In the month since Mac and I had become official, I'd spent a good deal of time with her sister. We'd chatted at trivia and bowling league. The ladies had even invited me to their latest book club meeting. But Bonnie's husband, Danny, had been absent for most of that. I figured something was going on in their marriage that was none of my business.

"She's not answering?" I asked.

"No." Mac glanced at her unchanged text thread one more time before placing her phone face down on the table.

I reached for her thigh and gave it a squeeze. "Maybe something came up."

She nodded.

Nola and Junior were heading out to the lake after dinner, so Mac and I were back at her house tonight.

It was after two in the morning when pounding somewhere downstairs woke me. Mac was just sitting up as I finished buttoning my jeans. I hastily threw a tee shirt over my head.

"Grab your cell and stay here," I told her. "I'm going to see who it is."

"Wait," she hissed. The knocking hadn't stopped. "Be careful."

Nodding, I headed for the stairs.

When I reached the front of the house, I peeked out the window next to the door, unsure of what I'd find.

"Shit," I breathed, then hurried to unlock the dead bolt.

Bonnie practically fell into my arms. She was crying so hard I couldn't make out what she was saying.

"Bonnie, take a breath for me," I said softly as I led her over to the couch nearby.

"Brady," Mac called from the bottom of the stairs.

I met her gaze helplessly as she hurried over.

Bonnie's face was twisted in agony, her eyes puffy and cheeks flushed.

I knelt in front of her. "Are you hurt, Bonnie?"

But she couldn't answer me. Her breaths were coming too fast. She sounded like she was suffocating even as tears leaked down her face.

Mac was frozen at my side, staring at her sister like she'd never seen her before.

"Mac," I said quietly to get her attention.

She flinched, meeting my gaze.

"Help Bonnie get her sweater off. Get her purse too," I instructed.

I didn't know what had happened, but I thought it'd be better for Mac to be the one to touch her. I didn't want to scare her, but I knew the cardigan she wore might feel confining in the face of a panic attack, and the strap of her crossbody bag wasn't helping either.

Mac jolted into action while I spoke softly to Bonnie.

"Take a deep breath with me. Try to do what I'm doing." I exaggerated my inhales and exhales for her benefit.

When Bonnie was free of her bag and her sweater, I grasped her hands and kept talking. It was dim. The only light in the room was coming from the kitchen, and I did my best to calm her down.

"Should I call 9-1-1?" Mac asked from where she'd joined me on the floor.

"No," Bonnie choked out between gasps, her fingers gripping me tight. "No . . . ambulance."

Mac and I shared an uneasy look but left our phones in our pockets.

It took another five minutes for Bonnie's breathing to even out and her hands to loosen around mine. Mac sat quietly at my side and watched her sister struggle.

When I thought it was safe, I said gently, "I'm going to go get you some water, Bonnie. Mac will be right here."

I urged Mac to join her sister on the couch and then went quickly to the kitchen.

Judging by the way she'd frozen, I didn't think Mac had ever seen Bonnie this way. Her movements were wooden and uncertain, her gaze wide-eyed and frightened in the face of her sister's pain.

Once I'd filled a glass, I heard low voices.

I stood at the threshold of the living room, giving them some privacy, but heard Bonnie manage through a fresh wave of tears, "Danny wants a divorce." She hiccupped a sob. "He doesn't want to be married to me."

Mac wrapped her arms around Bonnie, shushing and rocking her gently. "It's okay, Bon. It'll be okay."

I approached quietly and placed the glass on the end table. Bonnie didn't look up, but Mac met my gaze and mouthed a thank-you over her sister's head.

I made my way upstairs to Mac's bedroom and shut the door, hating that her sister was suffering. Bonnie was a good person. Kind and thoughtful. She was a go-getter and a leader in the community. The first to volunteer for anything and dedicated to her family and her students.

Hours later, I felt the bed dip and opened my eyes. I checked my phone. It was 4:13 a.m.

"Is Bonnie okay?" I asked as I opened my arms and Mac burrowed into my side.

"I don't know," she whispered. "But she's asleep in the guest room across the hall. We talked for a little while, but I mostly just watched her while she slept. I was so scared, Brady."

My arms tightened reflexively upon hearing the tremor in her voice.

"I couldn't tell you the last time I even saw her cry," she admitted. "Bonnie is always so perfect and put-together and on top of things. She never even said they were having problems. I mean, I've gotten a vibe for the last few months, Danny being weird and absent. They've seemed distant, disconnected. But divorce . . . I never thought . . ."

"She's going to be alright," I said. "She has you and your family. Candace would do anything for her, too."

I felt Mac nod against my chest. "Seeing her like that, knowing she needed me, was the only thing keeping me from going over there and kicking Danny's ass."

"I know." I pressed a kiss into her hair. My fierce protector. My hellcat.

We drifted off after that, and when I woke the next morning, I slipped quietly downstairs, intent on making some coffee and letting Mac sleep in.

I was sitting at the kitchen table, halfway through my first cup when Bonnie came down. Her short blond hair was pulled back into a tiny stub of a ponytail. She was wearing a pair of Mac's sweatpants and a tee shirt.

Besides having the same upturned nose and dimple in their chins, the two sisters didn't look much alike. With her dark hair and light eyes, Mac took after her dad and the rest of the Clarks. Bonnie, who was short and petite, more strongly resembled their mother. Blond hair, brown eyes, and an infectious smile with a slight gap between her front teeth.

She wasn't smiling now, though. Bonnie's eyelids were puffy, and her face was pale and drawn as she shuffled into the room on bare feet.

"Mornin'," I called, wanting to announce myself.

Her head rose. "Hi."

Then, she surprised the heck out of me by walking right up to my stool and hugging me hard. "Thank you," Bonnie said, her voice thick. "For last night. I'm embarrassed you saw me that way, but I appreciate what you did for me."

I squeezed her back. "Nothing to be embarrassed over. I'm glad you're okay."

With a final pat, she released me and went to pour herself a cup of coffee. "Not trying to cramp your style, but I think I might need to stay here for a while."

It wasn't my place to ask for details, but if that piece of shit was asking for a divorce *and* kicking his wife out, Mac was going to have some help in kicking his ass.

"Give me a list of what you need, and I'll go to your place and load it in my truck today."

"Thanks, Brady. You're a good one."

"Whatever you need."

She smiled, so weary and worn that my heart hurt for her. "I'm glad you and Mac found your way to one another. It's good to have someone who challenges you and makes you the very best version of yourself. I don't—I don't think Danny and I were that for each other. We gave one another permission to just stay the same."

"You deserve better, Bonnie. I know it doesn't feel that way right now, but I believe you'll find it."

"Maybe." She took a sip from her mug. She'd picked a Dollywood one that had three bears on it. "Maybe I'll meet someone who puts me first. You know, a fantasy."

I heard movement on the stairs and felt my heart leap a little at the prospect of seeing the woman who was walking down them. "Sometimes, the fantasy is real."

Bonnie eyed me like she thought I was sweet but wrong. It was the *bless your heart* of looks.

"Well, I'm going to get to work on some pancakes and bacon." Mac walked into the room, so I added, "Sound good to you, ladies?"

"God, yes," Mac groaned.

"That would be nice. Thank you," Bonnie said. "I'm going to grab a quick shower. I'll be right back."

I placed a griddle pan on the stove and noticed Mac staring after her sister, gaze still fixed on the corner she'd disappeared around.

"She'll be okay," I said. "Your sister is tough."

Mac turned toward me. "That's the problem. She's always been the responsible one. The caretaker. She keeps everything together. I'm worried that she'll focus on everyone else and let herself fade into the background. I want her to be happy."

"She'll get there, but you've got to let her grieve. She was with Danny for half of her life."

Mac scowled and reached for the coffeepot. "I know. She just deserves someone great. Someone who realizes how fucking amazing she is. Danny always took her for granted. He didn't support her." And then, while she was pouring the steaming liquid into a mug, she added, "I want her to have what we have."

She said it so casually, but I had to steady myself from where I'd crouched down for a mixing bowl.

Mac and I might have done things all wrong. Our journey was made up of twists and turns, pitfalls and minefields. But what we did have was a connection born of history. I had her back, and she had mine. She was my best friend, and I'd do anything for her. And I knew Mac would defend and stand beside me in any battle.

I straightened carefully, placing the bowl on the counter. Then I grabbed the milk and the eggs from the fridge. On the way back to the mixing bowl, I kissed Mac on the temple and said, "I want that for her too."

We spent the next few minutes in comfortable silence. I mixed up the batter and then let it rest. Bacon went into the oven, and Mac topped off my coffee.

"By the way," I said as I added butter to the griddle pan, "I took a picture of you drooling in your sleep the other night on the couch. I'm going to post it on Chatter today."

We were back to lovingly roasting each other on the app.

"That's fine," she replied, unaffected. "I have a revenge post ready and drafted."

I grinned. I planned on keeping this woman on her toes for the rest of our lives.

"Don't forget, Mac Attack. We have our first planning meeting tonight when you get home."

It was my day off, but Mac had to be at work in approximately one hour and fifteen minutes.

When she stayed quiet, I glanced over my shoulder to see her smiling.

"I remember," she replied shyly.

Tonight, we were planning our first vacation together and getting Mac's passport application in order. We would be narrowing down locations and picking from her extensive wish list. All those websites saved and bookmarked. The travel magazines with dog-eared pages, ready for the hypothetical to become reality.

She'd made me promise to give my input. She didn't want it to be just a trip for her. But all I wanted was for her to be happy—to have the experience she'd always dreamed of. And to experience it with her, of course.

Our love was already an adventure. One that had been unexpected at almost every turn. I hoped our relationship would keep growing and keep changing and that we'd do it all together. I felt unbelievably lucky to take these next steps with her. To see her dreams unfold and be by her side through it.

We'd travel, and we'd come home. We'd love, and we'd fight. We'd stay busy for apple season, and we'd welcome tourists to the town we loved.

Every step forward would be a step remembered. A girl with one pigtail and a boy with a death wish. Two people who'd been connected for so long they couldn't recall a before and after.

I flipped another pancake and felt Mac's arms come around my waist as she pressed a kiss to the center of my back. I didn't try to hide my smile. It wouldn't have worked anyway.

Mac was mine, and I was hers, and the good part was just getting started.

MAC

Two Months Later

Grandpappy's was closed on a Saturday afternoon in August for the first time in twenty years.

But today was an important day.

Chloe and Jordan were getting married. While the bride had asked to use the gazebo at the pond for a small ceremony during the week, Aunt Maggie had taken over and insisted on a Saturday wedding so that all the people who loved Jordan and Chloe could attend. Chloe was Maggie's Bake Shop assistant, after all, and Maggie loved the woman like the daughter she'd never had.

It was hot as hell, even at six in the evening, but there was nowhere else I'd rather be.

I shook my head and fought a grin as Brady caught my eye and winked from his position under the gazebo roof. The guy had gotten himself ordained online and begged Jordan and Chloe to let him marry them. He was ridiculous.

But when, a few minutes later, he went slightly off script and spoke about second chances and how true love—like Jordan and Chloe's—was worth waiting for to get the timing right, I had to fight the wobble in my chin as I reached over and squeezed Bonnie's hand.

My sister was . . . doing fine since the split with Danny. She'd become the hyper-efficient, best version of herself that I'd been worried about. She showed up to staff and committee meetings at the elementary school with homemade snacks for everyone. She was all smiles at family dinners. She nailed all the art history and pop culture trivia questions on Monday nights without missing a beat. And she didn't do a single thing for herself.

Aside from that first horrible, frightening night, I hadn't seen her shed a tear. It was only because I'd known her my whole damn life that I got the distinct impression she was trying to fake it until she made it.

Jordan drew my attention as he struggled through his vows. He wore suspenders, along with the rest of the wedding party, and I was sure Brady Judd was to blame. But the emotion was evident on Jordan's face. His brother, Seth, and Will stood at his side, and those of us gathered gave a sweet chuckle when Will passed his best friend a handkerchief.

Chloe looked radiant in her cream wedding gown. It was strapless and sleek and wrapped around her thin frame beautifully. Her bright red hair was pulled into an elegant low bun. And she looked at Jordan like there was no one else in the world.

I was happy for them. They had a long history, too. Best friends through child-hood and adolescence until Jordan's best friend, Keaton, had swooped in and stolen Chloe away. They'd married too young, and Keaton spent the next ten years controlling her every move. He'd hoarded her time and isolated her until her friendship with Jordan—and nearly everyone else—faded away. But all that ended last spring when Chloe left her cheating husband and started working at the Bake Shop. She'd reclaimed her life and found love with the man who'd never really forgotten her. The one currently choking back tears under the August sky.

Finally, Brady announced the pair partners in life, and the groom dipped his bride low and kissed the hell out of her.

The crowd cheered, and I let loose a whistle that had Brady looking my way with undisguised love, right there for everyone to see. I had a feeling it wouldn't be long before he started casually mentioning marriage-adjacent things. He wasn't subtle, and I knew him better than anyone. Except for maybe Abby. He'd been the one to recognize what was going on between me and Brady in the first place. And after we'd publicly admitted at a Friday night bonfire that he, the wise and intuitive Cole Abernathy, had been right all along, he'd forgiven us for keeping our relationship a secret behind his back.

Men were dramatic creatures, bless their hearts.

The reception was being held in the big barn in the center of the property. We'd spent the last two weeks prepping and cleaning it out, setting up chairs, a dance floor, and decorations. The doors were open wide on either end. And with the sun setting over the mountains in the distance and the twinkle lights sparkling overhead, it looked otherworldly.

I was already planning my pitch to keep it like this to host weddings and add it to our event-planning repertoire. Mom usually handled small-scale events for locals —book clubs, the Kirby Falls women's league, the festival planning committee, and fellowship groups from around the area. But I was actually looking forward to expanding what we offered. We could bring in a part-time event planner to manage things, and we could host folks who appreciated the magic of our tiny mountain town. I kind of liked the idea that some happily-ever-afters might start right here.

"Here you go," Brady said, passing me a glass of sparkling wine.

"Nice job up there, minister."

He made a face. "Ew. Don't call me that. I'm not into it."

I laughed.

I knew now that his goal had always been to make me laugh. It was a relief not to have to hide it anymore.

"Countdown?" he asked out of nowhere, as was his way.

"Only 145 days," I answered without checking my phone.

"Nice," he said, clinking his glass with mine.

We had a running countdown to our first trip. We were going to Iceland in January. Seeing the northern lights surrounded by snow and visiting the black sand beaches on the southern coast had been on the top of my list for years. And

I was excited that Brady hadn't been yet either. It was something we could experience together.

We stood shoulder to shoulder, watching folks sway on the dance floor. We'd get out there soon enough, but right now, I just wanted to take in the beauty of the place—my home—and the people I loved.

My eyes drifted to a spot of stillness at one of the tables.

Larry was wearing black, of course. But she'd ditched the combat boots for sparkling stilettos. Her dark hair was loose and curled, hitting the tops of her shoulders. The longest I'd seen it in years.

She was unmoving, and I followed the tilt of her head to where her attention was focused.

Kayla stood in the circle of someone's arms—a guy I didn't recognize and had never seen before. My heart sank as the man leaned in and whispered something. She smiled in response and kissed him in a way that would have had me covering the eyes of anyone under ten. *Jesus.*

Larry visibly stiffened, and I fought the urge to go to her, to comfort her. I didn't know how to make things better. I'd never loved someone from afar the way she did.

Oh, I had experience with secrecy, but the one-sidedness of her feelings broke my heart. She was still unwilling to talk to Kayla or come out to her, certain that the truth would push her friend away, and she'd lose her forever. To Laramie, that would be worse than never having her the way she wanted.

"Well, would you look at that," Brady murmured.

I looked over, but his attention was focused on a woman who'd approached Larry. She was holding a camera and smiling down at my cousin.

I recognized her as the wedding photographer, someone Chloe had hired out of Greenville. She was tall and curvy and beautiful, her black maxi dress flaring dramatically around her hips.

After a brief back-and-forth, the newcomer pulled out the chair next to Larry and perched on the edge of the seat. Her body curved toward Larry, and they looked like parentheses closing in on one another.

The woman angled the back of her fancy digital camera and showed my cousin something, scrolling through several images I couldn't make out from here.

"What do you suppose—?" I cut myself off as the photographer passed Larry a card, smiling widely the whole time. Then, she looped the camera strap around her neck once more and stood.

Larry watched the woman walk away, then quickly glanced around to see if anyone had noticed. Her wide eyes collided with mine, but I smiled reassuringly and offered a wave.

She waved back awkwardly, then tucked a strand of hair behind her ear, turning back to face the dance floor. Kayla and her date were nowhere to be seen.

"Very interesting," Brady said quietly, shooting me a sly smile.

Larry had come out to him a few weeks ago. She'd said it was because he and I were in a "committed relationship" and she didn't want me to have to lie to him and "be responsible for turning us into idiots again." But she'd said it all with a teasing tilt to her lips, and I suspected she was testing the waters to see how it might go should she decide to come out to the rest of the family.

"Very interesting indeed," I replied.

The music changed, and the opening beat of "Love Shack" came from the speakers next to the dance floor.

"That's our cue." Brady held out his hand.

I took it, grinning.

"Let's snag Larry on the way," he said, as we maneuvered around tables and chairs.

I drained my glass and looped my arm through my cousin's despite her protests. But by the time Becca dragged Will out to join us, Larry was laughing as Brady spun her around and around.

We stomped our feet in time to the lyrics. Jordan and Chloe hurried out to the middle of our circle from where they'd been making the rounds and garnering well-wishes. The dance floor filled up as we danced and sang. The deejay kept things going with "Y.M.C.A." and "Celebration," classic reception songs that we all knew by heart. Candace and Mercer then made their way out, as did my sister, Bonnie.

When the tone shifted and "Don't Stop Believin'" by Journey filtered through the barn, Brady didn't hesitate. He held out a hand for Bonnie and spent the next four minutes making her laugh.

"Do you ever just hate how charming he is?" Larry chuckled.

We had our arms on top of each other's shoulders and were swaying like middle schoolers.

I laughed. "Yes."

She raised a single dark brow. "You know it wasn't hate all that time, right?"

I'd gotten a fair amount of I-told-you-so-ing from her as well. Nothing as ridiculous as Abby's public acknowledgement, but it was still pretty annoying.

"I know," I said. "But in the end, it doesn't matter. Whatever we were doing, no matter how unhinged or absurd, brought us together."

And that was the beauty of it. I never saw my twenty-five-year feud with Brady as wasted time.

He'd been right today, standing under that gazebo. Timing mattered. Love might find you when you least expected it, but it was undoubtedly meant to be. And I was tired of regretting my life away over missed opportunities and misplaced expectations.

I'd never try to undo the pranks and the public spectacle. Couldn't even if I wanted to. It was who we were, and I loved it almost as much as I loved Brady.

Our rivalry was what lassoed my heart. Sure, there might have been a little rope burn. At first, I'd been dragged along, kicking and screaming. But I never claimed I wasn't stubborn.

Brady and I had history—boatloads of it. But we weren't supposed to fall in love until it happened. Like a lightning strike or a flash flood. A kiss in the front seat of a truck that changed my life forever.

I'd never wish it away, and I wouldn't change a single thing about the path we'd taken.

Except for the Elmer's-glue thing.

We could have maybe skipped that one.

The fun in Kirby Falls continues with Bonnie's story in Leaf You Hanging, *coming this fall.*

Want more of Mac and Brady? Well I have TWO bonus scenes for you!
First up is a sweet bonus epilogue featuring Mac and Brady traveling together for the first time. Get the bonus scene HERE when you sign up for my newsletter.
If you have trouble with the link above, scan the QR code:

Were you curious about that Elmer's Glue Incident of 2009? I have the flashback bonus scene for you right HERE! Enjoy teenage Brady and Mac and their prank shenanigans!
If you have trouble with the link above, scan the QR code:

acknowledgments

To my amazing authenticity and sensitivity readers: Emily, Jon, and Krista. Thank you for your role in providing realism to Brady. It was my intent to approach this character with well-informed sensitivity and accuracy. I appreciate your willingness to guide and instruct.

To Nathan: You have no idea that one Facebook post, years ago, inspired so much. Thank you.

also by laney hatcher

Kirby Falls Series

Take It or Leaf It: A Grumpy Sunshine Slow Burn Romance

Leaf It To Me: A Small-Town Slow Burn Romance

Leaf and Let Die: An Enemies to Lovers Small-Town Romance

Leaf You Hanging: A Reformed Bad Boy Small-Town Romance

Cozy Creek Collection

Fall Me Maybe

Bartholomew Series

First to Fall: A Friends to Lovers Historical Romance

Second Chance Dance: An Enemies to Lovers Historical Romance

Third Degree Yearn: A Second Chance Historical Romance

Last on the List: A Surprise Pregnancy Historical Romance

Smartypants Romance

London Ladies Embroidery Series

Neanderthal Seeks Duchess

Well Acquainted

Love Matched

Find bonus content, reading order, and other news at my website:

https://laneyhatcher.com/

about the author

Laney Hatcher is a firm believer that there is a spreadsheet for every occasion and pie is always the answer. She is an author of stories both old and new where the HEAs are always guaranteed. Often too practical for her own good, Laney enjoys her life in the southern United States with her husband, children, and incredibly entitled cat.

Find Laney Hatcher online:
Facebook: https://bit.ly/3s6KnuY
Newsletter: https://bit.ly/3SbXg2v
Amazon: https://amzn.to/3IaOwU7
Instagram: https://bit.ly/3s4IRcS
Website: https://laneyhatcher.com/
Goodreads: https://bit.ly/3BD0Gme
TikTok: https://www.tiktok.com/@laneyhatcherauthor
Threads: https://www.threads.net/@laney.hatcher

Newsletter sign up

www.ingramcontent.com/pod-product-compliance
Lightning Source LLC
Chambersburg PA
CBHW020233010826
48973CB00006B/1493